STANLEY & HAZEL

BY

JO SCHAFFER

STANLEY & HAZEL by Jo Schaffer

EPub ISBN: 978-1-946700-83-4
Mobi ISBN: 978-1-946700-82-7
Trade Paperback ISBN: 978-1-946700-65-0

Published by Month9Books, Raleigh, NC 27609
Cover design by AM Design Studios

Gabe, Nate, Colin, Quinn, Jack, Emily and Jonathan.
Kiddos. Loves. Hooligans.

STANLEY & HAZEL

The summons came in the usual way.

An old hymn that would arouse no suspicion. Outside, a high-pitched voice sang, "Oh, love the veil, he spreads it over us."

Legion looked out of his second-story mansion window at the street rat standing just beyond the gate in a tattered coat, ridiculous Irish style cap, and pants with holes in the knees. A scrawny arm raised and waved the white feather in its filthy hand.

The Master used these disposable things for his work. No one particularly bothered with these children of the street, winding their way amidst the hungry masses standing in soup lines, other than to kick and swear at them when they got in the way. And, when they finally disappeared into The Winnowing, no one would miss them. Someday, the operation would be out in the open and the little vermin would no longer be needed.

Legion smiled into the ornate mirror that hung on the wall as he put on a tweed jacket. He sprayed on cologne and slicked back his hair with sweet-smelling hair cream. No one would guess that he was the Protector of the Faceless One, the strong arm of his destructive power. Instead, they saw the image he chose to present to the world: a model citizen from a prestigious family, interested in money, cars, and dames, and whose only passion was the tiny columns in the Wall Street Journal.

Frowning, he straightened up his coat and wondered why the Master would summon him now. All the pieces had been strategically put into place. The machinery of mass persuasion was already doing its work, and the next step would be obvious: eliminate the unworthy. It would only require a nudge to get people to do the right thing once they understood it was in their self-interest.

But too many still had compassion for the rabble of the streets and backwoods, so The Winnowing had to remain secret for now. Only an emergency would warrant a summons to the caves. Something threatening, a situation that required his unique skills.

He left his room and made his way down the large marble staircase. Thankfully, nobody was home to ask questions about where he was going. The Master did not appreciate tardiness.

A few servants scurried about down below but would only speak to him if invited. They knew their place and would never dare to question him or talk about his comings and goings. The new house girl avoided his gaze as he passed her on the staircase. He turned to watch her ascend, smirking as he did. She stayed away from him, but he could have her if he wished. That long black hair bound tightly on the top of her head would fall like glossy waves around her slender neck. He briefly closed his eyes and breathed in the faint sweetness of her scent as she passed.

Giving her a mock bow, he made his way down the rest of the stairs, across Italian tile floor, and out the large mahogany door. He walked along the illumined brick pathway as the sun dipped below the tree line. The rattle and roar of automobiles sounded from beyond and the whining call of a newsie floated on the breeze. "Extry, extry! New evidence found in the Lindbergh kidnapping! German immigrant had accomplices!"

Legion rolled his eyes. The papers were nothing more than entertainment for the masses. The truth was hidden in the shadows of the three-ring circus that served as a decoy.

"See the new photograph by London doctor that proves the Loch Ness monster exists!" the young voice piped next.

Case in point. It was all a colossal game of misdirection. While people fixated on fantasy, the real power to be feared operated beneath the surface. Some people knew and the rest didn't. He was one of the chosen. He knew. Legion had a swelling in his chest, and he took a deep breath.

The messenger bounced up and down at the gates, shaking the white feather in his right hand. Clearly the rat didn't like waiting. Legion took his time, whistling as he strolled with hands in his pockets.

"Hey, mister," the rat said in a hoarse whisper, "I got a message for ya. Some guy told me to give you this feather. He said you'd pay me for it." His dirty face scrunched, puzzled.

Legion smiled. "I see it, boy, you've done well. I'll make sure you get your reward."

The rat grimaced, showing mossy-green teeth. "Ain't you gonna take it? The guy said you'd pay me. And I don't trust richie riches like you."

Legion frowned at his disrespect. It didn't seem to care who he was or where he was. The boy fidgeted and moved; all it wanted was its next meal. Like an animal.

"Ah, how frustrating for you. Yes, of course, I do have payment, but I don't need the feather."

The rat glanced around, nervous, flaring his nostrils. "Say, what's this all about? Is this some kind of set up? I want my money now, mister."

Flexing his hands, Legion forced a smile. "In payment for your trouble, I'll give you an address to something better. They'll have food there and more. You'll be able to start a brand-new life."

The boy dropped the feather with a scowl. "I need money. I ain't had nothin' to eat in a few days."

"I understand. That's why this place will help you. They like good boys like you. They have food," he said, slowly this time.

He didn't have to pressure or persuade. The sunken cheeks, hollow stomach, and trembling limbs would do that for him. Hunger would override any instinct for safety. Legion kept a pleasant smile and hands in his pockets as he watched the rat fidget and then take a step forward.

"Ah, gee, all right, mister. Can I have that address? Don't worry, I can read a little."

Handing the rat a slip of paper, he said, "There you go, kid. Enjoy the food. You won't have to worry about starving anymore."

The boy slipped away into the dusk without looking back and Legion stepped out onto the avenue heading away from his home and toward the bustle of the city, the rhythmic clack of his heeled shoes like a metronome. He turned down a deserted alleyway and a prickle ran down his back. The faint whiff of cigarette smoke made him whirl around, hands ready, but there was nobody there. Just a stray dog with protruding ribs sniffing around some garbage. Legion covered his face with his sleeve to block the stench as he moved away from the useless scavenger.

Emerging from the alleyway, he hailed a black taxi that took him all the way to the beer district. He talked loudly the whole way about the joys of post-Prohibition parties and the best booze in St. Louis, how the good times were coming back and the stock market would rebound. The cabby chuckled at a few ignorant remarks, the usual resentment toward the rich cloaked in his dark eyes, but it was no matter. The driver would write him off as another privileged swell and not give him a second thought.

Finally, the cabby dropped him off at the Soulard open-air market, which had just begun to close. He blended in with the crowd, keeping his hands in his pockets, annoyed every time a person touched or jostled him.

He dodged into dark alleys, knowing nearly every street in this area of St. Louis by heart. Finally, he arrived at the large, brick Lemp mansion. No one came in or out much these days. They'd become recluses, the guardians of the gates to the kingdom of the Faceless One, who'd taken over the caves that honeycombed beneath the entire city.

When he knocked on the door, a short, fat man opened and said, "Welcome. He is waiting on you."

Without a word, he made his way through the pristine house, which smelled of wood polish, and down to the basement. Two muscled men, fellow members of the Guard, stood by a doorway with an iron gate and bowed as he went through.

Descending into the stone carved tunnel, he squinted as his eyes adjusted to the flickering candle light that lit his way; no electrical lights were allowed in the domain of the Master. After winding his way through the underground tunnels, Legion finally found himself in the throne room. Water dripped down from the ceiling and echoed through the chamber. The candles dimmed as a familiar, cold darkness swirled around him. Legion feared and welcomed it. Before he announced himself, a voice echoed in the rock chamber.

"Welcome, Legion. Come and sit with me."

His eyes adjusted again, and he saw the wooden throne at the center of a large room. The Faceless One sat on the throne, clothed in white with a white veil covering his face. Legion approached and knelt, kissing the ruby ring on the right hand.

"We have a problem, my son. And perhaps you can answer for it." The cave resonated with his words.

Legion's heart beat faster but he kept his head bowed. "At your service, my lord."

"The traitor has returned."

He resisted the urge to glance up. *Her*. She'd come back. Why? How could she be so ignorant? Surely, she knew that it meant instant death?

"My lord, I had no idea."

"You may look at my veil."

Legion looked up and still couldn't make out any features. The cloth indented and expanded with breath, the only indication the Faceless One might be human.

"I have a hard time believing that you did not know. The two of you were so close; there was a time we thought to bestow her on you for your faithful service, until we discovered what she was up to with that ballplayer. She was unworthy."

Clenching his fist, Legion took a deep breath and calmed his anger. He couldn't lose control of his feelings and make things worse. He remembered her beautiful face and their long walks in the park. Maybe he'd loved her at one time, he couldn't remember, only that her betrayal felt like a punch to the stomach and drained her of humanity.

"My lord, I swear I didn't know she was back. And I thought I knew her. I thought she would make a beautiful asset to your Court. But, she lied to me and I missed it. I should have known."

The veiled head rested back against the throne. "Yes. Yes, you should have. You lead my protection and guard our holy person. And yet, you let someone in so close as to almost destroy everything we've worked for. And now, she has come back. My sources tell me she intends to tell everything and has proof."

Legion rose, forgetting himself. "What proof, my lord?"

The Master didn't speak for a long moment. "And who told you to rise in my presence?"

Trembling, he knelt, face to the stone floor. "I'm sorry, my lord. My surprise got the best of me."

The Faceless One's pale hands touched Legion's shoulder. "It is well, my son. Even the elect can make mistakes. You must neutralize the threat, however. I will not tolerate a second failure."

Legion nodded. He didn't fear dying, but being cast down into the lower ranks was unthinkable; to not be able to approach the Master and sit at his service …

"Yes, my lord. I will make sure everything is taken care of."

Chapter One

Hazel pulled back the heavy satin curtain and a square of bright sunlight landed on the towering bed. "Mumsy, get up. It's past two o'clock." Not that this was anything new. The rest of the household had already lived a full day and her mother still lay heavy and motionless in her frilly, canopied bed like a corpse in a fancy casket.

Mumsy startled and shifted around amid a dozen fluffy pink and cream pillows. "Say, what's the big idea?" she groaned, squinting in the light. "Peggy, get Peggy … "

Hazel snorted and tugged on the tasseled cord beside her mother's bed. "She'll be here with a bromo-seltzer for that headache." She flipped on the torch lights and the crystal chandelier that hung high over the center of the room. The mix of striped and floral patterns in her mother's spacious bedroom were probably not helping her aching head.

"Thank you, darling." Her mother clasped both hands over her curly blond hair. "Had another doozy last night." She yawned, releasing the faint smell of gin and vermouth. It had been the martini madness again, a real bender.

Hazel noticed a stack of her mother's belongings in the large marble fireplace across from her bed. "I can see that … Planning a bonfire?"

"Eh?" Mumsy squeezed her eyes shut. "Oh, that. I need Peggy to put all of that away … made sense to us at the time … "

"Well, hold your brains in while you wait." Hazel shook her head and smiled. Her mother knew how to kick up her heels like no other. It seemed as if lately she was determined to reclaim her youth. Days of bathtub gin and an occasional handsome stranger, cocktails, champagne, and society playboys. "That's what you get for your wild ways."

"Darling, you sound like your father," Mumsy moaned.

Hazel shrugged. Pops was a model citizen, and she admired him, but somehow the comment stung. She scanned the room to make sure there was no evidence of a second occupant. Her mother's party clothes from the night before were the only ones scattered around. Hazel sighed in relief. None of her wild flings were serious, but they drew Hazel's dad's attention, who was otherwise too busy to notice much at all. Mumsy had to be noticed.

Her mother let out a moan and sat up. "See here, you gotta live a little before you die."

"You look more dead than alive." Hazel bent to pick up a turquoise party dress, silk cape, and heeled shoes strewn across the floor.

"Just let Peggy do that. Oh, I must be a sight." Mumsy sighed and covered her face, groaning.

"Peggy has enough to do." Hazel dropped the pile in her arms onto the bed. She kissed her mother's cheek. "And you're lovely."

"Oh, sh-sh-shh. Too loud." Mumsy shut her eyes and massaged her scalp. "You're a riot. Ha. Ha." She made a funny face and then smiled. "Don't you have anywhere fun to be? Your friend … Silvia is having a birthday party?"

"Sandy. That was last Saturday."

"Ah. Was it the bee's knees? Boys and booze? Hot music? Gimme the scoop."

Hazel shook her head. "Sure. It was a great party. The police didn't raid it or anything." She rolled her eyes and tossed a round pillow at her mother. Ever since Prohibition was repealed the year before, it seemed like her mother was obsessed with the freedom of drinking without having to go to a speakeasy.

Her mother sighed. "Your boyfriend there?"

"Haven't got one." Hazel watched her mom grimace, yesterday's makeup streaked across her face. Sometimes, she seemed like a complete stranger.

"Well, men come and go." She lay back, closing her eyes and let out a deep sigh. "Don't tell your father about my headache. He'll only scold."

Hazel patted her mom's hand. "He's no fool. And your face will give it away."

Mumsy pulled the blanket over her head. "Swell."

Hazel half-smiled and left her mother making headache sounds. On her way back down the long hall, she snatched a cookie off a silver tray that Roberts carried toward the guest wing. Mumsy must have brought friends home last night after all.

Roberts turned and nodded his graying head. "Miss Hazel."

"Hiya, Robbie." She popped the cookie into her mouth and skipped down the sweeping wooden staircase. She crossed the parquet floor and paused with a hand on the door of the informal dining room beside the kitchen.

Her father's voice vibrated against the wood. "Nonsense! I don't give a hang about the Securities Act. Trade it!"

Hazel pushed into the room where her father sat at his lunch, a smoldering pipe beside his plate and a carefully creased paper on the table. Nicholas Peter Malloy II held the black telephone to his ear like a club with one hand and to his mouth with the other.

He nodded vigorously a few times. "Right. Sell copper. More lumber … Forget that. And you tell Pierce to listen up. I know stocks." He crashed the two sides of the telephone together as he hung up.

"Problems?" Hazel slid into her chair and made a kissy face at her father.

"Hmph. The market is rebounding. Happy days are here again." His face showed no mirth. This was business.

Happy days? It all seemed the same to Hazel. Ever since the stock market crashed when she was a kid, all her dad and his friends talked about were the hard times. But the cloud of misery seemed to hover at the fringes of her life as she moved from her elegant house to the sleek, rounded lines of their Buick to the clean interior of the Mary Institute, where all the girls floated in the healthy glow of ease. It made her feel like she was only dreaming … or that there was something in her closet with dark, hungry eyes watching her sleep in her comfortable bed. Not a sunny thought. She pushed it away.

"What's for lunch, Pops?"

"It's Father. And we're having kippers. Your mother joining us at last? Had this late meal just for her … "

Hazel shrugged. "Once her room stops spinning."

Her father made a face, straightened his necktie, and picked up his pipe. All of his attention went back to his paper. Hazel wondered again just how much Pops regretted marrying a beautiful jazz baby from new money all those years ago instead of some debutante, a refined girl from the right family. The kind of girl he desperately hoped his own daughter would be.

She waited as the kitchen maid served her lunch with practiced grace. Hazel hoped Peggy wouldn't be busy upstairs for too long, so they could talk about the new Clark Gable picture playing at the Fox Theater downtown. Hazel had seen it with Sandy and Mrs. Schmidt the week before it had become an obsession. Gable played a newspaperman with plenty of spunk. And that smile …

"We'll need the evening paper," her father said.

Hazel lit up. "I can get that for you, Pops—uh … Father." Maybe that tall boy with the faded flat cap would be on the same corner with his papers. He had the bluest eyes she'd ever seen.

"Nonsense. Roberts will see to it." Pops clenched his pipe in his teeth and held up a copy of the morning paper, a barrier declaring the topic was closed.

Hazel wrinkled her nose and stuck her tongue out in her dad's direction. He never allowed her to go anywhere alone—as if she couldn't take care of herself. She took a bite of her lunch and stared at the back of his paper, reading ads for the latest picture shows. Maybe Sandy would catch one with her tonight. Hazel could wear her new lilac dress—it made her eyes really shine.

"I'd like to go to the movies with Sandy tonight," she said.

Pops lowered his paper. "Tonight? The Sinclair family is coming for dinner, Hazel." He looked at her for the first time since she'd come into the room. "Your hair. Set it. And," he waved a hand at his own face, "do something with all of this."

"Oh, you'd like me to shave your mustache and wax your brows?" Hazel fluttered her eyelashes.

Pops grunted away the small upturn at the corners of his mouth. Hazel loved it when he almost smiled.

"Lipstick and whatever else your mother has," he muttered, face back in his paper.

"I see." Hazel sighed.

Ever since she'd turned fifteen, the swanky families had come swarming, blatantly parading their eligible, suitable sons, most of them dull as dirt and alike as can be: polo-playing, Ivy League-attending, sharp dressers with slicked-over hair and little to say to Hazel. They mostly clung to every word her father said and tried to impress him with their knowledge of stocks, bonds, and all kinds of boring talk about money.

Hazel cringed at herself. Money might be easy and dull for her but maybe she was spoiled. She'd seen the forgotten men on the streets as she'd passed in the chauffeured car, even if she tried not to … their heads down, hollow-cheeked, wearing dirty, threadbare clothes. In the papers, there were pictures of scrawny children begging for food with filthy, empty hands outstretched. She looked down at her perfectly manicured fingers as they gripped a fork and knife made of pure silver. The food on her plate was more than she could eat. She didn't want to think about that.

"Ever think about hungry people?" Hazel questioned, almost without meaning to.

Her father nodded as he spoke. "Hard not to. They seem to clutter the sidewalks everywhere these days. It's unfortunate." He gave a slight grimace as if he felt sorry about it, but saw no solution.

Hazel bristled at his apathy. "The Sinclairs funded that new medical clinic for the poor."

Her dad nodded again. "That young doctor they put in charge is milking them no doubt, but it's good for image if you're considering running for mayor. It's also a handy tax shelter for them, I'm sure." He put down his paper and smirked to himself.

Knowing the Sinclairs, their reasons for opening the clinic probably weren't out of the goodness of their hearts. But it was still a good thing. Hazel wrinkled her brow. "Sandy's family gives to shelters."

"Well," her father cut into his filet, "I'm sure the Schmidts are well intentioned and probably trying to redeem themselves in the public eye, as well they should."

"Nobody who really knows them would think they were dirt." Hazel hated it when people got that preachy tone when they talked about her best friend's family. It wasn't their fault their oldest daughter caused a scandal.

"Of course not. They are still a wealthy, positioned family. Although, you might do better to mix with Brigitte Slayback and her friends. You've been invited to the Veiled Prophet Ball, Hazel, and so has she. That's an honor."

"Sandy was too." Hazel furrowed her brow. Sometimes she wanted to poke her dad in the eye. Brigitte was a know-it-all flirt and a snob.

His face registered surprise for briefly. "Well. I suppose her father has paid his dues," he muttered. "The point is, people often are exactly where they belong."

"You mean all those hungry people? In the gutters?" Her stomach clenched. Sometimes her dad said things that felt … wrong.

"Hazel, I don't like it either, but life has a way of … " he paused and stroked his mustache, " … sorting these things out."

"Sorting?" Hazel frowned. How is starvation sorted?

He cleared his throat. "Ever wonder why they are poor and we are not, Hazel?"

"Because you make three hundred thousand smackers a year like Granddad before you?"

He rolled his eyes at her slang. "Well, yes, I do. I make that money through hard work, using my God-given intelligence. If we just gave money to everyone out there on the streets—who would do the work? It's a case of survival of the fittest. The cream always rises to the top."

"Cream." Hazel wrinkled her nose. It made sense in a way, but it seemed cold to talk about people as if they were soda fountain toppings.

Pops grunted and picked up his paper again. "Anyway, focus on what's important here; the Sinclairs are the cream. And they are coming tonight, so I'm afraid taking a show with the Schmidt girl is not on the schedule."

"They won't miss me. The Sinclairs are coming to see you." Suddenly it seemed intolerable and unimportant.

"Gabriel is coming with them this time."

Hazel bit her lip. Last year she met Gabriel at a dance, before he left for his first semester at Yale. She'd been intrigued then. There was something different about him. A sardonic glint in his eyes behind those black-rimmed specs. Something almost dangerous about his smile. Then she'd heard rumors that he and Regina Peck were caught necking in the back of the Slayback's Cadillac limousine after the dance. Hazel didn't want to find out for herself what he was like on a date.

"I don't like him much. He's a snore."

Her dad slapped his paper down on the table. "What's that got to do with it? He's a fine boy. His family is very influential."

"I know." She pushed at a tomato with her fork. It popped open and bled. Her appetite died.

"Hazel, don't make up your mind about anything before you give it a try."

Funny. That had sort of been her mother's message today too. Live a little. Take a leap. Just maybe it was time to try something new. "Fine. Have it your way, *Father.*" Hazel stood and curtsied.

He grunted. "That's my girl."

Not this time, Pops, she thought.

Hazel strolled out of the dining room and made her way through the cavernous house that echoed with her footsteps. She trotted up the stairs and past her mother's room, which always smelled of roses and champagne.

The murmur of Peggy's voice with its Irish lilt came through the door. "Ma'am, I need you to stand on your own two feet that God gave ya if we're to put this on. That's right. There now … you're a pip."

Mumsy was having a hard time recovering. She never seemed to learn from all the post-party headaches. Hazel sighed and retreated to her room.

She opened the tall window and looked down at the ivy trellis that would be her escape. Some of the leaves had gone from dark green to red and pale gold. Hazel felt like a character in a movie. Could she really do it? She reached out and shook the trellis frame—it felt sturdy. She imagined sneaking out under the moon. Alone. Then maybe something interesting would finally happen to her, like in the movie *It Happened One Night.* Hazel sighed.

But the moon wasn't out. The afternoon sun shone on the

perfectly maintained grounds of the Malloy estate; trimmed hedges, blooming flowers, lush green grass, and garden statues. Willy, their gardener, had raked up any trace of fall only a few hours before. Everything was as it should be.

She caught her reflection in the vanity and cocked her head at the girl with dark unruly hair and wide blue eyes. A moment of shame paralyzed her. She looked all wrong. Oh, how she wished she looked like the actress Myrna Loy, whose hairdo was never out of place. Pops was right about her hair. Hazel patted it down and fiddled with the bobby pins. Maybe she should bleach it like Jean Harlow; it worked for Mumsy. Maybe a beauty spot. She poked a finger over her lip and tried to imagine it.

A soft knock sounded at the door. "Missy?"

"Come in, Peggy."

The door opened, and Peggy peeked in her wavy auburn head. Her light brown eyes sparkled as she chuckled. "Oh, your mother is pickled."

"Tell me something I don't know." Hazel smirked.

Peggy bounded into the room and gave Hazel a quick hug. "There now, Missy. There will come a day when your mother steps off the merry-go-round." As she spoke, she played with Hazel's hair, tucking stray curls and patting it down.

"Mumsy thinks she's still a flapper. She's beautiful and carefree. Wish I could be more like that. But Pops is disappointed in me enough as it is."

"Psh. Now, now. He treasures you and you're a fine-looking miss. And even finer on the inside. Nobody in their right mind could be disappointed in you." Peggy had such a sweet face, her pert little nose, smooth skin, and rosy cheeks almost made her look as young as Hazel, though she was probably old enough to be her mother. "Give me another hug, lass."

Hazel smiled at her maid and wrapped her arms around her. Peggy was all lovely and soft. "You're a dream."

Peggy pulled away and giggled, dimpling her round, pink cheeks. “Oh, you. I haven’t had a moment ’til now—tell me about that Clark Gable movie.” Peggy fanned her face.

Hazel let out a squeal. “He burns me up.”

Peggy listened while Hazel told her all about the movie. It was funny and romantic, and Gable was the perfect combination of tough wise-guy and tender lover. Claudette Colbert played the spoiled debutante who falls for him. They were all wrong for each other, and it was wonderful.

“Clark Gable makes all these society frat boys look like porridge.” Hazel sighed.

“True enough.” Peggy nodded. “But they’re real, lass.” She touched Hazel’s cheek.

Hazel frowned. “Not to me.”

After Peggy left, Hazel picked up her red-striped baton and twirled it around, letting her mind clear. She had to figure out a new routine for the next pep rally; this one was too easy now. Hazel usually loved practicing her majorette skills, but today she was restless and distracted.

Hazel put the baton away, flopped onto her bed, and opened a copy of *Photoplay*, featuring beautiful, famous people in black and white. She lost herself in the glamorous world of Hollywood.

She examined a Max Factor ad. Peggy always told Hazel that she was a lovely girl “without all that war paint.” She continued to turn the pages as if the answers were all there. The secrets. How to be beautiful, high class, and refined. A debutante. Somehow, no matter how Hazel had been trained and schooled, it never seemed to stick like it did with the other girls in her set. Maybe because of Mumsy—she wasn’t like the other mothers.

She flipped another page. A sexy and mysterious woman smoked a cigarette in a Camels ad. Hazel held her fingers up, pretending to take a long drag of a cigarette, and then blew it out slow and sultry. If she wasn’t cut out to be a debutante, perhaps Hazel could be a femme fatale.

"What do you say?" she asked the silver-framed signed photographs on her mantle.

Clark Gable and Jimmy Stewart smiled back at her. Jimmy almost seemed to wink. Hazel sat up and stretched, looking at the clock. Only a few hours until dinner with the Sinclairs. The late lunch had thrown off her day.

Hazel thought of how eager Pops had been about her fraternizing with Gabriel Sinclair, who was the perfect example of all the things she couldn't be: poised, proper, and predictable. Gabriel belonged with a girl like Regina Peck or Brigitte Slayback. Hazel just couldn't do it. The walls seemed to press in on her and she jumped off the bed, pacing the gleaming wood floor. Hazel didn't want to tame her hair or anything. She wanted to have some fun.

"Okay, boys. Let's step out." Feeling reckless, Hazel snatched her handbag, tossed in a tube of lipstick, and leaned out the window. She could be wild and have fun like Mumsy. She didn't have to be Daddy's perfect socialite daughter.

Just before taking the leap, Hazel grabbed the latest feathered thing Pops had bought her and crammed it onto her head over her uncooperative hair.

A proper girl never left the house without a hat.

Hazel then knelt on the windowsill and looked down. Her head started to spin; the ground looked too far. She just had to do it without thinking. A swoop in her belly later and she'd turned around, still clinging to the window. She reached down with one leg, trying to find a foothold. Her foot seemed to flail in space and she teetered, losing her balance. Hazel clung to the sill and froze, afraid to move. She took a deep breath, squeezed her eyes shut, and pushed herself backwards.

Hazel let out a yelp while she hung by her arms. "Oh, gee, oh, gee … " She kicked her legs until one slippery shoe found support. Hazel grasped at the leaves and the trellis shook. With a cautious step down, the other foot anchored itself below the first. She made her way down a couple more steps before an impudent autumn breeze let her know her backside was on display. Her dress had snagged on the ivy.

Bananas. Ranting to herself, she yanked her skirt free, almost losing her balance. Her heart pounded and her brain became fuzzy.

Hazel looked down at the grass below and wiped a hand across her damp forehead. Her arms trembled. Little by little, she made her way down, trying not to think about how one misstep could drop her like a rock.

At the bottom, Hazel slumped against the side of the house, breathing hard, her head resting against the ivy. With a sigh, she looked down at the state of her clothes. Her silk stockings had snags in them. Hazel removed both shoes and then, feeling wild, yanked her stockings off. She looked up at her open window as her bare feet flexed in the cool grass. Hazel grinned as she put her shoes back on.

She had done it.

The sun hung high in the sky. Beyond her immaculate yard, cars passed on Lindell Boulevard. What lay outside the safety of her stately home, the Buick, and the wall of chaperones? She felt impetuous and clever—was this how Mumsy felt when she went on a spree?

The Sinclairs would arrive soon, but she was one dame who wouldn't be on display tonight.

Chapter Two

Stanley gripped his copies of Sherlock Holmes mysteries as the trolley car clanked down the tracks to Sportsman's Park. He took a deep breath of clean autumn air. It smelled like freedom; a perfect day for baseball.

He smiled as he glanced over at Vinnie, who stretched his legs into the aisle, a battered fedora pulled down over his eyes. His best friend looked relaxed and asleep; time to get him up and moving. The day was too excellent to be wasted and a brisk walk to the park would do Vinnie some good. He was starting to look fat; doing shady business with the gangs was keeping him well fed. Plus, Stanley would be able to do some scouting for the meeting of the Knights later.

Reaching up, he pulled the wire to signal the driver. When the bell clanged, the trolley rolled to a stop.

Vinnie started, pulled off his hat, and asked, "Say, what gives? Are we there already?"

Stanley gave him a friendly kick. "Nah, move your lazy ass. We're walking the rest of the way. I need to stretch my legs."

"Why is it when you feel like you gotta stretch those stupid long legs of yours, I've got to suffer for it?" Vinnie grumbled as he scratched his arm and grimaced.

"We're Catholic. Suffering is what we do. Now move it; you're sixteen, not sixty. So stop your whining."

They paid the conductor and stepped out onto Lindell Boulevard, one of the wealthiest neighborhoods in St. Louis. The road was lined with large stone mansions, every house closed in by iron gates shutting out the rest of the world. None of them, Stanley would bet, had been touched by the desperate hunger most of St. Louis felt.

Stanley let out a low whistle and laughed. "Check them out. They think the rabble will storm their castles and behead them."

"Now there's an idea," Vinnie said, not really paying much attention.

"Until you get led to the guillotine for making them eat cake," Stanley muttered to himself. Sometimes St. Louis seemed on the verge of some kind of French Revolution craziness.

Stanley squinted at the wristwatch Vinnie was wearing and wondered if his sticky-fingered Italian buddy had stolen the thing. It looked a little too shiny for a guy like Vinnie. "Old Man Seable isn't going to like it if we're late. The game is starting soon." Stanley took off his cap and ran a hand through his reddish-blond hair. He had that uneasy tickle in his stomach that usually meant something was about to happen, and Stanley hoped it wasn't that they were about to get fired.

His friend shrugged, his eyes elsewhere. "You wanted to walk. Check out the window dressing," Vinnie said, cocking his head toward an open window on the side of a gray brick mansion covered with ivy.

A girl about their age in a blue dress and a hat with a long feather gripped the ivy at each side of the window. Her brown hair poked out from under her hat as she tried to maneuver her way out. Finally, she threw one leg over the ledge and her dress caught on a branch of the ivy. It lifted her skirt a little and gave the boys an excellent view of her legs.

"Say, I'll have some of that," Vinnie leered.

Stanley elbowed him in the ribs. “This is exactly why I don’t let you in the Knights of St. Louis. You have to be a gentleman.” Stanley looked away to give the girl some privacy. Still, most of him really did want to look. She had pretty amazing legs.

Vinnie snorted. “Gentleman. Says the kid who’s kissed half of Dogtown, the Hill, and most of the dolls in Gaslight Square.”

“Shut your cake hole.” He collared Vinnie, turning him away from the scene and counted to ten. When Stanley was sure the girl had made it to the ground, he glanced back, catching her straightening her dress and ridiculous hat.

Stanley allowed himself a good look. The girl was drop-dead beautiful. Her face glowed from her climb down the ivy, and she had a little smile on her face while she put on her shoes.

He evaluated the situation and rubbed his chin. Something about her gonked him. The girl had class but also some kind of wild streak. Stanley wondered what her story was.

She’s sneaking out. Why? From her dress, she planned to hit the town. By herself?

“You getting an eyeful?” Vinnie punched him in the shoulder.

Stanley shook his head and smiled. “Sorry, she’s like a work of art. I was just wondering what would motivate such a daring escape.”

Vinnie rolled his eyes. “Why can’t you talk like a normal person for Pete’s sake? But, yeah, she’s like a painting in a museum, all right. Pretty to see, impossible to touch.”

“Yeah … like the Mona Lisa,” Stanley muttered.

“Come on; Old Man Seable is gonna beat us senseless,” Vinnie said as he started walking.

Stanley joined him but kept glancing back. The girl was cutting through the hedges between houses. He wondered again what she was doing and why she hadn’t left by the front door. Running away for some fun? Escaping a tyrant father? He couldn’t help but form stories in his head all the time. When he became a reporter someday, he’d get paid for it. Then he’d get his own place and not have to answer to Uncle Seamus and his bottle anymore. Unconsciously, he ran his hand across his jaw where a bruise had faded to yellow.

By the time they got to Sportsman's Park, Stanley wished they'd taken the trolley the rest of the way. They made it right before the game started and Old Man Seable yelled until they climbed up the ladder to the catwalk. Vinnie took the first inning, giving Stanley a chance to read.

He finished *The Adventure of the Speckled Band* as he sat on the catwalk under the large wooden scoreboard. His long legs stretched in front of him and his polished black shoes hung out over the metal edge. The fall sun warmed Stanley's face while he munched on salty, sweet Cracker Jacks. Between the Cardinals and his favorite mysteries, a Saturday afternoon didn't get any better.

"Bookworm. I can't figure why you read and watch baseball," Vinnie said as he sat down beside him. He scratched his arm, and Stanley saw a bluish-green mark that he couldn't make out before Vinnie covered it with his sleeve.

He tried not to smile. Vinnie must have gotten a tattoo and not told him. That probably meant he cried like a little baby and didn't want to talk about it. Stanley decided to lay off at least for a little while. Getting the tattoo on his own chest hadn't been a picnic either.

"As if you read," Stanley said. "Just keeping my mind sharp." He had plans for the future. Someday, he'd be a detective or reporter instead of just delivering papers and working the scoreboard.

The crack of the bat made Stanley drop his book on the catwalk and leap to his feet. His stained tweed cap blew off in the breeze and his hair flopped in his face. He watched the ball fly over the left field fence just below them. The rest of crowd came to their feet with a roar as Joe Medwick, the St. Louis Cardinals' left fielder, trotted around the bases.

"Holy Smokes, Ducky murdered that ball!" Vinnie shouted as he thrust his fist in the air. Medwick waddled around the bases in his trademark duck-like trot and spat out a wad of tobacco, getting it on his hands. Stanley watched, amused when the player wiped it on his uniform and kept jogging.

"Score change. Old Man Seable will give us the business if we slack on the job," Stanley said and pointed at the white numbered metal placards beside them. He didn't want the cantankerous old guy to lecture him. He got enough of that at home these days.

"I'm still in heaven over that homer by Joe. You get this one, huh?" His friend leaned back, hands behind his head, elbows out, with a pleased grin on his face.

Stanley punched him in the shoulder. "Gotta earn your keep."

"Yes, *Mother*. Look, just because you think you're such a man, doesn't mean we ain't still kids," Vinnie said, picking up one of his comic books.

"*Aren't* still kids," Stanley corrected as he grabbed the "3" scorecard and made his way to the metal ladder. He suddenly realized his hat wasn't on his head. He ran back and breathed a sigh of relief when he saw it lying next to Vinnie. Leaning over, he picked it up, flipped it in his hand, and put it on backwards.

"You and that hat—it's like your security blanket."

"It was my dad's. You know that." He reached up and ran his fingers over the frayed brim of his cap.

Vinnie nodded and fanned himself with the comic as Stanley walked back down the catwalk to a metal ladder at the end. With a quick pull of his muscled arms and thrust of his legs, he made his way up to the scoreboard, onto a wooden walkway, and changed the numbers.

Stanley stood at the end of the platform and looked out at the ball field. Not a bad way to make a few extra bucks. Selling papers was his bread and working at the ballpark was his butter. For now.

The Cardinals had taken their place on the field, warming up for the next inning. Stanley took off his hat and twisted it in his hands. Glancing down at it, he noticed some of the threads had started to fray and he found a small hole in the back before he put it back on.

He'd had it as long as he could remember but didn't want a new one. Even if he could afford one. Which he couldn't.

The old hat and the necklace of St. Jude, patron saint of lost causes, given to him by his mom the day she walked out of the house for the last time, were all he had left of his parents. He couldn't even remember their faces or voices. The cap and necklace were like clues to a great mystery he'd never been able to solve. Stanley doubted even Sherlock Holmes could get to the bottom of it all.

Stanley leaned his head against the scoreboard. He knew that baseball was only a game. But sometimes it seemed almost holy, like a source of mysterious joy sent by God to everyone trying to make it through bad times. The smells of the pinewood that held up the stadium, the freshly cut grass, and grilling hot dogs swirled together like an offering of incense. He breathed in deeply and smiled. Nothing ever bothered him here or at the parish.

"Hey, wadda ya doing up there, Fields? Get your butt down here."

Old Man Seable stood on the catwalk beside Vinnie looking up through the scoreboard opening, hands on his hips. His white hair stuck out in all directions and his coke-bottle glasses were blurry with grease. Stanley tried to hide a smirk.

"I was just thinking about ways to steal your job, Mr. Seable."

The old groundskeeper shook his head. "Better watch that mouth, son. I'll knock it clean off ya."

Stanley chuckled as he climbed down the ladder. "You'd have to catch me first, old man. That'd be a feat for the papers."

He strolled over, took off his hat, and bowed.

"Look at you. Think you're the man, do you? Think every girl's eye is on you because you look like a movie star or something?" Old Man Seable demanded, mouth twitching.

Vinnie snorted as he munched on a half-eaten sandwich. "Thing is, sir, every girl does love him, including your … "

Stanley shot Vinnie a look. Old Man Seable would pound him if he knew that Stanley had kissed his granddaughter last week. She'd trapped him in one of the underground tunnels, and Stanley didn't like to disappoint a girl.

The old man stared at him with watery eyes. "Better watch yourself, boy. Kissing all those girls will bring nothing but trouble."

Stanley nodded. He didn't want to argue with the old man. Besides—he was right. Girls were trouble. Maybe that's why he could never really fall in love with any of them. Then again, he couldn't complain about the kissing, their warm skin against his, or when they'd whisper in his ear. And, the way girls smelled … How could he resist something soft and sweet in this crummy world where everything was so rough?

Vinnie laughed. "I keep telling him that."

"Listen, you bums, I need someone to go down into the tunnels and get me some green paint. The scoreboard needs touching up after the game, and my leg is bothering me more than ever," Mr. Seable said, grimacing as he leaned against the metal railing.

Stanley knew a walk down the tunnels meant missing two innings. But he was starting to feel kind of guilty for kissing the old man's granddaughter.

"I'll get it," Stanley said as he made his way toward the stairs that led down to the stadium.

"Thatta boy. Vinnie, you could use more energy like that, you no-good lazy …"

"He's only doing it so you won't ask …"

Stanley grabbed an empty tin can resting on the metal railing and whipped it at Vinnie's head. It hit him with a dull metallic thud, and the boy yelped in pain.

"Gonna make you pay for that one, Stanny boy." Vinnie scowled, rubbing his head.

"Yeah, like the last time we boxed. You were in bed for two days."

Vinnie groaned with indignation. "I was not."

Old Man Seable broke in. "Boys, stop it. Stanley, get the paint. Vinnie, get the ticker and update all the out of town scores. Move, both of you, before I knock out your brains and do the world a favor."

Stanley made his way down the stairs and into the stands. The smell of hotdogs and popcorn drifted on the breeze. He breathed in and wished he had some spare change to buy all the stuff he wanted to eat.

He showed his pass to the ushers and made his way through all the rich people sitting behind home plate. Stanley smirked to himself. They came to the games dressed up like it was some kind of fancy garden party. The men wore three-piece suits and their best fedoras, while the women put on smart dresses and wore silly hats. He thought of that girl he'd seen climbing out the window. No reason why something so pretty should be topped with such a ridiculous hat.

The saying may be that clothes made the man, but Stanley always believed work made you a man. About the only thing that looked good on him were his black shoes, a gift from the *St. Louis Post-Dispatch* staff for selling the most papers last year on his street. He'd earned those shoes with his own two hands. It may not be the best work, but he was grateful. These days finding work was no easy thing. Soup kitchen lines of tattered figures with downcast faces seemed to grow every day. The city rushed around them as they faded against the crumbling brick buildings, useless and going invisible. A man without work was a forgotten ghost.

Stanley found the tunnel entrance, showed his pass, and the guard let him through. He made his way down the brick tunnels into the bowels of the stadium. The dim lights led him toward the supply room. Stanley shoved his hands in his pockets and thought about the night ahead. He'd learned there were four families on the brink of starvation in the neighborhood. He and his gang, the Knights of St. Louis, wouldn't let that happen. They'd raid the trash cans over on Lindell tonight. Those people had so much money; they threw perfectly good stuff away.

"Stanny, I'm here."

He stopped short and turned to see Margaret Seable, Old Man

Seable's granddaughter, leaning against the wall, her curly blond hair flowing to her shoulders like liquid gold and framing a heart-shaped face. Even though she wore a plain brown dress like most girls in Dogtown, she managed to look dolled up. Her painted lips slid into a smile that was all for him.

"Heya, Maggie. What's shakin'?"

"We could be, if you wanted." She sauntered up to Stanley and put her arms around his waist. As she got closer, her sweet perfume started to shut down his brain.

He didn't resist and drew her close. Her body pressed hard into him and memories of their last electric encounter rushed through his head. As Stanley ran his hands along the sides of her body, he forgot about his resolve to stay away from her.

Maggie leaned in and kissed him lightly on the lips. Stanley closed his eyes and let out a soft breath as his heart surged into overdrive.

"Aren't I more fun than those stupid old books and papers?" she whispered against his lips.

Stanley paused. Margaret sometimes laughed at his reading and plans to be a reporter. She'd promised to cure him of it by marrying him and making him get a "real job." Her idea of ambition was to marry a guy with a lot of dough.

Stanley leaned back and forced a smile. "I'd better get back up to the scoreboard. Your grandpa would murder me if he knew I was down here with you." He was being a coward. Stanley needed to come clean and just tell her how it was. "Look … I like you, but I'm not sure we're … a fit."

She furrowed her brow. "So, you got your hands all over me and now it's all over?"

"No, it's not like that. We just don't work." He wished he felt something for her. But Margaret didn't know him. Not really. She liked that he was the leader of the Knights, but she had no idea what was going on in his head. If all he was to her was Sir Paycheck and all she was to him was Miss Feelgood, it probably wasn't love.

"What if I tell Grampy that you tried to take advantage, how do you think your precious job would look then?"

Stanley swallowed hard. He hadn't thought about that. He couldn't risk losing his job.

"You wouldn't do that to an okay guy like me, would you?" He smiled on one side and looked straight into her eyes.

Margaret's cheeks colored as she stared at him, crossing her arms. The dim light of the tunnel made her eyes gleam. Stanley thought he saw tears. "You hurt my feelings, Stanny."

"Sorry, Maggie. I'm just trying to stay out of trouble with the old man. You know I care about you." He put his hands in his pockets and avoided her eyes. He hated to see a dame cry.

Maggie sighed with relief. "Leave Grampy to me. Promise to take me dancing next week and I won't make any trouble for you." She smirked. "I'll make it worth your while."

Stanley let her burrow into his arms. He sighed. "It's a date."

"I can never stay mad at you," she murmured into his chest.

He kissed her hand. "Now, fair maiden, I must fetch paint for the King, forthwith."

Maggie giggled and kissed him on the cheek. "I'll be seein' ya."

Stanley smiled until she disappeared out of sight. Then he slumped against the wall and let out a deep breath before he continued down the tunnel toward the supply room.

At the end where two passageways broke off to his right and to his left, Stanley heard low voices drifting from his right. His stomach tickled, and he strained to hear what they were saying but couldn't make anything out.

Usually no one came down here during games; everyone was too busy watching the Cardinals. His curiosity got the best of him and he followed the voices down the passageway. Stanley found what everyone called "the engine room," which was really the place where they brought all the broken signs, old bases, and other cast-off items from the stadium. He often nicked a broken bat or two. No one would miss a few old bats, and he could get a good price for them on the street. Local gangsters loved Cardinal stuff and it helped the Knights buy food for people.

He crept down the passageway until he could start making out words.

"Baby, I know you wanna help me, but you're gonna get into trouble. I can take care of it myself, Evie," a man said in a low, hurried tone.

Stanley recognized the voice of Paul Duncan, a third-string catcher who worked in the bullpen warming up relief pitchers. He was a good guy; he got Stanley an autographed ball from Dizzy Dean after Stanley cleaned Paul's cleats.

"Let me help take care of your gambling debts so we can be free," a woman pleaded. "It's taking too long, and Iowa is awful. My grandmother is a beast—she always has to remind me how lucky I am that she took me in after—"

Paul's voice was gentle as he said, "I know. You've had it rough. But I'm uneasy about all this, and that's a fact."

"I had to come. All I could think about was you, baby," she whispered in a soft, soothing voice.

"But, what about those hooded guys you told me about? They might do something to hurt you. I'd go crazy if something happened to you," Paul said.

Stanley peeked around the corner to see Paul in his white Cardinals uniform. The birds on the bat stretched across his broad chest. In his arms was a dame. She was beautiful, with her hair cut in a tight, dark bob. She wore a knockout red dress and her eyes shone as she stared at Paul, her full lips pulled into a slight smile. No doubt, Paul was a lucky guy.

Stanley suddenly realized if he stayed where he was, they'd see him. He ducked back into the shadows of the tunnel and stood there, wondering what he should do.

The woman's quiet voice echoed off the cement walls. "I know you're worried, but I have a plan."

"What plan?"

"My diary, Paul. There's a code in it. We need to get it from my little sister. Give it to the Egan Gang, the Raven's Flock, or whatever they're calling themselves now. It'll be just what you need to get out of hock with them. Pay your debts, and then we can run away. Disappear. Let them all eat each other alive."

Paul's voice was louder. "Why would they want your diary? I've been paying them back slowly. I don't like welching on a debt. It ain't me."

"This will pay your debt by giving them information. Believe me, they'll want it. You know what I did for the Veiled Prophet when I was his queen," she said with a bitter laugh. "Well, it's all connected. We can bring it all down by using the gangs against them."

Paul shook his head and fidgeted with his cap. "I just don't know, Evie."

Stanley mouthed a silent "Oh" as he realized who the dame was: Evelyn Schmidt, a former rich girl who'd messed up bad and gotten thrown out of paradise. She'd been crowned the Queen of Love and Beauty at the Veiled Prophet Ball a few years ago but had fallen into some sort of trouble. They'd taken her crown away for "unsuitable behavior." The papers had used words like "disreputable" and "shameful," and even, "things that can't' be described in this family newspaper."

He shook his head. That line ensured everyone would fixate on those "unseemly" things, like Evelyn having sex in the back of Paul's car or in her bedroom at her parents' palatial house on Lindell. He'd watched editors at the *Post-Dispatch* tell writers exactly the right phrase to spark people's dark side. And, he had to admit, it's how he got people to buy papers. The nastier the story, the more people wanted to read about it. Stanley peeked around the corner again to get a better look at her.

Paul spit tobacco on the ground and pulled away from her. He paced the room muttering to himself and then said, "You shouldn't have come. They won't like it if they find you here."

She scoffed. "Once everyone knows about the numbers they won't be able to do anything to us. The numbers are the key to the whole business. It is beginning, Paul. They've started their plans. You know what that means … for people like you."

The ballplayer turned pale. "I know … But my ma was an immigrant—not me."

"That doesn't matter to them," she said.

"But, I mean, what can we do? Ain't it dangerous? I might be fine with the Raven, but they ain't likely to be happy to see me at the Rookery. They told me to stay away."

"Show some spine, will you? A few days of danger and then we can be free. St. Louis will explode, and we can be together," she said.

Stanley shifted his leg and bumped against a shovel behind him. The tool fell to the floor with a clatter, and Stanley held his breath, pressed tight against the wall.

Evelyn startled, her eyes wide. She grabbed Paul's arm. "It's them," she whispered.

"Nah. Don't worry, baby." Paul glanced around, nervous.

"They watch. Sometimes you can't see them. It's not … natural." Her voice came out strangled and breathless. Her previous courage seemed to be trapped in her throat.

Stanley wiped sweat from his brow and crouched down, trying to control his breathing.

"That's a load of hooey. They ain't ghosts." Paul walked toward the doorway and leaned out. Stanley said a quick prayer to St. Jude for protection as the ballplayer called out, "Say, anyone out there? Show yourself, and I promise not to hurt ya."

At that moment, a rat ran across his foot and into the room past Paul.

"Ah, it's just a rat," the ballplayer said as he walked back to Evelyn.

"We won't have any peace until we've stopped them," she croaked.

Stanley peered out to see the couple embrace. A flash of light caught his eye, and he noticed a large gold ring with a glittering red stone on Evelyn's hand where it pressed against the ballplayer's back.

"I know, baby. I won't let them keep us apart again."

"So, what do you say? Get this diary to the Raven? Help me set Lindell Boulevard on fire?" Evelyn pulled back and looked into Paul's eyes.

"I just can't, Evie," he said with a gentle voice, caressing her cheek. "I got a life with the team. Let's wait 'til the season is over in a few weeks. Go on back to Iowa where you'll be safe—just for a little longer and then we'll see. I'll come see you soon. We could take the pennant and go to the Series. Imagine that!"

Stanley knew Paul had said the wrong thing; he could hear the tears in Evelyn's voice. "You're a coward, Paul Duncan, and not a real man. Do you know how much I've given up to be with you? Everything. You want me to keep hiding? I want to be with you. It's the only way we can be free. And you talk about the pennant? Baseball … baseball! How dare you." Her lip trembled and she raised her fists in frustration.

"Okay, baby. Calm down. Shh … shhh." He held her wrists to keep her from beating his chest. "You win. Let's meet in Forest Park tonight after sunset, at the statue of St. Louis, in front of the art museum. You need to explain it all to me. I wanna know exactly how those numbers work and what Legion is planning to do. We'll plan then, okay? I gotta get back to the game."

Stanley could hear them kissing. He didn't want to see anymore, so he crept to the other branch of the tunnel and walked silently toward the supply room.

His mind raced with what he'd just heard. Evelyn wanted to bring someone down. But who? And what about those numbers she kept talking about? How was that gangster, the Raven, involved? What the hell was Legion? And what was the plan? Did it have something to do with the gangs? Evelyn said everything was connected with the rich people on Lindell. Was it some kind of new alliance between the gangs and rich merchants? That couldn't be good. At all.

Stanley's head spun with the possibilities. Something else was going on here other than a disgraced beauty queen coming back to town. He knew that'd he'd have to talk to Vinnie and that stunk. They usually avoided talking about the gangs. It's how they stayed friends.

Taking a small leather-bound notebook from his back pocket, Stanley wrote down, *Meeting at St. Louis statue tonight. Veiled Prophet? Gangs? What sort of information does her diary have? What are the numbers? Who/what is Legion?*

Stanley kept the notebook full of things he observed on the street for possible stories to pitch to the city editor at the *Dispatch*. None of his ideas ever got taken, but Stanley knew he'd hit the jackpot one day. And this one had all kinds of promise, full of sex, lies, cover-ups, and maybe some kind of alliance between rich people and the gangs of St. Louis.

Grabbing the paint from the supply closet, Stanley rushed back through the tunnels, up through the seats, and back to the scoreboard.

Old Man Seable met him when he reached the top and boxed him in the back of the head. "Took ya long enough. What were you doing, runnin' for president?"

Stanley grinned. "Nah, looking for wood to build a coffin for your funeral, old man."

"No respect. Get outta my sight before I belt you good."

Stanley found his way back to Vinnie, who'd just finished updating the out of town scores. "Hey pal, thanks to you, I got a large knot on my head. I owe you one."

"Whah, whah, whah. You've had worse from your older sisters."

"I oughta ... " Vinnie drew back his fist and then winced. He glanced down at his arm and then covered it up, but this time Stanley saw the red, swollen skin and tattooed 01 on his forearm.

"Are you still hanging around with the Raven's Flock? Is that who gave you the tattoo?"

Vinnie frowned and lowered his eyebrows. "Why do you wanna know? You turning copper like your uncle?"

"Nah. Just wondering. I want you in the Order, but I can't as long as you're hanging with them."

"I can hang with whoever I want. They're not bad fellas, you know. They keep my family fed when I do jobs for them. We gotta eat. Besides, what makes you think I want to be in your stupid gang anyhow?"

"Like what kind of jobs?" Stanley asked, picking a sliver of wood from a post and chewing on it.

"Mind your own beeswax, reporter man. You ain't gonna get me to rat out anyone."

Stanley let it go, knowing he wouldn't get any more information out of his friend. Still, Vinnie's evasiveness about his tattoo bothered him. They spent the rest of the game changing the score, talking about the Cardinal's chances for the pennant, and about the new girls who'd moved into Dogtown.

Stanley thought about the conversation he'd overheard in the tunnel. He remembered that Evelyn Schmidt had lived in a fancy pile of bricks on Lindell. He wondered if she'd gone home, or even if she could. Frowning, he tried to imagine living in her world. Cast out whenever you did the slightest thing wrong? No thanks. All the money in the world wasn't worth that.

The girl from the window crossed his mind again. There was something attractive about a girl escaping on her own, one who didn't act like a princess waiting for a white knight to rescue her. Both the window girl and Evelyn showed spunk. Seemed as if not everyone from Lindell were stuffy snobs.

The secret meeting with the disgraced Veiled Prophet Queen and Paul could be the scoop that got him a respectable job on the newspaper. Then he wouldn't have to scrape for food or live with Uncle Seamus and his pal, Jack Daniel.

A familiar tickling in his stomach caused Stanley's pulse to jump. With growing excitement, Stanley stared out at the Cardinals on the field, not seeing the game. Maybe this was going to be his big break.

Chapter Three

The Schmidt family lived in a red brick Colonial-style mansion just a few houses down from the Malloys on Lindell Boulevard. The green shuttered windows and gabled rooftop seemed to stand aloof, gazing over the tops of the surrounding trees which were painted in yellow, orange, and red. Hazel rang the bell and then glanced down at the state of her clothes. She smoothed the skirt of her blue dress and bent to straighten the seams of her stockings, then realized she'd taken them off.

Ah, bananas.

The large wooden door opened and Meyers, the silver-haired butler stood there, a polite smile stretched in place. After a quick glance over her bare legs and back up at her face, he raised his brows, amused.

"Good afternoon, Miss Hazel."

Hazel shrugged and gave him her sunniest grin. "Meyers, you're a mess." She reached out and made his perfectly crisp, straight bowtie crooked. "There now. What would you do without me?"

The old man opened the door wide. "Come in, Miss," he said, fixing his tie. "Miss Alesandra is in the north parlor."

"Thanks!" Hazel knew the way. She skipped toward what she and Sandy thought of as the blue room because of the blue, striped wall papering. She heard a radio playing schmaltzy music through the sliding wood doors, then a familiar voice.

"And now, *The Romance of Helen Trent,* the real-life drama of Helen Trent, who, when life mocks her, breaks her hopes, dashes her against the rocks of despair, fights back bravely, successfully, to prove what so many women long to prove: that, just because a woman is thirty-five or more, romance in life need not be over; romance can begin at thirty-five."

Hazel rolled her eyes. Why did Sandy listen to that show about old people?

She slid the doors open. Sandy lay on her back on the floral couch facing the glowing domed radio. Her honey-blond hair spread out around her head in glossy waves. She didn't look up.

"Set it on the desk, Flora." Her friend waved an elegant hand at the other side of the room.

Hazel glided over to the tall writing desk and boosted herself to sit on it. "Like this?"

Sandy barked a laugh and sat up. "Hazel Malloy! What's new? Where's your escort?" She glanced around as if searching.

Hazel kicked her feet, letting them swing. "I jumped out the window, and I'm on the loose. Want to go see a movie tonight? Let's sneak out."

"You're pulling my leg." Her brown eyes popped wide. "You straying over the lines?" Sandy's smile widened in surprise and delight.

Hazel shrugged, feeling a bit foolish. "Oh, foo." She was used to being the predictable one; maybe it was ridiculous to try to be anything else.

"Well it's a first, but I think it's marvelous." Sandy wrinkled her nose. "Too bad the new one is a baseball picture." Raising her slender eyebrows, she pretended to yawn into her hand.

"*Death on the Diamond.* It's Robert Young, and it's what's playing, so who cares? Let's go." Hazel hopped onto her feet, restless and ready for fun. She'd escaped out of her window, and she didn't want to waste her chance. Her friend lay back down on the couch. Sandy was beautiful, lazy, and good for nothing. Hazel smiled. "C'mon. Why not?"

Sandy shrugged. "Don't want to. I'm cozy right here."

"Well that's a curve." Hazel folded her arms and frowned.

Her friend smiled back, wide and slow, nestling into the cushions. Sandy rarely bothered to explain herself. Like when she'd showed up at the Spring Swing dressed in a top hat and tails. Hazel never heard her reason for any of it. She supposed at the time it had something to do with Sandy's love of tuxedo-wearing actress, Marlene Dietrich. They'd just laughed like mad together until the school headmaster asked Sandy to leave. It was a scandal.

The sound of the radio program continued and the Schmidts' plump maid, Flora, entered the room carrying a silver tray with a chicken sandwich and glass of milk balanced on it. "Here now, Miss Alesandra." The maid's teeth gleamed like lamps from her cocoa skin.

"Set it on the desk." Sandy didn't even look up from her manicure.

"You're delightful, Flora," Hazel said.

"Mm-hm. I'm the tops. You hungry, Miss Hazel?" For such a large woman, Flora moved with grace as she set down the tray, her skirt and apron swaying gently around her thick legs.

"I'll eat some of hers. She's watching her figure." Hazel leaned over the tray and picked up half of the sandwich.

"She's not the only one watching her figure these days," Flora chuckled. "All them young men swarming like bees. You 'spectin' one tonight, ain't you, Miss Alesandra?"

Sandy sniffed. "That will be all. Thank you, Flora."

The smile on the older woman's face froze. "Yes, Miss Alesandra." With an abrupt turn, she left the room.

Hazel clicked the radio off and, chewing a bite of sandwich, dropped down onto the couch. "Why the snootiness with Flora?

She's a peach. And who's coming tonight?"

"I'm missing my radio program." Sandy pursed her lips.

Hazel gave her friend a stern look. Something had put Sandy in a peevish mood. She was her closest friend, but she was difficult to really know—unpredictable.

Sandy let out a sigh. "Flora forgets her place. Daddy is thinking of giving her the kiss off. But never mind that," she sat up again, her eyes glinting, "you sweet on Charles Chouteau, or is he up for grabs?"

Hazel was about to object to Flora possibly losing her job, but Sandy's question distracted her. "Charles? You don't mean that quiet boy who follows Gabriel Sinclair around? Is that who's coming over?"

"I wish. It's just Simon Busch and his family. The boy has a nose like Jimmy Durante—how's a girl supposed to get around that beak for a kiss?" Sandy stuck out her tongue. "But I wouldn't complain if Charles escorted me to the VP Ball—he was approved." She sighed. "I like the shy, mysterious kind, they're always the best kissers in the end … all that hidden passion." Sandy smiled slow and dreamy. "Gabriel ask you yet?"

Hazel let her head fall back against the couch. "I suppose that's why he's coming over tonight." Since learning she had gotten the gilded invitation, Hazel'd had an uneasy excitement playing in her stomach whenever she thought of it. The Veiled Prophet Ball was the biggest event in St. Louis society. But the subject made her uncomfortable, especially in the Schmidt household.

"Have your gown yet? I do. Mother had mine shipped from New York. It's lovely and just a little, tiny, smidge daring. Can't wait to be seen in it. Hope yours isn't a rag, or I'll be forced to stand by Brigitte." Sandy loved being the center of attention, and she hated Brigitte Slayback.

"My dress is still being made. Don't worry, I'll be togged to the bricks." Mumsy's dressmaker was taking care of it, and Hazel's dad had shelled out some serious money for it. Seemed like a waste under the circumstances.

Hazel regarded her pretty friend and sighed. “I hate to be a pill, but you know the Veiled Prophet won’t pick either one of us.” There. She’d said it. Hazel shoved the last bite of sandwich into her mouth. Her dad probably had high hopes, but Hazel would never match up.

Sandy scowled. “Says you. Did Madame Zelda look into her crystal ball and tell you that? Why wouldn’t we be chosen?” Sandy acted as if she didn’t know—now she was in a huff.

Hazel rolled her eyes. She swallowed and licked her lips before answering. “My mother and your sister.”

“Evelyn was crowned Queen of Love and Beauty when she was about my age.” Sandy rose and paced over to the tray of food, taking a swig of milk. “We have as much chance as anyone. Maybe.”

Hazel was sure it was the business with Sandy’s sister that made her act crazy sometimes—like Sandy wanted to show everyone she didn’t care what they thought, which wasn’t true. “What do you hear from your sis these days, anyhow?” After Evelyn Schmidt had been given the greatest honor a girl in St. Louis could get, things went south, and that didn’t mean Arkansas. It had been all over the papers. Hazel still heard the servants’ gossip and occasional rumors at school about it.

Sandy shook her head. “Not much … a letter now and then. I miss her, Hazel. Sometimes I go into her room and pretend she’s going to come in and snit at me for going through her stuff—remember how she used to do that to us?” Sandy smiled but her light brown eyes were wet.

Hazel nodded. “Yeah.” When she was a kid, she thought Evelyn was the most glamorous girl she’d ever met. Her room always smelled of Chanel perfume and Golden Glint Shampoo.

“Anyway, all of her things are still in there. Daddy didn’t let her take anything with her—and you know she’s not welcome back. The last letter I got from her just said she missed me and she asked me to look for—”

“Alesandra.” Mrs. Schmidt’s alto voice cut through the room.

"Oh, hello, Hazel. How are you?" Sandy's mother stood in the doorway, slender and poised in pearls. A soft ivory evening dress pooled at her feet, and her chestnut hair was in a wavy up-do. So classy. Not like Mumsy.

"Hello. Just fine. And you?" Hazel glanced down at her own disheveled appearance and heat rose in her cheeks.

"Very well, thank you." Mrs. Schmidt's smile was polite but she shot a look at her daughter. "I'm afraid we have visitors coming, and Alesandra needs to dress for dinner."

"Okay. Well, I'll see you around, Sandy."

Sandy didn't answer but nodded at Hazel. There was something tight about her movements as she strolled to the radio and turned the knob. Sandy was upset but Hazel wasn't sure why. The sounds of Cole Porter lifted from the wooden radio and filled the room, masking the tension with jumpy music.

There's something wild about you child
That's so contagious
Let's be outrageous
Let's misbehave!

Hazel let herself out with the sound of Mrs. Schmidt's disapproval and Sandy's rebellion fading behind her.

"Turn off that clatter, Sandy."

"You're just a tin ear."

"Don't use that slang on me, young lady. I have excellent taste in music. I don't like those lyrics. You know what it's talking about."

"Sex, sex, sex! It's 1934!"

Hazel cringed, shut the front door behind her, and descended the steps of the high porch, disappointed she'd be out on the town alone.

Hazel knew how to get to the Hi-Pointe Theater but had never walked there or gone alone. Ever. She walked up Lindell Boulevard along the edge of Forest Park as cars passed, and the houses seemed to shrink as she approached North Market Street. A woman in a drab brown dress holding a baby wrapped in newspapers sat in the grass on the edge of the park. The woman stared at Hazel with deep-set eyes. A shiver went down Hazel's back, and she clutched her handbag tight, quickening her step. Surely that woman and her baby took no comfort that their situation would be "sorted out" as the "cream" floated to the top, as Pops had put it.

Hazel kept an eye open for the tall newspaper boy who sometimes stood on the corner of Lindell and Skinker Boulevard. Several times, as Jennings took her to school in the Buick, they'd passed the boy and Hazel had felt a slight tugging in her belly. She didn't know why, out of all the people she passed, she wanted to know what his life was like and who he was. He never seemed to notice her pass in the automobile; his bright blue eyes flicked about as if impatient with the people walking by as he waved the front page and called out the headlines.

Further down the avenue, a few young boys in red baseball caps played catch in the street with a blackened ball. As cars approached, they'd shout to one another and run to the sides of the road to let them pass. Across the street, a man in a worn-out gray suit puffed a cigarette, leaning against a lamppost. He watched Hazel with narrowed eyes. She looked away and hurried on.

Chapter Four

When the game ended, Old Man Seable gave them their pay and told them not spend it on booze like every other darn Irishman or Italian he knew. The boys walked out on the bustling street and waited for the next trolley car. Automobiles rattled past, belching out black smoke, and a worn-out busker sat on the curb playing a hot piece of jazz on the saxophone with an empty felt hat at his feet. Stanley bobbed to the music and tossed a coin into the hat before climbing into the trolley.

Several minutes later, they got off the trolley at the usual stop and walked past the St. Louis Art Museum, one of the only buildings left from the 1904 World's Fair, dominating the top of the hill in Forest Park. A statue of King Louis IX of France perched on top of a rearing horse stood in front of the museum. The statue had become the rallying point for his gang after their nightly raids of the trash cans on Lindell. Stanley had a familiar surge, like a call to arms, as he looked at it. He'd chosen the saint as their patron because Louis IX of France had done so much to help the poor.

Now it would be the meeting place tonight for Evelyn and Paul for whatever they were cooking up. It was time for a little late-night sneaking around. He had to know what they were up to.

"Tell me something, Stanny boy," Vinnie said as they walked around the hill.

"Sure."

"Wasn't King Louis a rich boy with money and power? Don't you hate all those things? Why'd ya name the gang after him?"

Stanley almost made a sarcastic remark about how well-read Vinnie was, but he caught himself. Taking off his hat, he stopped and stared at the statue. Vinnie had a good point. He thought and then said, "It's not money or power that I hate, Vinnie. It's how it's used, you know? Rich people have a lot. They should help people with it, just like Father Timothy says in his talks on Sunday. They've got an obligation to help people."

Vinnie nodded. "Guess so. But I doubt I'd agree if I weren't poor myself."

Stanley smiled. "Yeah." He shrugged. "It's their choice. I wonder why anyone with plenty wouldn't choose to help. I have nothing, yet I do what I can."

They made their way to the other side of the park, past the stench of the St. Louis Zoo, where Stanley scanned the bushes for one of the scruffy kids who always seemed to be playing there. A little boy with a dirty face and ragged pants that were too short caught his eye. Stanley pulled out a small bag of peanuts he'd found on the ground at the stadium and tossed it at the kid.

Leaving the park, they crossed Oakland Avenue into Dogtown, their neighborhood.

"All right, Stanny boy, this is my station. Later, gator."

They shook hands and Stanley walked toward St. James the Greater Catholic Church. His brain was going faster than the Indianapolis 500. The walk past the fancy pants mansions hadn't improved his mood. It was hard not to want to throw rocks at the swells living in comfort while so many others scratched in the dirt for food not far away. He'd also sort of hoped to see the girl from the window again.

Stanley kicked at the weeds that strained up through the cracks in the pavement. Poor weeds. He knew how they felt. Why did he and everyone he knew work so hard for so little? It didn't seem right. He knew Father Timothy wouldn't want him to hate the swells, but he couldn't help it. Every time he gave a starving kid bread he'd found in a Lindell trash can, his anger grew a little more.

Up ahead, the spire of St. James pierced the sky, pointing to the sun. Stanley decided to stop in the church and say a quick prayer. As he climbed the stairs, shouts echoed from the alley next to the church. It sounded like someone in his neighborhood was in trouble. He jumped off the stairs and raced around the corner.

Four kids about Stanley's age stood around a small boy with pale white skin, blond hair that stuck out in all directions, and a few missing teeth. He only came up to their chests, but he'd put up his fists to defend himself.

"Come on, kid, join us. The Raven could use a good kid like you. We gets lots of meals and all you gotta do is deliver some messages, see?"

Stanley clenched his fists. He'd told these goons to stay off his street and away from Bobby "Teeth" Guido. They'd taken out more than their fair share of his choppers. He stepped into the alley behind the group and walked toward them.

"I ain't joinin' you, and you can tell the Raven I said so. I'm a Knight," Teeth declared in a high-pitched voice.

The four teenagers laughed as their leader, a tall kid with a thin mustache who went by the name of Jericho, said, "You ain't got much of a choice, pal. Join us or get a beating."

Teeth raised up his fist. "I'll take the beatin'."

Without hesitation, Jericho struck out with his right fist and hit Teeth square in the face. The kid went down, holding his mouth as blood trickled through his fingers.

"Wow, I think that's the bravest thing I ever saw, hitting a little kid surrounded by your gorillas," Stanley drawled, taking off his coat and hat and throwing them on the ground. He rolled up his sleeves, taking a boxer's stance, and counted to slow the rush of adrenaline that pumped through his veins. *This may not end well*, he thought. But at least Teeth would get away.

The four meatheads turned around, and Jericho said, "This ain't your concern, Fields."

His heart beat harder, and heat rose to Stanley's cheeks. "I told you brainless vagabonds to stay out of my neighborhood, didn't I?"

Jericho cracked his knuckles. "Ya talk like a swell," he sneered. "Anyways, the Raven don't take kindly to being given orders, see?"

"Not giving orders to him. They're to you, ignoramus," Stanley said, furrowing his brow.

"Whatcha gonna do about it, book boy? You're all by yourself," said a fat teenager with pimples.

"No, he ain't."

Stanley turned his head to see his friend Arthur, one of the Knights of St. Louis, walking up behind him. His bowler hat, pulled low over his dark eyes, was cocked to one side and a cigarette dangled out of his mouth.

"Why ya hanging with this guy and his stupid Knights? You should be with us," Jericho said.

Taking a long drag on his cigarette, Arthur took off his hat and put it on the ground. "I decide my business, not you. Now get outta here before we take yous apart."

Trying not to smile, Stanley turned back to the teenage gangsters. "Yeah, beat it."

Jericho smiled. "Still four against two, Fields."

As the aspiring gangster got closer, Stanley could see a blue tattoo with the numbers 0203 on his right forearm about the same place as Vinnie's. The ink looked inflamed and infected.

"Nice tattoo. The Raven giving that out to all his little chicks?"

"He ain't givin' those out. Shut your yap," Jericho said, pulling down his sleeve and grimacing.

"No? So where are they coming from?" Stanley asked without much interest as he relaxed his boxing stance.

The thug took a swing at Stanley then, and it caught him square in the mouth. Staggering back, the world spun a little, but he didn't fall. Arthur launched himself at Jericho, grabbed his head, and head-butted him in the nose.

The fat kid and a short and stacked redheaded gangster came running at Stanley. He crouched in a boxer stance again, held up his hands, and blocked all their punches. Raising his right leg, he kicked the fat kid, who crumpled in a heap clutching his stomach.

"Let me have Jericho," Stanley shouted as he moved between Arthur and the gang leader. "I told you to stay out and leave Teeth alone. Didn't I? I told you to stop picking on little kids."

Stanley launched his right fist into Jericho's stomach, left hooked him to the side of the head, and kicked him in the knee in quick succession. The guy went down in a heap, groaning in pain. Stanley didn't care about God. He didn't care about Father Timothy. All he wanted to do was hurt this kid as much as possible.

He kicked Jericho hard in the stomach once. Then again. And then again.

"This is what you get when you pick on people smaller and weaker than you, and who can't fight back. This is what you get, you pile of horse crap."

Stanley saw red and his ears roared from the blood pumping in his veins. With each blow, the gangster grunted and tried to block the next one.

"Don't. Ever. Come. Back. Here. Again. See?" Stanley growled.

"Please … stop … Fields … " Jericho groaned, curling into a ball. He held up one hand covered in blood from his gushing nose.

Stanley didn't want to stop. He wanted to keep hurting him. But as he drew back for another punch, Arthur grabbed his arm. "He's had enough, boss. He ain't worth killin' and yous gettin' sent to the chair."

Breathing hard, Stanley looked down at his handiwork. His stomach tightened. The gangster scooted away and left a trail of blood on the ground.

"The Raven … he's gonna … I'll get you … " Jericho grimaced and pressed a hand to his belly.

"Gonna finish that threat or just mumble?" Arthur asked, lighting another cigarette.

Stanley turned to the other gangsters, who stood back staring at him like he was a loaded gun. "Take this piece of trash and get outta here."

The others hurried to grab Jericho, pulled him to his feet, and carried him out of the alleyway.

Stanley's heart thumped hard in his chest as he tried to calm down. He sat on the curb and closed his eyes. Taking deep breaths, he started to shake as the adrenaline rush slowed down and the cold crept in. The inside of his lip bled into his mouth. He spit into the gutter.

Stanley slicked back his sweaty hair as he looked up at his friend. "Thanks, pal."

Arthur picked up his hat and took a drag of his cigarette. "That was somethin' else. You did what I would've done. Ya hurt him bad." He stuck out a hand and helped Stanley to his feet.

Stanley rubbed his head and looked at the blood on the ground. Vomit rose in his throat, and he swallowed hard.

"Easy, rookie." Arthur smirked. "It's only blood. We all got it. Even the swells bleed red."

Arthur had a rough life, Stanley knew, with his father never leaving his bed and the bottle and his mother in the nut house. They'd been okay once, years ago, until someone from Lindell decided otherwise. Arthur had only shared bits about how it all went down; he wasn't exactly chatty. One day, Arthur's family had money to spare and then the next they were struggling to stay off the streets. Nobody seemed to know anything else about it.

Stanley understood where Arthur's rage came from. Still, he couldn't get over Arthur's love of beating the crap out of guys. And now, he'd become just like him. He'd lost control and given himself over to anger.

Teeth came up to them, grinning, another tooth gone, and blood smeared on his chin.

"Fellas, that was aces! I want to fight like you!"

Arthur waved him away. "Get outta here, pigeon, before I beat you myself. Don't you have things to do? You better get what I asked you or I'll thump you good. Now scram." Pigeons were what Arthur called his informants: kids who ran around and gathered information. All of them were orphans and looked up to the Knights as big brothers. Without them, the Knights wouldn't know much that was going on in town. Stanley had to admit that their information saved their asses more than once. Still, he didn't always feel right putting kids like Teeth in danger.

Teeth stared at Arthur but didn't argue. "Yeah. Okay." He turned and started down the alleyway.

"Hey, hold on," Stanley said, picking up his coat and pulling a baseball out of the pocket. He threw it to Teeth, who caught in midair and grinned.

"Stanley, this is aces. Where'd you get it?" he lisped.

"At the ballpark, dummy. Now get outta here," Stanley said, shooing him away.

Teeth ran off as Arthur said, "Good thing I was looking for yous. Yous mighta had some trouble."

Stanley nodded, his stomach still churning. "Something wrong?"

"My pigeons. They keep disappearing on me, and I don't like it."

Stanley shrugged. "It happens, doesn't it? I mean, I'm sure they're okay. Probably some moved on to another city or something. Going to California for work and all that."

Arthur took a huge puff of his cigarette. "Nah, Professor, it ain't like that. Gimme some credit, will ya? I don't pick flighty birds.

Something strange is going on. And seeing that gorilla's tattoo … I've started seeing those around town. I've got the pigeons flying around, trying to see what they can pick up."

"Any ideas?"

"Nah. Not yet. Just wanted to tell ya about it. I don't feel right, that's all." Arthur stared at him, puffing on his cigarette. "Was wondering when yous would beat someone bloody. Welcome to the club. Feels good, don't it?"

Frowning, Stanley said, "I just lost control. Won't happen again." He didn't understand why he lost control of his anger, and that scared him more than anything. Every time, in every fight, he had a handle on it. Anger got you hurt. Why was today different? Was he finally losing it and turning out like Arthur? Would he beat someone to death someday? The terror of that idea overwhelmed Stanley and made him afraid of himself.

Smiling, Arthur took the cigarette out of his mouth, examined the lit end, and then took another drag. "It gets easier every time. Soon you love it. Besides, we're at war, Stanley. And you know it." He nodded. "See ya soon." Arthur strolled down the alley and disappeared.

Stanley put his hands on his knees and breathed hard. He didn't want it to get easier. But Arthur was right: a part of him enjoyed smashing Jericho's nose and watching the blood flow.

Shuddering, he straightened up and ran into the church. Dabbing his finger in the holy water, Stanley crossed himself and found a pew toward the back. He bowed to the altar, entered the pew, knelt, and bent his head in prayer.

Please. Please forgive me for my anger and my rage. Help me understand.

After a few Glory Bes, Hail Marys, and Our Fathers, Stanley said a quiet "Amen" and felt at peace. Not that he had the mystery of God figured out any more than the mystery of his parents suddenly disappearing. At times, his anger flared up at all three of them, and he would confess it to Father Timothy. A good person wouldn't resent their parents. And no one should be mad at God.

But, sometimes, a lot of the time, he was guilty of both.

Sighing, he left the pew, bowed to the altar again, and went outside. As he walked down his street, neighbors sat on the porches of their brick houses and duplexes to gab with each other. Everyone gave him a wave and a "Hi Stanley, how was the game?" when he walked by.

"Watch out, Stanny!"

A ball came hurtling from the street ball game, and he caught it with one hand. The group of younger kids cheered as he tossed it back to them. He looked back to see an automobile coming down the street, and he yelled, "Car."

Everyone scampered out of the way until the car passed spewing black smoke and loud jazz. The game resumed despite the oncoming dusk and the possibility of dinner. Some of them wouldn't have much to look forward to anyway. If baseball was the food of life—play on. Stanley watched for a minute and then continued toward home.

Women with scarves tied on their heads beat rugs to get out the dust, and men smoked as they cut the grass. Somehow, being around the people in his neighborhood cleared away the rest of the dark clouds in his head, as his uncle liked to say.

Finally, he reached home, sweet home. Ralph O'Sullivan, the man who shared the other half of their brick duplex, sat outside on the porch wiping his large forehead with a handkerchief.

"Stanley, how about that game, eh?"

"We murdered 'em," he replied with a smile.

"Be careful, son; your uncle ain't happy with you," Ralph said.

"Oh, why?"

"Loose lips sink ships, sonny boy." The man chuckled and coughed.

Stanley swallowed hard as he went inside. If Seamus wasn't happy, he might be in for another beating. He could never tell with his uncle. On one hand, Stanley wasn't living on the streets, had a room to himself, and Seamus let him do what he wanted. But, the bad side was when Seamus felt like knocking him around. The way Stanley felt right now, he probably should just take it. Probably he deserved it after the fight with Jericho.

As he walked from the small foyer into the living room, the wooden floors creaked. Taking off his coat, he threw it on the old, red couch that occupied the wall to his left. He went to turn on the radio when his uncle said from the dining room, "Hey, boyo, can you bring me that anatomy book from the middle shelf?"

He breathed a sigh of relief because the request meant his uncle was on a case. Maybe he wouldn't have time to get sore at him. Turning to the wall of books opposite of the couch, he found what Seamus needed. His uncle was a big-time reader and insisted Stanley read too. As a kid, he'd fought his uncle hard because all he wanted to do was play in the street. Seamus didn't give in and now Stanley was glad for it.

He went through the doorway and into the small dining room occupied by a wooden table big enough for four. Seamus was looking over some papers and taking occasional drags on a smoldering cigarette. He was a small, compact man with flaming red hair, a living Irish stereotype, and the younger brother of Stanley's father. He could box guys twice his size. Seamus dressed smart even with his small paycheck. He wore a suitcoat, silk waist jacket, and wire-rimmed spectacles when he read. He told Stanley the only way to get people to respect you was to dress to the nines. It bothered Stanley that his own uncle bought into that peacock philosophy. A man was what he did, not what he wore. No amount of smart clothes changed the fact that his uncle drank too much.

"Hey, here it is. Want me to start the food?" Stanley asked, trying to keep it light.

Seamus took the book from him, laid it on the table, and frowned. "I did already. Stew is a cookin'. Want to gab at ya for a wee bit," he said with a broad Irish accent.

Stanley looked to his right into the small kitchen just off the dining room. The smell of beef stew wafted through the room. He tried to look unconcerned as he sat down at the small table, but his heart thumped hard in his chest. Stanley scanned the room for any empty bottles or evidence that Seamus had been drinking.

"What's up?"

Seamus didn't smile. "You, from what I can figure out. I'm gonna ask you directly. You been smooching with Sean McDaniel's daughter?"

Stanley didn't see any point in lying about it. "A little. Just messin' around. But … "

"And why you goin' and doin' that? You know Sean. He could make things hot for me at work, you know," Seamus said, blood rushing to his face; not a good sign.

"I dunno. She kissed me first. What was I supposed to do?" It sounded stupid to Stanley as soon as it came out of his mouth.

His uncle sighed, took off his glasses, and squinted. "That's the excuse I always hear from your gob. 'It wasn't my fault, Seamus.' And 'She couldn't keep her hands off me.'" He paused. "For someone who thinks he's a knight, you don't act much like one."

Stanley looked up, hands gripping the table. "What do you mean?"

"Knights don't go around kissin' girls and gettin' them into trouble. Sean won't let his wee innocent gal," his uncle snorted, obviously not believing that lie and making Stanley feel a little better, "out of his sight for the near future. You come close, and he'll take a baseball bat to ya, and that's a fact. Plus, he threatened to file a report on me, some made-up pile of garbage. Won't stick, but it'll cause trouble for a while. And I wanna keep the peace around here."

Stanley's faced burned as he bowed his head. He really did feel ashamed. It seemed like every choice he'd made in the past year had been all wrong. At the same time, he couldn't help but feel a bit resentful toward his uncle. It wasn't like he was ever around to help. "I'm sorry, Seamus. I didn't mean to cause trouble."

"Well, it's all past, boyo. But enough is enough. Get a hold of it, or it will ruin you." His uncle stared at him. "Look it, I know you've had a rough go of it. Practically havin' to raise yourself and all. I know I'm not around much, but I've done the best I could."

Stanley nodded without listening. He'd heard this speech before.

"But you know around here, it's all about politics: on the force, in the city, whatever. People watch you. You're kinda hard to miss—not only because you command a room but also because you're my nephew. You got responsibilities, ya know."

Responsibilities. That's all Seamus preached. Stanley tried not to make a face, knowing it might get knocked off.

"Yeah, well, I live up to them, don't I? I go to school, serve at the church, work two jobs, and bring in as much money as I can." *And I don't waste it on booze*, he added to himself.

Seamus held up his hands. "All that's aces. I'm proud of ya, and your da would be too. But don't use that excuse to get into trouble elsewhere. You know what I mean. I know all about your little Order of Knights. That stops now. No more of it. Get me?"

Stanley nodded. The girls would stop, but the Knights wouldn't. Stanley made a fist. No way would he give it up just because his uncle was afraid. His uncle talked about being a good Catholic, but he was too much of a politician to claim that with any honesty. Seamus, while being a good cop, bowed the knee too much and to the wrong people. And the drink made him weak.

"Listen, boyo, no shame. We all got our things. I smoke and drink a wee bit too much. Part of the stress of the job. We just gotta go to Mass, confess, and live a little better than before, like Father Timothy says." He paused. "But still, I gotta punish you, lad. So, no going out for the next few evenings, and disband your Knights."

Stanley almost leapt out of his chair but instead gripped the underside of the table. Opening his mouth would get him nowhere.

He could sneak out easily enough, but not if Seamus was watching his every move. Plus, any sass talk, as Seamus called it, often resulted in a punch to the face. While Stanley stood about five inches taller than Seamus, the little detective packed a wallop. Not that he got hit very often, at least in comparison to his other friends. One day, he would stand up to the wee man himself. But, until then, Stanley would need to control his temper.

"Yeah, okay. It's all aces. I'll just do some reading and listen to the radio. No big deal."

Seamus eyed him. "I'll take your word as a man. I've got the late shift for the next few nights, so you're gonna have to fend for yourself."

Stanley nodded and gave his uncle the thumbs up. "No worries." Sometimes the late shift meant a stop at O'Malley's. But now, instead of whispering a password to get through a trapdoor for booze, his uncle could stroll in, sit at the bar, and guzzle at his pleasure. At least now the guilt of being a cop and being a drinker was not an issue. Problem was, he'd had to compromise and make deals with unsavory types for years to keep up his habit. For that, Stanley couldn't respect him.

Seamus nodded, stood, put on his suit coat, straightened his tie, grabbed his black fedora, and put his hand on Stanley's shoulder. "Good man. I'll wake you for Mass tomorrow."

Sure you will, Stanley thought. *If you can peel yourself out of bed that early.*

With that, Seamus left the apartment. Stanley went into the kitchen, helped himself to a bowl of stew, and sat at the table. He forced himself to eat, but his brain would not shut off. He thought back to Evelyn and Paul, sorting through their conversation in his mind.

Stanley shoved his dinner aside and realized he couldn't stay home, no matter what he promised his uncle. Too many questions gnawed on his brain. He decided to sneak out through the alley to avoid his neighbors, although everyone was probably inside eating dinner anyway. There was just enough time to walk to the movies at the Hi-Pointe, catch the sports highlights, and watch *Death on the Diamond*, a mystery flick that centered around the Cardinals. The money he'd gotten from Old Man Seable would be enough to pay for the film and some popcorn. By the time the movie ended it would be after sunset. Hopefully, he could make his way to the St. Louis statue, find Paul and Evelyn, do a little spying and then head home before Seamus got wise.

He went upstairs, grabbed a flashlight and put it, along with his notebook, into an old knapsack. Looking in the mirror, he straightened his flat cap.

All right, Stanny boy, time for a night of adventure.

Stanley crept down the bricked alley, hiding behind trash cans and blending in with his surroundings. He'd trained his Knights from the stuff he learned in his mystery novels and other books he read; how to use ordinary scenery to blend in and hide was an important skill to use when they raided the garbage bins on Lindell. He was proud of all the work they'd done without getting caught.

He arrived at the Hi-Pointe Theater and breathed a sigh of relief. Red neon signs framed the marquee that proclaimed the strange combination, "*Death on the Diamond* with cartoons." Stanley smiled on one side. A little distraction from life was a good idea.

Stanley stood there for a moment, checked both directions for people he knew, and saw no one. Straightening his cap, he went into the theater.

Chapter Five

It took longer than Hazel thought to walk to the theater. It seemed like such a short distance in the Buick. Although the fall temperatures were a nice break from the heat of summer, sweat beaded on Hazel's face—partly from nerves and partly from the humidity. Her eyes stung from the dirty air and grime seemed to coat the inside of her throat.

By the time Hazel reached Clayton Avenue, she'd counted dozens of people who looked hungry. She felt exposed to the desolation outside of her comfortable world, and it clung to her clothes like dust. Blisters were forming on both feet. Three miles was certainly longer on foot in heels with no stockings. Exhausted and tense, Hazel looked up to see the brick façade of Hi-Pointe Theater, the marquee lit up like a Christmas tree against the dusky sky.

As soon as Hazel pushed her way through the front doors, her weary journey was forgotten. The buttery smell of popcorn and the framed posters of her favorite stars caused her pulse to race. There was only a small crowd in the lobby, but Hazel loved the excitement in the air.

"Hello, miss," the young ticket girl greeted her, eyeing her clothes. "Not the most romantic movie, miss." The girl seemed to be looking for who she had come with. "How many?"

Hazel smiled. "Just one. Robert Young is a dream. Besides, I love a good mystery."

After Hazel bought her ticket, she headed to the concession counter for popcorn but stopped short. Hazel's heart jumped, and she lost her breath.

The boy.

The tall, blue-eyed newsie strolled past her eating popcorn. He never looked up, he seemed to be so deep in thought Hazel almost expected him to walk into a wall. He wore a flat cap backwards over his reddish-blond hair, black shoes that looked as if they'd just had a spit shine, and a ratty knapsack on his back.

A couple, dressed really fine, blocked his way. The boy tapped his foot with impatience as the man in an expensive suit and black fedora stood in front of the doors talking to a woman with a mink stole around her neck. Hazel wondered why they weren't at the Fox Theater downtown.

"Darling, we could go someplace else. Just thought you'd have a lark doing something different."

The woman sniffed. "Slumming is not my idea of evening entertainment. This place serves *popcorn*," she said with a sneer. "They let anyone in here." She lifted her chin with disdain at a group of kids Hazel's age. They seemed okay. Average. Their clothes, although not expensive, were neat and clean, and they seemed like a spirited bunch—laughing and free. Hazel almost envied them.

"Well it isn't the Park Avenue class you're used to but … " The man continued talking to the woman as he led her way.

The newspaper boy's shoulders stiffened, and he watched them go. "Swells," he growled with a stormy look on his face.

"Did you want some popcorn, Miss?" the old man at the counter asked Hazel.

She forgot about getting something to eat when the boy disappeared into the auditorium. "Uh, no thanks," she said as she made her way toward the auditorium.

Inside the dark interior of the theater, newsreels already played. The announcer talked about strikes on the docks somewhere out west. Black and white images of men in baggy clothes holding signs marched across the screen. Hazel didn't see the uniformed usher with a flashlight who was usually there. She searched the seats in the glow of the flickering silver light.

The backwards hat gave the newsie away. He sat by himself munching popcorn. Now what? She had no experience talking to boys outside of her set—or any boy she didn't know. Hazel pressed her lips together and shifted her hat. She was a Malloy. This was just another leap.

Stanley stood in line to get his popcorn with his head down, deep in thought. He looked up, and his stomach did a flip. The girl he'd seen climbing out the window on Lindell was standing in line to buy a ticket for the movie. He took a deep breath. There was something about her, something more than just beauty. Thing was, he couldn't figure out what that something was. It could only mean trouble.

He avoided looking over at the girl again, waited for his turn, bought his popcorn, and made his way to the theater. When he reached the doors, he heard a rich woman sneer at the Hi-Pointe crowd.

She's just a rich snob. Looking at the Hi-Pointe like it's some Hooverville or something. Why don't they go back to the Fox Theater where they belong?

He resisted the urge to glance back at the window girl and went into the theater.

Maybe the girl just wanted to slum it at the poor people theater like those other swells. Wanted to prove how compassionate she could be or maybe she was an old-school flapper thrill seeker. It felt like a violation for swells to wander into places that belonged to regular folk. Didn't they have claim on enough, with all those fancy restaurants and clubs where normal people weren't allowed? Stanley just wanted to relax and enjoy himself and not have to look at those high-hat snobs. Well, he couldn't let them spoil it for him. Flexing his hands, he let out a breath and decided not to care tonight. He had to admit that window girl was a real dish though. Maybe he didn't mind so much that she'd turned up.

Finding a seat about halfway up, he moved over to the middle of the row. With a sigh, Stanley sat down with his large bag of popcorn and started to munch on the delicious, salty kernels. It was a splurge, but he needed it tonight. The whole day felt off. He had that nagging feeling that a storm was brewing. Trouble with Maggie, the mysterious conversation he'd heard in the tunnel, the fight with Jericho, his uncle's sermon, and this girl. He forced his attention to the screen. So far, the pre-show entertainment, as the theater called it, was just a bunch of crummy commercials.

Stanley leaned back into his soft chair. He tried to shut off his brain for a moment and closed his eyes. He started to breathe deep and his body began to relax. He could feel himself drifting off to sleep before he heard the rustling of a dress. He opened his eyes, and there she was.

The girl stood in front of him, smiling, with her blue eyes and hair shining in the light from the projector. She looked even better up close, her wavy hair sticking out from under a brown, feathered hat and in a knock-out dress. She had the gonk, all right, the ability to render him speechless. This was new, and he didn't like it much. It meant he wasn't really in control anymore.

She spoke first. "Pardon me, is this seat taken?"

With an effort, he tried to recover his smart mouth.

"Yeah, well, a G-man was in here earlier scoping the place for

President Roosevelt. Hasn't come back, though. So, you're probably safe."

The girl wrinkled her nose at his rudeness, and he wanted to kick himself. "Well, I'm sure the president wouldn't ask a lady to give up her seat for him," she said.

Stanley shrugged. "He's the president; he can do anything he wants."

Stupid, he thought. *Don't be a jerk. She's trying to be nice.*

"Well, that'd be a feat for the papers, getting his huge wheelchair in here and all," the girl cracked with a hint of laughter in her voice. Without another word, she sat down right in front of him and the long feather from her hat trembled in his view of the screen.

Stanley scratched his head. He was surprised that someone outside of the press knew about the wheelchair. He'd heard of more than one cameraman who had their camera smashed by the secret service for taking a picture that showed the president's disability. It was all about protecting the image. This girl must have some important friends. He bristled.

"Say, girl, do you mind removing your hat? I don't think it was meant to be a part of the movie."

She turned around and made a face at him. "This isn't just a hat, wise guy, it's a Henri Bendel." It sounded like "On-ree" Bendel.

Oh brother, Stanley thought. Swells named their hats? Just what he wanted to hear right now. His temper simmered, and Stanley leaned forward, seized the feather, and shook it.

"Nice to meet you, On-ree, I'm sure you're nice and all, but take a seat, eh?"

Turning, the girl scrunched her nose at him. "You're not a very nice boy."

Stanley shrugged. "I'm nice to my friends and to people who don't name their hats."

She turned back around and didn't say another word. He expected her to turn up her nose and make another smart comment. But she didn't. Instead, she removed her hat and placed it on the seat next to her. Further, she didn't storm out of the theater and fetch the manager like most swells would have done. Instead, she glanced back at him and raised a brow.

Huh, he thought. *This girl …*

As the cartoons started to roll, he stared at her outline, lit up by the flickering movie screen. Her shoulders shook as she laughed at the cartoons. Everything about her reeked of money and privilege; things Stanley resented. But her twinkling eyes and sly smile were like clues to a deeper mystery. She had a light inside her.

Get a hold of yourself, Stanny boy. What did Vinnie say before? She's like a painting. I can look, but I can't touch. Besides, didn't you resolve no more dames?

His little pep talk didn't work because how he felt about this girl was like the difference between the Cubs and the Cardinals. The other girls would never win the Series. For no rational reason, he wanted to take her hand and stare at her like a fool. His skin tingled like she was shooting sparks.

She glanced back at him again and caught him staring. Flushing hot, he busied himself with his popcorn and tried to act like he didn't notice her, while his heart ran all the bases.

The girl gave him a slight smile and whispered, "I'm sorry if I was rude earlier. My name is Hazel, Hazel Malloy."

Stanley took off his hat and bowed in his chair. "Stanley Padraig Fields, at your service, madam."

She gave a small chuckle and said, "I adore your hat."

"Well, he doesn't have a name. I hope that's okay."

Hazel let out a blast of laughter. Someone from up front turned to shush them; a newsreel had begun. She covered her mouth and snickered quietly. After a moment, she dropped her hand and sighed. Hazel looked at his popcorn. "I wish I would've gotten some. It looks so divine."

"If you let me, I'll buy you some. I've gotta use the bathroom anyway," Stanley blurted, and then mentally counted the change in his pockets. It should be just enough.

Hazel blushed and shook her head. "Oh, no, I couldn't let you do that. It's way too much trouble."

Stanley furrowed his brow at her false pity. "I don't mind. Happy to do it."

She shook her head. "It costs too much money. Please don't."

Stanley stiffened and sat back in his chair. "Think I can't afford it, is that it?"

"Oh, no, nothing like that. I just meant—"

Stanley held up his hand. "You think I'm some poor slob who can't afford to buy a girl some popcorn, don't you, you snobby swell? Why don't you sashay back to Lindell?"

Hazel rose to her feet and put her hands on her hips. "Hey, now listen here. You've got a chip on your shoulder the size of King Kong. I was just trying to be thoughtful, so cram it."

This girl had sand, no doubt. Stanley tried to find a snappy comeback but all he could do was grin.

"Sit down!" somebody called out.

Stanley almost laughed, anger gone. Hazel plopped back into her seat, her back to him.

Maybe he should have left it at that. But his pride stung. He also didn't want her to ignore him. He leaned forward to talk to the back of her head. "Think you're entitled to me being nice, do you?"

She turned and glanced at him from the corner of her eye. "No. I expect you to have manners, even as a smelly Irish boy from Dogtown. Don't they teach those over there? Given your rudeness, I'd say no, no matter how well you may articulate." Hazel sniffed, raised her chin, and faced the movie screen.

Stanley didn't know what else to say. She beat him but good by reminding him of his manners, and he felt a little ashamed of himself. He couldn't believe he gave a scrap about what any swell thought.

He tried to focus on the News of the World, which was all

about that Hitler guy, who'd just become dictator over in Germany, meeting with some American businessmen. He frowned at the images of the small man with intense eyes shouting and waving his hands. Something about that guy creeped him out, even though many people thought he would save Germany. *Not with that moustache.*

Hazel cleared her throat and tucked a curl behind her ear. Stanley shifted in his seat. He had been rude and he wanted to make it up to her … see that smile again.

No, he told himself. He needed to steer clear of this one. It would bring all of Lindell down on him, and the politics … His uncle would box him good and Stanley would never be able to keep raiding trash cans for his neighbors.

Stanley moved a few seats over, so he could watch Hazel from the side; the clip onscreen with Dizzy Dean and his brother Daffy talking about their chances at the World Series wasn't even enough to make him look away. She chewed on her bottom lip and her slender fingers fidgeted with the strap of her handbag. She was upset.

He stood without a word and went into the lobby. Digging into his pockets, he took out a nickel, just enough for one small bag of popcorn. He looked at his half-empty bag and wondered if he could combine them.

Stanley approached the counter, placed his nickel on it, and said, "I'd like a small bag of popcorn."

The counter boy handed him one. "Here you go."

"Thanks, bud."

He combined the two bags into one and went to the restroom to take a few moments in the mirror. Stanley took off his hat, straightened his hair, and practiced his smile. He looked down at his hands and decided to wash them.

"Well, that's gonna have to do."

Stanley made his way back into the theater and sat beside her with his heart pounding. The sleeve of his jacket brushed her arm and she turned to him in surprise but didn't frown at him or tell him to go away. She smelled good.

"So, um, I got some more popcorn. We can share. You know, to make up for my rudeness. On-ree can have some too, if he wants."

Hazel let out an unladylike laugh and clapped a hand over her mouth. "Shh! The movie's about to start."

This boy was outrageous. She glanced around, hoping nobody she knew was there to see her sitting by him. What would Pops do to her if someone told him she had been at the movies with a strange boy?

"I'm not the one braying like a donkey." He cocked an eyebrow and shoved a fistful of popcorn into his mouth. Several pieces escaped and fell into his lap.

"Classy. And it's *Henri*, the French form of Henry." She reached into the popcorn bag, took a kernel, and delicately put it into her mouth. Hazel raised her chin and chewed with her lips closed.

He froze for a second, embarrassed, but then he slapped his knee and stifled a laugh, his cheeks full of popcorn. "This ain't caviar, dollface."

Hazel sniffed. "Don't call me that. You, who needs a vacuum cleaner handy when he eats." She glanced down to his lap full of popcorn and gave a *humph* of satisfaction. She'd put him in his place, again.

Stanley wiped his mouth and then brushed the contents of his lap onto the floor. "Not a problem. You're the one who can't get dressed without a maid."

"I do so dress without a maid!" The very idea. What did his kind know? She wasn't some helpless princess. She folded her arms in her lap and hoped he didn't notice how wrinkled her dress was. "Been dressing all by myself for as long as you have, wisey." She pursed her lips.

A sly look glinted in his eyes and he dropped his gaze to her legs. "You forgot something."

Hazel blushed hard and tucked her legs under her seat, yanking down on the hem of her dress. "I had stockings on … " It wasn't as if she could tell him she climbed out of a window and ruined them. "It's a funny story … " She fidgeted with her handbag; the wild feeling when she'd removed her silk stockings was long gone, replaced by shame—in front of a Dogtown newsie.

To Hazel's mortification, a saucy grin stretched across his face. "Oh, I happen to know this one."

The man sitting in front of them craned his neck around and scowled. "You mind not yakking during the show?" he growled.

"Pipe down. It hasn't even started yet." Stanley gestured at the screen just as the seating lights dimmed and the MGM Lion appeared.

The man's angry answer was covered up by the roaring lion on the screen.

"Oh, yeah?" Stanley cupped a hand to his ear. "Your sister's a cheap what?"

Hazel sank into her seat; his gutter talk made her cringe, although a part of her wanted to laugh at his wicked words. Her pulse sped up when the man's wide face contorted in anger.

"Why you little—" The man sputtered.

She sat forward and unleashed her sunniest smile. "I'm sorry, Mister, he isn't right in the head. His mother left him at a soup kitchen when he was little and when they found him, he had eaten so much soup it was leaking out of his ears." She patted Stanley's head and nodded at the man. "He's been *different* ever since."

The man rolled his eyes, but she saw how her smile softened him. "Ah, you're nutty." He waved a dismissive hand and turned back to the screen.

The opening credits glowed white, and Hazel settled into her velvety seat. From the corner of her eye, she noticed the boy, Stanley, watching her with a goofy grin on his face.

"You're something," he whispered low as he leaned toward her ear.

A little thrill went through Hazel. He made her skin tickle. Sitting by him in the dark seemed so daring and yet somehow familiar. Stanley was an interesting mix of funny and nice, but also rude and common. Her father would detest him even if he didn't talk like most newsies. Hazel decided to ignore him for the rest of the picture, resolving not to eat any more of his popcorn. They weren't pals and never could be. Besides, he was a troublemaker and she didn't need any of that. Especially with the Veiled Prophet Ball coming up; all eyes would be on her, eyes that waited for any misstep. The Schmidt family had learned that in the worst way—Sandy's sister especially.

Hazel sat tall, chin up, and soon was swept away by her one true love: cinema magic. The film had romance, mystery, and action. Robert Young made her sigh. What a man.

She tried not to pay attention to the boy beside her, even though he shifted around and bounced his knee through most of the film. Now and again, he'd mutter under his breath. At one point, he raised his voice at the screen.

"Look behind you, Einstein! Guy with a gun on the roof—right-field pavilion!"

A lot of people in the theater called out this way at the exciting parts. Hazel was always amused but never felt comfortable doing it herself. Other than Mr. Grumpy in front of them, it was a lively crowd, gasping, clapping, and laughing along with the story. Hazel liked that about going to the Hi-Pointe. This kind of fun and spirit was not acceptable at the Fox downtown.

As the story unfolded, Hazel found herself gripping Stanley's arm when the third murder took place. His arm flexed, and she snatched away her hands, folding them in her lap on top of her handbag. He didn't react, just stared at the screen, holding the now-empty bag of popcorn, slack-jawed. She leaned away from him, her face warming. Stanley was like magnetic energy sitting beside her in the flickering light of the theater and she wanted to turn and stare at his face. He was nothing at all like the slick-haired boys she knew. He was messy and alive.

Ah, bananas.

By the time "The End" appeared on the screen, Hazel sat on the edge of her seat feeling jumpy. When he leaned down to grab his knapsack, she stood and tried to hurry out of the theater, so she wouldn't have to talk to Stanley again, but the crowd clogged up her escape. For some reason, she just wanted to get away from the tall, smart-mouthed, newspaper boy with those eyes that reminded her of July skies.

He was at her elbow before she could make her way to the door. "So that guy in the movie figured it out. Did you? I mean, the clues were there but he took some leaps. I had it figured out, though. My uncle's a copper. He can't watch pictures like this without blowing his top."

She nodded, unsettled by the way her skin prickled when he stood close. "Yeah. I guess real police work is different than the movies. The Cardinals sure couldn't stand to lose many more players at the rate the killings were going. Do you suppose a thing like that could happen?" Hazel's experience with violence and organized crime was strictly entertainment. It seemed unreal to her that people could be that way in real life.

As they pushed through the crowded lobby to the outside, he walked behind her and spoke to the back of her head. "Of course. Our city is crawling with rats. Some of them I know by name."

Hazel shuddered. "Oh." It occurred to her that Stanley could be one of them, even if he didn't sound much like one.

As people dispersed out in front of the theater, she examined him by the glow of the bright marquee lights. Stanley's clothes weren't dirty, but they were worn thin at the joints. His hands were large with scarred knuckles, probably capable of strangling a man. A bruise purpled one cheek and his bottom lip had a small split in it—she hadn't noticed that before in the dim light of the theater. There was something hard about the set of his jaw. Nervous, she stepped away from him. It was dark now, and she remembered she had a long walk home.

"Yeah. Sure. My uncle deals with bums like that all the time. They're all over. Like that guy over there—he's probably packin' heat." He lifted his chin to a figure across the street—a silhouette in a fedora and long coat leaned against a lamppost, smoke pluming up and obscuring his face.

Even though she suspected that Stanley was just trying to show off his street-smarts, a cold shiver ran down Hazel's back. Was that the same ratty man she'd seen as she walked to the theater? She couldn't tell. They both seemed to be from the wrong side of town. Her throat tightened.

"Gee. You really think so? Packing heat? A gun?" Her voice trembled.

Stanley chuckled. "Nah. I'm pulling your leg, doll—uh, Hazel."

He said her name, and she felt calmer. "Well, I gotta head home. It was nice meeting you … Stanley." She stuck out her hand for a shake, and he furrowed his brow.

He looked up and down the street. "You got a ride? Some long, black hearse-like thing with a haughty-faced chauffer?"

She pointed her chin up. "I walked here myself."

"You don't say." That twinkle came into his eyes again. "Well, seeing as you seem like a nice kid, how about I walk you home?"

Despite herself, relief rushed through her body. *Bananas.* She hated to seem fragile. He already thought she was a princess. "I'll be fine." Hazel turned as if heading home.

The tall boy blocked her way after two steps. "Hey. No point in you ending up in the meat wagon. A girl like you shouldn't be out alone at night."

To her surprise, he seemed entirely sincere. He bowed and offered his arm as if he were a gallant knight. Stanley's jaw might have a hard set, but his eyes were kind. She hesitated a moment, but that man still stood on the other side of the street, and she'd just watched three brutal murders. "Well, I guess I could do you the honor." Hazel didn't take his arm, but she gave him a smile and a nod.

He straightened with a chuckle. "Let's make like Houdini and get outta here. I know a shortcut."

Chapter Six

Stanley looked both ways down Skinker Boulevard as Hazel walked next to him. A breeze danced around them, swirling the scent of her. She smelled sweet and expensive. He couldn't figure how he was walking with this rich girl and why it somehow seemed right. With her, he felt more like a man than a boy trying to make time with a girl.

"So, tell me, do you walk strange girls home often?"

"You're not so strange." He turned and winked at her.

Hazel looked down at her shoes. He'd made her uncomfortable. Stanley stared at the street trying to figure out the rules with a girl like her. After a few cars passed, they crossed in a hurry.

"So, this is a regular thing for you?"

Stanley smiled. "Sure."

She stiffened a little. "Oh, so I'm the latest catch, is that it?"

He laughed. As if he could consider a girl like Hazel to be catchable. "Not like that, I mean, I try to keep girls safe and all. Well, okay, it's been like that before, but not now."

Hazel side-stepped away from him, causing Stanley to curse

himself inwardly. They entered the park and followed the path leading to a small grove of trees.

Why was he having such a hard time talking to her? Stanley didn't know what to say to a girl like Hazel. It was stupid, really. To break the tension, he decided to have a laugh.

"So, uh, I've seen you before, you know." Stanley smirked and stuck his hands in his pockets.

"You have?" Hazel asked, backing further down the path. The speckled lamplight filtered through the trees, revealing the wary look on her face.

He shuffled his feet. "You're not easy to miss. Your beauty surpasses the stars." That was a good one—girls loved it when he said stuff like that.

Stopping, she turned back to him and rolled her eyes. "I suppose that usually works on perfect strangers. I thought you were cleverer than that, even though you have dubious manners."

He hadn't expected that response. It stung a little to be talked down to. It's what he hated about all the swells. "Sorry, I don't have her ladyship's airs. Don't have much money to buy any," Stanley snapped, but instantly regretted it. He wasn't going to make a very good impression on her if he kept mouthing off this way.

Hazel stood there and stared him down. She crossed her arms and wrinkled her nose. "What do you mean you've seen me before? Are you some creep who stalks innocent girls, seduces them, and then takes advantage of them on long walks in the park?"

Stanley chuckled to hide his panic, and she sniffed loudly. This wasn't going well at all. He didn't get it. Where had his skills gone? He tried to keep it light.

"What's so funny, wise guy?" She marched further down the path into the shadows.

"Hey, stay close. This place is dark and can be rough at night." He approached her and offered Hazel his arm, but she ignored it, frowning.

"Hm. I never expected an Irish street thug to have such manners and to be able to put together an educated sentence."

That sparked his indignation again. It was like she had no idea she was being insulting. "Oh. I see. I don't fit the stereotype. My uncle insists on proper grammar, among other things," Stanley said as he raised his chin. He realized that she was smiling. Hm. She was teasing him. Was she flirting?

He must have been staring because her expression changed to uneasy and she backed away again. He needed to say something, reassure her. "Say, look here, I'm not gonna hurt you." He wasn't used to having to convince girls that he was safe. Usually they hung onto him like he was a kind of life raft.

"Well, you're not … not … " she stuttered.

"Not your kind? I'm supposed to be an ill-mannered newsie from Dogtown with no social graces?" he asked, using a mocking fake English accent and holding his nose up high. Stanley took off his hat and held it in front of him. "What is my lady's complaint?"

Hazel narrowed her eyes at him. "You seem … insincere. You're nice and then rude and then you try to be funny."

She was right. He was acting weird and it embarrassed him that he couldn't be smooth. Stanley stuck his hands in his pockets, wanting to think straight.

They stood staring at each other. She sure was pretty with the moonlight making her eyes shine. She walked back to him a little.

"Tell me what you meant when you said you saw me before."

Stanley shrugged, not sure how to act anymore.

"Spill it, boy," she said, frowning.

Okay. He just had to be real with her or he'd only make a bigger fool of himself. "Easy. I was heading to the baseball game with my pal, Vinnie. We saw you climbing out of your window. And, uh, I told my friend not look at you because … well … "

Hazel blushed a furious red. "Oh, bananas. You saw that?"

Stanley cocked his head. "Bananas?"

"It's a silly thing I say," she sighed.

Stanley liked how Hazel talked—open and not too flirty or brainless. This girl didn't seem to fit his view of the high-class set. And she hadn't fallen for his knight act. For some reason, he really liked that.

She stepped close, eyes cast down, and gave a shy smile as she looked up. "I've seen you before too," she said softly.

Stanley's heart skipped as their eyes locked. "Yeah?"

She nodded and sauntered back a few steps. "It's getting darker," she said.

"Okay, Bananas. Nice to officially meet you."

Stanley held out his hand, glad he'd washed them in the theater. The black ink of the papers, the dirt at the ballpark, and the thin layer of coal dust that coated St. Louis made a fella's hands grubby pretty quick. He'd bet dirt didn't stick to Hazel. She glowed.

Hazel stared at his hand, mouth twitching. "Hm. Did you really tell your friend to turn away?"

"Yep. As a Knight of the Order of St. Louis the King, I saw it as my duty."

She chuckled a little, then reached out and shook his hand. Her grip was strong but her skin was soft. He held on a bit longer than normal.

"A knight? What's the Order of whatever you just said?" Hazel tucked a stray curl behind her ear.

Stanley wasn't sure how much he wanted a swell to know about his gang, but the warmth of her hand still tingled in his palm. He walked past her before he started to blab. When she didn't follow, he looked over his shoulder. "Are you coming or not?"

Hazel hesitated and then walked fast to catch up with him. "So, how about it?"

Stanley didn't answer at first as he looked around him to make sure things were safe. They'd come to one of the large open spaces of the park. Little fires had sprung up all over the field, and figures huddled over them against the evening chill. The sun had almost disappeared, and the shadows dominated the entire field. He hoped there wouldn't be any trouble. Desperation could make people do crazy things. Some of the people out here he probably knew, and they wouldn't bother them. Still, Stanley would need to be on his guard. You never know who moved into a Hooverville on a regular basis. He strained to see in the darkness for anyone making a move toward them.

"Well, the Knights are my little gang, I guess."

"Ha! I knew it. I knew you were in a gang! You dirty rat. Have you ever shaken someone down for money? Given anyone the business? Been in the slammer?"

Stanley laughed. "Who talks like that, except people in the movies?" He couldn't remember when he'd been more entertained by a girl.

As she chatted on about some gangster movie she'd recently seen, they made their way past people cooking whatever dinner they'd managed to scrounge up. The smell of boiled cabbage filled the air as the wind began to stir.

One of the greasy bearded men at a fire gave a loud wolf whistle at Hazel and said, "Hey, there, beautiful, why don't you come here?"

Hazel let out a gasp and clutched her bag but raised her chin with a fierce expression on her pretty face.

Stanley's heart thumped. Nothing would happen to her while he was around. He stepped between Hazel and the guys by the fire. "Mister, if you're gonna open your gob again, I might put my fist through it. Mind your manners." When the man scowled at him, a feeling rose inside Stanley, the one he'd felt earlier that day—right before he'd beaten Jericho bloody.

"Oh yeah, kid?" The man stared at him, and Stanley stared back, feeling as if his whole body vibrated.

Just make a move … Stanley clenched his fists and waited. The man shuffled backwards and then glanced at the fire. He was just a drunken bum who didn't get what he was saying, most likely. *No point in beating this guy up.*

Stanley let out a breath and turned around to see Hazel giving him a nervous half-smile. He led her away, trying to calm himself down. It was a good thing Arthur wasn't there. It would have turned into a real rumble.

"I knew it. Gangster," Hazel said.

He rolled his eyes. "You *do* watch too many movies. No, the Knights aren't that type of gang."

"Then what? You were pretty tough back there. What do you guys do?"

He furrowed his brow and didn't answer. Art Hill was still a bit of a hike, and he wanted to walk by there to see if Paul and Evelyn were hanging about. They'd never said what time specifically, but he couldn't imagine either of them would be there too late. He should have never offered to walk Hazel home; he might just miss out on the story of a lifetime. Still, he couldn't turn his back on a girl in distress. Especially this one.

"Well, we help people who need it. Find them food. Protect little kids from real gangs, make sure no one hassles dames, that sort of thing." He sounded too much like a hero and for some reason he cared if he gave her the wrong impression. Smiling on one side he said, "And shoot peas at the swells who parade in the city and try to tell us how to live our lives."

Hazel gave him a sideways glance as they finally reached the end of the field and found the road that led to Art Hill.

"So, nobody but you is allowed to hassle *dames*?" She smirked. "I've been on those floats. I'm the girl twirling the baton. I bet you hit me."

He shrugged. "Probably. Wish I could say sorry, but I'm not really." If this girl didn't like his gallant act, then he'd just have to be himself, whatever mix of things that happened to be.

Hazel seemed unruffled. "Do you have an actual peashooter?"

He stopped walking and turned to her. "Why?" She was a major distraction. He should be sniffing out the story of the year, but he wanted to keep hearing her talk.

"So I can see what keeps pelting me in the head every year." Hazel laughed.

Stanley watched her a moment; her laugh washed over him like warm water. The mystery of who she was had him fixated. He pulled out the peashooter from his coat and handed it to Hazel.

"There it is. Feast those blue peepers."

She took the peashooter and held it up to examine it. For a moment, she didn't say anything. He watched her, fascinated by her face. She was pretty in an effortless way, and expressed everything she felt. A million thoughts seemed to swim through her head and they flitted across her face. It reminded him of sitting and watching the Missouri river, imagining what was under the surface causing the ripples. Stanley was curious; wishing he knew what caused her expressions was far more compelling than wondering what created the ripples that broke the river's surface.

"What's in your head, girl?"

Hazel looked up at him as if startled out of a daydream. "Do you have a pea?"

Stanley pulled out a little leather bag and pulled back the drawstrings.

"Hold out your hand."

When she did, Stanley took it and held it. Heat radiated from her palm and gave Stanley goose bumps. He poured out a pea.

"How do I shoot it?"

"Uh, well, put the pea in one end and then blow it through the other. Hit that." He pointed to a tree with a twisted trunk not too far from where they stood.

Hazel did what he said, inhaled deeply, and with a burst of breath sent the pea into the night. It hit the tree with a solid plunk.

"Say, that was a heck of a shot." He scratched his head, surprised she'd hit anything on her first try.

She handed the peashooter back to him with a grin. "Thank you, Sir Knight."

They walked in silence for a long time. Stanley wanted to ask her a flock of questions, but he also realized the futility of that. He'd probably never see this girl again. It was too bad. She was really something. But Lindell and Dogtown didn't mix and it was pure chance that their paths crossed at all.

Stanley turned to her, curious. "Tell me. Where did you see me before? Perhaps on the golf course or having martinis at the club with the mayor?"

Hazel scoffed. "Selling papers, silly."

Stanley's face warmed. "Oh. That's just my cover. I'm actually an international spy."

"There's no shame in selling papers," Hazel said.

"Yeah. Someday I'm going to write for the papers. Then, I'll work my way up to be a regular columnist. Someday I might even move into radio journalism or write for the newsreels."

"I bet you'd be good at it," she said.

That made his chest warm. "Yeah?"

"Sure. You seem smart. And you have a great voice for radio."

Stanley blushed. It was a good thing it was dark. "What's it going to be for you? Ivy League college and marry a prince?"

Hazel let out a ragged sigh. "I hope not. I kinda had my heart set on becoming a pirate."

Stanley chuckled. "Is that a fact?"

Her eyes twinkled when he looked at her and then her face went serious. "Well, to be honest … I don't know. There's what's expected of me and then … there's that part of me that's just mine. The part that's a wild gypsy or an actress or a world traveling explorer who brings medicine and education to native tribes in exotic places."

Stanley grinned, liking her more every second. "Sounds like the interesting part."

Hazel nodded, a little frown tugging down her full lips. "My world is so little, Stanley."

He supposed it was. Seemed like being a swell would open the world up to you but maybe it didn't. Maybe it just confined you to Lindell and the "right places."

"Well it just got bigger, dollface," he said, gesturing to the large, dark expanse of the park.

"Yeah," she breathed. "And I can't see a thing."

"Just follow me." Stanley shoved his hands in his pockets, deep in thought.

After walking in silence awhile, Hazel stopped. "Stupid shoes. I'm starting to get blisters; how much farther do we have to go?"

Stanley turned around and smiled. "Just up and over the hill, really. Not much farther. Take off your shoes. It will hurt less."

Hazel scrunched up her face. "I will not. It's unseemly."

He shrugged. "Unseemlier than parading the town with bare legs?"

Hazel grimaced. "My stockings tore … I need to preserve what dignity remains." Her smile was embarrassed and cute.

They climbed the stone driveway up to the top of the hill. The art museum rose above them like a Greek temple. Stanley paused to wait for Hazel to catch up and a stocky copper appeared from behind a tree.

"Say, you kids, you can't stay at the top of the hill. City is clearing everyone out. Too many people sleeping up there and causing problems, so scram," he called out to them.

Stanley recognized the voice of Liam Reagan, one of the guys who worked with his uncle.

The last thing he needed was Uncle Seamus hearing that he was walking a pretty swell home in the dark. He'd get smacked for sure. Liam was a good guy, so he may not tell Seamus.

Stanley grinned. "There's one of St. Louis' finest."

The copper came closer and then he smiled. "Stanny, is that you?

What in blue blazes are you doin'? Is that a dame with you? Gonna do some smooching?" He clapped a large hand on Stanley's shoulder and let out a guffaw. Stanley's cheeks heated again.

Hazel stiffened and opened her mouth as if to say something.

Stanley tried to sound casual. "Nah. This poor girl got lost in the park, and I'm walking her home."

The copper gave him a wink. "Sure, sure, Stanny boy. Another flower for your collection."

Stanley's reputation had apparently gotten out of hand. He didn't look at Hazel, but he felt her eyes boring into the side of his skull. The sooner this conversation was over the better.

"Can we at least walk up the hill? It's a shortcut to her pile of bricks over on Lindell."

The copper scratched his head. "Lindell is it?" He eyed Hazel and then gave Stanley an impressed look. "Guess it wouldn't harm anything. Just be quick, boyo. The city is pretty serious about it, and I don't want no trouble."

"No worries. And no need to tell my uncle, right?"

Liam nodded. "Square deal. Be safe. Some dodgy people in the park tonight, Stanny."

He tipped his police hat to Hazel. "Be careful of this one, lass. He's a heartbreaker, and how."

"Good night, Liam," Stanley said, giving the officer a sarcastic salute. He didn't bother denying anything to her.

"I guess I'm supposed to feel honored," she muttered.

He shouldn't care what kind of impression he made on her. All rich people thought he was dirt. But he found himself being bothered. Maybe he should have stuck with the knight routine. Nah, she'd be out of his life forever in a few minutes anyway.

They walked at a slow pace up the hill. Hazel kept stealing glances at him and making *pshing* noises.

"Did you spring a leak?" Stanley asked as they reached halfway up the hill.

"Many conquests, eh?"

Stanley didn't say anything. He'd rather box six rounds with Barney Ross than answer that question. It's one thing to talk about it with the guys, but quite another thing to do with a doll. Besides, how could he explain he was trying to walk the straight and narrow now? She'd just scoff.

"Let's go to the St. Louis statue and look out on the lake for a moment," he said, pointing up the hill.

Hazel walked a few steps away from him. "Is this where you bring all your little flowers, Stanley the Knight?"

He sighed. "Okay, I've brought a few girls here. Just forget about it."

She glared at him. "I'm not another one of your conquests."

"It's just a great view of the lake. Come on." Stanley held out his hand. While she didn't take it, Hazel headed up the hill.

She turned to him and said, "Your uncle is a policeman?"

"Yeah, detective. He would skin me if he knew I was out right now. I'm kinda in trouble with him."

"For what, if I might ask?"

"You know, stuff." He scanned the hill for any sign of the lovers' rendezvous.

"Hm. How incredibly specific."

Stanley suppressed a laugh. They were getting close, and he didn't want to make any noise if Paul and Evelyn were already there.

They walked up to the steps of the art museum. On their left, the large statue of Louis IX of France dominated their view. So far, no Paul or Evelyn in sight.

Stanley turned his back on the statue of the saint and looked up at the museum. He loved walking around inside, seeing what the artists created. Streetlights illuminated the entire plaza and the large stone columns that dominated the entrance. There was an eerie stillness, and Stanley had that tickle on the back of his neck that told him something wasn't right. His uncle called it the Second Sight, but that was old Irish superstition. Stanley just called it street sense.

Unaware of his mounting unease, Hazel sighed. “Oh, I adore it here. I love all the beautiful paintings. I could spend hours looking.”

Stanley nodded, trying to play off that he was fine. “Me too. My favorite is the medieval art.” Distracted, his eyes scanned for movement behind the columns.

Hazel smiled at him, opened her mouth to say something, and then looked over his shoulder in horror.

“Stanley, look,” she gasped.

He spun on his heel, thinking some muggers had caught up with them. Stanley’s heart dropped into his stomach. Standing on the low concrete wall behind the large St. Louis statue was a shirtless man wearing a black hood. His bare chest was smeared with a dark brown substance.

“Who the hell are you?” Stanley shouted. Shapeless shadows hovered around the man and Stanley tried to focus on what he looked like. It was as if the darkness stared back at him, blocking his view on purpose.

The figure didn’t say anything, just turned and jumped off the concrete wall. Stanley grabbed Hazel’s hand as they ran to the rail. By the time they got there, the man had sprinted down the hill and there was no way they’d catch him.

“What’s that all about?” Hazel asked, freeing her hand from his grasp. She obviously thought she’s just seen a crazy homeless man—and not the shifting shadows that Stanley saw.

“No clue, but I … ” He turned toward the statue and saw a person slumped against the base. A baseball bat lay on the ground right next to the limp body. Stanley walked over with quick strides and Hazel followed him. When they got close, he saw bare legs with a dress pulled up to the knees. A mashed flowered hat lay on the ground.

“Lady, are you … ” Stanley stopped when he saw the woman’s face. He crouched down to examine her. Hazel let out a terrified yelp from behind him.

The right side of the woman's head had been smashed with the baseball bat. The broken bones caused her face to sink in and blood still poured out of her nose. Stanley touched the girl's cheek and grimaced as blood coated his fingers. The chunks of bone moved under her skin, broken to pieces. His stomach turned, and he took a few deep breaths as the world spun a little. Fainting was not in the cards. He steadied himself with his hands on the ground and tried to keep himself in detective mode.

Stanley felt her neck just to be sure … no pulse. "She's dead." Behind him, Hazel let out a strangled cry.

"No. No. No. No." The look on her face crushed him.

"You recognize her?" Stanley asked.

Hazel didn't answer as her hand went up to her mouth. Her body started to shake. Tears flowed down her cheeks as she fought for control.

"She's my best friend's older sister, Evelyn," Hazel gasped out between sobs.

Stanley looked closer. It was the dame from the tunnels, Evelyn Schmidt. Beaten to death by a baseball bat. This didn't look good for Paul.

"Please. Please. Let's go get your policeman friend. This is awful." She shook and backed toward the gravel drive. Tears ran down her face and she wrung her hands together.

"Okay, okay … " Stanley's mind was spinning. He was worried about Hazel, but he couldn't stop the questions running through his head. What happened here? Was that Paul's bat? Who was the guy in the hood? Stanley scanned the scene and then looked down at Evelyn's legs. Written in black were the numbers 010106. Just like the tattoos on the gang members.

His skin prickled. "What the—"

"What are you doing? Stanley, please. Please," Hazel said as she motioned to him, not coming any closer.

"Hang on." A strange calm came over him. Stanley wiped the blood from his hand on the ground. He shrugged his knapsack off his back, opened it, and took out his notebook. Reaching toward the numbers on Evelyn's leg, he dragged a finger across the black substance.

Charcoal ash, he thought to himself. Stanley wrote the numbers down in his notebook and the words: *More numbers. Are they linked to the conversation in the tunnel?*

"Don't touch her. Please. I know her family. We have to tell someone," Hazel pleaded, eyes huge and glistening in the dim light.

Stanley nodded and stood. "Let's find Liam."

Hazel stumbled down the grassy hill of the moonlit park. Stanley glanced at her from several steps ahead. "You with me, Bananas?"

"Yeah." She swallowed back the urge to be sick. Hazel's legs moved her forward, but nothing seemed real. She was in Forest Park at night with a newsie boy she'd just met, and Sandy's runaway sister was back there, slumped against the statue of St. Louis with her head cracked open.

She couldn't make her brain take it all in. Evelyn's face—caved in on one side, her mouth slack, teeth showing like gravestones covered in blood. Gripped with panic, Hazel quickened her step to catch up with Stanley—her only guide in this darkness. He was a part of it. This was his world, not hers.

The lanky boy marched ahead of her, calling out. "Liam! Heya, copper!" He stuck his thumb and pointer finger into his mouth and blasted a loud whistle that echoed through the park.

Away from the lights of the plaza, where the trees blocked the moon, the darkness deepened.

"Liam!" Stanley pulled a flashlight out of his old knapsack, and the beam swept across the grassy hill and several forlorn looking people in rumpled clothing.

From the trees, near a bonfire surrounded by huddled figures, a voice called back. "That you, boyo? What's the ruckus?" The policeman from before emerged from the shadows, his wide face scrunched in question when the beam from Stanley's flashlight stopped on him. Liam squinted and raised a hand against the light. "Say, put that out."

Stanley clicked the flashlight off and gestured in the direction they had come. "There's been a murder! A girl. Her head is smashed in—there's a baseball bat and there was a guy in a mask," he rushed, his voice breathless.

The policeman's eyes grew round. "Been reading too many of those dime novels? This ain't funny."

"She's dead," Hazel blurted. "It's awful." A sob caught in her throat and she pointed toward Art Hill, blinking back tears. "Up there."

The policeman examined her face. "Say, you're on the level."

Hazel wiped fresh tears away, breathless. "There really was a man in a mask—a hood." Hazel shivered.

"A hood?" Liam's brows dipped.

Stanley's chest rose and fell as if he'd run a mile. "C'mon. He's getting away." He turned and they all hurried toward the statue.

"Which way did he go?" the policeman wheezed as they climbed.

Stanley pointed the way they had seen the mysterious man run.

"Well, let's see the body before we run after this masked fiend." The way the policeman spoke made it clear he didn't buy the whole story.

As they got closer, Hazel prepared herself. She had never seen a dead body in real life before tonight, and her stomach twisted at the thought of seeing the slumped over, bloodied form of her best friend's sister again.

Hazel still remembered the last time she'd seen Evelyn alive. It was just days after being crowned the Queen of Love and Beauty and before the scandal had hit the papers. Even though they were too old, she and Sandy had been playing with dolls, perched on the towering aquamarine satin bedding in Evelyn's room. They stopped to watch as the older girl sat at her vanity. In silk and lace underwear with a filmy robe draped around her pale shoulders, Evelyn was impossibly glamorous.

Evelyn gazed into the oval mirror applying red lip rouge. "It's our duty to be beautiful, girls," she'd said, rubbing her plump lips together.

Sandy snorted and twirled her long braids. "I don't think I care if I'm beautiful."

Her older sister raised slender eyebrows. "Don't be a silly goose. Everyone has a purpose. And luckily for us, being beautiful and privileged is ours."

"Who says?" Sandy tugged on the yarn hair of her doll.

"The Veiled Prophet." Evelyn smiled. "I met him. And he told me that I'm a shining example of what other women should aspire to be." She lifted her chin proudly.

"Yeah, until next year when they crown a new Queen." Sandy stuck out her tongue.

A thrill had run through Hazel. The Veiled Prophet. It was like hearing Evelyn had met Santa Claus. He was mysterious and important. He chose his favorites and gave them precious gifts. A large ruby ring glittered on Evelyn's hand. She was so lucky. Hazel doubted she could ever be chosen—she was too awkward.

Hazel saw herself in the mirror beside the elegance of Sandy's big sister. "I'm not sure I want to be an example to anyone. I always fumble things when people are watching me."

"You're young—you'll grow out of that. Come here … you have such lovely eyes. And your mouth … " Evelyn gestured for Hazel to sit beside her on the tasseled bench. "And just look at your graceful hands. I bet you'd be a pip of a majorette."

Twirling a baton in front of crowds of people seemed like disaster waiting to happen but when Evelyn said it—it seemed possible to learn.

Hazel still remembered the cool, light touch of Evelyn's fingertips as she applied red to her lips and kohl to her eyes. The floral scent of Evelyn's perfume had filled Hazel's head with visions of Hollywood romance and moonlit garden parties.

Now, Hazel found herself staring at Evelyn's pale, lifeless hands, illuminated by a harvest moon that cast shadows across her once beautiful face. "Her ring, it's gone," she said in a whisper. It was as if everything that had given Evelyn life and glamour had been stripped away from her. Now it was all blood and battered bones.

With a buzzing in her head, Hazel backed away from the body of Sandy's sister. Forcing herself to breath deep, she swallowed the lump that rose in her throat. *Don't vomit.* Her brow perspired, and she wiped it away. She breathed in the cool night air and slowly the buzzing in her ears subsided. Hazel became aware that Stanley and the policeman were talking.

"What kind of maniac would do such a thing?" The officer shook his head and then stepped closer to the body. He seemed to notice the numbers on Evelyn's leg. He went rigid and muttered something that sounded like the Irish Peggy used when she was angry.

Liam glanced over his shoulder. "MacDonald and Ferguson are on beat around here. Somebody needs to call this in." He blew the whistle that hung around his neck a few times. Answering whistles sounded from somewhere nearby in the darkness of Forest Park.

The policeman dropped to a squat beside Evelyn's body, took out a notepad, and scribbled something down. Stanley moved to stand beside Hazel and put a hand on her back for just a moment, steadying her.

Liam pulled a handkerchief out of his pocket and wiped the numbers off the body.

Stanley made a noise in his throat. "Isn't that evidence?"

"Listen, boyo, I'm the cop here. Now, out of respect for your uncle I'm asking you to keep your trap shut. See?" He straightened and faced them both, eyes flashing.

Hazel swallowed. Something wasn't right. The kindness Liam had shown before was gone. It seemed like the policeman was threatening them. "But … I don't understand," she stammered.

"Exactly. You don't. Leave it be." He turned his eyes to Stanley. "It's bad enough that you've been out here with the likes of her … I don't think Seamus would like to know what you and your Knights have been up to." He sneered.

Stanley's hands curled into fists, but he nodded. "Don't want any trouble. We're aces. I'm no stool pigeon." He motioned as if zipping his lips closed.

Liam nodded. "There's a good lad. Smart, boyo. Leave the police work to me. We'll catch the slime who done this."

Two other policemen came from out of the night and within minutes Hazel and Stanley were being questioned about how they found Evelyn, what the hooded man looked like, and whether they knew the victim. In a blur, Hazel answered as best as she could under Liam's watchful glare. She didn't mention the numbers, and Stanley didn't either.

Sirens brought more policemen and a few men in trenchcoats and fedoras who crowded around the body. Cameras flashed like lightening, fixing the image of Evelyn in Hazel's mind in bright colors.

Red. So much red.

A man in a black fedora holding a notepad approached Hazel. "So, you see what happened here, Miss? What's the scoop? Who's the dead dame? Someone said you knew her. Who would blip her off? What were you doing here at night—you don't look like the kinda tomato from this part of town? What's your name?"

Hazel stepped back, confused by the barrage of questions. "I-I'm Hazel Malloy," she stammered.

"Malloy? Like Nicholas Malloy? Hot dog!" The man scribbled in his notebook.

"Back off, Jackson. You buzzard." Stanley grabbed Hazel by the arm. "Don't talk to this guy," he said to her.

"B-but the detective asked me some questions." Hazel had no idea what was going on. Stanley spoke down to all of the adults, so she couldn't tell who was in charge.

"He's not a detective. He's a newshound."

The man grinned. "Aw, Stan. You wouldn't deprive me of this scoop. Let her barber."

"Barber?" Hazel touched her hair, nervous.

"He means talk, doll," Stanley said. "Keep her out of this, okay?"

"Not a chance." A wolfish grin stretched across the man's sharp face.

Stanley pulled Hazel away as two policemen started to argue with the newspaperman.

"This is a crime scene, you bum. The coroner hasn't even come yet," Liam said.

"Stick your beak elsewhere," said the other cop.

Everything was in commotion. Hazel found herself staring vacantly at the columns of the Art Museum across the plaza. It was like a mausoleum to her now. She clutched her bag and turned to the tall newsie at her side. Stanley's eyes darted around as more cars arrived. "Let's get outta here. Don't want to run into my uncle if he gets called over. He'll need some time to blow off steam."

Relieved, Hazel nodded. She had seen enough. Nobody seemed to notice as they slipped away from the scene of the crime and down the long lawn that led to the large pool and fountains of the park. The moon reflected ghostly light onto the water. Stanley walked with long, brisk steps. A little dizzy, Hazel hobbled to catch up, the blisters on her feet stinging. Her mind was too full to carry on a conversation, and Stanley seemed to be deep in thought.

A baby cried somewhere in the dark. The murmur of voices

reminded Hazel that the shadows hid people within them. A small barefoot boy scampered across her path. Even in the moonlight, she could see that he was filthy and too thin. From a short distance were the shouts of an argument and more crying. Hazel shivered, keeping her eyes on Stanley's back as he marched forward into the night as if there was nothing alarming about any of it.

When they reached the street, Stanley slowed and gave her a half-smile. "Atta girl, keep up." He shifted his hat with one hand and stopped to look at her. Under a streetlight, his blue eyes searched her face. "That was pretty rough stuff for a dame like you … " He squinted at her, concerned. "You look pale as milk. When's the last time you ate? You barely touched the popcorn."

"I haven't had much of an appetite today." Hazel's hands shook as she tucked a strand of hair behind her ear. She didn't feel hungry. Her stomach twisted, and her knees wobbled. "It's been quite a night." Hazel fought the urge to cry. Everything was a tangle in her head, and she wanted to go home and forget everything she'd seen since she'd gone out her window. Yet her mind raced over the details as if trying to figure it all out despite her wishes.

"You need food." Stanley took her by the elbow. "I know just the thing."

Hazel stumbled along, allowing the boy in the backwards cap to lead her down the street to Gaslight Square. A bar, a café, a club with music playing, and people without faces passed her on the sidewalk seemingly unfazed by the sirens that had screamed past just minutes before. None of them knew that a girl had been murdered not far from where they all went about their lives. Stanley stopped in front of a shabbily dressed boy in a dusty bowler hat who smoked a cigarette and stood beside a wheeled cart. His face would have been attractive if it were not so hard.

"Hiya, Stan," the boy said, blowing out a cloud of smoke. He looked Hazel up and down with a mix of disgust and surprise before turning back to Stanley. "The usual?"

"Thanks, Arthur."

The boy, Arthur, nodded and opened the top of his cart. A cloud of steam came out which smelled like baked bread and hot dogs. He reached inside, pulling out a large pretzel that he wrapped in a page of newspaper. "Here ya go. What's the word?"

Stanley took it and handed it to Hazel. "We need to gather the Knights. Something just happened."

Hazel held the warm pastry and wondered what she'd stumbled into as she desperately tried to keep her mind from memories of Evelyn. Stanley seemed safe, but if he had a gang, maybe he was dangerous. He'd been strangely calm at the scene of the crime, examining the body and writing things down as if he saw things like that all the time. Hazel clutched her purse tighter, and the smoking boy smirked at her, then shook his head.

"Yeah. Got a thing or two for you, too. Had some interesting customers lately." Arthur squinted as he blew out more smoke. "Who's the fancy dame?" He jerked his head toward Hazel.

Hazel frowned. "The *dame* is Hazel Malloy," she said, irritated that her voice shook. These people could be so rude, but she was in no condition to pull off classy indifference. Hazel's hands still trembled. She couldn't fathom how Stanley seemed so casual after what they'd just experienced.

Grinning, Stanley pointed at her. "She speaks for herself."

"She's a swell." Arthur sneered with slightly crooked teeth.

"You got that right. But she's okay."

Arthur pinched his cigarette between two fingers and tapped the ashes away. He narrowed his eyes at Hazel and then lifted his chin to Stanley. "Just the same, I'll save what I have to tell yous."

"I'll see you around." Stanley raised his hand with his pinky and ring finger curled and his other three fingers pointing up. Arthur nodded and did the same thing back.

The newsie took her elbow again and propelled her down the street. "Ever eat one of those before?"

In her daze, Hazel had forgotten about the pretzel in her hands. "Oh. No, I haven't."

He stopped to gape at her. "You don't know what you've been missing, Haze. Take a bite."

Haze? She wrinkled her nose. "I'm not hungry." How could he be thinking about food?

Stanley rolled his eyes. "You're about to faint. Eat. Besides, pretzels are good for you."

"Yeah?"

"Sure." He tugged the pretzel from her grip and removed it from the paper. "See the three parts? Father, Son, and Holy Ghost," he said.

"I'm not particularly religious."

"Doesn't mean they like you any less. And," he turned the pretzel in his hand, "it looks kinda like a heart too." He gave her a wink.

A surreal feeling, as if Stanley spoke to her from the end of a long tunnel, made Hazel blink her eyes to focus on his face.

"I see. So this is 'the usual' and you give it to all the 'dames,'" Hazel said mechanically.

Stanley shifted his cap again. "Only the ones I find dead bodies with."

He was trying to cheer her up. As if that were possible. She wanted to burst into tears. "Hm." Hazel took the pretzel back and bit into it. The warm, salty dough was delicious. "Why, this isn't half bad," she said, trying to rally.

"Would I steer you wrong?" He smiled but there was tension in his blue eyes and across his brow. He was feeling screwy too.

She ate the pretzel and walked beside Stanley toward home. Hazel tried to pretend they were just a girl and a boy out for an evening stroll, but the night pressed in on her and horrifying images of Evelyn appeared whenever she looked away from Stanley.

He started talking about his uncle, the cop, and the sick feeling returned, along with all of the questions. Hazel couldn't stop wondering over every detail; she wanted to know what happened the same way she had earlier at the movie—but this was real.

"Seamus is a pretty good cop," Stanley said. "He's got instincts, ya know? And a mean right hook." He paused and rubbed his jaw. "But sometimes, I don't know. It's like he's holding back. Something's got everyone scared—even the cops."

Hazel could see why. Life on the streets was a nightmare. "Stanley, what would your uncle say about the evidence that Liam destroyed? Maybe those numbers were important."

Stanley scratched behind one ear. "I was thinking the same thing. Earlier today, I heard Evelyn arguing with one of the ballplayers—I work at the ballpark, see. They were in the tunnels. She mentioned something about numbers and a diary. I got the idea that the gangs are involved. But there's something else too. Can't figure it." He gazed ahead, chewing his lip.

Hazel's pulse sped up. As horrible as everything had been, there was something exciting about all of it too. "Did you know Evelyn would be there?"

Stanley nodded. "I heard them plan to meet there by the statute to talk. Just figured I'd overhear something good for the papers."

"I see. Well, where was he?"

"That's an excellent question."

Hazel thought about this and took the last bite of pretzel. It really did seem to make her feel better. "Evelyn shouldn't have come back to town—seemed it was through with her back when she left. Maybe she just couldn't stay away from her man, but he was the wrong sort. Everyone said so." Had Evelyn's baseball-playing boyfriend killed her with the bat? But what about the hooded man and the numbers? "There's more to this mystery."

"Yeah. And we're going to solve it. I got a feeling about this, Haze. I don't believe in coincidences. I met you, then all of this happened, and you know the victim. I think we're supposed to fix this." Stanley slipped a finger under the collar of his shirt and pulled out a necklace with a medallion on it. He rubbed it between his thumb and forefinger, whispering to himself.

"What's that?"

He glanced over at her. "St. Jude. He's the patron saint of lost causes. It was my mother's."

She didn't want to disrespect anyone, but it all seemed far-fetched. "You think us meeting and finding the body and all of that was not an accident? You think God had something to do with it?"

"Sometimes there's no other explanation." Stanley's jaw tightened.

Hazel shrugged. "Maybe." She suddenly felt exhausted.

They walked on in silence. When her house loomed into view, it seemed foreign to her—something from a happier time. Without warning, tears filled her eyes and ran down her cheeks. She wiped her face with the back of her hand. A part of her just wanted to hide inside of her big house, wrapped in satin sheets, and be fed from a silver platter, forgetting all the grime and horror of the night.

But somebody had killed Evelyn and she had to know who.

Chapter Seven

Hazel sniffed and brushed the wetness from her cheeks. Her feet hurt, and her eyes burned with unshed tears. When they arrived at the gates of the Malloy estate, Hazel felt conflicted. She wanted the comfort of her room, but she didn't want to say goodnight.

"This is your place," Stanley said, gazing up at the strong walls of her home. He turned to her. "Hey. You crying?" His tone was gentle.

Hazel nodded, not trusting her voice.

"Sorry about your friend." His hand rose toward her face as if he might wipe her tears, but he dropped it back to his side.

"It's not that we were close or even friends, really. It seems like ages ago that she left. But she was beautiful and kind. And mostly … her sister Sandy will be devastated, and she's my best friend," Hazel choked out, her throat squeezing around the words. "I just don't know how anyone could do … "

"Well, something stinks. I can tell you that. From a certain angle, it makes sense. Rich girl gets mugged. But there are other factors at play here. Like the Lindbergh kidnapping a couple years ago—it doesn't all add up." Stanley frowned.

Hazel watched his face as he thought. Stanley was no average newsie from the streets. He was obviously well-read. "Yes. There is something more going on here."

Stanley nodded and gave her a sympathetic glance. "Anyway, I'm sorry about your friend."

"Evelyn was so lovely," Hazel whispered. "Why did he do it?" She pictured the man in the hood and shuddered.

"That hooded jerk can't hide from us. We're gonna avenge her." Stanley put a fist to his chest. "I swear it."

Hazel wanted to believe that this wise-talking newsie really could help find the man who had taken Evelyn's life. Nobody was safe with maniacs like that on the loose. And there was something not right with the police. Those numbers on Evelyn's leg. They meant something, yet the officer had erased them. What had Evelyn known about numbers that she'd told the ballplayer?

"I want to help. Something tells me we can't trust anyone," she said as more tears rolled down her cheeks.

Stanley removed his cap and twisted it in his hands. "No crooked, dirty copper can stop us from figuring it out. We have clues. And my uncle will help too—he's clean."

"I hope so."

He paused and looked her in the eyes. "And," Stanley glanced at his feet and then back up, "I don't want to give you the wrong idea. I'm also doing this for me. My dream of being a reporter someday … I need good stories to make a career for myself. I'm not a hero."

"I don't want a hero; I want a partner to help me figure this out." Hazel needed the man who did this to pay. She wanted to help make that happen.

Stanley grinned, his whole face lighting up. "Meet me at ten o'clock Mass at St. James tomorrow and we'll talk it all out. Can you do that, partner?"

Hazel nodded. Stanley reached out and touched her cheek for just a moment. "Well, get back to your ivory tower, Princess."

Her heart fluttered but she huffed. "Go back to your slum."

He tipped his hat. "On my way."

Hazel watched Stanley dart away into the shadows. That tugging in her belly happened again—as if a string attached to him pulled at her as he went. She brushed away fresh tears and walked across her lawn. Hazel stared up at her window. It was shut and the light inside her bedroom was out.

Bananas.

Her goose was cooked and how. Hazel circled the house and climbed the steps up to the servants' entrance. The clatter of glass made her jump as she stumbled over a wire basket of empty milk bottles awaiting pick-up beside the door. She slipped into the kitchen, the aroma of dinner still strong in the air. She had missed dinner and Pops would be furious. The mess from food preparation cluttered the counters but the cook, Mrs. Flannigan, was not in the room.

On her way up the backstairs, Hazel heard the murmur of voices coming from the den beside the dining room. The Sinclairs were still visiting. Maybe she could hide in her room and nobody would bother her.

"Well now, look who's been larking about." Peggy looked down at her from the top of the stairs. "Where on God's green earth have ya been?"

Hazel froze a moment and then rushed up the stairs and threw herself at Peggy, arms wrapping around the warm, soft body of her maid. "Peggy, Peggy it was horrible!" Hazel burst into tears.

Peggy held her fast. "Now, now, Missy. I'm not angry with you. Been worried sick is all … " She pulled back and her light brown eyes looked Hazel over. "What's happened to my gal?"

"I met a boy, and we found … something," Hazel blurted through her sobs.

Peggy's eyes grew large. "Slow down, dearie. Come up to your room with me and you can tell me everything."

In Hazel's bedroom, Peggy turned on the light, pulled back the comforter, and patted the mattress. Hazel sunk into its softness, wincing at the ache in her feet.

"Now what's this about you hanging about with unknown boys? What would your father say to that? Don't you know it isn't safe?"

"Oh, Peggy, I never knew how it really was out there. I mean … I know there are hungry people, and I hear what Pop's friends say about the economy, but … " Tears stung her eyes again. The woman she'd seen with the baby wrapped in newspaper and the families huddled around fires in the park were images she couldn't shake. Had one of those desperate people attacked Evelyn to take her ring and handbag? She shuddered.

Her maid bent and gently removed Hazel's shoes. "Yes. It's different when you put a face on hunger and lives to the talk about economy."

"Yeah." Hazel's mind jumped all over the place. She kept seeing tattered, hungry people and images of blood. She didn't want to tell Peggy about Evelyn while snuggled in her own bed. It would bring it home. Make it real. She wanted to keep it out there in the dark of Stanley's world. Her teeth chattered like the time she rode in the back of a Model-T with Sandy and some friends on a bumpy country road going to a picnic. Hazel clenched her jaw to stop them.

Peggy's face grew concerned. "Now, now. You've had a terrible shock. Tell Peggy all about what happened." She pulled the blanket up around Hazel's body.

Hazel closed her eyes and waited to feel calm. She thought of Stanley—how safe he made her feel. "I met a boy at Hi-Pointe Theater. A newsie. He doesn't seem stupid or lazy like most poor people." She was stalling, afraid to put into words what they had found.

Peggy gave her a look. "Know many poor people, do you, Missy?"

Hazel's cheeks burned. "Well, I mean, Pops says … Sorry, Peggy. That was horrible. I don't think I even believe that—I don't know why I said it." She rubbed her forehead.

Peggy's smile was patient. "I know, lass."

Hazel felt like she needed to make up for her slip. "Nobody works harder than you, Peggy. And you're sharp as a tack."

The Irish maid wrinkled her nose. "All right then. Don't work yourself up. Tell me more about this hardworking, Einstein newsie of yours—and what you found." Her expression more tense than curious, Peggy picked something out of Hazel's hair and waited. But Hazel couldn't put words together. There was no clear way to start.

"I … There was … in the movie there were murders … and … "

Peggy sighed and smiled. "Ah. Did your mind get away from you, then? Something gave you a fright in the dark?"

Hazel shook her head. If only that were it. "He was walking me home from the theater—to keep me safe. And she was there—dead. Under the statue of St. Louis." Hazel swallowed a sob. "There was a baseball bat." She squeezed her eyes shut but still saw the blood.

Peggy gasped. "A dead woman? What a terrible thing for young eyes to see." The maid wrapped her warm arms around Hazel. "Our Lord be praised that you're safe and that the evil man who did this didn't touch you."

"We … we saw him."

Peggy stiffened and pulled back. She stared at Hazel. "Did you?"

Hazel nodded. "It was dark, and he wore a hood. He ran away before we could find the police."

Peggy's eyes widened. "A hood? That's a terror. You haven't been watching too many pictures, have you?"

"No. It's true! Ask Stanley. We saw him, I tell you," Hazel almost shouted. "We told the police—and I don't know if they believe it either, but … " Hazel stopped herself. She couldn't talk about the numbers. Fear gripped her chest. It felt like somebody was watching her.

Peggy's lips tightened. "Stanley, is it?" The maid blinked several times and straightened Hazel's blanket.

"Yes … he-he found the policeman, and we answered questions.

Stanley knows all about how the police do things—his uncle is on the force. He walked me home."

Peggy flinched then nodded several times. "I hope you'll never run off alone again. You can't be messing about at night with ruffians. Just think of what could have happened."

"He's not a ruffian. And we're going to solve this murder. Together."

Peggy put a hand on Hazel's cheek. "So, and sure he brought you home safe, but, Missy, you mustn't be foolish. This isn't the movies. You won't be solving murders with the likes of him. It isn't your place."

"What is my place? To be beautiful and privileged? A shining example of love and beauty? Look where that got Evelyn Schmidt." Hazel's breath hitched. It made her sick how disposable Evelyn had been to good society.

"Now what's got you thinking about her? She's been gone years now." The older woman tilted her head.

Hazel stared. She hadn't told Peggy who the dead body was. "It was Evelyn." Her mouth went dry. "Evelyn is dead. Murdered on Art Hill."

Peggy's lips parted as if she'd speak and her face went pale as she touched her forehead and each of her shoulders in the sign of the cross. She stood and then sat again.

Hazel realized Peggy had met Evelyn before and was taking it hard. "It's a shock. We all liked her … " Hazel trailed off watching Peggy compose herself.

"Thank the Blessed Mother you're safe," she finally said. "That's all that matters; you're both safe."

Yes. It was a close call. If she and Stanley had arrived only a minute before, maybe that man in the hood would have killed them too. For several moments, neither of them said anything while Hazel lay cocooned in her comfortable bed and Peggy paced the room.

"I told your father you were in bed with a headache and would come down later. You should go down now, Missy. You know how these folks always stay late. Change your clothes, freshen up, and make yourself pleasant." Peggy stopped pacing and eyed Hazel. "Do you think you can do that?"

Relieved that Peggy had covered for her, Hazel shut her eyes and relaxed into the pillow. "I don't know. How can I go back to parties and idle chatter after tonight? The Sinclairs care about nothing but money and power. They need to know what's going on out there."

"Ah, so now you're the voice of the people because you got your shoes dirty, is that it?" Peggy put her hands on her hips. "Get your lipstick on and keep that chin up. If you shout or rock the yacht they'll only throw you off." She stepped closer, her face serious, eyes bright. "Things will be made right in time, dearie. But you need to stay out of trouble. Change starts here." Peggy tapped a finger on her temple.

Hazel bit her lip. "So … people need to change their minds before anything else will change."

Peggy smiled. "Well and if all else fails, there's the fist." She winked and held up her fists. "Now put away what happened for now. Go be your beautiful self."

When Hazel descended the stairs, the seams of her new silk stockings were straight up the backs of her legs and her rose-colored dress was wrinkle free. Peggy had tamed her wavy hair, powdered her nose, and painted her lips. Hazel stared down at her hands, pink from washing them over and over. She still felt dirty from her adventure but knew her Lady Macbeth moment was not about physical filth or guilt. Her shiny world had changed. She could not unsee what she'd seen.

Roberts stood at the door of the salon. For the first time, Hazel noticed how old he was. His gray head bent slightly, and his wrinkled face hung slack and … bored. The man seemed tired, leaning back and forth as if his feet ached. When he looked up and saw Hazel, he straightened and smoothed on a smile. "Miss Hazel, I hope you are feeling better."

"Why, yes I am, Robbie. Thank you."

He opened the polished wooden door, and Hazel entered the large, elegantly furnished room. The smell of tobacco and bourbon filled the air. Nicholas Malloy stood by the carved marble fireplace, in the position of power, smoking his pipe. His attention was on Mr. Sinclair, a tall, blond man, and the two young men with him. They sat in wingback chairs facing Hazel's dad. Mumsy lounged on a couch further away beside Gabriel's mother, who sat stiff and aloof.

"I disagree. Manufacturing will lead us out of this recession. Coal, paper, Bulova watches, Zenith radios. Going up." Mr. Sinclair leaned forward in his chair and raised his glass to take a drink of the amber liquid. He held a cigar in the other hand, which had burned down halfway. They were well into the discussion.

Gabriel Sinclair glanced over at his father with a proud look on his face. "Professor Cornwell agrees with you. I've been buying up Crown Zellerbach, myself." He pushed his dark spectacles up his nose as if to emphasize his cleverness.

Hazel's dad nodded. "Yes. Yes, those are fine. But," he held up his pipe and glass of bourbon, "tobacco and, despite the Noble Experiment," he smirked, "spirits are as popular as ever. Music, movies ... no matter what happens, everyone wants these."

"Beer." Gabriel smiled. "I've invested in plenty of that lately."

They all chuckled. It was obvious that the comic relief had been needed. Mr. Sinclair reached over to clap his son on the shoulder. "A true Yale man."

"I'll drink to that." Hazel's dad raised his glass. "To the end of Prohibition."

"Here, here. How we survived it, I'll never tell." Mr. Sinclair winked.

They all grinned and drank from their glasses. It hadn't really affected them much in their circles. Their wine cellars were always well stocked.

"Actually, the real hope for the future of our economy, is, well, the defense industry." The voice was slow, considering, and a bit hesitant, like Jimmy Stewart. It was Charles Chouteau, a handsome boy with shiny brown hair and big green eyes. Hazel thought about how Sandy confided earlier that day that she hoped he'd ask her to the Veiled Prophet Ball. That was before—when such things seemed important. She faltered a moment as sadness washed over her, thinking about how Sandy would feel when she heard about her sister. Hazel swallowed and dug her nails into her palms, taking a deep breath.

"It's true. The defense industry is strong. Electric Boat, Douglass and Honeywell. We just need a good war to jumpstart everything." Nicholas Malloy took another puff from his pipe and caught sight of Hazel as she came further into the room. "Ah, gentleman, my daughter must be feeling better." Her father's face reflected pride at her appearance.

"Hi, Father." It was nice when Hazel could tell she pleased him, but she felt like an actress coming onto the stage. Ready to say her lines and behave as if nothing terrible had happened behind the curtains.

The men stood up from their chairs. Gabriel gave a half-smile. "Hazel."

"Hello, Gabriel. How have you been?" She strolled over to him.

"Peaches." He let his eyes sweep from her face, down her body, and back. "Say, you look swell."

Hazel's cheeks warmed.

"Hi, there, Hazel. I-I hope your headache has gone." Charles gave her a shy smile.

"Yes, thank you, Charles." Hazel tipped her head to the side. "It's nice to see you. I didn't realize you'd be here."

"I invited him along. Otherwise he'd spend all his time with his nose in a book." Gabriel grabbed the other boy's shoulder and gave it a shake.

Charles' face reddened. "Now see here—"

Mr. Sinclair interrupted. "Hazel, you look like a grown woman these days. I hear you've been invited to the Veiled Prophet Ball?" His voice was sharp, and he stood very straight,

Hazel nodded. "Yes. I'll be going."

From across the room, Hazel's mother piped up. "She's going and how. You should see the gown—cost a handful of clams, I can tell you."

Hazel noticed Pops cringe, and she smiled to cover the awkwardness in the room. "Mumsy is very proud of her dressmaker."

"As well she should be." Charles turned to where Hazel's mother lounged on a couch.

Mumsy let out a screeching laugh. "Oh, you!" She wobbled as she sat up. A long white, cigarette holder balanced between two fingers, swirls of smoke dancing from the end. "What a lovely thing to say." She ran a hand over her purple silk dress with the feathered collar. It was a bit much—but that was Mumsy.

Mrs. Sinclair, with light brown hair to her shoulder and wearing a simple, pale green gown, sat in uncomfortable contrast beside Hazel's mother. She kept her chin raised as if to stay above the water of unsuitable company. Hazel figured Mrs. Sinclair only tolerated Hazel's family because they were swimming in money and, for some reason, Mr. Sinclair had taken a liking to her dad.

Mrs. Sinclair barely masked her disdain as she said, "You use a local dressmaker, don't you, Gertrude?" Only the Lindell set called Hazel's mother that. Mumsy's wild friends all called her Gertie.

"Eduardo is a pip! And he won't bleed you like those New York grifters. Not saying he's cheap—but I've got my butter and egg man right here." Hazel's mom cast a flirtatious look at her husband. His ears reddened, and he cleared his throat.

"Well, what do I know about dresses? As long as you're happy."

Hazel's dad stroked his moustache in a nervous gesture.

Mumsy lowered her eyelids and gave a vampy smile. "You're all man, Mr. Malloy," she purred.

There was a silence in the room so full of electricity that Hazel felt her face burning. The "almost smile" that she loved to see tugged at the corners of her father's stern mouth, but his expression tightened back into its usual mask of decorum. He gave Mumsy a scolding glance.

Mr. Sinclair coughed and raised his glass. "To a very wise man. Nicholas, we salute you." They all chuckled and drank.

The men had funny grins on their faces. It seemed to bother Mrs. Sinclair. With a miffed snort, she set down her glass instead of drinking with the rest of them.

Mumsy continued to rave about her dressmaker, using all possible slang and expletives, and the men resumed their talk of the stock market and politics.

"What's your take on what Hitler's brownshirts are doing over there? Do you approve of his violent methods?" Charles asked.

"Ah, yes … His struggle to be the one man with wisdom in a sea of blockheads, as he calls the rest of the world. He's nothing but a bully." Mr. Malloy shrugged.

"Well, when he finally started talking sense a few years ago, I have to admit he caught my ear." Mr. Sinclair rubbed his chin. "I agree that the capitalists who have worked hard to make the money should have the authority."

"Hitler has always opposed socialism," Gabriel said.

"But he changes his tune depending on what he needs. To the working class he talks of tax cuts and redistribution of wealth … to industrialists, the take down of Communism. Of course, he couldn't fund his cause with all those stormtroopers if he didn't chum up to the people making all of that evil money." Hazel's dad snorted.

Hazel stood between the two conversations, out of place. She didn't care about any of it. All she could think about was Evelyn and how horrible Sandy was going to feel when she heard the news that her sister was never coming home again.

Hazel sat beside one of the tall built-in bookshelves and pulled out a book. She flipped through the pages, not seeing what was written there.

"You-you know, the original was published all in Latin. I believe it was in 1516." Charles stood over her, gazing at the book she held in her hands. "*De optimo rei publicae statu deque nova insula Utopia.*"

"Oh, yes. Thomas More. I remember something about that from school." Hazel smiled.

"And what do you think of More's philosophies?"

Hazel barely remembered when they discussed *Utopia* in class last year, but she didn't want to seem stupid or naïve. "Well … he had high ideals and … "

"Always has his face in a book when given the choice," Gabriel interrupted. "Don't mean to crust you, Charles, but you sure can be a wet blanket."

Hazel sighed with relief. "Well, this is high thinking here … perhaps not for beer investing types," she teased.

Gabriel straightened his glasses and rolled his eyes. "There are some absurd notions in that book. Thomas More has been dead a long time. We live in a modern age and have grown past those things. We have planes, radios, electron microscopes; there are advances in science that More never could have dreamed of."

"So, you're saying that philosophy and politics are obsolete only because of our strides in science?" Charles folded his arms in challenge.

"I'm saying—how is what he said relevant to now? We're a new kind of people. We're smarter—above that sentimental, starry-eyed dreaming. Humans, especially Americans, are like an advanced race. The rest of the world has an eye on us for good reason."

Hazel frowned. Advanced race? The starving, desperate people she'd seen and the brutal murder of a beautiful girl did not seem to jive with Gabriel's view of modern human superiority. If things were so ducky why were there so many people suffering and why did the rich not seem to notice? How was that a sign of intelligence and advancement?

"I think when people are eating out of trash cans and being murdered in the streets we still have a lot to learn," Hazel said.

"Well, let's be realistic. There will always be people on the bottom and people on the top. That's reality. We can't change the way things are. We can't start from scratch." Gabriel seemed to pat her on the head with his words.

Hazel bristled but held her tongue.

Charles furrowed his brow and spoke in his low, slow manner. "Thomas More says it's the duty of philosophers to work around in real situations and, for the sake of political expediency, work within flawed systems to make them better—not from scratch. Grow your change in the current soil."

"Sounds like a smart approach." Hazel thought about how Peggy had said that change starts in the mind.

"Well, More's *Utopia* also encouraged slavery, ease of divorce, euthanasia, and free hospitals. Can you imagine the chaos? Even if you had plenty of money, you'd be waiting to see a doctor with crowds of the disease-ridden masses. Plus, More was a Catholic. Consider the source, I say." Gabriel pursed his lips.

"More's society tolerated atheists, which should please you," Charles said.

"But he despised the idea of private property. He'd have everyone living in shacks. No thank you."

"Some sacrifices must be made for the good of all. Have you read *Mein Kampf?"* Charles switched his gaze to Hazel. "Sorry, we must be boring you with all of this."

"Not at all. I'm thinking … " Hazel flipped a page and a passage caught her eye: "*… for in courts they will not bear with a man's holding his peace or conniving at what others do: a man must barefacedly approve* *of the worst counsels and consent to the blackest designs, so that he would pass for a spy, or, possibly, for a traitor, that did but coldly approve of such wicked practices."*

Hazel wanted to find out what happened to Evelyn, but it was so much more than that. There was something wrong at the heart of the world she lived in. It was obvious to her now. The Lindell set were like sleepwalkers. And there was something else … something unseen and corrupt—she sensed it. The idea had started to grow inside her ever since she watched that policeman erase evidence from the body of her dead friend, the fallen Veiled Prophet Queen of Love and Beauty. Somehow, it was all related.

Like the book said, could she be a spy—pretend that everything was roses while she figured out what was really going on? It would be hard to bite her tongue and giggle like a silly girl. But Peggy was right. If she rocked the yacht, nothing would change. The infiltration of ideas was how changes had to be made.

Fine. Maybe she could play the model debutante. Wear her designer hats and lip rouge, say please and thank you, agree when everyone said the cream rose to the top and the gutter rats were there because that's where they belonged. She thought of Stanley; if he belonged in a gutter then so did she. But she would never say so in these circles.

She slammed the book shut. "Well, boys, I don't know about you, but I'm dizzy from thinking." She giggled like a fool. "You ever play that new game that just came out? It's all the rage." Hazel flashed an appealing smile, and both Gabriel and Charles lit up. "It's called Monopoly. A couple of ambitious boys like yourselves should enjoy buying up the world."

"Say, I've heard of that. The Slaybacks have Monopoly and it was quite a splash at Brigitte's last party," Gabriel said.

She stood and reached out to straighten Gabriel's bowtie. "I'll just have Roberts toddle off and bring it, then." Hazel gave a wink and went to find the tired, hardworking butler.

Chapter Eight

Stanley walked back through Forest Park with questions pounding him like right hooks. Just as he sorted through one question about Evelyn and Paul, another hit him. By the time he made it back to Art Hill, he felt like he'd sparred with Samson the Troll for twelve rounds at Freese's gym.

Can't make all the pieces fit, he thought. *Why can't I think straight?*

The feel of Hazel's skin still lingered on his palm from their parting handshake. He held up his hand to his nose and breathed in deeply. Her lingering sweet scent brought images of her smile, her laugh, her crinkled nose when she was huffy, and the way she made him feel at ease. *Partners.*

She was the prettiest partner any detective ever had. Stanley let out a deep sigh, shook his head, and shoved his hands in his pockets.

Now that she wasn't with him, he felt all the turmoil rolling in him again mixed with anger. She'd been a kind of anger tonic, one that kept him from having to flex his hands and control his breathing like he otherwise had to do when things got tense.

Stanley brought his thoughts back to Evelyn. Whoever beat her to death wanted to make a statement and not just kill her. He knew enough from his pulp magazines and Seamus's dark hints about murder to know the difference. Everything about her death shouted that someone wanted to send a message to someone else. To him, it seemed too public, too brutal, and too theatrical to be anything else. Question was, why?

Stanley shuddered as he remembered the crunch of the bones when he had touched her face, her blood oozing everywhere, and her blank stare.

Get a hold of yourself, Fields. Don't be such a muffin. You've seen people die before. Old news.

But all the other deaths he'd seen from a distance. He'd never seen a body up close or smelled the blood. Seamus always told him it was much different in real life than in Stanley's detective stories. He hated to admit it, but his uncle was right. Stanley didn't like his first brush with murder.

As he walked, Stanley realized the blood and shattered bones didn't bother him. It was Evelyn's blank stare, the look of a body with no soul, as if someone had left the building and shut off the lights, that made him never want to close his eyes again.

Stanley stopped and knelt. He crossed himself, said a quick prayer, and looked up at the art museum. From the flashlights crisscrossing the top of the hill, he could tell the police were still working the crime scene. He wondered if they'd taken Evelyn's body away or if it was still propped up against the statue of St. Louis, staring off into the night sky.

As he walked around the base of the hill, he thought about Liam and the numbers. What was it all about anyway? Did it have anything to do with the numbers mentioned in Evelyn's diary? Gambling? Gangs? Rich business types? Both? Did Paul beat his girlfriend to death with a bat to get rid of her? Stanley had to admit that was a possibility, and the police would probably go after Paul first. But if it was not the Cardinals catcher, who was the creepy guy in the hood?

And why did the darkness seem to gather around him? … Stanley felt it in his gut. He was someone much more sinister than the bullpen catcher from the St. Louis Cardinals. He pushed away the uneasy feeling that always came with his street sense.

He tried to focus on other details of the case. Who or what was this Legion that Evelyn had been telling Paul about?

Stanley guessed he would have to spill his guts to the coppers. They'd need to know everything he knew, eventually, including the conversation he overheard in the tunnels. Still, after Liam's little erasing evidence trick, Stanley didn't know who he could trust unless it was …

Seamus.

He wondered if his uncle was part of the investigation. Stanley gazed toward the hill. Cops swarmed the place like ants. This whole business would be splashing the headlines tomorrow and his chance for the big scoop had been snatched away by a lunatic in a hood. Now he'd never get to the bottom of whatever Evelyn had been doing back in town.

He'd snuck out for nothing. Once his uncle read the police report, he'd see Stanley's name on the paperwork and know the score. He couldn't hide it from him. A breeze carried the barking voices of the policemen on the hill. Stanley realized it would be better to talk to Seamus at home and not in front of a bunch of his fellow cops. But what if he'd already heard about him and Hazel poking around the scene? Better let Seamus calm down.

Stanley finally made his way past the hill. No way could the Knights rally at the statue, he realized. He'd have to send Teeth out after Mass and tell everyone to meet at the Castle instead.

No telling when the coppers would be done with the place, and he didn't need the hassle just now.

Plus, people would be visiting the statute by the bushel. It'd be a circus. Everyone would want to see where the disgraced beauty queen got whacked, and newspaper reporters would be crawling all over trying to get all the scandalous details; the worst would sell a lot of newspapers, after all. Folks got their kicks in the weirdest ways. They'd imagine the beating that took her life. Stanley saw the results and didn't need to speculate. He just wanted to forget about her dead eyes.

Still, he realized he was the only one in the city who knew about her conversation with Paul. He had the threads in his hands, as Sherlock Holmes liked to say. Maybe the story didn't die with Evelyn. He wanted to follow those threads to see where they led. This was his story, and he didn't feel like turning it over to anyone, not even Seamus.

Besides, he had a partner now. He didn't mind sharing it with Hazel. The girl had guts all right. She'd agreed to meet him at St. James. Whoever heard of a rich Protestant dame going to a poor Catholic church? That seemed screwy to him. But he liked it.

He found his way to Dogtown and its familiar streets. Most of the time, he didn't even need to look up to figure out where he was going. Stanley knew every marker, stone, and sidewalk crack by heart. The sounds of radio shows drifted out of open windows. The Lone Ranger was galloping toward certain doom, and Jack Benny was making stupid jokes.

Stepping back through the dark alleyway, he found his way to his back door and inched it open. Stanley stumbled around trying to find the light switch until his uncle's voice cut through the darkness.

"And what, boyo, do you think you are doing?"

Stanley's heart jumped. Seamus was supposed to be working the night shift. Swallowing hard, Stanley closed the door and turned to his uncle. "Thought you were working."

Light flared in the darkness as Seamus struck a match and lifted it up to the cigarette dangling from his mouth. "I was."

"Oh." Stanley had an uneasy feeling. Seamus sat on the living room side of the table, blocking Stanley's escape to his bedroom. The lines around his eyes were more pronounced than they'd been a few hours ago, and his uncle's cheeks were bright red, a sure sign he'd had a few before Stanley got home.

"You wanna tell me where you been, or do I need to spin that yarn?" Seamus asked.

Pulling out a chair, Stanley sat down across from his uncle. "I was out doing some stuff. Don't you want the light on or something?"

"Nah, I don't. Too bright. This will do, sure." Seamus struck another match and lit a candle. The flickering flame revealed a bottle, half-empty of amber-colored whiskey.

Stanley took off his hat and tried not to shake. He ran his fingers through his hair. Seamus stared at him, took a sip of his whiskey, and said, "I know where you were, so I'm givin' ya a chance to tell me the truth."

"I was at the movies and met a doll there from the rich part of town. Really didn't want her to walk through the park alone, so I took her home." He swallowed. "Saw someone murdered, well, saw the victim just after he crushed her skull. That's the truth."

His uncle stared at him. "And what did you think?"

Stanley tried to control his shaking hands, but he looked away. "It was the worst thing I've ever seen. I shut my eyes and … I see her … blank stare … "

Seamus nodded. "Ya never get used to it, boy. Not ever. God's very image, destroyed and vacant. There is nothing worse."

His uncle took a drink of whiskey, staring off into space. Stanley relaxed. It had been at least a week since he got his ears boxed for doing something wrong. Indeed, with his lessons at the gym, he could probably take his uncle down. Still, the man knew how to street fight unlike anyone Stanley had ever seen. He'd watched him bust a few rowdies at the pub who'd whistled at a nun walking down the street. Seamus had taken the broomstick from behind the bar, twirled it, and beat the rogues senseless.

"Who was on patrol, boyo?"

Stanley sat back in his chair. "Um, Liam was. He let us go up on the Hill for a short cut."

His uncle didn't say anything as he swirled the whiskey glass.

"Do you know who got the business up there?"

Stanley shrugged. "The rich dame I was with knew her." He tried to sound casual. Evelyn and Paul's conversation in the tunnel was his ace in the hole for now. That story was his chance for a real job.

Seamus didn't talk much about any of his cases or encourage Stanley's curiosity. Mostly, he just told Stanley to work hard, go to Mass, and attend school. Seamus hated the very idea of his nephew becoming a newspaper reporter.

"Lindell's very own Evelyn Schmidt. You know who that is from selling your papers, yeah?"

Stanley nodded. "Yeah, that rich dame who was mixed up in some scandal. What was that all about anyway?"

His uncle gulped the rest of his whiskey and poured another.

"Never ya mind, lad. Nothing you need to worry your noggin about."

Stanley pressed harder. "Who killed her? Did you catch the hooded guy we saw?"

Seamus grimaced. "No, not yet. Everyone thinks you kids have an overactive imagination."

"That's not fair. Both Haze and I saw him. We're not stupid, you know," Stanley said, gripping the table.

His uncle laughed. "So, it's Haze, is it? How much smooching did you do tonight on the way home?"

Stanley shifted in his seat. "None. She's not that kinda girl. Don't think I'm her type anyway. No money and all." Something inside him sank.

Another gulp and another pour. With each sip Seamus's face turned a darker shade of red.

"Are ya ashamed of who ya are?"

"Nah. Just stating facts. I'm never gonna be able to date someone from Lindell."

His uncle stopped smiling and made a face, shaking his head as he said, "That's the least of your problems, boyo. I'm gonna have to take the strap to ya for not listening."

Stanley clenched his fist and stood up. His body shook, but no way he'd get strapped again.

"No. You're drunk, and I'm practically a man. I make my own money. I go to school. You can't tell me what to do."

His uncle stood, stumbled a bit, and removed his belt. Seamus snapped it together and said, "You'll do as I tell ya, boyo."

Stanley scooted the table into the wall so hard that it made a dent. He put up his fists, bent his knees, and said, "You put your meat hooks or that strap on me, I'm gonna knock you on your ass, got it, copper?"

Seamus launched himself at Stanley. His anger flared. He struck out with a right cross that landed his uncle on the floor with a crash that vibrated through Stanley's body.

Horrified, Stanley bent down to his uncle and flexed his fingers. "You okay, Seamus? I'm sorry. I'm so sorry."

To his surprise, his uncle wiped blood from his cheek and chuckled. "Ah, now you're a man, sure. Welcome to it, boyo. Hope you enjoy it more than I have."

Furrowing his brow, Stanley got up and backed away a few steps. He expected Seamus to get up and start beating him without mercy. In a daze, he examined how his fist had gone red from hitting his uncle. He felt a little shaky and sick to his stomach.

"Ya gonna help me up, or am I gonna have to sleep on the floor tonight?"

He reached down and gave his uncle a hand. Grunting, Seamus pulled himself up. Blood seeped out of a split in his lip.

"Mary and Joseph, boyo, where did ya get a right hook like that? Freese is really teaching ya well. Get me that steak out of the freezer, if ya be so kind."

Stanley went into the icebox and got out the frozen meat. His brain was in a whirl; he expected Seamus to come at him at any moment. He could never tell when his uncle would explode, and he realized the uncertainty was almost worse than the hitting. He handed the meat to his uncle who placed it on his cheek and poured himself another whiskey. Seamus took a sip and laughed to himself, muttering something under his breath, then stared at the ceiling while holding the slab of meat to his cut, purpling face.

"Can I ask you something?" Stanley asked.

His uncle waved him to continue without saying anything.

"Numbers, Seamus. I saw numbers on her leg written in coal dust. Liam wiped them off. Hazel and I both saw it. And gang members are starting to show up with the same stuff tattooed on them. What's that all about?"

His uncle didn't say anything at first, and Stanley thought he'd passed out.

"Seamus?"

"Boyo, I ain't sayin'." His uncle took off the slab of frozen meat and looked at him. "Ya don't mind me much anymore. That's plain. But, I'm telling you now, leave those numbers alone. Nothing good will come of it. And it could mean the end of you and me. That's a fact."

End of them? What was his uncle rambling about? Was it the whiskey? Or was there really something going on that connected the murder, the numbers, and the tattoos?

"They are a message, boyo, a message to crooked coppers."

Stanley wrinkled his nose. "From the killer?"

To his surprise, Seamus nodded his head. Stanley examined his uncle. Seamus would have to be extremely drunk to be giving this information. He'd bet money his uncle would forget in the morning.

"It's a gang thing, isn't it? That's what it is," Stanley pressed.

Seamus laughed and his whole body shook. He leaned over the table.

"Use the head God gave ya, son. Gangs? Do ya really think so?

Are there any left in St. Louis? I mean, real ones, not the brats who hang out at the Rookery who go around talkin' tough but never actually do anything."

Stanley ran his hands through his hair. His uncle didn't know what he was saying. Sure, the gangs had lost a lot of power, but they were still a force in the street. And if the rich people were starting to give them money for something, they could get even more dangerous. He dealt with them all the time and their threats. He'd seen grocers, store owners, and even newsies pay them protection money.

His uncle let out a loud burp and then slumped over, the steak falling from his hand and landing on the table with a wet noise. Seamus probably wouldn't give him anymore useful information tonight.

"Come on, up to bed. I'll help you."

He took Seamus under the arm and led him through the living room to the closed staircase near the small foyer. The narrow staircase made it hard to drag his uncle up the wooden stairs. As they climbed up, Seamus started to mutter.

"Ah, William. Thanks, brother. I love ya so."

Stanley froze. William. His dad's name.

"They took ya, didn't they? Ya left me, and now you're haunting me. Why did you stick your nose where it don't belong?" Seamus slurred his words and Stanley could barely make out what he was saying. He strained hard to listen.

"Yah, boyo. You left me on your crusade with that woman. Ya both paid for it, didn't ya?"

Stanley swallowed hard and didn't say anything. He was afraid if he interrupted his uncle, whatever sober part of Seamus remained would stop the flow of information. He ached for more, anything, even if it was just the rantings of a drunk.

"Gotcha killed, didn't it? And what did it serve? Nothing. They still control everything. Ya dead and your wife gone … she still … "

A chill ran through Stanley and his knees almost buckled. What if his mother was still alive? Wouldn't she come back if she was? What did his parents stick their noses into? No way to know what was true when Seamus was like this. His uncle let out a loud belch that reeked of whiskey. Stanley turned his head away and propelled his uncle to the landing at the top of the stairs. The floor squeaked under their feet as Stanley shuffled to get his uncle turned in the right direction.

Maybe the numbers were gang code to tell the coppers not to look too closely. That seemed to fit with everything Paul told Evelyn. Maybe her death was a message from the gang to Paul about his gambling debts. Sure, the hooded killer was a bit odd, but then St. Louis gangs did crazy things. Maybe this was a new thing for them, a hooded hitman, kind of like those wastes of space Catholic haters, the Ku Klux Klan.

Seamus started mumbling in Gaelic and Stanley couldn't make out the words. He lifted his uncle on to his creaky bed and turned him on his side in case Seamus got sick. Stanley didn't want him to choke on his own vomit. He didn't bother with the covers as he figured Seamus would just sleep in his clothes.

Closing the door, he went downstairs, grabbed the whiskey bottle off the dining room table, and walked into the kitchen. He opened it and poured it into the sink. Stanley paused before the bottle was fully empty and considered drinking it. He shook his head. On top of everything else, he didn't need that vice to confess to Father Timothy. After the last of the whiskey was emptied into the sink, he went into the living room. With a deep sigh, he sat on the beat up old couch and looked at the clock. It was only 11:30, but he felt like he'd been up all night.

Turning on the radio, he flipped it to KMOX, and lay on the couch. The voice of Billie Holiday, his favorite singer, soothed him and he took a deep breath. He didn't want to think about Evelyn just now. He didn't want to think about the murder, Seamus' drunken rambling, or the numbers. He just needed peace.

Stanley looked down at his knuckles, still red from knocking

Seamus to the floor. He'd stood up for himself but now that meant he was a man. Seamus may have been a bit rough with him, but he was somebody he could look up to. Now there was nobody.

The whole day overwhelmed him, and tears flowed down his cheeks. Since no one was around, Stanley didn't bother wiping them away. Something else. He needed to think about something else. Something pleasant … something …

Hazel's face appeared in his thoughts. Her touch. Her eyes. Her smile.

Stanley turned over on his side. *Peace. She makes me feel peaceful but excited at the same time. Like being in church or at the ballpark.*

He got up, knelt by the couch, and prayed to the Blessed Virgin. Somewhere around the tenth Hail Mary, he fell asleep.

Hazel hadn't slept well at all. Dark dreams featuring hooded strangers and dead bodies ran like newsreels through her head. The victims kept changing faces. Sometimes it was Evelyn, then Sandy, Peggy, or vaguely familiar people she didn't know, the faces of hungry people from the streets.

It filled her with a horrible dread knowing that man was loose somewhere. It reminded her of the time that a large, black spider skittered across her wall. Hazel had screamed, thrown a shoe at it, and missed. The spider had disappeared behind her vanity. She made Roberts and Willy move the furniture around looking for it, but they never found it. Hazel hadn't slept well for days after that. She just knew the spider was somewhere in her room … waiting for revenge.

After dressing, Hazel blearily descended the stairs. The smell of sausage, eggs, and coffee led Hazel into the informal dining room. Breakfast lay arranged on silver trays atop the polished mahogany table. Her stomach twisted. Maybe just a cup of coffee.

Both her parents sat at the table eyeing her. Something was wrong. Hazel's father glared, arms folded across his chest. The way the smoke rose from the pipe clenched in his teeth, it looked like his head was on fire.

Mumsy picked at a piece of toast on her plate. She darted a look between her smoldering husband and Hazel. "Morning, darling."

"Um. Morning, Mumsy … Pops." Hazel sat in her chair and reached for the coffee.

Nicholas Malloy cleared his throat and snatched the folded newspaper from beside his plate. He shook it open, allowing the headlines to unfurl in Hazel's direction.

FORMER QUEEN OF LOVE AND BEAUTY SLAIN

Hazel lost her breath and then composed herself. She tried to seem casual as she took a sip of coffee that burned her tongue. "That's terrible—who?"

Dad held up one hand to stop her. He turned the paper around and read from it, his voice becoming more of a growl as he went. "The most shocking news to me was not the murder. Hazel Malloy, young daughter of wealthy and powerful Nicholas Malloy, found the body while on a nighttime stroll with her beau, Stanley Fields, a local newsie." He stopped abruptly and lowered the paper, revealing a red face trembling with rage.

Hazel swallowed and shrank into her chair. There was nothing she could say. "Sorry," she squeaked.

"Darling, that must have been dreadful to—" Mumsy began.

Her father interrupted. "Sorry? Hazel Frances Malloy!" His fist came down onto the table making the dishes rattle. "Am I to understand that you sneaked out alone with a boy from the gutter?" He growled, gesturing with his pipe.

Hazel straightened in her chair and talked as fast as she could. "He's not from the gutter! And I went to see a picture at Hi-Pointe, not to meet a boy. After the show it was dark, and he walked me home to protect me."

"Protect you? He took you through Forest Park at night, Hazel. Do you know what kind of people gather there at night?"

"Hungry ones."

"Dangerous ones, just like the kind of people who murder beautiful, wealthy girls with baseball bats." His eyebrows and mustache both seemed to glower.

"But we don't know who did it. The police—they're supposed to investigate it. They think it's that baseball player but there was … " Once again, Hazel felt her skin crawl when she considered telling her dad about the numbers.

Her father narrowed his eyes. "Was what?"

"The man … in the hood … "

Nicholas Malloy shook his head, his face still dark. "What man in a hood?" he sputtered.

Hazel pointed to the paper. "It's in there. They asked us what we saw; we told them."

"The foreign-looking man in the dark, tattered overcoat you saw fleeing?"

Hazel frowned. "That's wrong. That's all a lie."

"Enough. I'm not interested in the details." Her father scowled. "My name is in this paper. Do you understand what that means?"

"That you're famous?" Hazel tried to smile, hoping to relieve the tension.

Mumsy covered her mouth with her hand. "Hazel, don't make jokes. Your daddy gets angry when he's worried—"

He cut her off. "It could bring disgrace on this family to be touched by a scandal like this." He set down his pipe with a bang that sent sparks scuttling across the tablecloth. Hazel watched them wink out one by one.

"Scandal?" she whispered, incredulous. Hazel's voice rose as she continued, "Evelyn Schmidt is dead. That's not a scandal, that's a tragedy—a horror—and all you can think about is your reputation?" She stared at her father, unafraid, finally seeing him for the first time. He was scared, scared of being the next disgraced man, the next disgraced family, from Lindell.

"My reputation is what gives you the life you live, Hazel. And you need to appreciate it. Don't you know what could happen if you no longer had our good name to protect you?" The rage seemed to have drained a bit with her words.

Hazel felt her face burn. "Someone could chase me out of town—kill me with a bat?"

Her father stood. "See here, young lady, alter your tone. Now. I won't tolerate this."

"Well? What will happen? Tell me, Pops! What's worse than being murdered?"

"Shame. Disgrace." He pointed at her. "You will destroy your chances of marrying well by running around with newsies and gutter rats."

Mumsy shifted in her chair. "Nicky—"

"Gertrude." Nicholas Malloy shot his wife a stern look. "You know I want what's best for her. An advantageous marriage will make all of the difference in her future happiness."

Mumsy shrugged as if she didn't care and took a sip of coffee. But Hazel saw her eyes moisten.

"Gabriel Sinclair may not even ask you to the VP Ball after a thing like this." He leaned forward to emphasize his words.

"I don't give a hang about the ball." Hazel wanted to shake the table until all the fancy dishes crashed to the floor. Why was this conversation even happening when the real issue was that Evelyn had been brutally murdered?

Her father balled his hands into fists. "Hazel."

"Well, I don't!" She folded her arms in defiance. "Look how they treat their queens if they make a mistake." Hazel stood so that her father couldn't look down on her like a storm cloud. "I won't go."

"Yes. You. Will."

Hazel's mother set down her mug and finally spoke. "Our daughter saw a dead body and this is what's crawling into your cap?" She looked over at Hazel. "Darling, that must have been horrible."

A lump rose in Hazel's throat, and she nodded. Mumsy reached a hand across the table and Hazel took it. "It was the worst thing I have ever seen," she managed to say.

Mumsy squeezed her hand and then let go. "Try not to think about it, darling."

Yes. That's how Mumsy dealt with everything unpleasant. That and a good laugh and a little champagne fixed most things.

"I am sorry you saw what you saw, Hazel," Pops said in a softer tone. He took a deep breath. "But had you been doing what you are supposed to do, you never would have. You will never do something dangerous and foolish like that again."

The injustice of everything boiled inside but she couldn't keep talking back to her father if she wanted to solve this case. She had to play the part of the debutante. She took a deep breath. "Yes, Father."

He narrowed his eyes, suspicious. "You know that I have your best interest in mind. Consider carefully where this new line of behavior and attitude is taking you, Hazel," her father warned.

"According to you, wherever people end up is where they belong anyway," she muttered to herself.

"What was that?"

"Nothing."

Hazel and her father faced one another over their forgotten breakfast.

"You are forbidden to see that newsie again. And you are never to leave this house without an escort. Do you understand?"

"I'll decide," Hazel blurted before she could stop herself. *Bananas.*

Her father's lips moved without words. "This is Peggy's influence. She lied to cover your tracks last night. That insubordination will cost her."

Hazel shook her head. "Wait. No. She didn't know—I—it's my fault. She was just doing what I told her to do. I'm sorry." She swallowed her pride, hoping she could calm him down.

Nicholas Malloy raised his chin in triumph. "You wouldn't like

Peggy to lose her position here over this, would you?"

She shook her head again. "No, please." Hazel couldn't imagine her life without Peggy to talk to and give her warm hugs.

"Never see that boy again."

"Fine. Next time I'm with him I'll close my eyes." Hazel cringed at herself. Why couldn't she hold her sass?

"You will obey." Hazel's dad looked hard at her, drilling her to the ground with his glare.

Hazel hung her head. She knew she had to see Stanley again. They had a mystery to solve; now that the papers were printing lies about what happened, Hazel was even more determined to find out the truth. She had to, for Sandy. But she would have to be careful. She didn't want to lose Peggy.

"Okay, Father. I'm sorry. I'll behave; I'll even go to the VP Ball with Gabriel if he asks." She had one hand behind her back, crossing her fingers. She hoped he didn't notice that she hadn't promised to never see Stanley again.

Her father nodded, a grave expression on his face. He smoothed his mustache and sat back down. He took another puff from his pipe and examined Hazel through the smoke.

Hazel sunk into her chair. She took a deep breath. "All I wanted to do was see a show. The rest was unplanned—an accident. I swear it."

He nodded. "No movies for a month. You need to get your head out of the clouds, Hazel. Rid yourself of romantic notions. They only lead to trouble. Stick to what's best for you. Trust me."

Hazel's mother made a sound in her throat. "Well, I like that," she muttered, slamming down her fork. "Was letting your romantic notions take over really such a mistake, Nicky?" Her voice climbed. "Well my life isn't such a clam-bake either. All your high-hat friends looking down on me and trying to make me feel small." She stood, chin raised like a Hollywood queen. "Well, I've got a scoop for you, Nicholas Malloy. I've always been bigger than any of them. Wise up to that. I'm no gold-digger, and you know it. What would the other swells think if they knew my new money saved your precious family name when the market crashed?"

Hazel's jaw dropped. Her father's face changed colors. "Gertrude."

"It's Gertie, you bum. And if I weren't so dizzy over you, I'd have left a long time ago. I'm tired of being seen as your disgrace when I saved you from the gutters." Mumsy spun around and stalked out of the room. Nobody made a dramatic exit like her. A warm feeling rose inside as Hazel watched her glamorous mother go.

Hazel's father cleared his throat. A pulse beat in his neck as he watched his wife leave. Hazel had never seen him look so deflated, but when he faced her again his expression hardened. "As I said, no movies for a month and no newsies." He raised the paper and hid behind it.

Hypocrite. People in the gutters belonged there—unless they had someone to save them? Hazel left the room without another word. Up in her room, she lay in bed trying to digest her breakfast of new information. New doors seemed to be opening and all kinds of lights turning on ever since she'd met Stanley. When she thought of him, she saw him clearly in her mind with that mischievous, quick smile, and those dreamy blue peepers of his. Hazel sat up, restless.

Looking at the clock, she realized it was almost time to meet Stanley for Mass. She went to her window and opened it. Looking out she saw Willy, the gardener below raking leaves.

"Mornin', Miss Hazel," he called up to her, tipping his hat. Even though his dark skin shone with sweat, he grinned.

"Morning, Willy." She smiled and backed away.

Bananas.

Hazel couldn't climb down the ivy while Willy watched. She blushed just thinking about how unrefined that would be. Pacing the plush carpet of her room, Hazel thought of everything that had happened since she'd first climbed out that window. She had seen things that had changed her, and it drove her mad to be surrounded by all the fine things and easiness of her life as if nothing had happened. Her mind filled with questions that she needed answered.

She grabbed her handbag, put on a simple hat, and made her way down the hall to the servants' staircase, pausing when she heard voices echoing up from below.

"Mr. Malloy has left for the club, but he wants twelve dozen roses ordered and put in the Missus' bedroom right away," Roberts' voice ordered.

"Yes, sir. I'll fetch 'em myself," answered a voice Hazel didn't recognize. There were so many servants in and out she couldn't keep up.

Sounded like Pops was bent on mending things with Mumsy. Their relationship was a mystery. As Hazel rounded the corner, she stopped abruptly when her mother stepped in front of her. "Hazel."

Her heart pounded. "Mumsy."

Her mother glanced at her hat and handbag. "Going out?"

There was no point in lying. Mumsy may seem like a brainless flapper but she was sharp—when she was sober. "Why, yes."

Mumsy cocked her head. "To see that boy?" She pursed her red lips and blinked.

Hazel nodded. "That's right."

Reaching out, she tucked one of Hazel's curls into place. Mumsy smiled.

"Finally gonna live a little? Hard to stop once you get a taste, isn't it?"

"I just—well I need to … "

Her mother backed away. "No. Don't explain. It'll be more fun if you don't. Be sure to be back before your father returns." Mumsy gave her a wink and trotted down the steps ahead of Hazel.

Gee, Mumsy is swell.

Hazel followed Mumsy down into the kitchen, and as her mother rattled off dinner instructions to Mrs. Flannigan, Hazel slipped out the back door and made her escape.

The brisk autumn air tickled her face. A rush of excitement shot through her veins. Hazel realized that she was actually having an adventure. Murder, mystery … maybe romance? She stifled the thought. Stanley was all wrong; there was no place for him in her life. Once they figured this murder out—then what? He'd never belong to the Veiled Prophet crowd or the gentlemen's club. Thinking of that made Hazel smile because it reminded her of something Groucho Marx said in a movie: "I got a good mind to join a club and beat you over the head with it." That was more Stanley's style. Hazel sighed.

This time, as she made her way through town, she paid more attention to the people around her. She looked into their faces and tried to imagine if they were like Stanley, good folk who had fallen on tough times and were doing the best they could. Maybe they were rough around the edges, but they could also be brave and noble. Even after the fright last night, she realized it was a crapshoot as to who was good and who was bad. There really were so many kinds of people in the world. Why had she never considered their eyes before? It seemed that the people in the gutter were human too. Imagine that.

In her white, flowered dress, she got looks herself. Men tipped their hats and women smiled politely. In the bright morning, everyone seemed less menacing. She didn't see anyone who looked destitute on her way to the Catholic side of town, just a lot of hard working types. When she noticed a scrubby young boy selling pretzels she decided to have one on the way to Mass since she hadn't eaten breakfast. Besides, her eagerness to see Stanley made her hungry.

She fished a few coins out of her bag and handed them to the kid. He was frail and freckle faced. He didn't say anything when he gave her the pretzel.

Hazel gave him a smile. "Thanks, you're a pal."

He blushed and grinned. A small girl sat on the sidewalk behind him playing with a rag doll. "That your sister?" she asked. He probably had to watch her while both of his parents worked.

The boy nodded. "Yeah." He raised his shoulders as if defensive.

The little girl had neatly braided golden hair. Hazel noticed that she only had one leg poking out from under her faded blue dress. Her heart squeezed. The girl just played with her doll like any other kid would. Lost in her imagination, she had a dreamy look on her face as she rocked the patchwork baby in her arms. What must her life be like?

Hazel pulled out a dime. "That's a pretty baby you have there."

The little girl looked at Hazel with a shy expression on her face. "Her name is Anna."

"That's a pretty name."

"She's got a broken arm and she can't walk yet," she said in a tiny, serious voice.

"Yeah? Well, she's as sweet as honey anyhow, and you're a good mommy." Hazel tossed her the coin. "You can get Anna some candy."

"Gee, thanks, lady," the girl said, staring at the shiny coin with huge eyes.

Hazel said goodbye to the boy and girl at the pretzel stand, and headed down the street with a bounce in her step, eating the pretzel. Warm, salty, and divine. Mmm. Where had these been all her life? She examined the shape of the pretzel and her face heated. It was kind of heart-shaped. That boy was smooth as silk.

Rather than cut across Forest Park to get to St. James, Hazel took the streets skirting it. She finished the pretzel and breathed in deeply. Sunday mornings were quiet and calm. Many shops and businesses remained closed, people were out in their Sunday best, and the sun seemed to shine a little brighter.

When the church rose before her, Hazel stopped to look at it. The gray stone, tall, pointed windows and towering spire were intimidating. She had never gone into a Catholic or any church before, actually. She bit her lip. Well, whether or not God was inside, Stanley was.

Hazel clutched her handbag and marched toward the front doors. Her heart sped up. She hoped Stanley liked her dress.

Chapter Ten

Stanley woke with a start and took long, gasping breaths. Sweat coated his face, and his heart thumped hard. Getting off the couch, he went upstairs to his room. Shivering, he sat on his bed and grabbed a hand-knitted green blanket before leaning back against the wall and resting his head on a large Cardinal pennant. Breathing deep, he tried to clear his mind of the nightmare.

Stanley stared into his dresser mirror. In the reflection, he saw the pictures of Cardinals baseball players and famous detectives that dominated the wall above his head.

He studied his face and grimaced. Despite what he'd said to Seamus last night, Stanley didn't see a man staring back at him. He saw a scared kid who didn't know anything.

"Only a dream, Stanny boy, only a dream."

It had been so real, yet he could only remember the last part of it. Evelyn lay as they found her. When he and Hazel approached the body, the debutante had turned her head and begged through bloody teeth for their help.

He shuddered as he got up from his bed, stuck his face in the water basin, and threw back his head. Sputtering, he slicked back his hair. Stanley always imagined himself as a tough kid from the streets. Nothing bothered him. He'd seen it all. Or so he'd thought.

Stanley shook his head and removed his shirt. A white scar marred his right shoulder, complements of Arthur. The night they'd met, Stanley had stopped him from killing someone, and the bowler-wearing mug he now called his friend had plunged his knife into him in a blind rage. Stanley had never seen anybody off his rocker like that, and Arthur, in his own way, had been apologetic ever since.

Tattooed on the left of his chest was the Sacred Heart of Jesus, done by a kid near Tower Grove Park with a needle and blue ink. He'd done a pretty decent job, with detailed thorns weaving around and piercing the heart. Flames of light burst from the top, and it looked as if his chest was engulfed in blue fire.

He heard loud snoring coming from Seamus' room as he walked down the hall. Knocking on the door, Stanley opened it and said, "Mass time; you coming?"

The only answer he got was louder snoring. Stanley decided to leave Seamus alone and let him sleep it off. As he paused at the door, he realized what he'd done last night. He'd stood up to his uncle and something had changed. No longer would Seamus hit him. His uncle had called him a man, a title he didn't give to just anyone. Somehow, Seamus seemed smaller now.

Walking back to his room, he stripped off his pants from the night before and slipped on his black slacks, frayed at the cuffs. Stanley put on his best white shirt with slight coffee stains on it and gathered the suspenders around his shoulders. He tucked in his shirt, grabbed his hat, and headed out the door for Mass with a slice of bread for breakfast.

The cool September air chased away the last remnants of his dream, and he whistled as he walked quickly down his street. Stanley passed the familiar small houses of brick and wood and smelled bacon frying. Thoughts raced through his brain to match the pace of his walk. Mostly he thought about Hazel, her amazing eyes and bratty attitude that made him laugh. He stopped whistling when he realized the song that was running through his head: that new song by Cole Porter, *(You'd Be So) Easy to Love.*

Stanley swallowed and wiped a hand over his face. Maybe Hazel's parents wouldn't let her go to a Catholic church in the Irish part of town. He hoped she'd show, since she seemed to know all about Evelyn's life and family and stuff. Stanley needed more information if he was going to figure out what happened and why. That's why he wanted to see her again.

"Terrible murder at the Art Museum. Disgraced debutante with face bashed in. Read all about it," a voice with a slight accent called out. "Extra, extra!"

Despite the horrific announcement, Stanley grinned as he saw Anino, a member of the Knights, holding up newspapers and yelling at the top of his lungs on the street corner. People walked by, bought papers, and shook their heads at the headline. Stanley could almost guess what the article would say. They'd describe Evelyn as a tart, messing around with the wrong sort, who got herself killed. Don't be the same, young people.

Stanley spat on the ground and walked up to Anino.

"Hey, Stanny, how about this bag of worms? And you, in the papers. Ain't that somethin'?" The short, brown-skinned boy shook the paper at Stanley.

"You know, English lessons might be a good idea for you," Stanley said, as he took the paper from Anino's hands.

"Say, you gettin' all high and mighty on me there, Irish? Looking down on me cuz you talk so good?"

"Well, can't help it, you're so short."

Anino smiled and said, "Paper says you found the body, that so?"

Stanley nodded. "Yeah. Me and Haze."

Anino's eyebrow arched. "Hazel Malloy? Paper says she's a swell. Betraying the Knights for a dame? You know they're the enemy, right?"

Stanley unfolded the paper and didn't glance up. "Give me sass like that again, and I'll box you."

He hoped his attitude put Anino off the trail. Stanley would never tell the Knights what he thought about Hazel.

Anino patted the two sticks hidden under his shirt. "Don't think so, Irish."

His dad had been a master of the martial art escrima in the Philippines and was teaching Anino. Stanley figured the kid could probably beat him senseless before he'd even get in one punch. Still, he couldn't let him know that.

"I'd knock you out before you got your pretty little sticks outta your shirt."

Anino rolled his eyes. "So, what's with this murder? Why'd you go up to the statue without us?"

Stanley didn't respond as he stared at the large, black lettered headline. The by-line made his stomach constrict.

"No, no way, Paul couldn't have done it."

Anino nodded. "That third string catcher with the Cardinals. It was his bat, and I guess they'd been a couple a long time, eh? She had a thing for slumming it and all."

Stanley nodded as he read. "Says the bat was Paul's, had his fingerprints all over it."

"You said it, boy. It looks pretty open and shut. Bashed her pretty head in, but good."

Stanley flinched but didn't say anything. He didn't want to think about his dream or look soft in front of Anino. He wondered if he would ever be able to get rid of that memory. No wonder cops and reporters drank a lot.

"There's more to this business than meets the eye. We have to talk about it. You ready for tonight?"

Anino nodded. "I got the message from Teeth. Think he wants to join."

Stanley snorted. "Kid's tougher than half the boys I know. Still, we need to keep him with Arthurs's pigeons for a while. Someday, maybe, we can make him a Knight."

He handed the paper back to his friend and strolled toward the church.

"Later, Stanny boy," Anino said, as he raised the paper and shouted, "Hey, come read how our boy here saw a dead body. Read all about it."

Stanley poured over the article in his mind. Paul couldn't have done this. No way. He might've been rough around the edges, like all the Gashouse Gang, but not like this. Like Father Timothy said, it isn't an easy thing to take a human life. Still, when someone was in love, maybe it made them crazy. He'd read about that kind of stuff before, so he couldn't discount it.

Before he knew it, Stanley found himself on the steps of St. James. He went inside, dipped his finger in holy water, and crossed himself. As he walked up the aisle, he saw Hazel sitting in a pew, looking around at all the stained glass and statues of the saints. She wore a white dress decorated with bright flowers. As he got closer, Stanley breathed in her sweet-scented perfume.

Hazel and church at the same time. He sighed. If he wasn't careful, he'd never get angry or upset again. Then, how'd he survive the streets?

He leaned in from behind, chin inches from her neck. "Hey there, Bananas. Fancy seeing you in this part of town."

She turned her head and gave him a small smile. "Some smelly street boy invited me. How could a girl resist that?"

Stanley chuckled. "He sounds like quite a catch."

Hazel snorted. "He thinks he is."

They stared at each other, their faces inches away.

"So, are you gonna park it, Mister?" she asked and pointed to her hat. "Henri needs a pew buddy."

"Sorry to let him down. Gotta be the server for the Mass."

Hazel wrinkled her nose. "You can't sit with me? I'm gonna be alone? I don't know anyone here, and," Hazel glanced around, "I'm not even Catholic," she added with a loud whisper, a hand at her mouth.

Stanley shrugged with a grin. "Sorry. Duty calls. You'll be fine."

He walked down the aisle and looked back at Hazel. She made a face at him and stuck out her tongue. Holding back a chuckle, he knelt in front of the altar, crossed himself, and made his way to the sacristy, a little room to the right of the front of the church.

When he entered the room, Father Timothy wasn't there. Stanley grabbed his white server robe and put it on. Pacing around the room, he noticed an opened letter on the desk. The word "Legion" caught his attention. He glanced around and didn't hear the footsteps of Father Timothy, so he read closer.

It was in the summer of my twelfth year that the Hooded Legion of the Prophet came for me. It was at night and as you can imagine, I was terrified. They burst into my bedroom, threw a hood over my head and transported me to a secret cave south of the city. Stripping off my clothes, I stood in a vast cave with voices echoing off the cave chambers. There were unnatural, diabolical agents present. You can imagine my horror. Father Tim, you cannot know how grateful I am that the Jesuits are—

Stanley's heart raced as he searched the desk for the envelope. Finally, he found it, picked it up, and read the address.

Brother Martin, St. Meinrad Abbey, St. Meinrad, Indiana.

Who was that? he wondered. *Why did he talk about the Legion of the Prophet?* He didn't see how it couldn't be, but this seemed like too much of a coincidence.

"Ah, Stanley, early like usual, good lad."

He dropped the envelope and said, "Good morning, Father, was just looking for matches."

"Ah, I left them in the right-hand drawer last night. Apologies."

He pulled open the drawer, reached in, grabbed the matches, and turned around. A tall, muscular priest in a black cassock that flowed down to the top of his shoes smiled at him. His salt and pepper hair was slicked back with pomade, filling the room with a sweet smell.

"And how are you, my son?"

Stanley looked away from the priest. The man had known him since birth, having given him all his early sacraments, from Baptism to Confirmation. He'd listened to Stanley's confessions, knew his problems and his sins. The man could read him like a book.

"I'm okay."

The priest frowned. "Stanley, you look pale and ready to faint."

Stanley shrugged. "Rough night, Father."

"Talk to me, my son."

With a deep breath, Stanley told the priest everything, including meeting Hazel. He talked about her spunkiness, her reaction to the murder, and how he'd walked her home.

Father Timothy raised his hand. "I'm sure the young lady is lovely, but finding someone beaten to death seems to be the issue."

"Not really a big deal, Father. I've seen dead bodies before."

He doubted very much that Father Timothy would buy that load of horse crap.

The priest came over and put his hand on Stanley's shoulder. "My son, it's okay. Violence is never easy to look at, especially murder."

"Guess so," he said and looked away. Tears formed in his eyes, and Stanley wiped them away. He loved Father Timothy, probably the only real father he'd ever had. Seamus didn't really fit the bill, especially since he'd knocked him flat. Plus, it felt good to talk to someone who wasn't half-drunk or ready to beat him.

"No shame in crying. Our Lord did so himself. He was a man of sorrows, after all."

Stanley nodded, not trusting himself to speak.

"Whenever you want to talk about it, you know where to find me."

"Yeah." Stanley changed the subject, so he wouldn't melt down. "How do you think the Irish are gonna do this year?"

Father Timothy, a Notre Dame grad, former member of the football team, and a confirmed Irish fanatic, shook his head with sadness. "Terrible. Thank the Blessed Mother for the Cardinals."

Father Timothy led them to the back of the church, and they walked up the aisle to start the Mass. Stanley went in front of the priest, holding up the Book of the Gospels for everyone to see. When he passed Hazel, she arched an eyebrow and gave him a small smile. He wondered what was going on in that pretty, little head.

After they reached the altar, Father Timothy began speaking in Latin, and Stanley fell into the rhythm of serving the first part of the Mass. When the gospel was read, he perked up his ears. The text was from the Gospel of Mark where Jesus cast multiple demons into a herd of pigs.

Father Timothy stood, put on his reading glasses, and pulled out his sermon. He spoke in a loud, clear, Dogtown-tinged accent as he read from his notes. "In today's gospel, we see Our Lord doing battle with the forces of darkness who call themselves Legion. It's popular nowadays not to believe in the devil or evil. And, I can assure you, the devil probably doesn't have cloven hooves or a pointed tail. But the powers and forces of darkness are real, especially in light of the young lady who was brutally murdered last night, who had been cast from her home."

Stanley shot a glance at Hazel. She stared at the priest as she clutched a little handbag.

"No matter what Evelyn Schmidt's sins might have been, she didn't deserve to be thrown out of the lives of her family and friends then brutally murdered. I doubt it was the man they claim it was, but I have no doubt the forces of darkness, Legion if you will, are at work."

Stanley straightened and gaped at Father Timothy. Even though the word went with the text, he wondered if he was talking about the Legion in the letter he read from the mysterious monk. How did that all fit together?

"Yes, she was a victim of evil, of people who think they can play God and decide who lives and who dies. I know not many of you want me to talk about these things. We all know those who've been dragged from their homes, told they are trash, unfit, and then had their God-given ability to have children taken from them. What mortal man is allowed to judge these things? What authority is given to them to alter what God and nature made possible? Everywhere, this hideous strength is seeking to get rid of the poor, the destitute, the lame, the mentally handicapped, or those whom they say are slow witted or dumb. Even worse, they want to reach into a woman's womb and burn out her ability to ever have children just because they deem her unworthy."

Stanley looked up. Father Timothy was really on a roll this morning. Evelyn's murder must have really put a fire up his collar. He watched Hazel out of the corner of his eye. She was riveted, attention glued to the good father.

"All of this comes about through the colonization of ideas, that is, ideas take over our heads like Western countries took over places like Africa. If we don't think of ourselves as good Catholics under God, our minds can be corrupted like anyone else and Legion shall take over."

Every eye in the congregation was fixed on the priest as he raised his arms, his green robe sleeves falling to his elbow.

"So, my brothers and sisters, let us oppose the evil that has started to grow in this beautiful country of ours by being faithful to Our Lord. We must fight, but not with weapons or fists to the face. No, this is a spiritual battle. Powers and Legions rule this city. So, let us rise and confront the powers, as Our Lord did. Amen."

Father Timothy bowed his head. Stanley didn't hear any coughing, fidgeting, or whispering. He snuck a glance again at Hazel, who had a white handkerchief in her hand and was wiping her cheeks. Boy, something about Father Timothy's words must have really struck a chord with her. Stanley wondered what it was.

After the Mass, Stanley took off his robe as Father Timothy came into the sacristy.

"Uh, interesting homily, Father. Do you really think there is a literal Legion in this city?"

Father Timothy furrowed his eyebrows. "And why are you asking?"

Stanley shrugged. "I dunno, just sounded like you believe that."

The priest rubbed his chin. "And what do you think?"

Stanley wanted to tell him everything, but he didn't have evidence for anything yet. Plus, a part of him wanted to do this on his own.

"Yeah, I think so."

Father Timothy nodded and narrowed his eyes. "And you would be right. Legion has begun to move, Stanley. Be careful."

Not trusting himself to say anymore, he received Father Timothy's blessing.

Hazel was waiting for him at the front of the church. She turned to Stanley and smiled.

"Heya, Bananas, what's shakin'?"

She wrinkled her nose. "Do you have to keep calling me that?"

He grinned. "Yep."

Hazel crossed her arms. "Maybe I should come up with a nickname for you."

"You're welcome to try," he said, as he held out his arm.

Hesitating, she stared at him for a few moments, and then sighed. "Fine, boy. I'll think on that. Where are we going?"

She took his arm as they walked down the street. He smiled, feeling her warmth pressed against him. The peace of her flowed into him again, and he felt like Jell-O. Trying to recover himself, he said, "I thought we could go back to Art Hill and poke around. The cops may have cleared out by now. Plus, I have something to tell you."

Hazel stopped and turned to him. "You can't be serious. Why would you want to do that?"

Stanley shrugged. "I don't know; we could do some snooping around. Maybe the police missed something."

"There's your nickname. Snoopy Boy."

"If you shorten it to Snoopy, we're aces."

She laughed. "You're outrageous, you know that?"

"So I've been told. Now, spill everything you know about Evelyn."

As they walked, Hazel told him about the Schmidt family and how they didn't get along with some of the other rich families in town. Further, she didn't know why Evelyn had been in such disgrace or why she got cast out of the city. How did all these things fit together?

"I just don't think Paul did this. I think she had some dirt on somebody powerful," Stanley said.

"Why do you say that?"

"Remember the conversation I overheard?"

She nodded.

"Well, there is more. I saw something on Father Timothy's desk this morning that talked about Legion."

Hazel raised her eyebrow. "That seems farfetched. Maybe they were just notes for his sermon."

"Nah, listen … " And he told her everything he read.

She chewed her lip as she walked. "But don't you think it still could have been Paul? I mean, all this other stuff seems crazy and unreal. Wouldn't the simplest solution be the best?"

Stanley didn't say anything. "I dunno. Nothing is ever that simple, Bananas. Guess anything is possible. I can't imagine any man doing that to a woman, but maybe if he got sore enough. Who knows? But, somehow, I don't think so. Think the family would know? How about your friend, Sandy, was it? Can you ask?"

Hazel frowned. "How in the world am I going to ask that right now? Say, 'Schmidts, can you talk about Evelyn's boyfriend who just took a baseball bat to her?' That will not go over well."

"Okay, keep Henri on your head; I was just asking. So, tell me, when I saw Evelyn at the stadium, she had a shiny ring on that looked important, like a World Series ring. Do all the highbrow dames have them?"

She shook her head. "No. She got that from the Veiled Prophet when she was chosen as the Queen of Love and Beauty. Did you notice she didn't have it on when we found her?"

Stanley nodded and didn't say anything until they reached Art Hill. He poured over the strands of the case, but nothing linked. Furrowing his brow, he felt like the answer was right there in front of him.

When they reached the statue, only one policeman stood guard. They gazed at the murder scene.

"Snoopy, I had nightmares last night. Bad ones. They scared me."

He nodded, but didn't tell her of his own bad dreams; he wasn't ready to be that vulnerable yet. "Something stinks here. Bad." Stanley eyed the cop and wondered if he was one of the crooked ones Seamus mentioned. "I think we're the only ones who know the whole story so far, so we better figure it out. Plus, the killer saw us. We need to grow eyes in the back of our heads. It's not gonna feel very safe for either one of us until he's caught. Unless the killer is Paul, which given all this stuff with Legion, I doubt."

Hazel frowned. "Okay, but where would we even start?"

"Evelyn's diary. You need to get it. Evelyn said her sister had it, so it's gotta be in the house somewhere, right? I'll go to the gangs to see if they know anything about these numbers. My friend Vinnie can get me in, no sweat. Maybe between the two of us we can figure what the numbers mean. Maybe it's just a gambling deal with the gangs and this Veiled Prophet character. Somehow, I think it's all connected."

She held up her hands in exasperation. "You don't get it. You really don't. I can't interrupt a family in mourning, even if they are close friends, and ask about Evelyn's diary. It would be unseemly!"

Stanley shoved his hands in his pockets and said, "Don't you want to know why she died? Don't you want to understand? All of this might be bigger than Evelyn's murder. I'm sorry, but that's true."

He stared at Hazel while she stared off to her right. Waiting, he wanted to see what she would do. Would she get it? Did she have as much moxie as he thought?

Hazel squinted at him, her brow knit together. "Ergh, I really hate you, you know. You're so frustrating."

He smiled. "Why? Because I'm using logic and making sense? Plus, you're just as curious as I am."

Hazel punched him in the arm and then composed herself. Stanley tried not to laugh. He did see her, and he liked everything he saw.

"Fine. I'll help you. We'll figure this out together. I want to do this for Sandy, and also, I liked Evelyn. She was always nice to me. She didn't deserve this. And, who knows, maybe her no-good boyfriend did bash her head in; you don't know."

Stanley shrugged. "Maybe so."

Hazel gazed at the St. Louis statue. He decided to not interrupt her thoughts as she chewed on her lip and lowered her brow.

"So, you really think your priest was talking about the letter he received? About Legion and all that?"

Stanley nodded. "Yeah, how could it not be? Too much smoke, you know? But I don't see how it all relates. We just don't know enough yet."

Hazel nodded, not saying anything. "I think he's right. I've heard them, Stanley, talking about those whom they deem 'unfit.' I thought it was just parlor talk coming from the snobby friends of my father. I'd forgotten about it until your priest said those things."

Stanley nodded. "Kinda scary, huh?"

"It made me feel awful. I want to fight the powers he talked about. I do. Father Timothy is right. Evil has to be fought."

They regarded one another. Somehow, some way, even though they were from different worlds, they were on the same page. Stanley saw it in Hazel's eyes.

"That's why we gotta figure this out. Do you think you could meet me back here tomorrow with the diary?"

Hazel chewed on her lip some more. "I dunno, Snoopy. I just don't know. It'll be hard to get out after last night. Why?"

"Well, first, I want to see what's in the diary. We might have a story here and the goods on whoever killed her if it wasn't Paul. Second, I want you to meet all the Knights in my little gang. We aren't what you think, even if we aren't rich swells. If that book tells us what we think we already know, something big is going down, and we're gonna need their help."

"Who are these Knights you keep going on about?"

Stanley took off his hat and said, "All in good time, Bananas. I'll see you here tomorrow after school, deal?"

"I have no intention of going to school tomorrow. I'm too upset about everything, and my mother will let me stay home and won't care if I slip away." Hazel frowned. "But I want answers and soon, or I won't help you anymore." Her blue eyes met his with a defiant glint.

It made him smile. "Square deal, Haze."

Hazel's hips swayed gently as she walked down the path. She turned and gave him a small smile. Stanley felt the heat rise in his cheeks. He watched as she made her way down the hill toward Lindell. The bright Sunday sun reflected off her pale skin and made her glow like candles in a church. All the rich folks would be milling around in the park for Sunday picnics, so he knew she wasn't in any danger.

On second thought, maybe, the swells were more of a danger to her than any street rat. That thought didn't settle well at all.

Chapter Eleven

Hazel had gone over what to say to Sandy a hundred times in her head as she walked to the Schmidt's house. Nothing she'd come up with seemed right. Her heart ached when she thought of how Sandy must be feeling. She stood on her best friend's porch and glanced into the high windows. Hazel wrung her hands together. The house seemed heavy and silent with sorrow.

Stanley was set on getting that diary, but how could she bring that up? "Hey, Sandy—sorry about your sister … can I have her diary?" Hazel cringed and hesitated before she rang the bell beside the large wooden entrance.

Meyers opened the door, his usually placid face grim. "Good afternoon, Miss Hazel."

She plucked at her skirt and tried to smile. "Hello, Meyers. I've come to pay my respects."

The old man nodded, his bloodshot eyes avoiding her. "The family is not formally taking visitors; however, some have gathered in the salon for refreshments."

"Okay." Hazel didn't know how to behave. It seemed like making a joke or being her playful self was the wrong thing, so Hazel buttoned her lips and followed the aged butler as he led her with a stiff back and long, slow strides toward the salon. Soft classical music played on the phonograph. The murmur of voices made her stomach drop. She didn't want to face a crowd. Hazel paused at the threshold.

Flora came out of the room holding a tray of empty plates. The usually jolly maid didn't greet Hazel with a smile but kept her head low. She'd been crying. Her eyes were puffy, and she sniffled. Flora had been with the family for years and had watched Evelyn grow up. Hazel knew that Peggy would be devastated if anything happened to her. Sometimes maids were like family. Flora gave a quick nod and hurried away before Hazel could say anything.

Inside, the salon was like a floral shop with large vases full of arranged flowers on the ground, the tables, and the windowsills. There were a dozen or so adults she recognized from society events standing in groups whispering. They held teacups or small plates with bite-sized food on them. Gabriel Sinclair, Charles Chouteau, and Brigitte Slayback stood around the phonograph examining record albums. Hazel took a deep breath and thought about the part she had to play.

Be a debutante.

She wove her way through the room unnoticed at first, catching snatches of whispered conversations.

"I always knew her life would end terribly. She was wild."

"That ballplayer was bad news from the beginning—"

"She should never have tried to pretend to be something she wasn't. The Queen of Love and Beauty has to be a maid of highest virtue—"

"Well, you reap what you sow."

"Her family will never recover from this."

As Hazel approached the table of refreshments, her face burned with outrage. It was terrible to speak so rudely of the dead, and in Evelyn's own home. She reached for a glass of water to cool off, but was stopped by a high, grating voice.

"Hazel Malloy." Mrs. Slayback lifted her nose in the air, her double chin wobbling. "Brigitte, look. Your friend Hazel is here." Her expensive green silk dress rustled as she came toward Hazel.

All conversations stopped, and it seemed as if everyone stared at her.

"Hi, Hazel." Brigitte joined her mother. "So … " her eyes flicked up and down in assessment. "Is it true? You saw?" Her button nose crinkled in disgust.

This promised to be about as fun as flagpole sitting in a rainstorm. She took a deep breath. "Yeah, I saw," Hazel said it softly so that only the few of them could hear. She didn't want an audience.

"Oh my, that must have been dreadful. Why would you be out there at night? You're fortunate the darky with the bat didn't go after you too," Mrs. Slayback scolded.

"The *Post-Dispatch* said it was Paul Duncan who did it. Which is it? Which paper got it right?" Gabriel Sinclair cocked his head at Hazel, his eyes bright with curiosity.

"W-well, they've taken the ballplayer into custody, haven't they?" Charles set down the album he held. "Sorry, Hazel, this must be very upsetting for you … "

She swallowed. "Yes. It was awful." Hazel felt a little light-headed. The room was stuffy and full of the scent of flowers so sweet that her stomach turned. Even though most of the people had gone back to whispered conversations, she felt as if a spotlight shone in her face.

"But seriously—they said it was Duncan's bat at the scene of the crime, right? Probably the only time that bum didn't strike out." Gabriel pushed up on his glasses with a smirk.

Brigitte let out a snort and hid her smile with one hand. Gabriel folded his arms and locked eyes with Hazel. "So what's this story in the *Globe* about you and your fella seeing the murderer?"

"I don't think you should talk that way to Hazel; she's had a shock." Charles's low voice was halting and kind.

Hazel blinked, hoping she would not burst into tears. She was not prepared for the feelings rising inside her. Being in Evelyn's home and seeing the flowers and the gathered mourners, even if most of them were there for the gossip rather than out of love for the Schmidts, made it all real. It wasn't just a nightmare, or a lie printed in the papers.

"Was there a lot of blood? Ugh. Don't tell me." Brigitte stepped back as if to avoid catching something that Hazel had been exposed to. "All I know is that it has all the daddies on Lindell scared for our set."

"We do need to look after our women better." Gabriel's gaze rested on Hazel.

Brigitte sniffed, wanting attention. "Well, my daddy has the biggest Civil War gun collection in the whole country. I dare anyone to bother me."

It was a silly brag, but it worked. Gabriel lit up. "I would love to see that some time," he said to Brigitte.

She smiled. "Any time at all." She cast a sly look at Hazel as if she had won a prize. "So, I have to ask," her annoying, pretty face was sour with disdain, "what were you doing in Forest Park at night with a newsie? Is this a new type of slumming? Am I missing out on something?" she asked, wide-eyed with fake innocence.

Hazel pressed her lips together. Brigitte was loving this. They all hovered like vultures, ready to pick at her carcass for gossip. Hazel had resolved to be the perfect debutante, play the game, and not rock the yacht, but something inside her wanted to shake them silly. "Hadn't you heard, Brigitte? Newsies are all the rage."

Gabriel coughed. "Your father assures me that you don't know the boy. That he walked you home after a motion picture you sneaked off to." His eyes got that dangerous twinkle in them. "That was a naughty, wild thing to do."

Hazel's cheeks burned. "You talked to my father about that?"

"After I saw this morning's paper I came to see you—" Gabriel began.

"I see." She narrowed her eyes. He was checking to see if she had fallen from grace. "And are you satisfied with what you learned?" She hated how he assumed to have some claim on her.

He gave a crooked grin. "I knew it couldn't be true."

Brigitte scowled. "Well, I'm relieved to hear you haven't taken a street rat as a beau. Imagine him at the VP Ball in his tattered clothes and little flat cap." She forced a nasal giggle. "Read all about it!"

Hazel's face grew hot. She wanted to shake the whole room by the shoulders. "I find it interesting that you're all so keen to know who my friends are and not about why you're all here today, or what I saw last night." She raised her voice and some of the others in the room stopped their own conversations again to listen. "Don't you want to hear about how the body looked? How her dead eyes stared into the night as if scared to death by the Grim Reaper himself? And then how I saw him too? In a hood, staring down on us in judgment?" Hazel shivered; she couldn't stop the words coming out. "There was so much blood. And she was so still … her hands were like marble, pale, motionless. Remember how beautiful she was?" Hazel turned to Brigitte who watched her, jaw hanging open. "Remember? She was your idol. The Queen of Love and Beauty. An example to us all." Her voice broke and she stopped.

The room was silent. Maybe now they realized just how serious this was. Or maybe they just thought Hazel had lost her mind. Everyone stared at her with an almost gleeful horror. Brigitte had a funny look of victory on her face.

Gabriel furrowed his brow. "What about this guy in a hood? What else did you see?"

She thought of the numbers and the way the police had handled things. "I-I don't want to talk about it anymore."

Hazel ran from the room, her heart pounding. So much for playing the debutante. *Bananas.* She had just made a doozy of a scene, but there was something ridiculous and unreal about all of them and the padded little world they had all constructed.

She paced the hallway trying to get her breath back. Generations of portraits lined the walls in gilded frames. The Schmidt family had a proud legacy of hard work and prosperity, but it all seemed pointless. Did it matter that they were respected and wealthy if their reputation could be destroyed by the whim of the pack at any time? Were any of them safe?

"Hazel?" Charles stood watching her, hands in his pockets.

"Oh. Hi."

"Sorry about that. Sometimes people behave like animals."

"Yeah. Guess evolution is true. Bunch of apes," she muttered.

His smile was slight. "The good thing about evolution is that species can get better in time."

Hazel shrugged. "Better at what? Being top of the food chain? Being predators?"

He cocked his head. "What happened to Evelyn was terrible. It's a shame she trusted the wrong fellow."

Hazel shrugged. Everyone thought it was Paul and for now, she didn't have any proof it wasn't. "Yeah."

"Say, have you seen that new Cagney movie, *The St. Louis Kid*?" he asked as if grasping for something to talk about.

"Uh, no. I haven't yet. But I live for movies."

Charles stepped toward her. "Heard it's a good one. He's a truck driver who gets mixed up in a union dispute after one of the leaders is killed. His girlfriend is kidnapped after witnessing the crime."

"Oh. Sounds like a swell one." Hazel wondered what he had on his mind. Was he warning her?

"Yeah … I wondered … since you're her closest friend … " He cast his eyes down, shy.

"What? Who?"

"Sandy. Does that sound like a movie she'd like? I mean … well, I figured that since her life isn't a bowl of cherries right now she might want … " he halted and shrugged.

"Oh. Oh." Hazel released a sigh. She was letting paranoia creep in. "You thought maybe Sandy could use some fun?"

He nodded and shuffled his feet. "Sure."

"Well … I know she'd like it if you asked." She wondered if she should tell him that Sandy was sweet on him and wanted to go to the Veiled Prophet Ball with him too. Something sunk inside her. Maybe Sandy wouldn't want anything to do with all of that now.

His smile was slow, like the way he spoke. "You really think so?"

"Yeah." It was funny that Sandy, who was a bit of a wild card, was attracted to Mr. Straightlaces. But he was a nice guy, and as Hazel was recently learning, sometimes opposites did attract. "Well, guess I'll try to find her."

Charles gave her a sympathetic nod. "Tell her the white lilies are from me."

"Okay." Hazel gave him a small smile and followed the hallway to the black and white marble floor tiles of the foyer. She took the curving staircase up to Sandy's bedroom. Taking a deep breath, Hazel tapped on the door. "Sandy? It's me … " There was no sound from inside.

She opened the door and the frilly floral room was empty. The bed was neatly-made and the furniture gleamed with polish. It looked as if nobody had slept in there for a while. Hazel backed out of the room. Something pulled her further down the hall to the bedroom on the end. She hadn't been inside it since that day long ago, playing dolls with Sandy.

The carved wooden door to Evelyn's room looked like all of the others on that floor, but it gave Hazel the creeps. She put her hand on the knob and a chill went through her. A part of her hoped when she opened the door it would take her back in time. She would find Sandy inside stomping around in her sister's heels while Evelyn lounged around in a flowy pink robe pretending to be Greta Garbo.

When Hazel pushed on it, Evelyn's door opened without a sound. The room was a wreck. Dresser drawers hung open like mouths, vomiting out the clothes that hung over their sides and spilled out onto the floor. A coral colored lamp lay shattered at the foot of the bed. The aquamarine satin bedding was rumpled and twisted, and pillows were scattered everywhere. A large lump on the bed moaned.

Hazel froze in fear. But then the mound let out a loud belch. "Uh … Sandy?" She crawled up and pulled back the covers.

Sandy's golden hair tangled over her face as she peeked up at Hazel through squinty bloodshot eyes. "Hiya, Haze." Her breath smelled like brandy.

"Oh boy, Sandy." Strewn across the mattress were photographs. Evelyn and Sandy together on their family trip to the seaside, at a picnic, holding hands on Cahokia mound, capturing their smiles and laughter in silver, black, and gray. A lump rose in Hazel's throat and her eyes burned with tears. She wrapped her arms around her friend and lay there, letting the tears come.

"She's never coming home," Sandy whispered.

"I know."

"So … what's the point?"

Hazel looked at her friend. Sandy stared at the ceiling. "I was gonna be the perfect lady, make the Veiled Prophet notice me."

Clutched in Sandy's hand was the photograph taken at the Veiled Prophet Ball when Evelyn had been crowned. She sat glowing in her gown beside the mysterious figure of the Veiled Prophet on his throne, his face covered in a curtain of lace. It was the first time that Hazel realized the whole set up was eerie.

"Why would you want to be noticed? Maybe if we lay low nobody will expect us to be perfect." She smoothed Sandy's hair away from her face.

Sandy squeezed her eyes shut and gave a ragged sigh. "Because if I was crowned, my family would be tops again. Then Evelyn could come home … " Her slurred speech halted and she began to sob.

Hazel held her tight. "I'm sorry. I'm so sorry." She pressed a kiss to her friend's head.

"Nothing matters now. Who gives a hang?" Sandy hiccupped and wiped her face with the back of her hand. She regained control and turned toward Hazel. Her golden eyes searched Hazel's face. "You saw her."

Hazel looked away. "Yeah."

"Tell me," Sandy breathed.

It took a while for Hazel to get it all out because she kept choking up. She described everything about that night except the numbers; a cold feeling always gripped her when she thought about telling anyone about them. When she finished, Sandy's body shook with emotion.

"Why would he do it?" Sandy gasped between sobs.

"I don't think they got it right. The guy in the hood isn't the ballplayer, if you ask me." Hazel gripped her friend's hand.

"No. It can't be. They were in love … "

"Did you know him, Sandy? Did you know why they took away your sister's crown?"

She nodded. "Yeah. The diary gave that away too."

Hazel's heart skipped. "Evelyn's diary?"

"Yeah … in a letter she asked me to find it and give it to Paul. But I never got the word to him. After she let me know where she had hidden it, I read some of it. It was love all right."

"Where is it now?" Maybe she shouldn't be asking. But somebody had to do something.

Sandy's lip trembled. "I'm scared, Hazel. She wanted that diary—maybe came back to town just to get it and then a man in a hood killed her … "

"Do you think it's connected?" Hazel asked.

"I'm scared." Sandy hid her face behind her hands. "And I'm a little drunk."

"Yeah. I know. That boy I met, his uncle is a policeman. Want me to give the diary to him? Maybe there's a clue about who killed her in it."

Sandy sniffed several times before pulling a small leather diary from under her pillow. "Take it. I can't bear it. I always wanted to be close to my sister—she's been gone a couple years now. I always thought I'd have a chance, but now I never will. I'd rather not know what I'm missing; I don't want to read anymore."

Hazel nodded and took the diary in her hands. She had expected to have to convince Sandy to give it to her. It broke Hazel's heart to see such a strong girl with no fight left in her.

"I'm going to help figure out who did this, Sandy. I promise." Hazel pressed a kiss to her friend's forehead.

Sandy let out a sob and burrowed further under the covers. Hazel stayed, holding Sandy and trying to comfort her until she fell asleep. Even in sleep, Sandy's brow was creased and her mouth turned down. She looked a bit like Evelyn. Hazel swallowed and tucked the blanket around her beautiful, devastated friend.

Hazel placed the diary in her handbag and headed back down the stairs. She had it. Stanley would be so proud. Maybe it was an important piece of evidence. She almost reached the door when Gabriel Sinclair stepped in front of her.

"Leaving?" He slid his specs up the bridge of his nose.

"I need to get home." Hazel tried to step around him.

"Wait. I have something to ask you."

Hazel clutched her bag. "What?"

He came closer, leaning in. "Is something wrong?"

Her nerves jumped as alarms rang in her head. "Wrong? I saw Evelyn's dead body last night. And now my best friend is falling apart, and there are things that—"

He held up a hand. "Yes. I'm aware. I was hoping to give you something pleasant to think about."

"Such as? William Powell's taking me to dinner?" Hazel shook her head, impatient to leave.

"Or Gabriel Sinclair is taking you to the VP Ball." He grinned expectantly.

"Wha—you … Oh, for crying out loud!" Hazel pushed past him and opened the door. Sunlight spilled into the foyer and lit up Gabriel's hair.

"Is that a no?" Hazel heard him call as she shut the door behind her and ran down the porch steps.

He had some nerve.

At the bottom of the tall porch steps, Hazel paused and looked back at the house. She bit her lip. Well, she'd failed at the debutante act again, but everything was so upsetting. Hazel sighed and gazed up at Evelyn's bedroom window. It was shut with the curtains drawn. Her heart squeezed. Poor Sandy.

The sounds of the automobiles on the street seemed wrong. Everything seemed off kilter, crooked. Hazel swayed on her feet. She sat on the last step, exhausted.

With everything that had happened, Hazel was a nervous wreck. Now, on top of it all, she had a stick of dynamite in her handbag. She pulled the leather-bound diary out and stared at it. What was so important in it that possibly got Evelyn murdered?

Her stomach knotted. The killer was loose, and he'd seen Hazel. She stood and quickened her step to the sidewalk. Stanley was the only other person who knew what the police and the papers had lied about. They had to figure this out fast and stop the lunatic.

Hazel gripped the diary tight as if somebody would snatch it from her hands. She took a deep breath and then coughed on a mouthful of smoke.

A faint snort made Hazel turn her head, her heart jarring inside her chest. That boy Arthur from the pretzel stand leaned against the front gate of the Schmidt's house in a cloud of cigarette smoke, bowler hat cocked to the side.

Arthur's dark eyes seemed to stab at her as he scanned her from her feet to her face. She couldn't tell if he recognized her or not.

Hazel stared back. "H-hi." She fumbled to put the diary back into her bag.

His lips pulled into a snarl. Arthur squinted through the smoke as it trailed out of his mouth. He didn't answer but spat onto the ground, almost hitting Hazel's shoes.

Part of Hazel wanted to let him have it. She'd never seen such rude, low behavior toward a girl. And not just any girl. Hazel raised her chin, but her moment of brave outrage crumbled when Arthur stepped toward her, a scowl of disgust on his face.

Hazel turned away and hurried toward her house. She glanced over her shoulder as she reached the gate. Arthur was still there, trailing her, watching her. She ran up the walkway, trotting up the steps of her porch. With her hand on the doorknob, Hazel looked back, and her stomach sank. The boy stood shadowed by the gate, hands in his pockets, staring at her. Hazel couldn't understand why, but he hated her. She saw it on his face. Now he knew where she lived. A chill ran down her back and she retreated into the house.

Hazel had made it home before her father. But just barely. Over a brief and silent dinner, Mumsy winked at her from across the table while Pops ignored her completely.

Back up in the refuge of her bedroom, Hazel pulled the diary out of her bag. She wanted to read it before she gave it to Stanley.

She opened it, and the binding creaked. The slight smell of rose petals wafted from the pages. It was like a little coffin, holding the remains of a person who had once lived and breathed.

Skimming through several pages of Evelyn's graceful handwriting revealed breezy accounts of her day-to-day life: shopping, the weather, a garden party at the Busch mansion, something about Sandy being a pest. A passage caught Hazel's eye.

Daddy finally talked me into going with him to see a game. I don't know what all the hullaballoo is about baseball, anyway. But he seems so pleased to parade me around. He said it's good to be seen with important people. Especially this year. I'm invited to the VP Ball, and anything can happen! Mr. Sinclair joined us at the ballpark and he and Daddy were placing bets and ribbing each other a lot. It was fun in a way. We had the best seats and I wore my new lilac dress—the one with the big bow on the collar.

After the game, Daddy was so excited because we got to hang out with his favorite player. I thought Dizzy Dean was a bit crude and filthy, but he was friendly. Daddy kept shaking his hand and smiling. He is famous after all.

There was another player, of no consequence. Daddy ignored him. He came over to talk to DD and I can't explain why, but I couldn't take my eyes off him (P). Even after he finished relaying his message to DD, P stood there watching me in a particular way. He looks a bit like a movie star ... Gary Cooper.

I'm blushing just thinking about him. P is tall and has muscled arms and legs. The way he moved reminded me a little of Annabelle's prize stallion that won the Derby last year. I'm sure he's just a brute from the wrong side of town. But I felt—and I would only admit this in here—I felt all hot and feverish when he looked at me. So different from the society boys.

His smile. His eyes.

I'll probably never see P again, but I swear he felt it too. For just a moment.

Hazel paused and looked up at the ceiling in thought. Love at first sight. Just like the movies. She sighed. Even if Paul was from the wrong people, you just can't stop the real thing. Just like that Clark Gable picture she'd just seen. Except, that didn't end in murder.

A few pages later, there was more about P the ballplayer.

I'm not sure how he'd know where I shopped, but when I came out of the department store with Flora, he seemed to be waiting for me. He looked so handsome in a suit and hat, even if it wasn't tailored. P didn't say anything. Just smiled and then passed by me, letting his shoulder nudge mine.

My heart raced when our eyes met. He gave me a wink. I couldn't say anything because Flora was there. But when I got home, I found a folded piece of paper in my handbag. He had slipped it in there without me even noticing! It says he wants to meet me tonight at the statue of St. Louis. I hardly know what to think! What if he's a masher? He is certainly no gentleman. I'm not going, of course. I mean, he might try something fresh. But I can't stop thinking about it. What if I went?

Hazel shivered. Little did Evelyn know that someday, going to meet Paul at the statue would be the last thing she would ever do.

She flipped through the pages of the diary and stopped in a random spot.

Flora delivered my note to P. I just had to see him. It was driving me mad. I have no regrets. As soon as I saw him I felt better—like a glass of water on a hot day. We talked, and we have so much in common. Hours went by, but it felt like minutes. He knows so many things about the world that I don't know. He looks at me like I'm a walking miracle. We sat in the park, holding hands in the moonlight under the stars. P has a beautiful voice, low and soothing. He softly sang my favorite song: "All of me, Why not take all of me? Can't you see, I'm no good without you? Take my lips, I wanna lose them. Take my arms, I'll never use them."

Sigh.

I think that was his way of telling me how he feels. Is it strange that in so short a time, I feel the same? It may be shameful, but I let him kiss me. I have never felt more alive. It just felt right.

Hazel realized she was holding her breath. It was so romantic and daring. Just like the movies. Maybe it was possible to feel that way for someone who is all wrong, but was it a mirage that led to destruction? She continued to read through the details of Evelyn's life with her secret sweetheart. Pages of their meetings and outings. Little snatches of heaven in a world of their own. It seemed that Evelyn's maid, Flora, was the only one who knew the truth.

Hazel jumped ahead several pages. Weeks had passed.

I love him. I don't care what Daddy will say. He doesn't need to know about my plans with P until after the VP Ball. I wouldn't do anything to jeopardize that. P says it's all "hogwash," but he doesn't understand what an honor it is to just be invited. I'm trying to help P to be more and reach higher. He has so much potential. I'm helping him sort out some trouble he's gotten into with some unsavory street rats. I'm happy to use my shopping money to give him a better life—a new start. If everyone is to accept him, he needs to improve himself. Maybe Daddy will even give him a position in the company. It will be difficult to convince everyone that P and I do belong together, even if he is from the wrong people, but he's worth fighting for.

Hazel wondered what Paul thought of all of this. She knew it was a lot of pressure to live up to high expectations. Was he really in love, or did he just take advantage of a beautiful girl with money? Hazel thought of her parents. Her mother hadn't been from society but had helped her dad. Was that why he loved her, or was there more?

Skipping past the middle of the diary, Hazel found a folded piece of paper that looked as if it had been torn out of a book. She unfolded it and thought she was seeing funny for a minute. It was written all in nonsense with portions underlined. Was it a code? Hazel tucked it back between the pages where she found it and turned to the end of the diary, just before the pages went blank.

The top of the page read, The Winnowing, followed by columns of three-digit numbers with labels she didn't understand. Veiled Prophet … Feeble Minded … Traitor …

What did they mean? Her skin crawled when she remembered the numbers on Evelyn's leg, the ones the policeman had erased. Stanley had written them down. They needed to get this diary to his uncle.

A banging sound echoed up from outside Hazel's window. She hopped up and peeked out, but it was dark and difficult to see where the noise had come from. Then she heard voices, and she craned her neck out of the window.

"Pipe down. You'll rouse all the sleeping Fat Cats." It was Stanley's voice. Her heart sped up.

When Hazel's eyes adjusted, she saw the outline of two boys rounding the corner of the house. One wore a flat cap, and the other wore a bowler hat. The soft red glow of a cigarette flared. "Keep your trousers on." It was Arthur.

She froze. Maybe he'd only been lurking around the back of her house to scout out the trash cans. Hazel tried to comfort herself with that thought. In the still of the night, their voices bounced off the paved drive and into her window.

"This one has cornbread and potatoes," Stanley said in a loud whisper.

They were on one of their raids to feed the starving families in their neighborhood. Hazel wanted to shout down to them and then wondered if it would ruin their fun or embarrass them. Besides, Arthur scared her a little. But he couldn't be that bad if he fed the poor, could he?

Hazel backed away from the window. Okay, so girls got murdered with bats and certain circles in society could turn on you like a pack of wolves, but the age of chivalry was not dead, because somewhere out there was a band of newsie knights trying to give hope and a mouthful of bread to folks who were down on their luck.

Hazel settled back onto her bed, shut the diary, and smiled to herself. That's what she needed to see at the end of a long, upsetting day. Just a little hope.

Chapter Twelve

A whack on the head brought Stanley out of his daydreams of solving crimes and holding a grateful, blue-eyed girl in his arms.

"Mr. Fields, please come back from your fantasies and pay attention!"

Stanley looked up to see Sister Mary John, dressed in a black robe. A white nun habit covered her entire head except for her face. Wondering about her hair color (and remembering the bet he'd made with Vinnie about it), he straightened up, "Ah, sorry, Sister, long night."

She stared at him with hands on her hips. "And what were you doing up late, boy? Sinning?"

Many different sarcastic replies came to his mind, like, "I was smooching on a Protestant girl up at Gaslight Square with a bottle of whiskey in my hand," but Stanley glued his trap shut. The last thing he needed was to be kept after school to write lines. He had to meet Hazel and the Knights. Besides, talking back to a nun was an iffy proposition at best.

He stood, bowed to the nun, and said with a smile, "Sister, I was protecting the defenseless and the weak."

The room went silent as the nun's mouth drew into a very thin line. He tried not to stare, because looking a sister in the eye was just asking for trouble. Stanley never laughed at the rumor that nuns could read people's souls.

"See me when the bell rings, Mr. Fields." With that, she turned back to the chalkboard and began talking about the math lesson.

Stanley slumped in his desk and tried not to make a face. He should've realized his hammy acting job would land him in hot water. Now he would have to pay for it and miss seeing Hazel.

The bell rang. Everyone left. He slouched toward Sister Mary's desk with hands in his pockets. *Maybe begging would work*, he thought.

"Sister … "

The nun held up her hand. "Silence, Mr. Fields, and let me speak. I want to see your face, please."

Stanley looked up, expecting the nun to give him a ferocious scowl. Instead, she stood and laid a hand on his shoulder.

I'll be, he thought, *the ol' battle-ax has a soul.* He cringed inwardly and resolved to add that thought to his sins for confession.

"Mr. Fields, do you know men in hoods have started to roam the streets?" she asked, in an educated Boston accent.

He looked up in surprise. "Um, er, no, Sister, I didn't know that."

She looked around, walked to the door, and shut it.

Stanley furrowed his brow. The man who killed Evelyn? There was more than one? "Who are they?"

Sister Mary John shook her head. "My guess is that someone has noticed your nighttime raids on the trash cans on Lindell Boulevard. It's been known that men from that part of the town will go into poor neighborhoods to intimidate the people there when something happens that they don't like. Very often, people wind up getting beaten or disappearing."

"They are trying to get me to stop?"

"I don't know, Stanley. Maybe they feel like the poor need

a reminder to stay in their place. Whatever it is, you must watch yourself. Father Timothy believes something dark is getting ready to descend on the city. So, no more going out at night."

"To hear is to obey, O Bride of Christ," Stanley lied, giving her a half-smile. He would have to confess that one, too.

Her mouth twitched, and, for a moment, he thought she would smile back.

"Away with you. Go sell your papers."

Stanley nodded, grabbed his lunch pail, and ran outside. Looking both ways, he scanned the street for any suspicious characters. Almost as if summoned, he spotted a man across the street in a black suit wearing a black hood with eyeholes.

His legs felt like lead and he couldn't move. The man stared at Stanley and stepped back into the shadows of the alley as a bus passed between them on the street. When Stanley could see the other side again, the man had gone. Swallowing hard, heart thumping, Stanley ran down the street toward Forest Park as fast as he could. He passed food carts, small brick houses, and wove through parked cars. He even ducked into a few stray alleys to throw off anyone who might be following.

Stanley looked up and down Skinker Boulevard. The man in the hood was nowhere to be seen, but he still felt eyes on him. He crossed the street and into the park, glancing back a few times before stepping into the protection of the trees. When Stanley finally reached Art Hill, he found Hazel at the statue.

Stanley almost forgot to tell her what had just happened when he noticed her yellow trousers belted at the waist with a red flannel shirt. Not many dames wore trousers. She looked good.

She caught him staring and Stanley blurted, "I'm being watched."

Hazel turned white. "Are you sure?"

He told her about the man in the hood and what Sister Mary John had said. Hazel listened and gripped her handbag. "What're we going to do, Stanley?"

"I dunno. Whoever murdered Evelyn obviously isn't afraid of much, least of all the cops."

Stanley watched Hazel's face. It was so smooth and clean. Innocent. "No more walking alone for you, Haze. Either you get a servant to go with you or wait for one of my boys."

She raised her brows. "I'm perfectly capable of taking care of myself, thank you." Hazel lifted her chin, pretty face determined.

He shook his head. "Oh yeah? You can defend yourself against a gun or a knife? That takes practice."

Hazel's shoulders went limp. "Okay. I get it. So, what now?"

Stanley said, "Let's go meet the boys, and we can work it out." He walked over and offered his arm. Hazel took it with a half-smile as he led her to the deepest part of the forest that dominated the park. Sunlight shone down through the trees. The leaves had started to change color from green into orange, red, and brown. Despite everything, he loved walking with her; it almost seemed normal.

"Hey, where we walking to, Timbuktu?" she asked, gripping his arm.

"You'll see. Did you get the diary?"

Hazel stopped, freed her arm, and opened her brown handbag. Pulling out the leather diary, she said, "I only had time to look at bits and pieces last night. Mumsy wanted girl time today since I was home from school. I know she means well, but I couldn't shake her. Didn't have a moment's privacy. Sometimes her sobriety can be so inconvenient."

Stanley snorted. Life with a drinker could be quite a ride; he knew all about that. "Can I see it?"

Hazel slowed her step. "Are you going give it to your uncle?"

"Nah. Don't want to. I want to figure this out on our own," he said as he reached out for the book.

Hazel clutched the diary to her chest. "You promised to give it to him."

Stanley sighed. "Yeah, but I've been thinking. We can't trust anyone. Plus, my uncle isn't the most reliable person just now. He'd be mighty sore at me if he knew I'd been poking around in this business. So let me keep it."

Hazel bit her lip. "No, Snoopy. I can't give it to you. I told Sandy I'd give it to the police, so I feel responsible. Plus, I want to read it some more. I didn't get very far."

He opened his mouth to object but stopped when he saw her set her jaw. No point in arguing with a girl who's made up her mind, especially this one. She was almost as stubborn as he was, maybe more.

"Fine. Have it your way. Must've been tricky trying to get it."

"My so-called friends just acted like it was a party; they wanted the gossip. Sandy buried herself in Evelyn's bed with a bottle of brandy." Hazel shook her head. "The good thing is, she gave the diary to me without a fight when I told her I knew a policeman. She knew we were there and all. She's pretty shaken up."

Stanley furrowed his brow. "We're gonna make sure someone takes the rap for this, don't worry."

Hazel sighed. "I hope so. Think this diary will help?"

He shrugged. "I'm guessing so. Can I at least look at it?"

Holding it tight, she asked, "You promise to give it back?"

Stanley rolled his eyes. "Yes, cross my heart, hope to die, stick a needle in my eye."

She frowned. "Classy. Fine, here."

Taking the diary, he opened it and started to leaf through. Stanley had no idea where to start.

"Read here." Hazel reached over and turned to a page she had dogeared. "It's the part where she talks about Paul's gambling debts," Hazel said.

He flipped to the page and read aloud. "P has been so foolish with his money, and I'm worried. He's in deep trouble with the Rookery crowd, and they are making threats. I keep offering him money, but he refuses." Stanley scratched behind his ear. "See, this here makes it seem like the gangs were hot on his tail, doesn't it?" he said.

"Maybe this points to the gangs doing it. I don't know," Hazel said, furrowing her brows.

Nodding, Stanley stared off into space. "Yeah, maybe. That makes sense with the evidence."

Hazel watched him. "But you don't think so, do you?"

He held up his hand. "Gimme a sec."

Stanley rolled it over in his brain. Something didn't fit. What was it?

He shook his head. "No … it just seems off."

She crossed her arms and raised her eyebrow. "How come?"

"Gangs wouldn't go after someone so high profile for a gambling debt. No way. They'd be smarter to blackmail her, to squeeze her for more dough. I don't think they'd crush a dame's skull with a baseball bat, even if she was the one who owed them money. They might do it in a fit of rage, but not in cold blood, and not in public unless they had some sort of protection."

"They're gangs, Stanley, I wouldn't put anything past them."

Stanley nodded. "Sure, you'd be right in most cases. Not here. They'd never put themselves in this kinda heat just for cash. She's too high class and well known for this sort of thing. Plus, she'd be worth more to them alive than dead. Has to be something else. Maybe there's more in this diary than meets the eye. Wasn't Evelyn the queen of rich people or something?"

"Queen of Love and Beauty. It's a high honor, Snoopy."

"Okay, so what else is in here that's got Henri in a twist?"

Hazel chewed her lip. "There's a strange section in the back marked 'The Winnowing.' It's a bunch of numbers or something. I wonder if it might have something to do with the numbers on her leg."

Numbers. Stanley's pulse quickened as he flipped through the book.

Hazel continued, "There's also a folded paper stuck in there that looks like it was torn from something else—but it's written in another language or maybe in a code. I think it all has something to do with the Veiled Prophet." Stanley came to the last three pages. Written on the first page were the words *The Winnowing—What I've Learned so Far. List incomplete, need more information.*

(Ordered By)

Veiled Prophet	*01*
Court of Seers	*02*
Bengal Guards	*03*

(Don't know what this is)

Traitor	*01*
(Unknown)	*02*
(Unknown)	*03*
Black	*04*
Mongoloid	*05*
Feeble Minded	*06*
Agitator	*07*
Criminal	*08*
Deviant	*09*

(This list scares me)

Unknown	*01*
Asylum	*02*
Shock Therapy	*03*
Sterilization	*04*
Confinement	*05*
Unknown	*06*

(Location?)

The Island	*01*
The Rookery (pending)	*03*

Stanley looked up, his heart hammering. Pieces were coming together. "You've got something here. These numbers look kinda like the ones on Evelyn that Liam wiped away, and," Stanley hesitated a moment, "my friend has a tattoo with these kind of numbers."

She stared at him. "That list is absolutely horrible. But what could it all mean?" He tucked the diary under his arm, reached into his jacket and muttered, "Damn it, I left my stupid notebook at school. I got in such a hurry to run over here and forgot it."

"Can you remember any of it?"

Trying to picture the numbers on Evelyn's leg, Stanley rubbed his chin. "I think the first number was 01, and according to this, it can mean a few things."

"I didn't have time to look much at the end of the diary. I got sort of swept away reading about Evelyn and Paul," she sighed. "Maybe there's more about this Winnowing business in the pages near the end before the numbers."

Stanley stuck his hands in his pockets and started to walk down the path. "Maybe. So, you read the mushy parts about Paul? Were they all nuts about each other?" Warmth crawled up his cheeks.

"I'm pretty sure they were in love. At least, Evelyn was. She was crazy about him," Hazel said, panting to keep up with his long stride. "Say, long legs, give me a break, will you?"

He smiled and slowed down. "Sorry. Why do you think so?"

"It's obvious in her diary by the way she talked about him."

Not knowing how girls thought, he'd have to take her word for it. Still, he realized he'd never thought about what dames might write when they were in love; probably mushy stuff about a guy's eyes or something. Did Hazel think that way? Did she like his eyes?

Stanley cleared his throat. "Uh, um, do you think he felt the same?"

She shrugged. "You tell me. You knew him and saw them together." She searched his face, and he had to look away when his stomach did a somersault.

Stanley tried to recall every detail of the tunnel confrontation. Paul spoke to Evelyn in a low voice and stared at her like a fella should, gentle like. And the smooching was intense.

"Yeah, I think so. Or he's a really good actor, but he's always seemed to be an honest guy, at least with me." They walked in silence. "So, we guessing he didn't bump her off? Even with all the evidence against him?"

Hazel tucked her hair behind her ear. "I don't know. I can't prove it, I know. Just a feeling I have. Is that a dumb girl thing?"

Stanley shook his head. "You aren't stupid. Hunches matter. And I don't think the gangs would touch her. But, still, I can't shake the gambling stuff in here. Evelyn might have paid a lot of money to get Paul out of trouble. If the coppers saw that fact, his goose might be cooked. They'd think he took care of her to hush her up. But, for the record, I think you're right. Paul wouldn't take a bat to a woman. Maybe some others on that team might, but not him."

She crossed her arms. "So, what do we do, go to the police?"

Stanley furrowed his brow. "Not a chance. You saw Liam wipe those numbers. If those numbers are related to this Winnowing business, and if everything my uncle told me about the police is true, they can't be trusted. Not with this," he held up the diary, "not with anything."

"Then what?"

He shrugged. "We do it ourselves. Then, when we have enough evidence, we take it to the papers, maybe the *Dispatch* where I work. I got connections there."

She raised her eyebrow. "Is that so? Or are you exaggerating?"

"Fact. You poke around and see if there's any useful gossip in your circles, and I'll look into the Winnowing. I wrote down the numbers that were on Evelyn's leg in my notebook. And I'll start with the gang angle and visit the Rookery. See if they know anything—seeing that some of them seem to be sporting numbered tattoos lately. Evelyn seemed to think they'd be interested in what was in the diary when

I heard her talking to Paul—but I'm not sure what they'd want with information they may already have."

Stanley furrowed his brow. Going to that den of thieves wasn't something he really felt great about. He'd heard they put out a hit to beat the crap out of him. Well, he would just take the beating. Not like that hadn't happened before, and it would be worth it if he learned something to make sense of all of this.

Hazel gripped his arm, causing Stanley to wince in surprise and pain.

"That sounds dangerous. You can't just walk in there."

Stanley smiled and patted her hand. "It's a bit dodgy, I admit. But I got connections. Don't worry."

She wrinkled her nose. "Hm. I'm not exactly worried. And is that your answer to everything, 'I got connections?' Are you going to sell me the Eads bridge next?"

He grinned, shook her hand off his arm to grip his suspenders, and said, "Say, friend, I got a marvelous iron bridge that spans the Mississippi for sale. Interested?"

She playfully slapped him on the arm. "I'm serious, Snoopy. I don't want you hurt for no good reason," she admitted.

Stanley stopped grinning and lowered his brow. "A woman's been killed. That's reason enough for me. It's wrong, and I think we're the only ones who can figure it out. I can do the street stuff while you get the rich people to sing like canaries."

Hazel stared at him, and he wondered what was going on in her head.

"Okay. Fine. I doubt it will do much good, but I'll see what I can find out on my end."

Stanley nodded. They stared at each, and Hazel's eyes reflected the light of the late afternoon sun. *A guy could get lost in those*, he thought. She smiled at him, and his knees went weak.

Easy, Stanny boy, easy.

"Aces."

Hazel let out a long breath. "I'm not sleeping well," she admitted. "I want to be the brave gypsy and all, but I just can't stop seeing what we saw." Her pretty face darkened and her eyes misted over.

Stanley's heart constricted. He wanted to be a strong man and reassure her, but he also knew how she felt and he suddenly wanted her to know. "The nightmares aren't pretty."

She looked over at him. "It scares me. You too, Snoopy?"

"Me too." They locked eyes, and Stanley felt like she saw into his soul. It made him lose his breath. Nervous and exhilarated, he reached out and touched her cheek. Hazel blinked, a tiny smile curving on her lips.

"It's okay, tough guy. I won't tell anyone," she whispered.

If Stanley kept gazing at her while she looked at him like that he'd end up either crying or kissing her senseless. Clearing his throat, he dropped his hand and said, "All right, Lady Bananas, let's get to the Castle, shall we?"

He held out his arm and she took it. "The Castle? What's that?"

Stanley grinned. "What are knights without a place to hang their helmets?"

"That doesn't really answer the question."

"I hate ruining surprises."

They walked for a few more minutes into the heart of the forest and came to a large clearing. A red boxcar, worn to a rusty pink by the rain, stood in the middle of the glade on a large piece of rotting railroad track. He'd found it one day while looking for shortcuts across the park. It had seemed like a great place for a clubhouse and hiding place.

The door opened, showing Stanley four of his best friends. . Stanley wished Vinnie would drop the gangs and join them. Then everything would be aces. He loved these guys, even though he would never tell them. They'd think he went soft or something.

"The Castle, my lady, home of the Order of the Knights of St. Louis. You're the first girl ever to be here, as far as I know."

Hazel stared at it. "How … how did it get here?"

Stanley shrugged. "No clue. My guess is there was a railroad spur here or something."

Hazel nodded but didn't say anything. As they approached the open door, she whispered under her breath, "That's Arthur, isn't it? I don't think he likes me much."

Stanley chuckled. "He doesn't like most people. You get used to it."

Arthur stared at them, cigarette dangling from his fingers and a slight frown on his face. Stanley had to admit that even he didn't like how the kid stared at Hazel. He wasn't going let that be an issue. He'd have to talk with him about that later. Arthur would have to get over it.

The others jumped down with welcoming smiles.

Anino took off his hat and bowed. "Anino Torres, at your service, my lady." He grinned.

Stanley hid a smile; Anino seemed like such a gent. If only Hazel knew how many members from other gangs he'd beaten up.

An olive-skinned boy in a black suit and a white shirt with a yarmulke on his head smiled. "I'm Jakob."

She stared at him like he was a ghost or something. Stanley would bet money she hadn't seen many, or any, Jews.

Stanley smirked. "Try not to eyeball our Jew too much, Bananas. He's a guy just like us, except he's a math genius, like that Einstein."

She turned Cardinals red. "I'm sorry. I didn't mean … just never met … "

They all laughed, and Jakob smiled. "I'm used to it, Hazel. No skin off my nose."

Shuffles came up to Hazel and kissed her hand. He was a rail thin boy with freckles and a never-ending smile on his face. No one would ever guess he was a notorious pick-pocket and a con man before he went straight and joined Stanley's Knights.

He smiled. "Hiya, doll. The name's Shuffles. Anywhere you want to go, I can get you."

Stanley frowned a little. "Take it easy, smoothy. Hazel's a lady, not some hussy off the street."

Arthur snorted, took a drag of his cigarette, and glared. Hazel glanced at him and then stepped closer to Stanley.

"All right, listen up. Something's going down and we're in the middle of it. So I need your help," Stanley said.

He explained everything that had happened since the murder, including the encounter he'd had with the hooded man in Dogtown that afternoon.

Jakob shook his head. "So, what's it all about? Who's the guy poking around? Think he's the murderer?"

Stanley shook his head. "Maybe. But let's keep our eyes open. I need you to start shaking down the street. We need all the pigeons out there with big ears. The murderer is still out there and I don't like it. I want to know who he is."

Stanley looked at Arthur. "And Artie, I want you to stick around Hazel's house and watch for anything shady. Guard her."

Hazel colored and Arthur made a face. "I don't want to look after some highbrow swell. She's safe; don't worry. She's got servants and all."

Everyone turned to stare at him. Stanley balled his fists.

"You owe me." Stanley pulled the neck of his shirt aside to reveal the white scar on his shoulder.

Arthur narrowed his eyes and took a drag of his cigarette before pointing it at Stanley. "One of these days, that ain't gonna work on me no more."

"Just do it, Artie. You're the only one who can, and you know it." Stanley hated asking Arthur to do this. He knew the mere mention of Lindell Boulevard made Arthur want to beat people because of what happened to his dad and mom. But he was the best man for the job because he was both fearless and a little crazy.

Arthur stared at Stanley and then nodded. "Fine, I'll do it."

"Good, and now our business for tonight."

Shuffles cleared his throat. "Stanny, uh, well, I like ol' Haze here, but the Knight's business isn't open to just anyone, no matter how cute she is."

Stanley opened his mouth to argue, but Hazel laid a hand on his arm. "He's right, Snoopy. I don't need to hear about tonight. It's okay."

He looked at the other Knights, who avoided his eyes. Darn it, they were both right. Stanley had established the rules of no outsiders at Order meetings. He had to stick with it.

"I'll walk you back."

A rustle in the trees distracted Stanley. All the Knights ran to stand by his side, and Arthur shoved Hazel behind them while Anino took out his two sticks, twirling them in the air.

"Who is it? Show yourself," Stanley barked.

A short, dark-headed kid came out and gave them a toothless smile.

"Hey, Stanley. Glad I found you. Can I join now?"

The Knights relaxed and chuckled. "Go home, small fry, and play with your dollies," Shuffles said.

Teeth stopped smiling and held up his fists. "I can fight any of ya. I took on the gangs when they wanted me, didn't I?"

Not quite, Stanley thought. Without him and Arthur helping, the kid would have been beaten to a bloody pulp.

Before Teeth could challenge anyone to a fight, Stanley said, "Say, Teeth, I got a job for you. Can you take Ms. Hazel back to Art Hill? She needs someone to keep an eye on her. She's in trouble. And since you're our best pigeon, you're the right man for the job."

The kid's face lit up. "Gladly." He stuck out his little arm to Hazel.

She gave Stanley a sideways glance and said, "Sir Teeth, I'd be honored if you would escort me. I'd feel a lot less scared with a brave knight like you to protect me."

Anino groaned and shook his head. "Don't give him any rope. He'll hang himself."

She smiled and said, "Snoopy, can I talk to you a minute?"

Stanley nodded, and they went around the side of the boxcar.

"What's up?" He shoved his hands in his pockets.

Hazel stared off into the woods and said, "I know what you're doing tonight."

Stanley pushed back his hat and said, "How'd you know?"

She chuckled. "I saw you and your guys pass my window last night. Plus, people talk about the poor raiding their trash cans."

"Oh. You gonna rat us out?" he asked, heat rising to his cheeks. Did he misjudge her? Would she deny people food?

Hazel crossed her arms and wrinkled her nose. "No, silly, I want to help you. We always have more than we need. I'm going to leave more than scraps out tonight, if I can. How do full chickens and loaves of bread sound?"

Once again, she surprised him, and Stanley only managed to say, "That'd be something. A family could live a week on that. You for real?"

"Very. And it'll be easy as catching a movie, don't worry." She looked over at the boys. "I'd better go with Teeth before the Knights think I'm your filly or moll or something."

He looked over at his pals who'd gathered in a semi-circle. All of them looked busy talking about something else, but he knew from their glances he'd get the business when Hazel left.

"Yeah, maybe so. Here." He slipped the diary into her handbag. "It will be safer behind your castle walls."

Hazel nodded, nervous. "Okay."

"I'll be seeing ya, Bananas." He winked to reassure her.

She tucked her hair behind her ear and looked up through her eyelashes. "I hope so."

Stanley's skin warmed when Hazel touched him on the arm. She went over to Teeth, who took her by the hand, and they disappeared along the path into the woods. He half hoped that she would come back and smile at him again.

When he returned to the Knights, Anino said, "Say, Stanny boy, she's a looker, make no mistake, and a sweet kid. I can see why you're crazy about her."

"What are you talking about? I'm not sweet on her."

They all laughed, including Arthur.

"Please, Stanny, the headlines are all over you," Jakob joked, punching Stanley in the arm.

"Yeah, and she's loopy over you too. Great. That's all we need," Arthur said, spitting on the ground.

Stanley's face burned. He wondered how that could even be possible. *No way could she like someone like me.*

"Anyone else says anything, I'm boxing all of you."

The Knights burst out laughing and made catcalls. Anino said, "Whatever you say, boss. So, what's the plan for tonight?"

Stanley outlined the strategy to hit the houses around Hazel's house. They all nodded, taking their assignments and not asking many questions. They'd done this all before.

"All right, Arthur, you're with me. Let's go hang out in Gaslight Square until the sun sets. The rest of you mugs, I'll see you at the statue when we're done, and we can talk about who needs food tonight."

Everyone scattered through the forest, and Arthur fell in with Stanley. He didn't say anything until they reached the main road of the park.

"Think you can really trust her?" Arthur asked, shoulders slouched as he scowled at the ground.

Stanley bit back a brisk comment. "Maybe. Who knows? I don't trust many people."

Arthur snorted. "Unless the people have pretty, shiny blue eyes and lips ya wanna smooch forever."

"I don't know what you're talking about," Stanley said, swallowing hard. Arthur was way too close to the truth. He just wanted him to shut up.

"No? How about every time you get dizzy with a dame, we gotta help you out of the scrape? What about that?"

Stanley wanted to fight back, but he knew Arthur was right. The Knights had covered for him in more than one smooching encounter. Every one of the Knights had complained to him at one time or another. Arthur wasn't exactly pitching an original idea.

"Remember last time? With that Italian girl's brother? We all got our hides tanned and how. That guy was a guerrilla."

"Yeah, that was a bad one." Stanley bowed his head and frowned.

Arthur nodded, satisfied his point had been proven. "Maybe your swell's good and maybe she ain't. But she could make things hot for us if you're not careful."

Stanley didn't reply, and they kept walking to Gaslight Square. A cold breeze blew in from the north; the city would be freezing by the time the sun went down. After bumming two hot dogs from the kid at the stand who owed them a favor, they sat on the bench and watched all the swells pour in for a night of partying. No cold snap would make it stop. They all laughed, drank, ate, and carried on like they didn't have a care in the world. All the while other people starved, girls were murdered, and something big and dark rose up in their town.

"You get how much I hate her and all this, right?" Arthur asked, talking with his mouth full.

Chewing on his hot dog, Stanley paused. He got it just fine. After what happened to his family, Arthur was a knotted ball of electrical wires full of anger. Stanley would probably be the same way if he were in Arthur's shoes.

"Look, there's no reason to hate Hazel. She doesn't understand what's going on out here, but she wants to. We just gotta teach her. All rich people aren't bad, you know. Plus, she wasn't the one who did all that stuff to your folks," Stanley said, finishing his hot dog.

Snorting, Arthur said, "Maybe, maybe not. I think they're all in it together. They took away my dad's job at IBM and drove my mom insane. They did it because they wanted something my dad had, I'd bet the farm on it. And, I'm getting closer to proving that. It's all linked, Stanny boy. And now, we have people disappearing from the streets and mysterious tattoos appearing all over. Something ain't right. Now you're asking me to help one of them. The swells need a reckoning for what they done, Stanny. And we're gonna give them one. You promised."

Stanley nodded. He had said those things, no doubt. But he'd seen enough lately to wipe the dust out of his eyes. Poor people weren't any better sometimes.

"Maybe. Maybe we all do, ever think about that?"

Arthur took out a cigarette, lit it, and tossed the match. "Most likely. I'm ready for mine. I got loads of beef. And the Man Upstairs is my number one target."

Crossing himself, Stanley said, "Don't be stupid. God hasn't done anything."

Sucking on his cig, Arthur glanced at him and blew smoke out of the side of his mouth. "You ain't kiddin', pal."

Stanley took out his pocket watch and then glanced at the sky.

"Sun's setting. Let's get to our business."

The shadows around them deepened as night fell, and the boys snuck along, hiding behind trees and edging along buildings. Finally, they found the first alleyway and the full trash cans.

"What'dya reckon? You take the first alley and I'll take the next one?" Arthur asked, flicking his cigarette to the ground and stomping on it.

Stanley looked down the alleyway and saw Hazel's house. The light was on over the garage, and the trash can was in plain sight. A large sack slouched beside it. His heart warmed. She'd done it.

"Yeah, aces. Let's go," Stanley said.

Arthur patted him on the shoulder and ran down to the next alley. Stanley raided the first few trash cans, finding the usual assortment of bread, bits of cooked meat, and vegetables that had not gone bad.

Sounds of the various radio programs drifted through the night air, but no one seemed to be walking the alleys like in Dogtown.

He filled up his bag with food found at each trash can and finally came to Hazel's house.

"Just what, may I ask, do you think you're doing?"

Stanley spun around to see a college student wearing a sweater and slacks. His blond hair was neatly combed and black-rimmed glasses reflected the light from Hazel's garage.

"Salvaging trash so people can eat. Not a crime that I know about." Stanley straightened and put his bag down.

The guy had to be about six-foot or more with the build of a football player. Not taller than Stanley, but broader. He was pretty sure a fight with this fella would hurt.

"Well, street rat, I think it is, and so is pestering someone who is above you, at least in my book. You're the one raiding the trash cans. Peeping in on Hazel too, are you?"

Stanley made a fist as his anger rose. "I can talk to anyone I feel like, swell. By the way, you can stop following me around."

"Gabriel, leave him alone. Now."

They both turned to see Hazel in her night coat stepping into the alley. Her hair was in curlers, and she wore a ferocious look on her face.

"Oh, I see; this is why you gave me the air. Is this what you've been doing lately, hanging around with trash like this? What would your father think?" Gabriel asked with a smirk. "What about everyone else?"

Hazel didn't say anything for a minute as she looked from Stanley to the frat boy. "What he doesn't know won't hurt him."

Gabriel chuckled. "Is that so? Well, let's see." He removed his glasses and slid them into his shirt pocket.

Gabriel turned to Stanley, pulled back his fist, and delivered a haymaker to his chin. Stanley staggered from the force of the blow.

Hazel gasped and demanded, "Stop it, Gabriel. Right now."

Stanley wiped blood from his lip. "You gonna sucker punch me again?" The world spun a little, and anger started to take over. He wanted to beat this guy until he bled.

Gabriel swung at him again and this time Stanley was ready. He sidestepped the blow, and the swell sprawled onto the ground with a grunt.

"Done yet?" Stanley asked, holding up his fists.

Hazel let out a squeak and covered her mouth.

Gabriel got up, dusted off his clothes, and turned to him in a boxer stance. The guy bobbed around like he was in a dance class. Stanley would have loved to see him do that in Freese's gym. They'd laugh him out of the ring.

"Let's see how well you fight, rat," Gabriel said, swinging hard.

A quick block with his left hand, and Stanley nailed the kid with a right uppercut. Gabriel staggered back and fell on his butt. Stanley glanced at Hazel, and he started calming down. He wasn't going to boot stomp this guy in front of her. But he wanted to, that's for sure.

"You fight like a common thug." Gabriel rubbed his chin.

"That's how the fittest survive," Stanley said with a grin.

Gabriel spit out more blood and touched his mouth. "I'm going to call the police. You'll pay for this, you Dogtown rat, if I have anything to say about it."

He jumped back up and Stanley launched an uppercut to Gabriel's jaw. The college boy went down in a heap and lay motionless on the ground.

Hazel let out a cry and stared wide-eyed at Mr. Fancypants on the ground. But she hurried over to Stanley and touched his face.

"Oh, it's swelling up. Are you okay?"

Stanley nodded, heart pounding. She gazed at him with glistening eyes. They drew closer together and he felt the heat radiating from her body. When she got close enough, the now familiar scent of her sweet perfume overwhelmed his senses. He couldn't resist. Bending down, he went in for a kiss. Her lips were barely an inch from his when at the last second, Hazel turned her head so that he got the side of her mouth. Drawing away, she gave him a half-smile and then grabbed his hand.

"Snoopy, go before someone comes out of the house. I'll take care of it. Please."

Stanley stared at her, dizzy and floating. He could still feel her on his lips.

"I don't want you to get into trouble," Hazel said.

"What about you?" Stanley asked, taking off his hat with a deep sigh.

Hazel looked at the pile of groaning Gabriel and wrinkled her face. "Don't worry, I'll take care of myself. Take the food and go."

Stanley reached down, took her hand, and kissed it. "Be careful, Hazel."

Mrs. Flannigan took a red slab of steak out of the ice box. "There now. Hold that on your face. You may have a shiner in the morning." She wiped her hands on her apron.

Gabriel scowled at Hazel and pressed the piece of meat to his face. "This is disgusting," he said.

Hazel ignored him, her mind still spinning over that almost kiss. Stanley's warm lips …

"Strapping boy like you can take it fine." The rotund cook with curly graying hair clucked her tongue at Gabriel.

Hazel shrugged. "You shouldn't have stuck your nose where it didn't belong."

He grunted in reply. Gabriel was steaming mad. His mouth was set in a hard line, and he refused to look at her.

She would probably catch it big if her dad ever heard about this. "Poor people need to eat too, you know."

"That in no way excuses their methods."

He was impossible. Hazel watched as Mrs. Flannigan went back to whisking eggs in a bowl for the meringue pies she was making for

Mumsy to deliver to the Schmidts the next day.

"You're sweet on him," Gabriel sneered.

"No. I think he's a swell guy, but I'm not sweet on anyone." She fiddled with the curlers in her hair, knowing she must look a sight.

"Hm. Not the tune you were whistling at the dance." He smirked and then winced, moving the meat to his chin.

"When we met?" Hazel tried to remember. She had danced with Gabriel a few times and they'd gabbed about the music. She'd thought he was handsome, well-mannered if not arrogant, and a little mysterious.

"Yeah. You were quite the sweet patootie." He snorted.

"What's that supposed to mean? I'm not a flirt." Hazel felt herself blush. Being curious about a boy didn't mean you wanted to be his honey.

Gabriel's laugh came out harsh. "Well, I suppose your kind of fellah wouldn't need much coaxing. He's just trash."

Hazel wanted to smack him in the nose, but she realized she was not playing the part of debutante very well at all. What she wanted to say was *I don't give two bits what you think.* But instead, she took a deep breath and tried to be gracious. "Well, I can see why you think poorly of him, and I am sorry he hit you. But he isn't really all that bad. He did protect me the night we found Evelyn."

He raised his brows high. "Guess you didn't learn a lesson from what happened to her."

Something in Hazel sparked. "What a horrible thing to say."

He shrugged. "I only mean, look how she ended up. She started associating with the wrong people, and she wound up disgraced and dead."

Hazel's hands shook, and she clasped them in front of her. He wasn't making it easy for her to be sweet. "So—it's all her fault that she went and got herself smashed with a bat? How clumsy of her."

Gabriel tilted his head and let out a sigh of forced patience. "You know what I mean. She thought that he was a square guy and that she could trust him, and it ruined her. A leopard can't change its spots, Hazel."

Her mind spun. What if Paul *had* done it? Maybe he grew up too rough for a girl from Lindell. Maybe the fact that he had lovely eyes and a fetching smile had lured her in. She would never have gotten mixed up in the gangs if it weren't for Paul. Evelyn thought she was helping him, but maybe he was just helping himself. Hazel thought of Stanley and his Knights and how she wanted to help them. But maybe they weren't what they seemed. Like Arthur, who glared at her like she was a cockroach. A chill went down her back.

Her thoughts raced through the contents of the diary. Evelyn had been so happy with Paul. They were in love. It couldn't be him. What about those numbers and the deal with the police hiding things?

"Well, maybe it wasn't him or the gangs." Her voice came out louder than she planned.

Gabriel shook his head. "And who else could it be? Think about it."

"Well, um … " She couldn't mention the numbers. "I mean, it wasn't Paul who ran her out of town."

"No. True. It was her reputation that did that. Once everyone knew what she really was."

Hazel put her hands on her hips. "And what was she, other than a sweet, foolish girl who thought she was a queen because everyone told her that's what she was?"

"She should have behaved like one. She should have picked a king."

Hazel tried to keep the bitterness out of her tone. "You mean, like you?"

Gabriel ran one hand through his blond hair. It was the messiest she had ever seen it. "I didn't set my cap for Evelyn, but there were plenty of good fellows who did. She was a stunning girl. I remember the day they crowned her; when I escorted her into the ballroom all eyes were on her." Gabriel paused and shook his head. "She could have had anyone. She wasted herself on that gutter rat." The way he stared at Hazel behind his spectacles was a clear warning; he was talking about her now.

"Maybe she had the man she wanted."

Gabriel frowned. "She deserved better."

Had Gabriel known about Paul back then? Hazel wanted to read more in the diary to see if there was a clue about how the Veiled Prophet learned about Evelyn's relationship with Paul.

Hazel startled as her father entered the kitchen in his dark red smoking jacket. "Flannigan, if there's some of that cake … " He stopped. "What's this?"

"Hiya … Father." Hazel's heart still raced from her argument with Gabriel, and now it almost pounded out of her chest. She had to pull herself together.

Gabriel stood and assumed his usual cocky stance, but with a pound of raw meat on his face he looked whacky. "Good evening, Mr. Malloy."

"Good evening." Hazel's dad stared and cleared his throat. "Is that my filet mignon?"

Mrs. Flannigan bustled over to the master of the house. "No, no. To be sure, that's a porterhouse."

With an impatient sigh, Hazel's father folded his arms. "You don't say."

The old woman grinned. "Let me get you a nice big piece of cake."

"Hazel? Will you tell me what's going on here?" Her father visibly struggled to maintain his composure.

She was in for it now. Hazel chewed her lip and tried to think of something funny to say but nothing came.

"Quite simple. I was coming for a visit. I was going to ask Hazel something." Gabriel glanced at her and then back at her father. "Then I saw some commotion at the side of your house and caught Hazel's newsie friend stealing. When I tried to stop him, a fight ensued."

"What?" Mr. Malloy's face went dark. He turned to Hazel. "Please explain why that boy was on our property and why he would attack one of our friends."

Her dad was humiliated and furious on top of that. Hazel was sure he had visions of facing Mr. Sinclair over this. "Pops, it wasn't like that."

"It's Father. Go on." He glared at her and took the plate Mrs. Flannigan handed him.

"Uh, Father, Stanley was just trying to get some food for some poor people." She gestured toward the large slice of chocolate cake he now held in his hands. "We all have plenty to eat—they just want the stuff we throw away. That isn't hurting anyone."

"Apparently, it is." He pointed at Gabriel who still gripped the steak in his hand. "Hazel, I'll say this only once more. You may not associate with that boy. From now on, you will stick to appropriate members of society. Good, upstanding citizens. Is that clear?"

"As the Mississippi after a storm," she muttered. There it was again—everyone was trying to tell her who was good and who was bad. Was it really as simple as circumstance of birth?

"Hazel," his voice warned.

The whole situation made Hazel frantic. "Who decides what appropriate is? I'd like to know. Stanley is trying to help people. When's the last time any of your 'good upstanding' citizens did that?" That couldn't be wrong—no matter who was doing it.

"We provide jobs, make our city strong, and contribute to the culture and education," he sputtered, then gestured toward Gabriel. "His family, as you know, is funding a clinic to aid the poor." Her dad shook his head. "Regardless of what you may think you know, Hazel, you're probably mistaken. No more arguing. Your newsie fascination ends now."

Hazel stared at her dad. He was tall, well groomed, and wrapped in his crimson silk smoking jacket like a king. His eyes met hers, impatient; he was probably eager to get to the next important part of his evening: eating cake and pandering to Gabriel Sinclair to save his reputation while people starved in the gutter. She despised him in that moment.

Maybe her face betrayed her thoughts because her dad frowned and took a step closer. "Now, Hazel, be reasonable. I'm only thinking of you."

"Thank you. Good evening, gentlemen," Hazel muttered in disgust. She spun on her heel and left her dad and Gabriel to fret. She had to get away and think.

In her room, Hazel paced the floor. Life had turned upside down so fast. It was like Jennings always said, "Just when you think this is how things are, they change." He'd been the Malloy family chauffeur since her grandfather's time, before there were even automobiles, and always had stories about how things used to be and how quickly the world seemed to be turning. Now Hazel felt the rotations herself in her own life and it made her feel unsteady.

Hazel sat at her vanity and stared into the mirror: same blue eyes, unruly brown hair tied up in curlers, and full lips. She cocked her head. When she was younger, her less than neat and glamorous appearance bothered her because she wanted to fit in, be what her father wanted her to be. But now she just saw a girl. She blinked. Did Stanley think she was pretty? She sighed. What did that have to do with the price of bread? They had almost kissed; her heart sped up thinking about it.

Bananas.

She was in a fix. Stanley was off limits, but she wanted to spend time with him. Even if only to solve the mystery with him—which she had to do for Sandy. Stanley was her partner. People like Pops and Gabriel didn't understand what was going on. Not all people outside the Lindell set were bad eggs; she had looked into their faces, and something in her heart told her that was true. That idea was probably as unbelievable to her father as sightings of the Loch Ness monster.

No matter what anyone said, Stanley was a good person. Wasn't he? He'd protected her, helped the poor, and there was just something good about him. Sweet. And handsome. She sighed thinking of his eyes and his smile. A thrill went through her belly. Hazel smiled at herself in the mirror when she thought of how he'd socked Gabriel Sinclair in the chin. It reminded her of Clark Gable. She didn't care if it was forbidden; she would see Sir Snoopy again no matter what. But then, the things Gabriel said nibbled at her mind. What if? Would her friendship with Stanley lead her somewhere dark? Into his world of hunger, struggle, gangs, and late-night marauding? Evelyn had left the safety of Lindell, and it had destroyed her. She tried to shake her paranoia that maybe Stanley wasn't what he seemed and thought about the facts again. Evelyn's death was not just a crime of passion. The police were covering something.

So far, Hazel had found no evidence in the diary that Evelyn had done anything with Paul that was shameful. Kissing and holding hands was what sweethearts did. The slander about Evelyn's lost virtue was probably just to disgrace her. The Queen of Love and Beauty had to be a maid of highest virtue, and claims to the contrary meant losing her crown. The public humiliation had driven her away. Obviously, somebody wanted to discredit Evelyn. Was it because of what she knew about the numbers?

Everyone seemed outraged at the very thought of crossing lines between the classes. Loving the wrong person was not looked upon with approval, scandalous or not.

Ugh.

Playing the perfect debutante was quite a trick. Hazel couldn't seem to stop speaking her mind. She made a rotten spy. Maybe she needed to hone her acting skills. What movie star should she pretend to be? Bubbly, mindless, and sweet … Carole Lombard maybe? Sandy was always a better actor than she was.

Hazel wondered how Sandy was doing. The last time she'd seen Sandy cry was when they were ten years old at a birthday party for Simon Busch, and that was only to get more cake. But seeing her friend, drunk and mourning her sister, was no act. It hurt Hazel just thinking about it. Enough brooding.

Hazel pulled the diary out from under her pillow and opened it. She didn't know what the numbers or code meant, and nothing she'd read so far explained them. She skimmed through passages toward the end. More about love, parties, shopping for new dresses, and then the date of the ball. Evelyn wrote about how elated and honored she was to be chosen to be the Queen of Love and Beauty.

I still can't believe he chose me out of every girl there! As I sat on a throne beside the Veiled Prophet, my heart swelled with pride. Everyone clapped and smiled for me. I wished Paul could have been there to see me. His Eminence whispered to me through the veil that he was sure I was special, that the others must look to me as an example and that he had great plans and honors in store for me. If I keep myself in good standing and do what I am supposed to do, I will be part of some big wonderful changes that will benefit everyone. Makes me feel like Joan of Arc or Florence Nightingale.

It was so thrilling!

But it has made me start to worry too. What about Paul? How will my new status affect us? I have a feeling that these people will never accept his kind. Maybe it's best that only Flora knows the truth for now.

Hazel stopped reading. The Schmidt's maid, Flora. Maybe she could tell Hazel something that would help her figure out who killed Evelyn.

Something whistled softly from outside. Hazel sat up and pushed the diary into its hiding place. She heard the sound through the window again. Hazel went to the glass and looked out. It was dark, but somebody was down there, waving an arm. Her heart jumped; maybe it was her favorite newsie. Then, she stepped back, nervous. Maybe it was the man who had been stalking Stanley. What if the killer was keeping an eye on them both? He would have read the papers, too, and knew their names. A cold fear crept through her veins.

Hazel cautiously peered from the side of her window.

"Hazel … it's me," a low, hesitant voice floated up to her.

She pushed the window open further and looked out. "Charles? What are you doing out there?" The night air carried her hushed voice down to where he stood.

"I—wanted to ask about Sandy. She wouldn't see me today." The dark figure below slouched his shoulders. Hazel glanced over her shoulder, grateful that the house was so large, and the servants slept in another wing. She peered back down at Charles.

"Oh … well, she was a bit … " Hazel didn't want to say that Sandy had gotten drunk.

"I know. She must be in pieces. I feel just awful about it. I wish there was something I could do." His voice was so quiet, Hazel had to strain to hear it.

"Of course." Hazel hesitated. "Well … you could maybe … you know, after the funeral and some time has passed, maybe ask Sandy to the VP Ball."

Charles cleared his throat. "Do you suppose she would want to go? With me?"

"Yeah. I do."

"Thanks, Hazel. I think I will ask her. I hear that Gabriel asked you but … "

Hazel groaned. That was probably why Gabriel had come over, to get her answer. "Oh, yeah. I guess I need to talk to him about that, but we're not friends right now."

"That so? What's the story? I always thought the two of you got on just fine."

"I don't know him that well, really." Although he was of the right set, according to her father, it wasn't until recently that Gabriel had really crossed paths with her much. The Sinclairs went back generations as one of the wealthiest families in St. Louis.

"He thinks the world of you, though."

Hazel shook her head. "What? That's news to me." She couldn't imagine Gabriel Sinclair thinking highly of anyone but himself. "Anyway, after tonight I'm sure he's changed his mind."

"That bad, huh?"

"Well, Stanley and he got into a scrap. Stanley punched him."

"The newsie?"

Hazel blushed. "Yeah. He's an okay guy, really, but Gabriel confronted him and it went downhill fast."

"I see. Jealousy. But I'm surprised he would be. Surely, he knows you're not the kind of girl to run around with a fellow like that. Other than to be gracious, of course."

Charles was trying to be nice, but Hazel felt ashamed. He was right. Sure, Stanley was a nice boy, but that was all. Maybe he wouldn't lead her to ruin, but they were from different worlds. That would never change. Her heart sank a little. She could see how Evelyn felt when she realized that maybe there was no way to bring Paul into her world.

"I like Stanley, but he's not my beau." She forced a low laugh as if the idea was absurd. "Can you imagine?" She stifled another fake laugh with her hand. Hazel's stomach twisted; she sounded just like Brigitte Slayback.

Charles chuckled quietly. "Well, I'm sure things will settle with Gabriel. He'll cool his heels, and you'll be friends again."

Hazel thought about that. Was a friend somebody who came from the same social class? Because really, that's all she and Gabriel Sinclair had between them. She had known him longer than Stanley, yet somehow, she felt like she'd known Stanley forever.

"I suppose." Hazel stared out the window. The stars and moon were covered by clouds now. Charles was barely visible below. Hazel rubbed her arms as a chill passed over her.

"Oh, I'm sorry, Hazel. You must be cold. Thanks for talking to me about Sandy, and I'm sorry that you have had such a trauma lately."

Hazel nodded. "It has been awful. I liked Evelyn, and nobody should go that way. I guess the hardest part is knowing there are people out there capable of doing things like that to other people."

"And I'm sure Sandy is devastated."

"Evelyn was her sister. And all that's left of the person she was is a pile of old pictures and her writings. Sandy is so sad that it will never be more than that. She always hoped Evelyn would be able to come home."

"It seems she tried to come home. I'm not sure that's a comforting thought or not." After a pause, Charles sighed. "Love is a funny thing. Getting mixed up with the wrong kind of person is no picnic no matter how romantic it may seem in the movies."

"I suppose." Hazel thought of the movie *It Happened One Night* again. Would the newspaper reporter end up drinking too much when he finds he can never live up to his debutante love's lifestyle? Would she regret marrying beneath her once the passion was gone? Maybe it would all be a mess. Even if two people in love found a way to make it work, the people around them might never accept it.

"Well, I should be going now. So long, Hazel."

"So long." Hazel watched the shadows engulf Charles as he moved away.

She shivered as she shut her window and crawled into bed. Thoughts of Evelyn and Sandy and the whole business overwhelmed her. Just when she thought she understood what was going on, she doubted herself and everyone else. She thought of the diary, feeling a little bit sick.

Hazel curled up into a ball, closed her eyes, and tried to imagine a blank screen. As she relaxed and the puzzle pieces whirling in her brain faded, she saw Stanley's smile: bright, mischievous, and adorable. She brought her fingers to where his lips had pressed at the corner of her mouth and warmth spread over her.

Bananas.

Chapter Fourteen

Early morning light lit up the clutter on the street and cast shadows across the sidewalk. Stanley gripped a wrapped roast beef sandwich as he made his way downtown. He wondered if Hazel was okay after last night and how everything shook out since that worthless gorilla tried to send him to the hospital. Stanley would never have left her if he didn't think everyone in the house was about to pour out of the back door. Something about that guy, Gabriel or whatever his name was, made his blood boil. He wondered what college boy meant to Hazel. Friend? Former boyfriend?

She almost let him kiss her. And even when she turned her head, he could still feel her lips touch his. She'd wanted to kiss him, he could tell, but she wasn't quite ready. That didn't bother him. Stanley realized he probably moved a little too fast, but he got caught up in the moment. He wanted to be careful with Hazel, didn't want to ruin anything. Normally, he would have been full speed ahead. But not with her. Not ever.

He approached the red brick police station and felt a surge of anticipation. Coppers in their blue uniforms and people in shabby clothes went in and out of the wooden doors. A few fellas wore regular suits; lawyers on their way to defend their clients. Looking closer, he guessed some of them were probably public attorneys hired by the state to defend criminals. The cheap tailoring of their clothes, scuffed shoes, and flimsy hats gave them away.

Somehow, Stanley needed to get past the desk sergeant, convince the guy who kept the jail to let him in, and take five minutes with Paul. All of it needed to be done before his uncle knew he was in the building.

Sure, and maybe I'll sprout nice legs and become a girl.

Still, he needed to try. Stanley realized he had to see Paul before going to the Rookery. He wanted to shake down the ballplayer about the numbers. He also wanted to see how the guy reacted when he mentioned Evelyn, just to make sure Paul really didn't do it. Seamus had told him how to recognize if someone was lying to him or not. Everyone had a tell when they lied.

Before he walked into hell tonight, he wanted to have all the info about the Winnowing that he could. Having more of the story about the numbers might give Stanley an edge. Not that he'd try to save himself from a beating. But if things got really ugly, it would pay to have an ace card up his sleeve.

Climbing the stairs, he controlled his breathing and forced his heart to slow. Stanley didn't want to seem nervous or concerned when he talked to the desk sergeant. He wiped his sweaty hands on his pants, adjusted his cap, and went inside.

To his relief, Jakob's dad, Levi Kopan, was behind the desk, his fleshy body bent over whatever he was writing. Not only did he like Stanley, he also wasn't fond of Seamus at the moment because of a scuffle they got into a few months ago. He wasn't likely to spill the beans to his uncle.

"Hey, Sergeant Kopan, what's shakin'? I see you had cherry-filled Clanton fruit pie this morning."

The sergeant raised his head and chuckled. "How in blue blazes do you do that?"

"If you wanna hide the pie from Mrs. K., better wash your hands. You gotta cherry stain on your right thumb."

Mr. Kopan examined his thumb and sucked off the evidence. "You're a regular Sherlock Holmes." The big man grinned. "Jakob says that you and that fancy dame who found the body are going steady now?" There was a note of caution in his tone.

Stanley sighed. "No, sir. She's just a friend." Great. Everyone was talking about it.

Sergeant Kopan winked at him. "Okay, Stanny. What can I do for you?"

"Er, well, you know I work at the ballpark, right?" Stanley asked, looking down while speaking out of the side of his mouth.

"Yeah, and?"

"I just, well, I know Paul, and I don't think he did it. The guy lost his dame and got locked up for it … So, I thought I'd bring his favorite sandwich. I know it's silly … " He tried to look as embarrassed as possible.

Sergeant Kopan stared at him. "Musta been awful for you finding her like that … "

Stanley put on a look of pain. "Yeah, it was."

Jakob's dad clucked his tongue and shook his head. "Well," he sighed, "that's good of you," he said, gesturing to the sandwich. "You don't by any chance have a metal file or a rod hidden in that thing, do ya?" Kopan smirked.

Stanley held up the roast beef sandwich. "Want a bite?"

He chuckled. "Nah." Taking out his keys, the sergeant called out, "Kelly, get your butt in here."

A tall, blond-haired copper, probably not much older than Stanley, rushed up to the desk. "Yes, sir, what can I do?"

Sergeant Kopan said, "Take Mr. Fields here to the holding tank. He wants to talk to that ballplayer."

Kelly took the key with eagerness. "You got it, boss. Anything else?"

Giving Stanley a sideways glance, the sergeant said, "Yeah, keep your trap shut about it."

The young officer clicked his heels and led Stanley down a hallway to the holding tank steps. Feeling relieved, Stanley decided to ask Kelly a few questions.

"So, uh, how long have you been on the force?"

"Oh, just a few months, not long. I know you, though; Stanley Fields, you're Seamus' nephew."

"Yeah, I'd appreciate it if he didn't know I was ever here, got it?" Stanley asked.

"Oh sure, Sergeant Kopan told me not to talk about it, and he's the boss. Must be a good reason."

Stanley shook his head and sighed. This fella wouldn't last long on the force. He knew enough about coppers to get that.

Kelly led him to the holding cell door, unlocked it, and said, "You've got fifteen minutes, just like everyone. I'll wait right here."

He went inside and almost scraped his head on the low ceiling. Stanley's eyes adjusted to the dim lighting. A row of ten jail cells, five on each side, stretched out in front of him. Taking a deep breath, he almost lost his lunch. The stench of pee, man sweat, and maybe scorched rat filled his nose and mouth. He hadn't spent time in the cellblock, but Stanley knew that jails could be awful, not fit for humans. It smelled more like the zoo.

Fighting back the urge to spew, he coughed and said, "Hey, Paul, you down here?"

A hand came out from the last cell on the left and waved. "Here; who is it?"

Stanley walked down the aisle and tried to not look at the other locked up pigeons. One hulking wreck, with his head shaved, stared at him and gave him a wolf whistle.

Ignoring him, he went all the way down to the end and found Paul sitting at the bottom of his cell. His pants were ripped in a few places, bruises ripened on his cheeks, and he was missing chunks of his hair.

"What the hell happened to you?" Stanley asked.

Paul grabbed the bars, and stood up slowly. "Hey, Stanny boy, whatcha doin' here?"

"I … uh … "

The ballplayer grinned and Stanley saw he had a tooth missing. "Well, let's just say the coppers gave me the business trying to make me confess."

"No. They didn't."

Paul nodded and then grimaced in pain. "'Fraid so. Why are you here?"

Stanley paused, looked down the hallway at the door, and said, "I know what's going on, I think."

Cocking his head, Paul asked, "How do ya mean?"

Starting from the beginning, Stanley told him everything, from spying on Paul in the tunnels to finding Evelyn's body.

The ballplayer shook his head. "The coppers ain't telling me nothing about you finding Evelyn. I had no idea. Is it true, was her face smashed in?"

Stanley closed his eyes and shook his head. He gripped the bars and leaned in to whisper, "Yeah. I'm so sorry."

Paul stumbled back in his cell and sank onto his wooden bed. He put his face in his hands. "Oh, my sweet Evie."

Shifting on his feet, Stanley waited until Paul stopped bawling and said, "I just need to know if you did it."

The former Cardinal backup catcher raised his head with tears in his eyes. "I ain't got no way to prove this, but no way. I loved Evelyn. Could never have … " Paul let out a sob.

Stanley looked away. He never knew how to handle crying fellas. He wished Hazel was here; she'd probably know what to say.

"Sorry. Sorry, Stanny. What else do you want to know?"

"The gangs. Could they have done this? You know, the ones you had debts with?"

Paul stood, gripped the bars, and whispered, "No, no, I don't think so. They're all square guys, and I'd been paying them back; they gave me a discount because I was a Cardinal and all."

Stanley searched the ballplayer's face. He spent enough time with newsies, hucksters, and grifters who made an art form out of lying. He was pretty sure Paul was on the level.

"If I find out you're lying, I'll tell Seamus everything I know, including the fight in the tunnels."

Paul shook his head. "Nah, nah, I'm not lying. I'm telling you, the gangs ain't in this. This was something else. Evelyn was scared."

"What did she mean by the Veiled Prophet stuff and burning Lindell to the ground?"

Wiping his face, Paul said, "She had some sort of diary. Said she kept some kinda secrets there, some kinda code."

Stanley nodded. "Yeah, we have it."

Paul backed away from the bars. "Where … how … ?"

"Don't worry about it. What's the Winnowing, Paul? What are the numbers? Did she say anything to you? And what is Legion? How does that fit in?"

The ballplayer leaned against the bars; glancing down the hallway, he whispered, "Stan, it's bad news for the city. It's a card system or something. Evie explained some of it to me. They're using it to, I dunno, take a census of the city or somethin'. She found out about it through some former salesman for IBM, I think. But she never got around to explaining all the details before she got banished, and she said it was too dangerous to put into letters."

IBM salesman? He'd heard of that company before some place, but where?

Just at that moment, Kelly opened the door and yelled, "Hurry, Stanley, your uncle is gonna get here soon. Better make tracks."

Stanley knew Seamus would throw him down here just to prove a point. He also didn't want to cause problems for Mr. Kopan.

"I gotta split, Paul. My uncle's coming."

Paul grabbed his hands and said, "Don't worry about me, Stanny.

Stop digging around about the Veiled Prophet stuff, and don't go to the Rookery; I ain't worth it. Your name is mud over there, I hear. Just let 'em fry me. I don't wanna live without Evelyn no more. And get rid of that diary. Burn it. Whatever the swells have planned, there's no stopping it anyway. Their Legion is coming and no one like us will survive."

Stanley cocked his head. Paul knew more than he was saying. He winced as the ballplayer dug his fingers in his arm.

He handed over the sandwich. "Here, it's a little smashed but good. It's from Rigatti's."

Paul grabbed his hand and the sandwich. "I mean it. Don't be pokin' around in the swells' business, Stanny. They don't like it when you cross the lines. Look what they did to Evie."

Stanley nodded without saying anything as he pulled out of Paul's grasp. The guy looked seriously spooked, and it made Stanley afraid. Jogging to the door, Stanley threw it open and said, "Thanks, Kelly. I'll be seein' ya."

He ran hard up the stairs, skipping two at a time. Heart pounding, he burst through the door, and Sergeant Kopan said, "Hurry, Stanny, he's in with the captain; get out, quick."

He dashed toward the door, and out onto the sidewalk, then ran all the way to St. James Church and sat on the stairs. With a few deep breaths, he calmed himself down. No, Paul hadn't done it, but they beat him to get him to sing. The ballplayer had given up and didn't really care to live. Stanley didn't understand that. Why wouldn't Paul want to fight? Avenge Evelyn or something? Whatever was scaring him must be big.

Stanley thought about Hazel. People she knew were probably involved in all this. They could hurt her or throw her into disgrace like they did with Evelyn. They could ruin her for life.

With a deep breath, he stood, shook the dirt from the jail cell out of his clothes, and started to walk toward Freese's gym to find Vinnie.

What an awful pit that jail is, he thought. How could they even cage an animal in there, let alone a man? Why didn't someone say something about the conditions? He knew the answer. No one wanted to take care of criminals.

He frowned. Seamus failed to tell him that little detail about his work: beating mugs and then making them rot in a stinking cell. Sure, he'd guessed Seamus took out a few guys with his fists when he was trying to arrest them as part of the job. But he'd never thought Seamus would hit a defenseless guy. Now he wasn't so sure. Someone had worked Paul over. A cop.

Were there any real good guys in the world anymore?

Stanley was so lost in his thoughts that he almost missed the entrance to the gym. Shedding his coat, he went inside and took a deep breath. Everything smelled like leather, sweat, cigs, canvas, and coffee. Jerry Freese never stopped drinking the stuff and always had a pot brewing.

The center of the gym was dominated by a large boxing ring. Everyone wanted to fight there, but Mr. Freese wouldn't let anyone until he said so. Stanley and Vinnie had just gotten the okay last month. All of the walls were lined with boxing gloves and pictures of various boxers who trained there. Hanging from the ceiling on all four sides of the ring were punching bags busy with kids from St. James's School working them with grunts and loud exhales.

Stanley scanned the crowd for Vinnie and then looked up at the ring. The Italian had his red gloves on and was clobbering a stocky guy with no neck. Not many could stand toe to toe with Vinnie. Even Stanley had a tough time taking him down.

Stanley climbed up in the ring and said, "Hey, why don't you pick on someone your own size, wop."

Vinnie gave his hapless victim one more whack to the body and the guy went down in a heap. His best friend looked up at him and gave him a smile.

"Yeah, get over here, and I just might."

Stanley scoffed. "Didn't bring my gear. But I need a favor, pal."

"Sure, whatever you need," he said as he walked over, took off his gloves and put them under his arms. "What's up?"

"The Rookery. I want to go there tonight. I want to see the Head Crow or whatever."

Vinnie frowned and looked sideways before asking, "It's the Raven, and why do you wanna go there?"

Stanley leaned over the rope. "Information."

"You mean about Paul and all that?" Vinnie asked, giving Stanley a probing stare.

"Kind of. But there's more to it than just him, like that tattoo on your arm for instance."

Vinnie rubbed his arm. "I don't want to talk about that. The Raven won't either."

Stanley shrugged. "I'm past caring or fearing the Raven, Vinnie. I think you know there's something much worse out there."

Hanging his head, Vinnie nodded. "I know it. The Raven knows it. But you still risk a beating even going there; you know that; right?"

Stanley put his head down and said, "Yeah, I hear you. But I gotta do it anyway."

Vinnie sighed. "It's really hard being your best pal, you know that? Can't leave it alone, like you should."

"I know."

"Do you also get that I ain't gonna be able to help you if you get into trouble?"

Stanley nodded. "I get it."

Vinnie held up the rope and climbed out. "Gimme a few minutes to clean up and change."

When Vinnie came out of the locker room, they walked outside and down to Manchester Boulevard to catch the streetcar. Grabbing the first train, they rode in silence, Vinnie sneaking glances at him every few minutes. Stanley ignored his friend as he watched the passing scenery. Even though he played it off with Vinnie and Hazel, he felt his stomach knotting the closer they got to the Rookery. The

Raven didn't forgive easily, folks said. A price would have to be paid. He needed to get ready for whatever came. Plus, if things went bad, he didn't want to tell Vinnie anything, in case the Raven decided to pump his friend for information.

Finally, they reached the end of the line and got off. Weaving their way through some rundown houses, they came to a wooden fence enclosing an old abandoned warehouse, not far from the Mississippi River.

Stanley glanced up at one of the broken windows and saw a lookout frown down at them as he called out. "Say, Vinnie, who's that with ya? Don't ever recall seeing his mug around here."

Vinnie yelled, "He's with me and all right. Wants to talk to the Raven."

The lookout yelled back, "All right, go on in. He's in the aviary."

Stanley shook his head. "What's with all the bird names?"

Vinnie punched him on the arm. "Shut your hole. This ain't the place for your smart mouth, got it?"

"Sure, *Mother*, whatever you say."

They entered through the broken doors and into the building. Vinnie led them down a long hallway with crumbling plaster walls. A strong musty scent made Stanley's nose itch and he sneezed.

So, this is where the so-called powerful gangs decided to hang their hat. Maybe Seamus was right; maybe they are broken.

After walking down a few hallways, Stanley lost all sense of direction. Part of him wondered if Vinnie did this on purpose or if that's what he'd been ordered to do. Sometimes he couldn't tell with Vinnie, and that made him uneasy. Even though they'd been best friends since they started working at Sportsman's Park two years ago, Stanley knew Vinnie was committed to his gang. He remembered the day Vinnie told him and the fight they'd gotten into. Now, Stanley thought that was pretty stupid. The guy was just trying to take care of his family. These were desperate times, and a man had to do whatever it took to put food on the table.

Finally, they arrived at a doorway that opened to a huge room that Stanley figured must have been the main manufacturing room when this place was a bottling company. Two men wearing black fedoras and cheap gray suits leaned against the door.

"Hey, Vinnie, how's it going? Who you got there?" asked the guy on the right, who had a few missing teeth.

"This is Stanley Fields, leader of the Order of the Knights of St. Louis."

The two men glanced at each other. "You brought that do-gooder here? What's the matter with you?" asked the meat sack on the left, cracking his knuckles. Stanley braced himself for the fight.

Vinnie raised his hand. "Hey, the boss said for us to bring anyone to him who might know about this thing with Paul."

The two mugs glanced at each other again. "The Raven ain't gonna be happy. This kid really gets under his skin, and he don't like that you're friends with him."

Vinnie shrugged. "Yeah, well, I wanna pop him in the face sometimes too, but that doesn't mean he ain't a good fella."

The guy with the missing teeth glanced at his partner and shrugged. "Your funeral, pal."

They stood aside and let Stanley and Vinnie pass. However, both of them put their shoulders into Stanley as he walked through the door. He clenched his fists, gave them a smile, and pushed through them.

If he weren't so nervous, Stanley would've been impressed by the work the gang did to make this place livable. Plush carpet had been rolled out in various places on the floor. There were wooden desks placed around the room, and lamps provided extra lighting.

A large wooden conference table surrounded by leather chairs dominated the center of the room. At the head of the table, a tall, thin man with a pencil mustache and pinstripe suit bent over a variety of files, muttering to himself.

Vinnie leaned in and whispered, "That's him, that's the Raven."

Seamus told him that the Raven consolidated his power a few years ago, after the last of Egan's Rats ate themselves during all the gang wars. From what Stanley heard on the streets, all the shattered gangs flocked to the Rookery, looking for a new boss to bring them together.

The Raven looked up from his paperwork and gave them a small smile. "Hey, Vinnie, how was the gym? Ready to go to work?" He glanced at Stanley. "Who's your friend, new blood?"

Vinnie squared his shoulders. "It's Stanley Fields, boss, he wants to bend your ear a little."

Sitting back in his chair, the Raven put his fingertips together as if he were in a George Raft flick.

"Is that right? You gotta lotta nerve coming in here, boy. Tell me why I shouldn't have my guys take you out back and beat you bloody."

Vinnie opened his mouth to speak, but Stanley put a hand on his shoulder.

"I'm here about Paul. I don't think he killed Evelyn, and I think someone set him up. I think I know why, too."

The Raven furrowed his brow. "Why do you care about him? He's a two-bit ballplayer who's no good and gambles too much. That's why he's forking over his money to us."

Stanley nodded. "Maybe he's done some stupid things, but he loved that rich girl, and it got him framed. I think you know why. Something is going on in this city, and I want to know what it is."

The Raven stood, buttoned his coat, and walked over to the boys. He looked Stanley in the eye and said, "You're a real hero, aren't you? I hear the stories. Giving food to people who are starving, robbing from the swells over on Lindell, beating up my guys who are just trying to help little kids."

Stanley scoffed. "Is that what you call it? Helping them? Helping them into what, living in this palace and hiding from the coppers?"

Vinnie muttered under his breath, but the Raven chuckled.

"Yeah, you gotta a lot of sand, boy, lotta sand. I think if you hadn't beaten up my guys, I'd like you. So I need to get this out of the way." He reared back and plugged Stanley in the stomach with his fist.

Stanley doubled over, sucking in air, but didn't fall to the ground. Instead, he straightened, held his stomach, and said with a burst of breath, "Now that I've paid the blood debt, you gonna answer some questions for me?"

The Raven stepped back, cocked his eyebrow, and said, "All right, kid, I'll give you this one free pass. It don't extend beyond an hour, get me?"

Stanley nodded, pain shooting through his stomach. "I got it. Can we sit?"

With a wave, the Raven led them to the table where they all sat. "So you don't think we did this, eh?"

Stanley shook his head and tried not to groan as he sat down. "Nah. If I did, think I'd be here? I'm not stupid. Besides, this is too much heat for you, I'm guessing."

Smoothing back his hair, the Raven gave him a half-smile. "You got that right, kid. We got half the flatfoots in the city breathing down our necks already, and we ain't even done anything. We're just trying to hold it together as it is. The papers ain't got a hold of the fact that Paulie owed us money, but they will. When that happens, it ain't gonna be pretty. Right now, they think he did it, but I don't even wanna know what will happen when they find out he worked for us."

Stanley raised his eyebrow. "He worked for you?"

"Yeah, in the offseason. He did some … persuading … for us when he needed to pay back the money he owed. Never gonna get actual hard cash out of him."

"So who did it?"

The Raven looked at Vinnie and nodded. "Hey, scram, will ya? Wanna talk to your pal alone."

Getting up, Vinnie gave Stanley a grimace as if to say he was sorry and then walked out.

The Raven took out a bottle of whiskey. "Want some? You're Irish, aren't you?"

Stanley smirked. "Yeah, but not that kind. Too much baggage, and I need my wits."

"Smart kid," the gangster said as he took a big gulp. "So, what do you know?"

Shrugging his shoulders, Stanley said, "I think something is going on with a thing called the Winnowing. I'd wager Evelyn the Queen found out about it, which is what got her pretty face bashed in. Then, possibly, just possibly, the people who did it wanted to frame Paul and then maybe you for it."

The Raven stared at him. "Listen, what I got to say, I'll deny ever telling you, see?"

"Yeah, I got it."

The Raven shook his finger at Stanley, light glinting off his pinky ring. "I'm serious, if any of this hits the papers, I'm gonna break every bone in your body, even though I like you, understand?"

Stanley shifted in his seat as his stomach pulsed with pain. "Reading you loud and clear."

"Good. Now, question, why do yous think the gangs are all gone from St. Louis, or at least, living around here in this dump?"

"I don't know, to be honest. Seems to me that your handy work is all over the streets," Stanley said.

The Raven chuckled and poured himself another glass. "That's what we want you to think, that we're powerful and can shake down anyone we want. Truth be told, we can barely keep this place up and running. And I can't even really protect my own guys anymore, thus the tattoos."

Stanley leaned forward on the table. "You mean you didn't force Vinnie and your other guys to get them?"

The gangster shook his head. "No. They're from the people we work for now. They required it, you might say."

"Why?"

The gangster didn't answer as he got up from the table and walked around it. "Kid, I got a family, and I'd like to keep them safe. So, I'm not gonna tell you. You're smart enough to figure all this out, if you dare. Just know that the gangs didn't go away. Someone set us against each other, and we almost killed each other off. That's what they wanted, see? They wanted us weak and at their mercy."

"Who's them?" Stanley pressed.

"I'll say this, there's a new breed of killers in the streets; well, they ain't exactly new, but they scare me. Me, a guy who's killed fellas with my own two hands."

Stanley leaned back, staring at the gangster with his mouth slightly open. Whatever spooked the Raven and Seamus must be something else. Something that made the hardest guys he knew into kittens.

"So, where do I start looking? How do I find out about these people?

The Raven laughed. "Didn't you hear me, kid? My advice? Don't start at all. Let Paulie fry. He knows he's gonna anyway. He's made the wrong people mad. Let it go and live your life stealing from rich people's trash cans. Keep doin' good and stop beating up my guys."

Stanley stood, shoulders back, and said, "I won't let it go, so you can forget it. The killer is following me and my partner. I have to get the answers before it's too late for both of us. Just give me something I can use and I'll go."

Sighing, the gangster walked back to his chair and sat. He stared at Stanley. "If they're followin' you, then you're already marked. Don't you get it? These tattoos … these hooded freaks running around … Legion they call themselves. They got money and influence, kid, more than you can possibly imagine."

"Do you know who they are? Legion?"

The Raven nodded. "I know some of them, yeah. They come here to give us orders and hire us out. I do it to keep them happy. To stay alive."

"I need to know a name, just one," Stanley said, gripping his chair.

The Raven shook his head. "Nah, not gonna give you that. But I'll give you a hint. One of them, his family goes back generations in this town. In fact, all the way to the start of the whole blasted place. You find that family, you'll find your guy and maybe some other things too, like why your pretty friend got killed. Now, get outta here, before I call my boys."

Stanley knew not to press his luck any further or he'd end the day in the hospital. "You got it. I'm leaving."

He started to walk out but stopped when the Raven said, "Hey, kid."

"Yeah?"

"Remember, these people, they ain't got no code. They want total control. That's all that matters to them. And with that control, they want to decide who lives and who dies. That's who they are, kid. Pure and simple. If you care about your uncle or that pretty little thing my boys have told me you're with, you'll drop it. Now get out of here. I hope God, if he even cares, goes with you."

Chapter Fifteen

Hazel woke before the sun came up, worried that Stanley may have gotten in over his head trying to talk to the gangs. She wanted to see him as soon as possible to find out how it went. But her dad was enforcing her lockdown. Hazel was only allowed to go to school for the foreseeable future. No picture shows, no friends' houses, no car trips with Jennings, and absolutely no fraternizing with newsies.

There'd be no chance to get away. Old Robbie was always at the front door, Mrs. Flannigan was given strict instructions to guard the kitchen entrance, and Willy would watch the yard.

She'd discovered next to nothing from the diary or any gossip on Lindell and was unlikely to if she was stuck at home. She couldn't let Stanley be the only one taking risks to solve this.

Bananas.

The sun hadn't risen yet. Hazel knew Willy would not be out in the yard for another hour or more. This might be her only chance to see Flora. Maybe the Schmidt's maid could tell her something that would help her discover who the killer was.

Hazel quietly got dressed, slipped out her window and down the ivy trellis. It was easier this time, despite the fact that it was still dim outside. The dew on the grass soaked through her stockings as she rounded the house and sneaked past the garage.

The murmur of voices made her pause and flatten herself against the wall. She held her breath and listened. It was too early even for the servants.

"You're a real lifesaver. I really appreciate it, sir." The emotional voice of a woman echoed in hushed tones from within the spacious garage.

"Shh. Don't mention it. Everyone needs a safe place to sleep. I wish I could offer better." It was a man, but it was difficult to tell who was speaking.

"It's better than anything anyone has ever done for me," she said.

"Do as I say … take this money and tell the father I sent you. He'll take care of you."

"God bless you."

"You'd best be going."

Hazel watched as a woman, in a tattered wool coat that reached her ankles, emerged. She looked both ways, crossed the yard, and disappeared through the front gate.

Inching forward, Hazel peeked into the garage and saw the elderly chauffeur, Jennings, bent over, pulling blankets out of the back seat of the Buick. There were so many little stories of survival and folks helping each other happening in the shadows of the castle Hazel lived in. It made her feel ashamed that she'd never even noticed before.

Hazel waited until Jennings had gone in before she darted past the garage and into the hedges that marked the edge of her yard. She'd be in deep trouble if anyone saw her. It would be a trick to explain sneaking around in bushes at strange hours. The clip clop of hooves coming from the alleyway made Hazel freeze and then duck down.

The white Pevely Dairy wagon appeared, pulled by the two

famous zebras she'd seen in the advertisement. Hazel had never seen milk delivered before; this was feeling like a real adventure. She watched as the cart passed and then sneaked down the alley and past a few houses until she reached the back of the Schmidt's estate. The maidservants lived in a little cottage in the back, beside the old carriage house.

She crossed her fingers for luck and approached the small white building. From inside, she heard the buzz of conversation. Servants woke long before she and her family ever had to. It must take an hour or so to get the household up and running and a lovely breakfast on the table. Hazel hadn't considered just how pampered she was until recently.

Staying out of sight, she leaned against the trunk of a nearby oak tree as an older woman in an apron, the cook, came out and hurried down the brick pathway toward the big house. A young woman, with her hair twisted into a braid and a black and white maid's uniform, came out next, skipping to catch up with the cook.

A moment later, Flora emerged, her white frilly cap and pinafore glowing in the early morning rays that peeked through the branches overhead.

"Flora," Hazel called out softly.

The large woman spun around, her eyes wide with fear, white globes against her dark skin. When she saw Hazel, Flora slapped a hand to her ample bosom. "Lord, Miss Hazel, you gave me a fright."

Hazel gave an apologetic smile. "Sorry," she said, walking toward the maid.

"Now, Miss Hazel, why're ya hidin' out here at this hour?" Flora placed her hands on her wide hips.

"I wanted to see you."

"Mmhm." She pursed her lips. "Why is that? You worried about Miss Alesandra?"

Hazel nodded. "Sure. But my biggest concern is that the man who killed Evelyn is still out there."

Flora took a step back, her eyes darting around as if checking the shadows. "'Spose that's true … "

"Yes. I want to stop him, and I need your help," Hazel said.

Flora swallowed. "What would I know about that?"

"I don't know, but you knew about Evelyn and Paul. Do you think he did it?"

Flora clapped a hand over her mouth and squeezed her eyes shut. She shook her head.

"No? You don't think Paul did it?" Hazel gently pulled the woman's hand down from her face.

"No," she whispered.

"Who did?"

"I don't know nothin'." She wrung her hands. "I don't know who done it."

Hazel felt bad for the woman, but it was obvious she was hiding something. "Flora, Paul may die for something he didn't do."

"I'm sorry … I'm so sorry … " Flora backed away a bit. Her face pulled into a grimace as her eyes filled with tears.

"Don't you want to stop the man who's hurt so many of us? You should've seen what he did … " A lump formed in Hazel's throat. "She was beaten to death with a bat."

Flora let out a sob. "I know, Miss, I know. And you had to see that with your own eyes."

"Who else knew about Paul?"

There was a crackle in the bushes and Flora let out a little scream, looking around wildly. Hazel startled and then pointed as a squirrel zipped up the tree.

"Help me, Jesus," Flora gasped. "I'm all jangled."

"What are you so afraid of? Don't you want to help if you can?" Hazel reached out and touched the maid's arm.

"It's all my fault. I did it," she groaned.

Hazel's heart jumped. "You did what, Flora?"

Flora spoke very quickly. "I told him. I told him 'bout Miss

Evelyn and that ballplayer. But he frightened me, Miss Hazel. Scared for my life. I didn't know what would happen, what they'd do to my beautiful baby girl." Flora moaned, bringing a fist to her mouth to stop the sobs.

"Who?"

Flora shook her head violently. "He—he's like the devil himself." She glanced over her shoulder. "I ain't said anything. I don't know nothin'! I'm confused."

"Tell me a name." Hazel's pulse raced.

"I can't do that. Please take care, girl. It's dangerous asking such questions. Now, go back to your beautiful home and let the cops do what they gotta do. I don't know nothin'." Her chest heaved and a sweat had broken out on her forehead. She was terrified.

"Flora ... just tell me—"

"I gotta get to work. Go home, Miss Hazel, and quick. You never know who's watchin'." Flora dashed away, heavy legs churning under her dress.

Hazel watched the maid go and then went back the way she came. Her brain whirled as she crept toward her bedroom window. Flora had told somebody scary about Paul and "he" had used it against Evelyn. But even if the man Flora told helped destroy Evelyn's reputation, leading to her banishment, that didn't mean that same person had reason to murder her. Maybe it was just Veiled Prophet politics. But the murder? Hazel didn't know what to think.

Back in her room, Hazel paced the floor, trying to figure things out until her mind was in a twist. She didn't feel like eating breakfast or seeing her father. School didn't start for another hour, but Hazel rang for Jennings to bring the automobile early.

She stood on the porch and waited until the gleaming black Buick rounded their U-shaped drive to the front of the house. Jennings got out, chauffeurs' hat over his balding head, and circled the purring automobile to open the door for her. Despite his age, he stood straight as a pin.

"Good morning, Miss Hazel. You look bright eyed and bushy tailed."

"Morning, Jennings. Guess I am wide awake." She slid into the warm, leather interior of the Buick. She thought about how soft the seats were and was glad that somebody in need had been able to sleep in comfort on them.

Jennings smiled at her, closed the door, and got back in behind the wheel. "Your father says I'm not to take you anywhere but the Mary Institute," he said with an apologetic glance over his shoulder.

"Yeah. I know. Just want to leave early for school today," Hazel said, looking into her book bag to make sure her homework assignments were inside. Her mind was scattered ever since finding Evelyn.

The Buick glided along for a while, and Hazel watched out of her window. Lately, the people they passed seemed more real to her. Any one of them could be like Stanley and his Knights or the kid with the crippled sister who sold pretzels. Good people struggling to get by.

She found herself searching for Stanley as they drove. But none of the tall fellows in flat caps were her newsie. No. She had to stop thinking of him as her newsie. Once they got to the bottom of what happened to Evelyn, it was farewell.

"And how is your friend, Sandy Schmidt?" Jennings asked. "We're all very sad about what happened. The Schmidts are good people."

"She's not coming to school. But I guess she's no better than the last time I saw her and that was the pits."

The old man nodded. "And so the pendulum swings."

"How do you mean?"

"Until this town finds a balance it will keep swinging. The powerful hurt the weak, and the weak rise up to even the score."

Hazel leaned forward. "You mean, you think somebody weak—or poor—killed Evelyn just for being who she was?"

Jennings didn't say anything. "I've seen how the rich and powerful bring down the fist on the working class. Parading their wealth and power every year. I think the tables are finally turning. It is a dangerous time for both sides."

Hazel thought about that. Was he talking about the actual Veiled Prophet parade? There really was a silent war on, and now she was aware of it. Stanley and his Knights with their peashooters were only the beginning.

"You mean the VP parade?"

The old chauffeur nodded. "That's one way they send the message that they're in charge. It used to be that he stood on the float, hooded and holding a rifle."

"What? The Veiled Prophet held a rifle?" That couldn't be right. Maybe the working class had their legends. Then again, it seemed like anything was possible.

"That's right." He grew silent as if willing her to think about it.

"I guess I never heard that before." The Veiled Prophet parade had been around since the late 1800s; maybe it was different back then. Things clicked and moved in Hazel's mind. Had the Veiled Prophet really stood like the Angel of Death as a warning to the poor to keep them in their place? But why? It made her think of the man in the hood who had killed Evelyn. Goosebumps raced down Hazel's arms. Maybe there really was a connection. Disgrace, discredit, and destroy. But she still couldn't figure out a reason or how it all fit together.

After Jennings let her out in front of the Mary Institute, Hazel headed up the steps to the arched doorways. Only a few girls walked the gleaming halls inside, so the sound of her shoes echoed off the walls.

Hazel went into the lavatory to check her hair. As usual she looked a bit wind-blown. Brigitte Slayback and Regina Peck entered giggling about something. When they saw Hazel, they stopped talking. *Bananas.* Of all the girls to run into on a day when Hazel didn't feel like hearing any snide remarks.

"Morning, Hazel. You look … keen." Brigitte stared at her own perfection in the mirror and rubbed her lips together.

Regina mimicked her blond friend, preening herself. "What's this I hear about Gabriel Sinclair asking you to the VP?" she asked with a heavy Southern accent. Regina spent every summer with her cousins in South Carolina and had adopted a clueless, drooling southern belle act. The accent increased when cute fellows were around. It made Hazel want to smack her.

Hazel almost groaned aloud. "Just a rumor."

Brigitte raised her brows. "Is it? Because Charles told me Gabriel had already asked someone."

Regina nodded. Glossy dark curls shaking. "And boy, was Brigitte upset as a kite in a hurricane."

Brigitte frowned and elbowed Regina. "Not upset. You see, Gabriel and I are having a little game. He dares me to do something outrageous, and I dare him to do something as well. If he actually does it I owe him something." She gave Hazel a wicked smile.

Hazel knew what she was doing. But she didn't care. Brigitte and Regina were the worst. They just loved being know-it-alls and stomping all over every other girl. "So you challenged him to ask me because it was outrageous?" Hazel folded her arms and looked Brigitte in the eyes.

"Well, when you put it that way it sounds simply criminal." Her fake smile was as annoying as her real one.

"So, tell us, sweetie, did he ask you or not?" Regina narrowed her eyes.

Hazel smiled. "You know, he may have. But lately I have had bigger things on my mind."

Regina snorted. "Bigger than the VP Ball? My daddy's in deep with the VP, and he says that this year's ball is going to be an extra important affair."

"I'm sure it will be splendid. But I'm considering skipping it."

Both girls gasped. Regina's mouth gaped open and Brigitte looked at Hazel with horror as if she'd said Stix, Baer & Fuller department store had closed down.

"You're pulling my leg," Brigitte said.

Hazel shrugged. "Sandy's sister was just murdered, and she's my best friend. If she doesn't want to go, I'm not going either."

"Hm. I see," Regina drawled. "I'd be careful if I were you, Hazel. This sudden rebellion of yours hasn't gone unnoticed. People in important circles are whispering about you."

Hazel tried not to laugh. "That's a sobering thought." Regina was all talk and loved to seem important and in the know, neither of which was true.

"It should be. You hanging out with newsies and running around with no chaperone. People might say you're up to no good. Not that I would believe the gossip." Regina went wide-eyed and placed a hand on her chest. "But maybe pulling a stunt like not going to the VP Ball would be less than clever of you, sugar."

It took all of Hazel's will not to roll her eyes. Anyone who was fool enough to get caught messing around in the back of a car with Gabriel Sinclair should probably spend less time faultfinding and gossiping.

Brigitte nodded. "Wouldn't want another fallen Lindell girl."

That was a line. They were all slobbering for another disaster. If Hazel fell into disgrace, it would only make these girls look better. Cut down their competition.

"I will be careful. Thanks, you gals are aces." Hazel batted her eyes and left. She could hardly stomach another moment with those paper dolls.

Sitting in Mr. Wren's history class, Hazel felt eyes on her again. Seems like everyone was still curious about what they had read in the papers about Hazel finding Evelyn's body. The girl behind her tossed a note onto her desk. Hazel looked back, and the freckle faced girl, Anne, shrugged to indicate the note was not from her.

Hazel covered the note with her hand as Mr. Wren turned back to the class after having written something on the board. He scratched his goatee and let out a ragged sigh as he always did right before launching into a lecture.

"The 1877 railroad strike in St. Louis grew into the first known general strike in United States history. Dissatisfied workers of commerce and transportation refused to work and demanded better pay. Remember, these were predominantly uneducated workers, doing menial tasks for which they wanted more money for the same amount of work."

A girl named Edith raised her hand. "Why did they think they deserved more than what they were getting?"

Mr. Wren raised his chin. "An excellent question. Unfortunately, it is quite common for people to want more than they deserve. However, one can hardly blame the desperate for wanting to rise above their chosen situation."

Hazel frowned. She doubted anyone chose to be poor. Sure, this was America, and hard work and gumption could get you up the ladder, but most folks were just born into a lifestyle and didn't know how to change it. She certainly hadn't done anything noble or difficult to have it so easy herself.

"The strike gained momentum with newsboys, boatmen, bakers, engineers, gas workers, brewery workers, cabinetmakers, millers, and factory workers joining the general strike. There was chaos in the streets and business came to a halt." Mr. Wren paced the front of the room. "The decisions of the few adversely affected the whole. Something had to be done for the good of all." He sat on his desk and rested his hands on his knees. "Any of you girls know what happened to stop the madness?"

Mary Cooper waved her hand until she caught the teacher's eye. She pushed up her spectacles and recited in a nasal voice, "The strike ended when three thousand federal troops and five thousand deputized special police killed at least eighteen people and arrested almost seventy of the strike leaders."

"Very good, Mary. With the leadership imprisoned, the strikers surrendered, the wage cuts remained, and more than one hundred thirty strike leaders were fired by the railroad companies. They accomplished nothing but losing lives and jobs." Hazel's history teacher shook his head.

"They had the right to stand up for what they believed. Isn't that what America is all about? The pursuit of equality and happiness?" Hazel blurted.

Mr. Wren gave her a scrutinizing glare. "Of course. They exercised their rights, but they were foolishly applied, as we see from the results. They were still free to improve their situations in life. But most of them probably went right back to the same work." He shrugged. "However, the leaders of business and politics offered an olive branch when all had settled down. To make peace and raise morale with the poor they created the magnificent parade and fair we enjoy each year. It still serves to boost civic pride." Mr. Wren grinned.

Something inside Hazel shrunk away from what he said. No, that sounded wrong. The people had been bullied, spanked like naughty children, and then patted on the head and handed scraps to eat. While people like her own father sat back smoking pipes and eating cake.

Let them eat cake. That's the same disregard the aristocrats had shown the peasants during the French Revolution, and then heads rolled. Things got ugly when people forgot to care about what happened to those less fortunate.

While Mr. Wren's attention turned back to the board, Hazel peeked at the note on her desk. "What do newsies kiss like?"

She crumpled the note in her hand. Hazel looked around the room, but everyone avoided her glance.

Bananas.

After school, Hazel practiced her baton twirling on her own while the track and field team ran laps around the grass. She flipped the baton over her head; it spun in the air while she turned in a circle on the ground and then reached up and caught it as it came back down.

That's the ticket.

A girl running by shouted, "Looking good, Malloy!"

Hazel grinned and spun the baton around from hand to hand, over her head, behind her back, and between her knees. After one final toss in the air, Hazel sunk into the grass, wiping her brow with the back of her hand. The thing about practicing with her baton was that it made her forget everything else. She lay back and stared at the blue scraps of sky peeking through the clouds. Like Stanley's eyes.

Chapter Sixteen

At home, Hazel hurried through her homework, so she could get back to the diary. So far, she'd learned about Evelyn's everyday life and her obsession with Paul but hadn't gotten to anything that would help unravel the mystery of her death.

Apparently, Hazel wasn't allowed to be alone anymore; every time she tried to hide and read someone would come in and interrupt her. Her father must have given strict instructions to the staff to keep an eye on her. It was hard to concentrate on the diary anyway as she worried about Stanley and thought about how Flora had acted that morning. What did Flora know that she wasn't saying?

Hazel knocked around inside her huge home like a caged bird. She had so much to think about, and she really wanted to see Sandy to make sure she was okay. Hazel slipped into her father's office. It was a large room paneled in dark polished wood and lined with bookshelves. A collection of pipes was displayed on the mantle over the fireplace, and various framed certificates and trophies stood as witnesses to the importance of Nicholas Peter Malloy.

She sat behind his desk and brought one end of the black

telephone to her mouth and held the other side to her ear.

Hazel gave the operator the number for the Schmidt residence and leaned back, propping her feet on her father's desk while the connection was made.

"You have reached the Schmidt household. Can I help you?" Meyers' voice came over the line.

"Hello, Meyers. This is Hazel Malloy. Can I please speak to Sandy?"

There was a long pause. "Miss Hazel, I'd be happy to give Miss Alesandra a message for you."

Hazel frowned in disappointment. "I'm worried for her, Meyers. I really think she needs a good friend right now. Couldn't you just tell her it's me?"

"The truth is … " the aged butler hesitated. "You see … we don't seem to know where she has gone."

Hazel dropped her feet to the ground and sat forward, abruptly. "How's that?"

"Flora took breakfast upstairs this morning, and Miss Alesandra was not there."

"Did you check Evelyn's room?"

"Yes, Miss. Mr. and Mrs. Schmidt are quite concerned. I had hoped that perhaps you knew where she was … "

"No. I haven't seen her since Sunday when I came to visit." Hazel's heart raced. Where could Sandy be? Was she somewhere blowing off steam? Her stomach knotted.

"Her parents have gone to speak with the police."

"Meyers. This is just awful. I've got to help somehow. I'll check back later to see if she gets back."

"Yes, Miss. I only hope you don't find her the same way you found her sister."

Hazel swallowed back the rising terror. "Maybe she's off on a spree. You know Sandy, she's a wild one."

After Hazel hung up, she pressed her fingers against her temples.

She couldn't bear it if something happened to Sandy. She stood and paced back and forth. There was nothing she could do trapped inside.

Stanley. She needed him. He could help; he knew the streets and the talk. If Sandy was somewhere out there he'd know or at least know somebody who knew.

What if Sandy hadn't just run off? If that hooded maniac had hurt her, Hazel would take him apart. Maybe something from the diary or what Flora said would help them figure out who the killer was—which might lead them to Sandy.

She ran up to her room, the late afternoon sun slanted across her bed through the open window, and heard Willy in the yard singing to himself. "I'm lookin' over a four-leaf clover, that I've overlooked before."

Hazel peeked out and saw the dark-skinned gardener resting the hedge trimmers on his shoulder as he strolled along the drive. As he continued to whistle the tune and make his way to the shed, Hazel knew this was her chance. She grabbed Evelyn's diary, threw it into her handbag, and ran back to the window.

Not giving herself time to be scared, she slipped over the edge of her windowsill and down the ivy trellis, praying she wouldn't miss a step. Hazel made it to the bottom and darted across the yard, avoiding the shed and the garage where Jennings might be having a smoke.

Out on the boulevard, she wasn't sure where to go. She hurried to where Stanley often sold papers, but he wasn't there. The Art Museum? Dogtown? She could search until midnight and never find him. Hardly noticing the people on the street, Hazel trotted down the sidewalk hoping to somehow run into him. When she realized she was near Gaslight Square, she decided to look for him there.

Weaving through the crowd, Hazel searched the faces. A black man in a top hat sat at a piano playing jazz out in front of the pool house, and some ragged kids who looked a lot like the Little Rascals danced to the music. A few passersby tossed coins at the kids. One freckle-faced boy caught her eye. He looked familiar. The minute he saw her, he grinned and danced closer.

"Hey, Haze! Whatcha doing out here?" Shuffles removed his hat and held it out to her.

"Oh, I don't have my coin purse with me."

He winked "Smooth. I'll take a honey cooler over Lincoln's ugly mug anytime." He tilted his cheek toward her.

Hazel hesitated and then planted a quick kiss on his dirty cheek. Shuffles' face lit up. "Thanks, doll. I'll never wash that."

"You never wash it as it is." Hazel smiled.

"Only on Sundays. Bishop won't let me pass the sacrament with a dirty face and hands." He grinned. "What do ya need, doll?"

Hazel couldn't focus; she felt an urgency to get moving. "Well, I really need to find Stanley."

The boy tipped his hat and gave her a wink. "Lookin' for Stan, eh?" His light eyes twinkled.

"Yeah. I am. I need his help in a hurry." Her anxiety increased as each second passed.

Shuffles pushed up his sleeves. "Say, you look worried."

"I am. Do you know where he is?" Hazel raised her voice to be heard over a sudden burst of clapping and noise from a rowdy bunch of sailors coming out of a bar.

Shuffles nodded. "Sure. He had to—" He hesitated. "How important is it you see him?" The small boy twisted his lips in thought.

"Please, Shuffles … just tell me where he is." It made her uneasy how dodgy the boy was being. Did Stanley not want to see her? Or was he hurt?

"Okay, Haze." Shuffles looked over to the group of tap dancers as one called out to him.

"Shuffles—you're gumming up the works. You're on harmonica for this one."

"Cool your pipes!" he called out to the kid. "Okay, Haze—he's meeting a friend at St. James. I gotta go." Shuffles blew her a kiss as he backed away. Then he pulled a harmonica out of his pocket and puffed away on it, dancing to the tune of "Ain't She Sweet" with the other kids.

Hazel smiled in thanks and went to find Stanley.

When Hazel finally crossed the street to St. James Church, she was startled to see Stanley right away. He stood out on the lawn of the church under the boughs of a tree that had turned gold and orange. Hanging on Stanley's arm was a beautiful girl with long, wavy blond hair. Hazel's stomach dropped. For a moment, her relief at finding him and the whole reason she wanted to see him disappeared.

As she approached Stanley and the girl, he looked up, surprised. "Hey, Bananas."

The girl pursed her lips and scanned Hazel's clothes; for once, she was proud to be wearing something expensive and fashionable.

"Hello, Stanley," Hazel said. Here she'd been worrying about his visit to the gangs and thinking he was busy investigating. She let out an involuntary snort.

He gave a nervous chuckle. "You turning Catholic?" He looked between the blond and Hazel.

"You're a wit. No, I need to talk to you." Hazel's heart thumped in her chest. She was just worried about Sandy; that was all.

"Sure, let's, uh … shoot the breeze." Stanley smiled.

There was a long uncomfortable pause while Stanley fidgeted with his hat and the blond girl leaned against him. Hazel's temperature rose.

"Alone," Hazel said.

"Hey, Margaret, suppose you take a powder, and I'll see you around the ballpark."

The girl sniffed and gave Hazel a scowl then turned to Stanley, purring like a cat. "Aw, Stanny boy, that won't be much fun with Grampy breathing down our necks … "

"That's the idea. I mean, we want to keep the old guy happy. Now … uh, make tracks, and I'll see ya." He reached out as if to pat her on the backside, then shoved his hands in his pockets.

"Bye, baby." Margaret smiled and kissed Stanley's cheek before she walked away, swinging her hips.

Hazel could barely look at Stanley. "That one of your high-class dames?"

"That's just Margaret. I work for her granddad. She's nuts." He waved a dismissive hand in the direction the girl had gone. "Anyway, glad you came along. I wanted to tell you about the Raven."

"She's beautiful," Hazel said, feeling short of breath. "But cheap." It was the only thing Hazel could think of to say.

Stanley's brows came down. "Okay, Haze, take it easy. She's a nice enough dame."

That did it. "Well I don't care if she is. You can like any kind of *dame* you want. That's not my business. She suits you."

"Oh, I hear you taking that high tone with me. Well, I'm not dirt and neither is Margaret. What's this all about, Hazel? You have a beef with me? Spill it so we can talk about the case."

"Sorry to barge in on time with your sweetheart." Hazel wondered what was coming out of her mouth. She was all stirred up inside and couldn't think in a straight line.

"I decide who my sweetheart is, dollface." Stanley shook his head.

Anger flared up inside Hazel, along with an irrational desire to punch Stanley in the eye. "Don't call me that. I'm not one of your street dames. Sorry if I gave the impression that I was. But you're every bit the street rat they all warned me that you were." Thank goodness, she had not let him kiss her.

Stanley stepped back as if she'd slapped him. His mouth dropped open as the color drained from his face. "What's got into you anyway? You're nuts, princess. You think because your daddy has money that you're better than us? I should've known you were a no-good swell, only born to live like a mosquito on the backside of the hardworking. Go back to Lindell and forget you ever met me."

Hazel felt tears sting her eyes. The things he said were awful. What a horrible boy. What had she ever seen in him? "Crawl back into the gutter and take your filthy mouth and ignorance with you."

Stanley blinked several times and then balled his fists. "Dames." His voice came out gruff and broken.

She fumbled in her purse for the diary. "You and your cop uncle figure it out. I don't want anything else to do with you." She threw Evelyn's diary at him; Stanley caught it before it hit his face.

"Yeah? Okay by me." He turned and stomped away, leaving Hazel in the yard of the church as shadows stretched toward her.

She stood, breathing hard, trying to calm down. How had this fire started anyway? She only came to Stanley to ask for help finding Sandy, and somehow, they'd gotten into a ridiculous fight over nothing at all. What was wrong with her?

Now what was she going to do about Sandy? And she hadn't finished reading the diary. Her foolish temper had ruined everything. Hazel wandered toward home, sick to her stomach. She kept wiping tears away and thinking about what had happened. Stanley was exactly what he appeared to be. He was no gentleman and probably only played the knight as a way to get smooches from silly girls like Margaret. Very impressive. She had almost fallen for it.

The sun lowered in the sky as Hazel walked aimlessly through a neighborhood she didn't recognize. A chill passed over her when she realized she was lost. Nervous, she looked around for somebody to ask for directions. A few people walked by, but they all seemed in a hurry or menacing somehow. Hazel was a fish out of water. What had she been thinking, running off by herself and believing she understood the way things really were? She knew nothing.

She walked through a neighborhood with small, brick houses. The smell of supper drifted in the air. Shouts came from one shabby looking house with a couple of broken down Model-Ts in the yard. The scream of a crying baby came out of another, and down the block the loud, shrill laughter of a woman raised the hairs on the back of Hazel's neck.

Even in Hazel's polite circles she had heard about muggers and rapists in Dogtown. Shadows seemed to trail Hazel as she hurried along. Every lamppost caught the corner of her eye—long and menacing, like a baseball bat held high. Evelyn had been a terrible reminder of what happened when a Lindell girl left the safety of uptown.

Hazel needed to find a place to hide. Filled with a panicky awareness that she was in the wrong part of town, she searched the long dark street for some sign of safety. A dim yellow light revealed a simple sign: *FAMILY CARE CLINIC.*

She hurried toward it, remembering it was the clinic the Sinclair family financed. The drab little building was like an oasis.

The knob turned when she fumbled with it. Pushing the door open, Hazel found herself inside a small white room with several chairs lining the walls. A ceiling lamp flickered above and the soft murmur of voices in an adjoining room made Hazel sigh with relief. Safety.

The door to the left swung open releasing the scent of rubbing alcohol and iodine. A middle-aged woman in a white pinafore and nurse's hat stepped into the room and eyed Hazel with surprise.

"Hello, Miss. Can we help you?" she asked in a thick accent. She rubbed her red lips together as she examined Hazel's clothing. It was clear she wasn't accustomed to people like Hazel coming around.

"I—uh—" Hazel wasn't sure what to say. She didn't want anyone to know she was out wandering again after how humiliated Pops was about her escapade in the newspaper. She had to have a purpose for being there. "I'm here because I need to talk to the doctor." Hazel swallowed, feeling stupid and awkward.

The nurse lowered her voice. "Are you in that kind of trouble?"

She glanced down with sharp eyes toward Hazel's stomach.

Confused, Hazel put a hand to her belly and shook her head. "Trouble … what?"

A handsome blond man in round spectacles wearing a lab coat stepped into the room. His eyes lit up when he saw her. "Ah, you're Nicholas Malloy's daughter. You must be here to … " he paused, his smile wavered.

Hazel blinked, surprised that he recognized her. His smile made her blush. "Yes, I'm Hazel Malloy."

"Hello, Miss Malloy. I'm Doctor Karl Galton. I met your father at a dinner the Sinclairs hosted when the clinic opened. You were dancing with the Schmidt girl in another room—very charming in your yellow dress if I recall," he teased. He seemed awfully young to be a doctor. Hazel remembered hearing that he was a recently out of medical school.

She smiled. "Oh."

He had kind eyes. "What brings you out here tonight, Miss Malloy? Are you interested in volunteering?"

"Uh. Yes." It was as good of an excuse as any, and why not? "I'd like to help"

The doctor's face brightened. "Wonderful. We can use all the help we can get here. Let me take down your information. Come with me."

Hazel followed the doctor back into a short hallway where they stepped into a tiny office with desk, lamp, and bookshelf. He motioned for her to take a chair while he opened a drawer and searched through files.

On the desk was a small stack of pamphlets with funny cartoons on them of black people and large-headed people with buckteeth. One read, "Selective Sterilization also protects children. For no child should be born to subnormal parents and denied a fair healthy start in life—or doomed from birth to a mental institution."

Hazel wasn't sure what to think of it … but it reminded her of what Father Timothy had talked about. She reached out and slid the pamphlet aside to see the one beneath it. She opened it and read the first paragraph.

Good genes make a strong man strong and an intelligent man smart, while bad genes lead to poverty, prostitution, and criminality. Improving the human race requires ridding the population of 'defective protoplasm' while encouraging the superior stock to breed more.

Hazel frowned to herself and set the folded paper down.

"Here we go." The handsome doctor placed some papers on the desk and held up his pen.

The nurse leaned into the room and said something to the doctor that sounded like German before picking up the stack of pamphlets from his desk.

"Thank you, Marie," Dr. Galton said. "And Miss Malloy here will need a size small candy striper uniform ordered."

"Very well." Marie nodded and left the room.

The doctor handed Hazel the pen and had her fill out a form. She told him she could start volunteering in a couple of weeks. She hoped her dad would let her. It had just fallen into her path but it seemed to be the answer she had been looking for. Stanley had his Knights, and now she could help, too.

"Do you have a ride home?" Dr. Galton asked as Hazel stood to go.

"Oh, yes. Jennings is waiting for me." She couldn't sneak back in if she accepted a ride.

He smiled at her. "I look forward to having you here with us, Hazel. There is so much we can do for those in need."

"Th-thanks." Hazel stifled a giggle and left his office before she could make a fool of herself.

As she left the clinic, Hazel heard the nurse speaking in German again. She wished she could speak another language. Maybe French or Italian.

She felt lighter now. This neighborhood would soon seem familiar to her. And she would know the people and help them—just like Florence Nightingale. If she weren't so angry at Stanley she'd run back just to tell him. Not all swells were self-interested parasites. She humphed to herself and slowed her step as a cold breeze brushed over her.

Her heeled shoes echoed too loud down the quiet street, forcing Hazel to remember her predicament. She was still far from home and unsure how to get there.

All at once, she knew she was being followed. Hazel's stomach flipped. Her eyes darted along the street, and she turned to see a figure pull back into shadow. Fear froze her in her tracks. Hazel broke into a run, her heart pounding. If the man in the hood was on her heels swinging a bat, she'd have a word or two for Stanley's Father, Son, and Holy Ghost if she saw them.

The sound of footsteps speeding up from behind spurred her on. She had no breath to scream with. Her feet slapped the pavement hard and fast, but she knew that he was closing in.

"Hey!" a masculine voice called out. "Where's the fire?"

Hazel looked behind her and the outline of a fellow in a bowler hat bounded toward her. She realized who it was and wasn't sure if she should be relieved or terrified.

"Stop. Didn't know swells could run so fast," Arthur grated.

Hazel stopped running, gasping for breath. "What, what are you doing chasing me?"

Arthur stopped a few feet from her and put his hands on his head breathing hard. "Stan told me to keep an eye on you, remember?" He scowled at her.

Hazel nodded, at a loss for anything to say. She wasn't sure what to feel or think at this point. Everything was a mess.

Arthur wrinkled his nose at her. "You run like a dame."

"Don't start with me, buster." Hazel put her hands on her hips. She was either going to burst into tears or wring his neck. "You think you're the only one with problems? You think just because my family is rich I don't? What's the matter with you anyway?" Hazel stared at Arthur, breathing hard.

A slight smile tugged at the corner of his mouth. He dug a cigarette out of his shirt pocket and stuck it between his lips. Without taking his eyes off Hazel, he reached down and struck a match on the bottom of one of his shoes. He lit up and took a deep drag, then let the smoke shoot out his nose. "Okay, princess. I don't like you either." His eyes narrowed, dangerous and hard.

Hazel swallowed. Arthur seemed entirely capable of taking a bat to a girl like her. She could tell by the way he looked at her that Hazel wasn't a person to him. Just a doll. A porcelain doll that he wanted to see broken into a million pieces.

"Fine with me. I have all the friends I need." Hazel raised her chin.

"All the cute little friends that money can buy," he said, the glow of his cigarette making his face a series of shadows and fiery outlines.

The devil himself could take a page from his playbook, Hazel thought.

"What business ya got in the clinic?" He squinted at her through smoke.

"I—was signing up to volunteer … to help."

He sneered. "Figures. Swells love to give *that* sort of help. What would we stupid, poor folk do without you?"

Hazel had nothing to say. It was as if Arthur would hate her no matter what. If she ignored the poor, she was his enemy; if she helped she was somehow worse. "Well, you caught me. Now what?" she asked.

"Now," he stepped toward her, "we walk you back to the paradise from whence you fell." He sneered and gestured her to follow him.

Hazel didn't know what else to do, so she trailed a few steps behind him as he wound her through the streets.

"Just out for a walk tonight?" Arthur asked.

"No—I was looking for Stanley; I need his help. My friend Sandy is missing. I'm scared something awful has happened to her."

"Guess you're running out of friends after all."

"It's not funny." How could he be so cold?

"I ain't laughin'." He blew another plume of smoke out. "Sister of the dead dame?"

"Yeah." Hazel stumbled over a broken beer bottle. Arthur reached out and steadied her, then kept walking.

"Well, I expect she'll turn up. One way or the other," he said with a shrug.

She shook her head. "You don't care either way, do you?"

Arthur paused and looked back at her. "Nah. One less swell is okay by me."

Hazel wrapped her arms around herself as another chill ran over her. There was nothing she could say to that. He scared her. All she could do was hope that he was leading her home.

Chapter Seventeen

"Cards closing in on the Pennant; read all about it!"

Stanley cringed at the stupidness of his sales pitch. He didn't feel like coming up with something catchy, and it showed by the few people who bought early morning papers. The fight with Hazel had given him a sleepless night, and he couldn't figure out why.

Mad, he thought. *That's what it is. I'm mad at her and her confusing female behavior. She doesn't have a claim on me. I can do what I want. Why do I care about some rich snotty girl, especially one who is so darn confusing?*

Taking off his hat and running his hand through his hair, Stanley realized he should never have started meeting with Maggie. He was just trying to keep his job at the ballpark, but maybe it was best to just tell Old Man Seable what happened, get fired, and start over.

He wondered why Hazel got so fighty and weird. It's not like they were boyfriend and girlfriend. They'd barely met. And why did he care so much? It was dumb, really. But the look of disgust on her face, like he was a rotting piece of meat or something, when she walked up to him and Maggie was burned into his skull.

Peace. For the first time after meeting Hazel, he didn't feel peaceful when he thought of her, and he realized how much that mattered to him. Shoving that thought aside, he finally sold his last paper and decided to skip school. He would have a good, long walk around the city to gather his thoughts and figure out what to do.

As he walked, he passed by soup kitchen lines, small kids selling coal, and the weird prophets of doom raving about how Jesus was going to destroy them all. Even though Stanley hated these guys, he had to admit that sometimes he wondered if Jesus wasn't doing that with all this stock-market-crashing-depression junk.

Furrowing his brow, seeing the dirty faces gaunt with hunger and mothers pleading for just a few scraps of bread to feed their kids, he remembered Father Timothy's words about not really knowing God's purposes for things; that he doesn't punish people like that.

One mother, with two kids whose dusty faces were streaked with tears, seemed almost crazy with desperation. Stanley went into a local bakery, bought two loaves of bread with his extra paper money, and took them out to her.

She didn't look much older than Evelyn, and he flashed back to the night of the murder. The hungry woman became a corpse with a smashed head. It opened its mouth to speak but Stanley didn't hear anything. He stepped back and shook his head.

The woman with two kids stood in front of him, staring at him.

"Are you okay?" she asked.

Stanley closed his eyes and said, "Long week, sorry. Here's some bread for the kiddos. Wish I could do more."

Without waiting for a thank you, he walked in the other direction, heart thumping against his chest. Taking deep breaths, he tried to concentrate and gather in his thoughts. He didn't want to panic or examine what just happened. Maybe he was losing it. Or maybe his brain was trying to tell him something.

This woman—Evelyn—everyone in St. Louis was in danger from this crazy jackass. The diary, the murder, the gangs being destroyed, something else was at work. This had gone from a simple murder investigation to something deeper. But what? He didn't know. He needed more information.

Stanley stopped walking. *The diary.* He patted his jacket pocket. It was still there. That fight with Hazel had blown his brain to bits. He needed to go someplace safe and read the diary.

The *Dispatch* archives. He could be alone there and also access any information they had on Evelyn and her scandal. He could've kicked himself for not thinking of it sooner. Feelings for Hazel didn't matter right now. Solving this crime did because she was in danger. He couldn't let it cloud his judgment simply because things were out of whack.

Turning around, he ran eight blocks to the Market Street trolley and caught it the rest of the way downtown. Getting off, he walked fast to the paper's headquarters.

As Stanley went through the glass doors, he was met by the chatter of dozens of typewriters. He loved the organized chaos of the newsroom floor. As he made his way through the maze of desks and rushing people, he said "Hey" to the cub reporters and the secretaries. All of them waved and went back to their work. His desire to be a reporter caused him to come in here often, and no one questioned him. He belonged.

Finding the stairway, he went downstairs and followed a long, narrow corridor to the archive room. He opened the door to a large room full of wooden shelves, about twelve rows deep. The room smelled of dusty paper and leather binding. Sitting at a wooden desk writing with a green fountain pen was Rickey, an ancient record keeper with wispy gray hair and coke bottle glasses who greeted him with a high, reedy voice. "Hello, Mr. Fields. May I ask what you're doing down here?"

Stanley took of his hat. "Sir, I'm doing research for school on ancient librarians, any help you can give me?"

Rickey chuckled. "Ya think you're funny, do you?"

"Most of the time, sir."

"What fool crusade are you on now?"

Stanley decided to tell the truth or a part of it anyway. "I'm looking for stuff on this whole Evelyn Schmidt thing. I was curious about when she was crowned the Queen of Fluff and Weirdness."

"That's Queen of Love and Beauty," the old archivist said, shaking a gnarled finger at him.

"Right, her. Can you point me in the right direction?"

Rickey sighed. "Yes, very well." He stood, body trembling as he leaned on his wooden cane. With slow shuffles, he led Stanley down the aisle to the second row of shelves and turned left.

"And what sort of information do you require? Articles?"

Stanley scratched his head. He needed to learn more about Legion. Raven dropped a hint that one of them came from one of the oldest swell families. Stanley would bet there was some connection to Evelyn and the Veiled Prophet Ball. "Pictures. I need pictures from the Veiled Prophet Ball of 1931."

Rickey cocked his head and searched the two rows of shelves that stretched out in front of them. Mumbling to himself about interfering young people, he finally exclaimed, "Ah, yes, I think that would be the top row of shelves."

He shuffled forward a few steps and turned around. "Get the lead out, young fella."

Stanley smiled and said, "Right behind you."

Rickey pointed up with his cane, "It's that box right there. You can take it down and look at it as you like. But, one rule, if I catch you taking anything, I'll kill you with my cane, got it?"

The bent old man glared at him with such conviction that Stanley worked hard not to laugh. "Right, gotcha, no nicking the pretty pictures."

Shuffling off, mumbling under his breath, the old man went back to his desk. Stanley took off his hat and started to sort through the files. Finally, he found one labeled, *Veiled Prophet 1931, Evelyn Schmidt.*

He opened the file and twenty black-and-whites scattered to the floor. Stooping to the ground, he sorted through them as he tried to straighten them up. Most were of various couples with names Stanley vaguely recalled. Finally, he came to one that gave him chills.

The large auditorium of the Hotel Jefferson had been transformed into a royal palace. Everyone was dressed to the nines with all the young girls wearing long white wedding dresses, as if they were going to their own wedding. All the older swells dressed in tuxes and the women in long, flowing dresses. Curiously, all the men wore a medallion around their necks.

Banners hung from the ceiling and garland dressed the balcony walls. At the center of all this waste of money was the Veiled Prophet himself. Sitting on a throne placed in the middle of the stage, he wore a long robe with flowers stitched into the front. A thin white veil obscured his face and the Prophet wore a golden crown with wings on each side. Stanley couldn't help but think about those Ku Klux Klan nutters who hated anyone different. Father Timothy rained down verbal fire on them on a regular basis.

The hair on the back of Stanley's neck stood up when he saw the spear in the prophet's right hand and his left resting on the hand of Evelyn Schmidt. Looking closer, he saw their fingers intertwined like sweethearts.

Evelyn beamed with an unsmashed face as if she'd been made queen of the world. Too bad she didn't know in this picture that world would throw her out in a few short months.

Stanley noticed the guards standing behind the Prophet and Evelyn. They wore ridiculous costumes of puffy-sleeved shirts, silk knickers, and turban-like hats. Fake beards hung down to their chests. To complete the weirdness, they'd smeared themselves with brown shoe polish.

Squinting and bringing the picture closer, he saw two of the guards with a hand on each of Evelyn's shoulders. Both of them wore huge smiles, but he couldn't make out their mugs.

"Hey, boy, are you done yet? Hurry up. I'm leaving soon," the old record keeper shouted from his desk.

Stanley walked to the end of the aisle and stuck his head out. "I'll be done in a few minutes."

He paced back to his spot and sat back down. Reaching into his coat where he'd shoved it the night before, Stanley pulled out the fat leather diary and his notebook. All the pieces of the puzzle were in his hands. He just had to fit them together.

Stanley flipped through the pages of the diary to the weeks leading up to the Veiled Prophet Ball. He figured Hazel had only read about halfway before throwing it at him. A bunch of stuff about Evelyn and Paul's romance mostly. Stanley scanned through a bunch of girl stuff about Evelyn's dress, what everyone else was wearing, and finally found a passage that hit him between the eyes.

Oh, and didn't 'Moe' and 'Larry' look fantastic in their Bengal Guard of the Veiled Prophet get ups? Moe keeps calling themselves 'The Legion,' whatever that is. Those two kept me in stitches all night, making jokes under their breath and making fun of everyone. But both of them had smiles on their faces when they led me to my chair at the left hand of the Prophet. I was so scared and trembling, but they made me feel calm and important. Who knew those two bums could be such gentlemen? I guess it runs in their families.

Moe and Larry. Two of The Three Stooges, obvious nicknames. He thought about that Gabriel jerk who tried to sucker punch him. He looked about Evelyn's age. Was he one of them?

He scanned the diary for other mentions of the two stooges. Finding them all over, most of the stories were just dumb things like going out on yachts or other stupid swell stuff. However, toward the middle of the diary, 'Larry' started to dominate the conversation. Checking the dates, it seemed as if they started getting close three months after the ball. One passage in February caught his eye.

Larry came to me tonight with my first request from the Prophet; he was to be my escort. We went and did the business that was asked of us. I found it distasteful, and I felt sick to my stomach. Yet Larry took me to the Veiled Prophet himself, and I knelt at his feet. He told me that he loved me and was proud of what I did. Then he stood me up and put his hands all over me. The whole time I just felt the urge to throw up.

When Larry walked me home, he told me I'd done great things and that the VP was more than pleased. All of this tonight made me start rethinking my role as Queen. Maybe, just maybe, the Veiled Prophet and everyone around him aren't as good as I perceived.

Stanley clenched his fist. Evelyn had been asked to do things she hated, things that made her want to throw up, and the Prophet had molested her. What could those things be? What did all of this have to do with bringing down Lindell? And the numbers, how did all that fit in?

I found out about the Winnowing tonight, and I've locked myself in my room. They want to remake the city in their own image. Transform it. Purge it. Everything is in place. I overheard a meeting with the VP and some men who spoke only German. I understood some because my mother insisted I learn our ancestral language. How I wish I'd studied it harder at school instead of daydreaming! I fear the Winnowing is not what I thought at all.

One of the hooded men caught me listening at the door. I hope I made him believe I was only looking for Larry. But I'm frightened that he'll report me and of what will happen if he does. I'm scared for my city. People need to know. I need to find out more while I have the chance. I want to tell Paul, but will that put his life in danger?

Please God, help me.

Stanley looked up and furrowed his brow. This was probably what got her tossed out. The Winnowing was about purging the city.

As he thought about it, he realized he'd heard the term "winnowing" from Sister Mary John's lesson on the gospel story about harvesting wheat by sifting out the worthless chaff. Looks like someone took that passage literally. He remembered what the Raven had said about the gangs being wiped out. Was that part of the Winnowing? Maybe the Veiled Prophet was cleaning up the city and that's why the cops were willing to take orders and hide any evidence.

He kept reading and started to shake.

The Winnowing is made up of a system of numbers, I know this much. I don't know how it works. It's how they'll decide and mark people. I will find out more if I can. Larry promised to help me become a part of it and understand what he does in the Legion. I must be a good actress; maybe I should go to Hollywood someday. He thinks I am still excited to serve the VP.

Stanley wiped his brow. He scanned a few more paragraphs about Paul and then read:

I was taken last night. I think they drugged me. When I woke up, I found a tattoo on my shoulder with the numbers 010107. I have this sense of doom I can't shake. I need to find out what these numbers mean.

A tattoo. Here it was again, them marking their own people. Evelyn. Vinnie. The Raven's gang members.

Grabbing his notebook, Stanley flipped to the page where he'd written down the numbers from Evelyn's leg.

Huh. *They are different,* he thought, *010107 on her shoulder and 010106 written in ash on her dead body.*

The next passage in the diary was written in smeared ink.

I went into the forbidden chambers to find answers. It felt all wrong in there ... like something cold and dead watched me. It sent chills down my back. There was a book in a language I couldn't read—I think it is written in code. There were numbers in it, too. I hoped to figure out the numbers on my shoulder, so I wrote down as much as I could. But I heard someone coming—so I didn't get them all. I did manage to rip a page of the code out of the book and hide my diary in my shirt before the door to the Holy Room opened.

Before turning the next page, Stanley pulled the loose piece of folded paper out of the diary and opened it. He couldn't make any sense of it. What was it all about? He stuck it back between the pages and read on.

It was Larry. He seemed very upset to find me there. I flirted with him to try to distract him, hoping he would keep it a secret. I know he likes me, and I thought it worked because he said he wanted to help. I thought he was going to show me something and tell me more about the Winnowing and the numbers on my shoulder. But when he took me to the caves under Lemp mansion, the VP was there. There were others. I couldn't see them, but I felt them there. Watching. The VP sat on a large wooden throne and Larry spoke to him like a prosecuting attorney. Told him I was a spy and that he caught me stealing information. Then he told the VP about Paul. I don't know how he found out about him! I realize now that Larry was the hooded man who caught me listening to their secret meeting, however, and that he's been watching me all along. I can't write what the VP said to me. Such awful things about me and Paul. He said I was a traitor and a disgrace—not fit for the crown. He promised that I would be cast out and made to seem like a scarlet woman, that the crown would be given to one more pure and deserving.

But, he gave me money. Told me to leave town and never come back if I loved my family. I'm writing this before I pack. But I know too much now. I'm afraid.

Stanley couldn't hold back a shiver. He flipped to the back of Evelyn's diary, to where she had started to decode the numbers.

(Ordered By)

Veiled Prophet	*01*
Court of Seers	*02*
Bengal Guards	*03*

(Don't know what this is)

Traitor	*01*
(Unknown)	*02*
(Unknown)	*03*
Black	*04*
Mongoloid	*05*
Feeble Minded	*06*
Agitator	*07*
Criminal	*08*
Deviant	*09*

(This list scares me)

Unknown	*01*
Asylum	*02*
Shock Therapy	*03*
Sterilization	*04*
Confinement	*05*
Unknown	*06*

(Location?)

The Island	*01*
The Rookery (pending)	*03*

As he scanned the list, Stanley could suddenly see how it all came together, and he wrote feverishly in his notebook. There were three sets of double-digit numbers. Depending on the order, they had different meanings.

01: That has to do with the Veiled Prophet. Evelyn figured it out—the first set of numbers tells who gives the orders.

Evelyn's tattoo had 01 and then another 01. Maybe the second set of numbers is what people did, their offense. That would mean that she was a traitor.

Then the third group of numbers: 06 on her shoulder and 07 on her leg. What are the third group of numbers for? Maybe their judgment?

Taking a deep breath, Stanley finally understood. The numbers were a way to catalogue people and what should be done to them. This kind of system would make it easy to find people and then deliver their judgment. The judgment of the Veiled Prophet. The Winnowing. People being branded like cattle and waiting their judgment to be executed.

He slumped against the shelves. All the pieces fell into place. Why Evelyn died. No wonder the Raven had been scared. This went all the way to heart of all the rich and powerful in St. Louis. They wanted to control everyone and maybe even get rid of them if they judged them to be unfit. He felt like puking up his breakfast right onto the archive floor.

"Boy, are you finished? I want to get home for my radio shows."

Stanley grabbed the photo, bent it in half, and tucked it into the back of his pants. No way would the old man go down there.

He came out from the shelves and made his way to the front desk.

"All right, Stanley, open your coat and let me see."

When he did, the old man looked closely at his shirt and felt his chest.

"Say, any closer and you're gonna have to buy me dinner." Stanley grinned.

Rickey grimaced but didn't stop the pat down. "All right, kid, you're clean. Those books in your coat you had when you arrived, yes? Good. Now get out of here."

Stanley went upstairs and made his way to Percy King's office.

The man had always been kind to him and kept encouraging Stanley to work on his writing skills. He never promised him a cub reporter job, but Mr. King would often drop hints.

Ethel, the editor's ancient secretary, smiled at him. "Hello, Stanley, what are you doing here?"

He took off his hat and gave her a smile. "I was in the neighborhood and thought I'd say hello to Mr. King."

She nodded and said, "Go on in, I think he has a few minutes."

Stanley walked up to the glass door with "Percy King, City Editor," emblazoned in black right in the middle. Knocking gently, he heard a voice say, "Come in, and hurry up."

Stanley walked in and found the editor at his desk. His gray hair was slicked back and glistening. Although he was a thin man, a slight stomach poked out over his belt.

"Stanley, welcome. Come in. You caught me right in the middle of trying to make a deadline. Don't want to rush you, but you're gonna have to make it lickity-split quick."

"Yessir. Thank you for seeing me. I've got a story pitch for you. It's a hot one."

Mr. King rubbed back his head and said, "Really, Stanley, I bet it's fantastic, but I really can't spare the—"

"Please, sir, it's about the Evelyn Schmidt case. I think I have evidence that Paul didn't do it. It could blow the whole thing wide open, and we'd sell so many papers your eyes would bleed."

Percy King rocked back in his chair and said, "Okay, go on, I'm listening. You have five minutes."

Stanley gave him a brief account of seeing Evelyn and Paul in the tunnel the day she was killed without mentioning the diary. Even though Percy King was a square dealer, Stanley knew enough about the newspaper business to trust no one until he got the okay to do the story. He closed his eyes, trying to recite all the facts from memory. Hazel's face kept popping up in his mind, and he had to force her out.

"Paul isn't the killer. You'll just have to trust me, chief. This all has to do with the Veiled Prophet and a secret group of swells running things."

Mr. King held up his hand.

"Wait a moment, son."

He stood, walked to the door, and shut it. Sitting on the edge of his desk, he pointed his finger at Stanley.

"I'm going to say this once and once only. Drop this story. Right now."

Stanley felt his heart sink to his toes. He'd always thought of Mr. King as fearless. He'd seen the editor have screaming matches with the governor, the mayor, and even a senator or two. It was pretty amazing.

"Why, sir, are you afraid of them?"

The man gave him a small smile. "I don't know what I am, to be honest. But these people you're talking about, they are some of the richest and most powerful people in St. Louis and, in fact, the rest of the United States. They've got the power to make my life miserable. I'm getting close to retirement and I want to get out of this town."

Stanley gripped the armrests of his chair. "So, you are scared."

The editor shook his head. "No, but you've got nothing I can use and no proof. You say you heard a conversation; that isn't solid proof. If I put this out there now, we would be vulnerable to lawsuits. Maybe worse."

Opening his mouth, Stanley checked himself. Something held him back from turning the diary over to Mr. King. What it was, he couldn't say. Maybe he was just afraid of getting his story stolen. Or maybe he was learning not to trust anyone. The cops were dirty, Vinnie was getting more secretive, Arthur seemed ready to flip his lid any day, and Hazel was mad at him for something he didn't do.

"Sure, whatever you say. I don't wanna cause any trouble."

Percy King smiled and said, "All right, Stanley. I got to get back to work. Keep selling papers."

Keep selling papers, Stanley thought. *Yeah, okay, sure.*

Stanley stomped his way out to the street. Leaning against a lamppost, he tried to calm down. It's not that he blamed Mr. King. Without the diary, the story didn't sound all that convincing. Still, Stanley didn't feel like giving anyone any slack. Everyone was to blame for looking the other way while evil rose to power. The whole world made him want to punch it.

A whiff of tobacco made him look up. Arthur stood beside him, puffing on a cigarette, his bowler hat tilting to the side. Stanley tried not to breath in the smoke.

"Heya, Stanny boy, I was hoping to find you here."

"You smoke more than a chimney in a coal factory."

"Last time I checked, you ain't my mama," Arthur said, blowing a smoke ring into the air.

Stanley suddenly straightened with the thought of Hazel. "What are you doing here? I thought you were supposed to be keeping an eye on Hazel."

Arthur nodded, the cigarette hanging from his lips. "Yeah, boss. That's why I'm here. I got Teeth keeping an eye on her."

Stanley made a fist. "Teeth? You gotta be kidding me."

"Keep your hair on. I got some information for ya about that Sandy girl and what's been going on with my pigeons."

Stanley straightened up. "Sandy? What's that all about?"

"Guess your little Haze didn't tell ya," Arthur said, drawing on the cigarette and sneering.

"She—I—" Stanley stammered. She'd come to tell him something and then they'd fought. His skin prickled. "What's going on?"

"I found your girl wandering in some pretty dodgy alleys last night lookin' for ya, so I walked her back home. She told me Sandy's disappeared. Vanished. Everyone thinks she went on a wild ride, but it ain't so."

Stanley's stomach dropped. No wonder Hazel had been a little nuts the night before. "You couldn't come tell me this last night?"

Stanley grabbed Arthur's arm, and his friend shook him off with a scowl.

"It ain't my concern. I got better things to do than rescue swells," he snarled. Then he tipped his head to the side and shrugged. "But, outta curiosity, and in case that dame missing is connected to my missing pigeons, I sent out my best little pigeons to nose around. Sure, as a Dizzy Dean fastball, they dug up a witness."

"What did they find out?"

"Enzo Fingers saw a hooded man sneaking around the Schmidt house. Fingers was casing the neighborhood, like he does, but was scared home by what he seen."

Stanley took off his hat and gripped his hair. "Why didn't you tell me sooner?"

Arthur gave an impatient puff on his cigarette and smoke billowed out. "I just got word back on this myself, and I've been trying to find your sorry ass ever since."

Stanley massaged his forehead. "Okay, okay, right. I bet this guy, Larry, took Sandy then."

"Larry?" Arthur asked, pulling the cigarette out of his mouth, his mask of indifference gone.

"A nickname for a swell who knew Evelyn. I'll explain later. For now, we need to get the Knights together. Get them to the boxcar as soon as possible. Send out the pigeons. Find out anything else you can. We have to find Sandy and this hooded guy. Or things are gonna get bloody."

Stanley closed his eyes and tried not to let the world spin. Hazel had come to him and tried to get his help. And he acted like a perfect street donkey. She had every right to call him names.

"Listen, we gotta move fast. Whoever killed Evelyn did it because of what was in her diary. And now, they took Sandy to try and get it back. My guess is when they find out she doesn't have it she'll crack like a thin piece of ice and tell them what she did with it and then they'll come for Hazel. This thing is getting ugly. And, if I'm right, it's not just about swells versus poor kids. It's something way worse."

Arthur puffed hard on his cig so that his face was obscured with smoke. Something more was bugging him, Stanley thought. He couldn't imagine what, and it couldn't be because he was worried about Hazel. "What is it?"

Arthur took a deep breath. "You know who Larry is, right?"

"No, but I'm hot on his heels. We just have to keep him away from Hazel while I gather the Knights, so we can rescue Sandy."

Arthur said, "Rescue a swell? Why would I wanna do that?"

Stanley set his jaw. "Because it's the right thing to do."

Snorting, Arthur flicked the end of his cigarette, the ashes fluttered to the ground. "You've changed since you met old blue eyes."

Stanley stared at Arthur. "Maybe. Let's just end this and get back to our semi-normal lives."

"That ain't gonna happen, Stanny boy. Listen. My pigeons have started coming back."

"The missing ones? Why didn't you say so?"

Arthur blew smoke at him. "Because it didn't start happening until today, that's why."

Stanley clenched his fist. "So, what are they saying? Why did they go away?"

The angry mask dissolved from Arthur's face. He paled, and the cigarette trembled between his lips.

"Guys in hoods kidnapped them. Stories are all alike. They're walking in an alley and a few hooded guerrillas jump them. Next thing they know, they're in some kinda doctor's office and being stabbed with needles. They wake up and have tattoos like the ones you been seein'."

Arthur looked down and took a drag of his cigarette. "Those numbers, they remind me of my pops."

Stanley gripped his friend's arm. "What do you mean?"

"When he worked for IBM … it looks like one of their numbering systems my dad was sellin' to the people on Lindell. When you were talking about that the other day, I had my ideas. But seeing them inked into the skin of one my pigeons, I knew."

Thoughts flooded Stanley's brain. That's where he had heard IBM from, the whole thing with Arthur's dad. Why hadn't he made the connection before? The Veiled Prophet people had stolen his work and renamed it the Winnowing. And Legion was their army.

"Now you understand: this is a war," Arthur said. "And I don't see how we can stop them. We should just get outta town and go west. Start over."

Stanley slumped his shoulders. He couldn't argue with anything Arthur said. It was all true. Yet he remembered Father Timothy's homily last Sunday. Good people were supposed to fight evil. They were never promised a victory or that it would be a glorious battle. They were just supposed to fight, even if they lost, even if the battle was grim and long.

Looking up, he said, "No. This is my town and yours. Maybe we can't win, Artie, but they took everything from you. And they want to do the same to everyone. I'm gonna fight. And we're starting by kicking the guy's teeth in who took Sandy, the guy who took your pigeons. So, are you with me?"

Arthur took off his bowler hat and smoothed out his hair. "Okay, let's go. Guess we all gotta die sometime." He dropped his cigarette and stomped it out as if it were a cockroach.

Chapter Eighteen

Hazel hadn't been able to make herself get dressed and go to school. She was positively sick with worry about Sandy; she'd cried herself to sleep thinking about her friend. On top of that, the fight with that stupid boy replayed in her mind dozens of times, and she kept adding things she should've said to put him in his place. But that only lead to confusing arguments with herself because she couldn't decide what Stanley's place was. She just wanted to go back to how life was before and to have Sandy back.

There was nothing she could do to change anything. The police were out looking for Sandy, but could they even be trusted? Whatever was going on with the town and whatever had happened to Evelyn and now Sandy was bigger than anything Hazel could handle. Before, with Stanley on her side, it seemed like they could carry it off, fix it all like he said. But now it looked hopeless. What could two kids do against the gangs and the politics of the city? Zilch, that's what.

Mumsy was in St. Charles visiting a friend, and Pops had business matters to attend to downtown. Neither of them seemed to have time for Hazel today, even with what was going on. The servants were pleasant enough, but she had never felt so alone. It was making her blue, and her head hurt from crying. All she wanted to do was nothing at all.

Hazel flipped through her magazines wishing she had the diary back, listened to several radio programs, and ate a full box of chocolates while reality blurred bit by merciful bit. That afternoon she lay on the couch in the sunroom, still in her nightgown, listening to music. It was a new record from Rudy Vallee. His dreamy voice filled the room and Hazel's mind slid into daydreaming.

You oughta be in pictures,
You're wonderful to see,
You oughta be in pictures,
Oh, what a hit you would be!

Hazel saw herself riding in the back of a limousine with Sandy and Evelyn; they laughed and gabbed together all dressed to the nines. After pulling up to Grauman's Chinese Theater, they stepped out into the bright lights and roaring crowd. They linked arms and walked down the red carpet while people screamed their names. Clark Gable and Bing Crosby greeted them with smiles and kisses on the cheek as if they were old friends. Little Jackie Cooper skipped up to Hazel and gave her a mischievous grin. Greta Garbo gave her a wink and wave. All the stars in Hollywood flocked around the three of them. Inside the theater, the lights dimmed and the show started. Hazel's name and face appeared on the screen, and Sandy clapped and whistled.

Evelyn turned to her and said, "I told you, you have lovely eyes."

Hazel felt someone sit beside her in the dim lit theater.

"Want some popcorn, Lady Bananas?" His warm hand engulfed hers.

Hazel smiled over at Stanley. He wore a tux with a black bow tie. His hair was slicked over and he had a pencil mustache. She sighed.

He leaned close and whispered in her ear, "Hiya, brat." That roguish side smile on his face.

"Kiss me," she whispered. Hazel pushed her hands into his hair.

His blue eyes came closer, the warm scent of grass and fresh baked pretzels, and then a shadow passed across the silver screen. A figure in a hood.

Evelyn screamed. It was the shrill sound of the telephone.

Hazel startled out of her daydream. *Bananas.* What was all of that? Her stomach twisted as all the darkness and horror of reality rushed back. She couldn't hide from it. But could she fight it? Not without Stanley.

Peggy swept into the room. "Oh, my dear." The round-faced maid gave her a sympathetic look. "Mrs. Schmidt is on the phone. She's asked to speak to you. Would you like to take the call in the den?"

Hazel's heart jumped. Maybe there was news about Sandy. Did they find her? Anxious, she disentangled her legs from her long white nightgown. "Yes, Peggy." Her hands trembled as she followed her maid into the den and picked up the phone.

Peggy patted her back. "There now, Missy."

It was enough comfort to give Hazel courage. She took a deep breath and brought the telephone to her mouth. "Hello, this is Hazel."

The voice on the other end was strained and hoarse. "Hello … Hazel. This is Mrs. Schmidt. I hate to trouble you … " she broke off.

Hazel swallowed. "No, it's no trouble."

"Hazel," Mrs. Schmidt didn't sound like herself at all, "I must know, did Alesandra confide in you? Please tell me. Was there someplace she would go?"

A cold heaviness dragged down Hazel's insides. They hadn't found her. The desperation in Mrs. Schmidt's voice made her heart ache.

"Gee, I-I'm so sorry, ma'am," Hazel choked out, trying not to cry. "I don't know where Sandy is."

A small moan and sobbing on the other end of the line made Hazel's own eyes fill with tears.

"I can't bear it, I tell you. Not Sandy too … it can't be true … " Mrs. Schmidt wept.

Hazel sunk into a wingback chair and closed her eyes, still listening to her best friend's mother fall apart. Such an elegant, refined woman, reduced to bawling like anyone else. Rich or poor, pain and heartbreak felt the same.

"I'm sorry," she whispered again. "I wish I knew where she was."

After Hazel hung up, she stared at the ceiling with tears running down her cheeks.

"Aw, now, Missy. Don't give up hope yet." Peggy stood watching her, wringing her hands.

"Come and hug me, will you?" Hazel sat up and held out her arms like a child.

She was soon engulfed in the warmth of Peggy's soft, strong arms. "There now. Dry those angel tears. Don't worry yourself," she cooed.

"I don't know what to do, Peggy. So much has happened. Ever since I took a walk with that boy, my life has turned upside down."

"Oh, and if I had a nickel for every story that began that way—" Peggy said with a smile in her voice.

Hazel pulled back and gazed into the light brown eyes of her maid. She was so kind, maybe the only true friend she had now, which was strange considering that she knew very little about Peggy, just that she'd come over from Ireland when she was a young woman about Hazel's own age. There was something about a husband who died in the troubles with the English landlords. Seemed the rich were grinding the poor into the dirt over there, too.

"I don't know what I'd do without you, Peggy."

"Aw, now that's sweet. But I'm just the maid." She winked.

The maid. Hazel thought of Flora. She had to make her talk, or the Schmidts could lose another daughter.

"I need to get out of here. I can't just sit here while my friend is missing."

Peggy patted her hand. "The burden isn't on you. Let the police—"

"I'm afraid Sandy will end up like her sister unless I help. I know this will sound whacky, but I don't trust the police."

Peggy blinked and smoothed a lock of Hazel's hair back. "And why do ya say that, dearie?"

"It's just … we saw them covering evidence the night Evelyn was killed. And there's more—some kind of plot that Evelyn came back into town to stop or bring down, I don't know. Stanley heard her talking to the ballplayer about it earlier that day before somebody shut her up with a baseball bat."

"And you don't think the ballplayer did it, then?"

"No. He loved her; there were other things going on with the gangs and maybe even the … " Hazel had the uneasy feeling that she was about to commit heresy of some kind.

"Yes?" Her maid cocked her head, her usually cheerful face very serious now.

Hazel glanced around, nervous, as if the walls were listening. But she just had to tell someone. Peggy was her rock. "The Veiled Prophet."

Peggy let out a slow breath. "Well, that seems like quite a tale."

"But it's true. Evelyn mentioned the VP and said she had information that would take everyone on Lindell down."

"So now you think that Sandy is in danger from the same man who killed her sister?" Without a bright smile on her face, Peggy looked older and Hazel noticed for the first time that there were gray hairs striping her auburn hair.

"Yes, I think he has her. But I'm not sure why unless … " Hazel thought of the diary. That had to be it. The hooded man who had killed Evelyn and who was probably stalking Stanley must know about the diary. Fear shot through her body. If the stalker was always watching them, he might know that one of them had it.

"What is it? You look as if you've seen the Grim Reaper himself," Peggy said.

"I—Stanley may be in danger."

Peggy shook her head. "One disaster at a time, Missy. There's no reason anyone would be after your newsie friend—is there?" She stared into Hazel's eyes; the pink in her cheeks had drained.

"Uh … no." Hazel had said too much, and paranoia leaked into her veins again, cold and unsettling. Anybody who knew about all this business was in danger, and as Arthur had pointed out, she was running out of friends.

"Well, I tell ya, if you really believe the police are good for nothin', maybe the best way to find Sandy is to ask your friend Stanley," Peggy said.

Hazel hung her head. She'd been foolish to throw the diary at him last night and let that silly girl get in the way of her asking Stanley for help. "I can't ask him for help. We're in a fight."

Peggy tsked and raised Hazel's chin with a finger. "Well, if he's the kind of lad you say, you can make amends, and this is no time for grudges."

Hazel nodded. *Stanley could help find Sandy and he might have better luck getting Flora to talk,* she thought. They could interrogate the maid together.

"Go and find him; he'll help ya." Peggy pulled Hazel up onto her feet. "Go and get dressed, find your newsie friend, and see what he knows and then get back here before supper so your da is none the wiser."

Hazel's pulse sped up. If the hooded man knew where the diary was then she was in danger as long as he was on the loose. The sooner she found Stanley and they solved this the better.

Later, after Hazel had dressed, she sneaked down the backstairs. While Peggy distracted Mrs. Flannigan with talk of how to get her dough "high as a Dubliner after a football game," Hazel slipped out of the kitchen door. She ran out onto the boulevard, heart racing.

She had to find Stanley. But what if she did and he was still angry at her? Would he even want to help find Sandy now? He and Arthur had nothing nice to say about her kind, but then she thought of some of the things she'd said and cringed. She had to apologize and make nice.

An idea came to Hazel, and she took a quick detour to find the boy who sold pretzels; the little crippled girl was not with him. She bought two of the doughy hearts—one to cram in her own mouth and one as a peace offering for Stanley. Hazel was half-worried she'd bump into Arthur selling his pretzels, but she never saw the angry boy in the bowler hat. *Whew.*

There was only one place she could think of where Stanley would be for sure at some point: the red boxcar. That was a place he wouldn't take a dame. She'd rather not see him with another one of his fillies. Not that she was jealous—he could do as he pleased—but she wanted to be able to talk to him in private. She didn't need a repeat of last time.

Hazel made her way across Forest Park, which seemed so different in the late afternoon than it had that first night. Sunshine filtered through the limbs of the trees colored by autumn. The light made the leaves glow in red and orange, reminding Hazel of the stained-glass windows of St. James. As she moved deeper into the woods, a sudden silence made her uneasy. The birds had been singing but seemed to stop all at once.

She spun around and searched the bushes and trees. Nothing. Then the birds tittered above again and Hazel sighed. She was going nutty. After searching and getting a little lost, she saw the rusted sides of the red boxcar peeking through the branches.

Relieved that she had found it, Hazel broke into a run. The Knights would tell her where to find Stanley if he wasn't there himself. Someone would surely be there.

"Heigh-ho! Hey fellas!" she called out as she came up to the hideout. The door was cracked open, and she thought she heard voices inside.

"Hello?"

"Hazel?" somebody asked.

"Yes! Stanley is that you?" With his pretzel in one hand, Hazel used the other hand to slide the door open—it took quite some effort to move. The screech of it echoed inside the old boxcar.

Sunblind, she stepped into the shadowed interior of the boxcar. It smelled of rust and cigarette smoke. "Stanley—is that you?" She blinked as somebody came toward her.

"No. Not Stanley," he said, stepping into the light that came through the open door.

Hazel froze in terror.

The man in the hood grabbed her and, before Hazel could scream, her world spun and she was on her back gasping for air. "Help!" she managed to rasp out.

He held a finger to his lips. "Shhhh."

The last thing Hazel saw was his shoe coming toward her face, then everything exploded in pain and went dark.

Chapter Nineteen

A dark cloud of dust and factory smog descended over St. Louis, and even though it was only the late afternoon, cars turned on their lights. Stanley coughed a little and spat out a mouth full of the city's smog. Everyone around him on the trolley coughed, hacked, and cleared their throats.

"Come on, you worthless bucket of bolts. Move!" Stanley pressed against the bracing bar of the trolley, muttering his frustrations. He'd never realized how slowly they moved. *Maybe learning to drive an automobile wasn't a bad idea*, he thought. That way he could go as fast he wanted.

He tried to calm himself down by praying a Hail Mary and an Our Father. Every time he closed his eyes, Stanley pictured a crazed hooded man with no shirt going after Hazel with a baseball bat. He tried not to imagine Hazel's pretty face smashed. It took a whole other level of craziness to beat a beautiful dame to death with a bat.

Stanley shook the bracing bar again out of frustration. "Move, will ya?"

Finally, the trolley stopped at Lindell, and he ran to Hazel's house. Peering through the gate, he saw the gardener, the chauffeur, and a tall man dressed in a suit pointing at Hazel's window. Dirty late afternoon sunlight pierced through the gloom, and the trees cast long shadows in the yard.

"How the devil did she get out?" the tall man demanded.

"Don't know, Mr. Malloy. She didn't come down this way, that's a fact. Maybe she snuck out a window somewhere."

Stanley stared at the tall man in the suit who had to be Hazel's father. He chuckled to himself and then froze. Hazel was loose on the streets somewhere. Taking off his hat, he ran his fingers through his hair.

Lady Bananas, what are you doing? And where is Teeth?

Not even knowing where to look, Stanley decided to head for the Castle. He hoped she'd have sense enough to go there first if she was looking for him. Breaking into a jog, he cut through the park and found his way into the forest.

As he stepped into the clearing, he felt it. The creeps. Something was wrong, but he couldn't put his finger on it. Glancing up, Stanley saw the boxcar door was open, something none of the Knights would ever do.

"Hazel?"

No answer.

"Hey, Bananas, come out and let's make up. I was a first-class heel."

Instinct and the lack of an answer made him hold up his fists as he walked slowly toward the doorway to peer inside. His stomach twisted when he saw a pool of red on the faded wooden floor. Something wrapped in white paper lay in the middle. Jumping into the car with one leap, he skidded to the ground, his face nearly touching the floor. Pushing himself up with his elbows, he touched the liquid.

Blood.

Grabbing the package, he realized it was actually wax paper protecting a pretzel. The blood seeped past the brown crust into the white dough.

Sitting on the floor, he gripped his hair. She'd come to see him and to end the fight. The pretzel made that open and shut. Trembling, he touched it and felt the warmth of her blood.

"Stanley? Is that you?" a moan from behind him asked with a lisp.

"Teeth? Are you … ?"

The kid came out of the shadows, holding his forehead. Stanley jumped to his feet and moved his hand. He tried not to flinch at the large red goose egg forming between Teeth's eyes

"What happened, kid?"

Teeth shrugged. "Can't remember, exactly. Was keeping an eye on Hazel when some guys in hoods jumped me. They tried to put something over my mouth, but I bit their arms. Gave me just enough time to give them the slip."

At least they didn't kill you, Stanley thought. *Thank God.*

"You didn't see anything else?"

Teeth shook his head. "It hurts, Stanley. Does that make me a big ol' chicken?"

Stanley gave him a half-smile. "Nah, just means you're brave."

The kid swayed a little and then threw up, nearly hitting Stanley's shoes.

"You have a concussion."

Teeth waved him away. "I'm okay, Stanley, want to go with you."

Stanley gripped his arms. "Kid, if you want to be a Knight, you gotta take orders. And I order you to go home. Get me?"

Teeth nodded. "Okay, Stanley."

"Go on, get out here. Go home. Stay there and don't leave the house. Things are about to get bad around here."

He watched until the kid disappeared into the forest, moving at a slow pace. Stanley paced as panic rose inside him. He had to figure out where Hazel was before that jackass hurt her even more. He slammed his fist into the side of the boxcar, shouting as his scabs reopened, letting out fresh blood.

"Stanny, boy, you okay?" Anino's voice popped in behind him.

"No. The killer has Hazel and Sandy. I was too late."

Falling to the ground, he folded his hands and put them to his head. Blood from his knuckles streaked his eyebrows and hair.

"What's the story?"

Stanley shook his head. "I'm only going to say this once, so let's wait until everyone gets here." Jakob came in a few minutes later, followed by Arthur and Shuffles. They all waited in silence until Stanley finished praying.

He stood up, walked over to the pretzel, and picked it up. He put it in his coat next to his heart. "Boys, it's time to go to war."

Stanley explained everything while watching the faces of his Knights. Each of them wore the hardened expression of a street kid knowing he was about to jump into a schoolyard brawl.

Arthur took a drag on his cigarette while he cracked his knuckles. "So where do we start looking for the princess and her lady in waiting?"

"No idea. But before we go searching, I'm going to Seamus. I don't even know if I can trust him but I can't go to any of the other cops," Stanley said.

Shuffles scoffed and messed with a deck of cards. "Ya sure you wanna chance it?"

"Yeah, your uncle is a little too law-and-order even for my pops," Jakob said.

Stanley shrugged. "Whatever he is, I … we need him. Something tells me this is way above our heads. We'll need the coppers, as much I don't want to say so."

"Yeah, but we still don't know where to look," Shuffles said, shuffling and folding the cards.

Stanley furrowed his brow. "We're gonna have to go to the Rookery. That's all there is to it."

All of the Knights glanced at each other. "Well, Stanny boy, we ain't afraid of a little rough stuff, but they outnumber us by, oh, like

Indians outnumbered Custer at Bighorn. I ain't one for the meat wagon, myself," Anino said.

"Yeah, we gotta use our brains," Jakob agreed.

Stanley placed his hand over his heart and felt the pretzel. "Unless I hear something different, that's all I got."

No one chimed in, and he nodded. "Then let's go see Seamus."

He led them out of the boxcar, through the park, and into Dogtown. He hoped Teeth got home safe. That kind of head injury sometimes killed people. He couldn't spare the time to check on him now and he needed all of his Knights with him. Who knew what the hooded crazy would do to the girls? Crossing himself, he took a deep breath.

Finally, they reached the house and Stanley said, "Wait here, fellas. I'll be right out."

Opening the door, he heard his uncle talking to someone.

"Peggy, why would you go and send that gal to him? Now you go sticking your Irish nose in this dog mess? Does Gertie know?"

"No, that's why I came to ya. Can't have her worrying after everything she's done for me. I sent Hazel to Stanley to get help. I knew he'd protect her, and I thought he might know where her friend was. But her da is on the warpath. So, can you help me find them?"

Stanley paused in his living room. They hadn't heard him come in and kept talking.

"Can't believe you did this, Peggy, after everything. We gotta protect him," Seamus said, pounding his fist on the table.

"Sure, like you're doing such a fine job of that. I hear the stories; I know what he's doing. I've seen him at it. The boy can't help who his parents were. He's gonna always help people, and you keep trying to prevent that."

His parents. Why were they talking about his parents?

"Ya knew them better than most, ta be sure." Seamus snorted.

Stanley couldn't take it anymore, and he burst into the dining room. A short Irish woman dressed in a maid's uniform sat at the table with Seamus. Her wavy auburn hair up in a bun had started to come unraveled, and she had light brown eyes. Only the gray streaks in her hair and the deep lines around her eyes said she might be older than Stanley. Everything else about her looked young to him. She seemed familiar somehow. When she turned to him, her lip trembled a bit before she got control of herself.

"Who are you?" Stanley asked, trying to figure out if he'd ever seen her before on the street.

Peggy stood and said, "Peggy O'Hara, I'm a housemaid at your friend Hazel's. And I knew your ma and da. Like family to me, you might say."

Stanley stared at her. "So, I guess I've seen you before."

She nodded. "But not since you came to live with Seamus, when you were a wee one."

"What did you both mean by keeping me safe?"

Seamus and Peggy looked at each other. "Well, your ma and da asked us to look after ya. It's me that's been telling Seamus about the Knights and their raids," Peggy said.

Stanley studied her face. "Why haven't I met you before?"

Seamus piped in. "I wouldn't allow it. We had a falling out long ago. She ain't a part of our lives."

Stanley had questions. Something was going on they weren't telling him. But there was no time for that.

Taking off his hat, he said, "Hazel's been kidnapped."

Peggy stood up, blood draining from her face. "What do you mean?"

Stanley told them about the boxcar, Teeth, the blood, and the pretzel. "She was coming to see me. And it's my fault she got taken by that hooded—" Tears welled up in his eyes, and he wiped them away quickly.

Shaking her head, Peggy started to sob. "No, I told her to go to you."

Seamus shifted his feet and pulled on his suspenders. "I better get to the boxcar. I'll check it out. Where you gonna be, Stanley?"

"Where do you think, flatfoot? Trying to find that hooded jackass."

Seamus nodded, then gave Peggy's hand a squeeze. "We'll find her, don't you worry none." With that, he opened the front door and said, "All right, fellas, come in. Stop hanging outside with your gobs open."

All the Knights filed into the living room and stood behind Stanley.

"When you find something, send me a message," Seamus said as he put on his suit coat and brown fedora hat. Nodding to Peggy, he left.

Peggy stared at the boys, tears streaming down her face. "You all look so lovely and handsome. May the Blessed Mother look after ya."

To Stanley's surprise, she rushed up and threw her arms around him.

"I'm so worried about Hazel. She's a good girl." Peggy blubbed into his shoulder. Stanley looked around at all the Knights who shrugged as he patted her awkwardly. A lot of help they were in this situation. He really needed Hazel.

"We will find her. I know where to start. Don't worry."

Peggy took out a large handkerchief and blew her nose. She patted him on the shoulders and left without a word.

Stanley rubbed his forehead as Arthur said, "Are we just gonna sit here basking in the love, or are we gonna go and get our teeth kicked in?"

They all chuckled a little, and Stanley led them out the door in silence. No one said a word as they took the trolley to the end of the line and walked to the Rookery. When they approached the abandoned warehouse, Vinnie appeared in the doorway and came out to greet them.

"Look who it is, the Italian who would be a gangster. Because that ain't a stereotype or nothin," Arthur said, waving his cigarette.

"Welcome to the Rookery, ya creepy bastard. Why Stanley let you in the Knights is something I'll never figure," Vinnie said.

"If ya want, spaghetti boy, I'll show you right here," Arthur said, taking off his hat as Vinnie crouched into a boxing stance.

Stanley held up his hand. "Shut your mouths. We don't have time for you two. Vinnie, I want to talk to the Raven."

Shaking his head, Vinnie said, "Nah, you can't. He ain't here. He's across the river doin' business. But I have a message for you."

Stanley crossed his arms. "Spill it."

Looking at Arthur with a smirk, he said, "The Raven wants you to know he likes you. Thinks you're swell and all. And for that reason, he wants you to know the person yous two discussed hired some of our boys for a job."

Stanley rubbed his head. "What kind of job?"

Vinnie gripped him by the arm. "Not what you're thinking. He just wanted us to guard the entrances to the Lemp caves for the next few days. No one in or out without his say so."

Breathing hard, Stanley said, "When?"

"Dunno. I ain't been out there myself. Makes no sense to me, but the Raven said if you came around here, you should know." Vinnie spat on the ground. "He also said he ain't gonna tell the boys you're coming, so it's gonna be a fight to get in."

Nodding, Stanley steadied his breathing before he said, "Boy, we gotta go to the caves. Fast."

Vinnie frowned. "What's this all about? The fellas will stomp you all good; is it worth it? Why would the Raven tell you all that?"

"I don't have time to talk. Got damsels to save."

Vinnie looked down as the Knights started to walk away. Then, he ran up to Stanley and said, "Hey, anything I can do?"

Stanley said, "Go find Seamus. He's at the boxcar. Just tell him Stanley says Lemp caves. You don't have to say more than that."

"I'm in like gin," Vinnie said as he took off running.

Stanley said, "All right, boys, let's go."

They walked a few miles as the sun started to drop behind the western horizon. Shadows crept over the streets as they approached what used to be the Lemp Brewery, shut down during Prohibition. Stanley looked up to see the International Shoe Company sign that dominated its side.

"Too bad they don't still make beer. I could really use some right now," Anino said, reaching into his shirt. He pulled out his fighting sticks and held them at the ready.

Jakob squinted. "Stanley, I think the best way to the caves is by the basement stairs."

"Anyone know how to get in there?"

Shuffles smiled and sorted his cards. "Ain't nothin'. That place is full of holes. Follow me."

He led them past the main gate and down the street to a gaping hole in the fence.

"So much for security," Anino snorted as he wiggled through. Everyone followed him except Stanley, who watched for anyone coming after them. When he crawled through, the wooden fence scraped his chest a little since he was broader than the others.

Shuffles picked the nearest lock and led them into the factory. The air smelled like stale beer, mold, and leather. The company had obviously been doing some work; some walls had been knocked out and others were being painted.

After walking down a long hallway, Shuffles held up his hand and a second later Stanley knew why. He heard voices from the factory floor.

"What's this all about? That rich boy gave me the creeps."

"Eh, who cares? It's money. You yellow or something?"

"Nah, I ain't yellow; your mother is."

Everyone in the room laughed, but the echoes made it impossible for Stanley to tell how many were in there. He scooted against the wall and leaned out as much as he dared. From his count, he saw Jericho and some of his goons standing in the middle of the factory floor. An even fight.

"At least we could have guns or somethin'. This place gives me the willies."

"What, you afraid of the Lemp ghosts? Better go home to Mama. The Raven said no guns."

Stanley took a deep breath and looked back at his Knights. He nodded to them, and they nodded back. Holding up all the fingers of one hand, he jerked his head toward the floor.

All of them nodded again. Anino twirled his sticks. Jakob took off his black coat and rolled up his sleeves. Shuffles drew out two switchblades, clicking the buttons so that the blades flicked out.

Arthur rolled his eyes and whispered, "Are ya gonna get on with it or what?"

Grinning, Stanley stepped out on the factory floor and said, "Heya fellas."

Chapter Twenty

A pounding in Hazel's head woke her. She kept her eyes squeezed shut, afraid of what she'd see. A metallic smell mixed with mold and dust made her nose itch. Shivering in the cold, Hazel realized she was tied to a chair. The taste of blood made Hazel's stomach lurch. She wanted to spit it out but was afraid to make any noise. An intermittent sound of drops falling and plunking into water came from somewhere near. Where was she? She felt dizzy and her face hurt, then she remembered …

The hooded man.

Hazel held back a scream. She heard voices—it sounded like young boys whispering and whimpering. She was too afraid to call out to whoever it was.

Footsteps sounded from the shadows and the voices stopped. She bit back the urge to cry out for help. Hazel had never been so scared in her life. Her heart froze when she heard whistling. A jaunty tune she recognized: *There's a New Day Comin'*. It echoed all around her, a frightening, cheerful sound that chilled her from head to toe.

The whistling came closer and then stopped, but the vibrations from the echoes still prickled Hazel's skin.

"What's the story, morning glory?" the man whispered in a gruff voice.

Hazel didn't move. If she opened her eyes or spoke, she might have a breakdown. He kicked her chair and a gasp escaped her.

"Open your eyes," he said in the excited way someone might use when about to give you a pleasant surprise.

Hazel obeyed. It took a moment to focus in the dark room. No, it wasn't a room but a cave. She could make out that one wall had an arched stone doorway. Candles were set about, each creating a small halo of light in the dark interior and casting shadow.

The man in the hood dropped to his haunches in front of her. "Do you have it?"

Hazel knew what he wanted. "Have what?" she managed to squeak out.

"The diary. We need it."

"W-what diary?"

He cocked his head—the hood still obscured his face. "Do you really want to drag this out?"

Hazel shook her head, afraid of what he'd do. He was like a snake about to strike. The taste of blood in her mouth reminded her that this psychopath had killed Evelyn with a baseball bat. If whatever was in the diary was worth killing for and worth Evelyn risking death, Hazel had to protect it.

"I don't want any trouble, Mister."

"Well you've got it in spades." He reached out and tipped her chin up with one finger, but she didn't want to look at the shadow under the hood.

"Please don't hurt me. I don't have a diary," she whimpered, closing her eyes until his hand left her face.

He stood, clucking his tongue. "Hazel Malloy, you're a smart girl. You know who I am and what I'm capable of," he said, no longer whispering.

The way he spoke was familiar. Hazel knew that voice. "You're the man in the hood who killed Evelyn."

"Yes. And?"

"And you took Sandy." Her heart ached at the thought of her friend.

"Yes. She told me your little secret. I persuaded her to tell me that you had the diary."

"Is she okay? Did you—"

"She's in pain, if that's what you want to know. What happens next is up to you."

He spoke so casually it made Hazel's stomach flip. She was gripped by fear and had to force herself to breathe.

"I-I don't want anything to happen to her. Tell your gang I can get them the diary if you let us go."

He laughed. "My gang. You're a pip. You think that's what this is? The gangs of St. Louis are dead men walking. It won't be long until we've taken care of all of them." He sounded so calm and friendly, as if he were talking about some favor he was happy to do for someone.

That voice. Soft, hesitant … like Jimmy Stewart. Hazel refused to believe it at first, but she knew who it was.

"Charles."

He shrugged and then removed the hood. "Well, this is no fun." The college boy with big green eyes stared at her. The scariest thing about the face of Evelyn's murderer was how normal and almost gentle he was.

Hazel's lip trembled. "Why did you do it?"

"He wanted me to. Sometimes sacrifices need to be made for the common good. You understand, don't you?"

Hazel shook her head. "I don't understand anything anymore."

It was hard to take in. Charles was the killer. He was probably also the one who frightened Flora and disgraced Evelyn.

He sighed. "I knew that night, when you and that newsie saw me with Evelyn that it would somehow come to this. I'm sorry for it."

It was clear that no matter what she told him, or whether he got the diary, Hazel would not leave here alive, wherever she was. The thought came with sudden conviction, and the initial horror of it quickly turned into a numb acceptance.

"Who is the Veiled Prophet? Why did he want one of his Queens killed? What do the numbers in the diary mean?" At this point, she just wanted to know—whatever he did, she would never tell him that Stanley had the diary now.

"So, you read it. We're very curious about what Evelyn jotted down in that little book of hers. This is so much bigger and more beautiful than you could ever imagine or comprehend," Charles said softly.

"Well whatever it is—wealth or power—it isn't worth killing innocent, good people."

"Money and power? We already have that. And as for Evelyn—she was a lovely girl. We were good friends, but she wanted to ruin things. She was foolish and ignorant. She didn't understand the importance of the Winnowing." He pulled something out of his pocket. It caught the yellow light of a nearby candle and glittered ruby red.

Winnowing again. What was it? "That's Evelyn's ring," Hazel breathed.

"She was no longer worthy to wear it." He seemed to lose himself in his thoughts, staring at the ring.

He was out of his skull.

Hazel's wrists hurt. They were lashed tight to the arms of the chair, causing her fingers to tingle. Her eyes had adjusted better to the dark, and she glanced around the barren space. A few wooden barrels set in a semi-circle around her held candles and some pieces of copper pipe were strewn on the ground. Through the arched passageway, there were no signs of other life, just the drip-drop of water. She wondered where Sandy was or if Charles had already killed her after she had spilled the beans that Hazel had taken the diary. She must have been so frightened. A lump rose in Hazel's throat. No way would she break.

"Is Sandy dead?" Hazel asked, her voice fragile.

"No. In fact, I'll probably bring her in here, so you can watch what happens when people try to interfere."

Hazel's anger flashed inside. "You're a monster! I will never help you and you'll never get away with it. Too many of us know what is happening! And maybe the cops have the diary. Ever think of that?"

"You mean your beau's uncle? Oh, we aren't worried about him. And I will get away with it. You don't seem to understand who I work for. What we can do. How powerful we are."

It was hopeless. The cops were in on it, maybe even the mayor. Her mind whirled with all the possibilities. She could not fathom why the Veiled Prophet was involved in murder. And if money and power were not the end game, then what was?

"I don't have your diary." Hazel felt like crying.

"Who did you give it to?" He stepped toward her; although he had no weapon, Hazel shrank back, looking up at him with stony defiance.

"I'll bring Sandy in here and you can argue about it. Shall I?" He seemed so detached, like somebody who had lived without consequences his whole life. Which he probably had. The Chouteau family owned a large portion of St. Louis and went way back to the roots of the city. They didn't seem the type to punish their only son for any of his faults or failings.

Hazel jerked against her restraints. "What do you think the papers will say to explain that three girls from prominent families were killed within a week? They can't all have been killed by Evelyn's unsuitable boyfriend; he's in jail! Don't you think people will wonder what is going on?"

"The papers?" He snorted a soft laugh. "They'll say what we tell them to say. And as far as you and Sandy … well, that's an easy fix. We know where your new boyfriend lives. We know about his

Knights, and we obviously have found their little hideout. They don't bother us so it isn't personal, but well-placed evidence will indicate the perpetrators. A gang of boys who regularly raid and steal from the rich would certainly rob and kill a couple of girls wearing jewelry and carrying handbags full of money. I think the jury will see that clearly enough."

"No!" If they framed Stanley and his gang, those boys wouldn't have a prayer.

"Yes. And actually, it rather neatly solves a personal problem of my own. You see, I would never use his power for my own agenda. No. My will is swallowed up in his. But sometimes fate is kind. In this case his enemy happens to also be mine."

"What did Stanley ever do to you?" she seethed.

"Stanley? Oh, I don't care two bits for your beau. But one of his Knights … I have a score to even there." He strolled toward the arched passageway and bent to pick up a piece of copper pipe.

Hazel wondered if Evelyn knew what was about to happen before she died. They had been friends; did she know that it was Charles when he came at her with the bat? Or had he been wearing the hood when he attacked? Hazel didn't know what would be more terrifying: to be killed by somebody you knew or by an anonymous masked madman?

Charles turned and looked over his shoulder at her, a slight frown on his face, almost apologetic.

She knew in that moment which was worse. It was beyond horror to look into the face of a person you thought you knew and then realize that he is a monster, a monster wearing the mask of a friend.

Charles looked out of the passageway and stood with his back to her, holding the pipe in his fist. He hung his head and took a deep breath.

The last shred of fight left inside of Hazel burst out and she screamed. Her voice was unrecognizable—so loud and shrill, the shriek of a banshee. It filled the space, vibrating and ear splitting.

Charles spun around and marched toward her, furious. Hazel's breath left her body.

"Shut your trap!" he shouted.

She had never heard his voice raised before, and she flinched. Hazel closed her eyes, expecting the pipe to swing down onto her head.

"I'm not done with you, Hazel," he said, quiet again. "Let's bring your friend in here and see if you like hearing her scream. Okay?" Charles smiled at her.

She shuddered. "No."

With a sigh, he reached over and yanked a handful of her hair. It burned her scalp as he shook her head. "You don't have a choice. Do you understand? I will bring Sandy in here and hurt her until you decide to tell me where that diary is."

Hazel let out a sob. She didn't want Sandy to suffer, but how could she cooperate with this animal and his master? The truth was, no matter what she told him, she and Sandy were never leaving this dark place alive. So why put Stanley in danger by telling Charles he had the diary?

Charles released his grasp on her hair and folded his arms. "Or do you want to tell me without going through all of that?"

Closing her eyes, she didn't answer.

"It's too bad. Even if I didn't have to kill her eventually, I would never be able to take her to the Veiled Prophet Ball; after I'm through with Sandy, she wouldn't make a suitable date. In fact, she would never want to be seen in public ever again." He sighed and walked away.

Bile rose in her throat, and she swallowed it back. "Don't touch her," she screamed. Hazel listened as the echoes of her own voice faded and Charles's footsteps got further away, reverberating through the tunnels. She burst into tears and babbled a prayer. "God if you're there, please help us. Please protect us and protect Stanley—you know him. He goes to church. I don't want to die … "

Hazel cried without restraint, and the sound of it echoed back into her ears, helpless and desolate. It seemed like several minutes went by and then a calm came over her, warm and soft.

Stanley's face appeared in her mind and she thought she heard his voice in her head. "Father, be with Haze … lead me to her before it's too late. Protect her … "

The words were soft and blurred with static like a weak station on the radio. Hazel thought she might be losing her mind, but it calmed her, and her body relaxed. One way or the other, the pain would be over soon. She hoped it wasn't too late for Sandy. Tears rolled down her cheeks in silence.

Somehow, she knew, Stanley was coming.

Chapter Twenty-One

Stanley stood facing down five teenage gangsters, four of whom he and Arthur had taken on to save Teeth. They gathered in front of a mountain of wooden crates full of shoes. All of them smoked cigarettes and frowned at him as if he were a piece of garbage who insulted their mothers.

"We meet again, Knight of Micktown. What are you doin' here?" Jericho asked as he smoothed out his thin mustache. He still had a black eye and a scabbed over split lip from the last time Stanley had faced off with him.

"I'm going into the caves and rescue the ladies," Stanley said, strolling forward with his hands in fists.

"What are you going on about, Saint Stanley? Ain't no dames there. Go play knight somewhere else."

Stanley grinned. "Wasn't really asking for your permission. I don't know what you guys think is going on down there, but it ain't good. He's got two innocent girls who haven't hurt anyone. It's kidnapping, like the Lindbergh baby. Remember what happened to the guy who did that?"

The teenagers looked at each other.

Jericho answered. "You're loony. It's just some gambling or something goin' on down there for rich folks."

A girl's scream echoed throughout the warehouse, cutting Stanley deep. *It's Hazel*, he thought; he had to make quick work of these jerks, so he could get to her.

He walked toward the thugs who were all looking at each other in confusion and said, "We can do this two ways: easy or hard. Personally, fellas, I'd like to not get any bruises on this pretty face. Did you hear that scream? That ain't gambling; it's kidnapping."

They muttered to each other, looking unsure.

Jericho spoke up. "We ain't leavin'. The Raven gave us this job, see?"

"It ain't personal," said a short, fat kid on the far left.

Stanley took off his hat and coat, placing them on the nearest crate.

"Sure, boys, I hear you. Then you won't take it personal if I got a few friends."

The Knights walked up behind him. He glanced to each side. Arthur and Anino were on his right; Shuffles and Jakob on his left. All of them had taken off their hats and coats.

"What is this, Boys Town gone bad?" asked Jericho. All the Raven's goons laughed, as they took off their coats and hats, too.

"Nah, just a good head cracking for you," Anino said, spinning his sticks.

The two lines drew closer to each other. Stanley and Jericho stood toe to toe.

Jericho sneered. "Last chance."

Stanley crouched into a boxing stance, his fists raised, and said, "Nah, I probably have a few more stashed in my mattress."

With that, Jericho threw a right hook that Stanley blocked and followed with a fast uppercut to the jaw. Falling back, the boy reached up to his chin and rubbed it. "All right, Stanley the Blessed, you got a mean swing; I'll give you that. Get 'em, boys."

Launching himself at Stanley, Jericho threw a combination of hooks, uppercuts, and jabs. Stanley blocked and parried each blow. The fella was fast but thankfully, he was dumb. He left his kidneys and his face wide open. Countering, Stanley hit each weakness hard; a hook to the kidneys, three quick jabs to the face, and a final uppercut to the jaw sent the boy to his knees.

"Don't feel so bad, chump," Stanley said, shaking out his hand.

"You're going down, Irish."

Stanley grinned. "In the good book, it's Jericho that tumbles down."

"Wise guy." Jericho grabbed a board, stood up, and swung it at Stanley's head. He deflected it with his arm, but the board skidded off and slammed into his eye. Grimacing in pain, he struck out with his right hand and the gangster went down in a heap.

Stanley held up his left arm to see a huge red welt, but it didn't look serious. He felt his eye and head. Blood ran down his face; his eyelid was starting to swell shut.

The world spun a little, but he steadied himself on a huge shoe crate. Panting, he turned to see how the others were doing. Anino fought the short, fat gangster who kept rushing at him like a deranged bull. When the guy got close to him, Anino whacked him in the head and the stomach until the kid went down on his knees. With a final swing of the sticks to the face, the kid went down for good.

Arthur went after his opponent with fury. He screamed out profanities while throwing punches, kicks, elbows. He unleashed himself with a rage that Stanley hadn't seen in anybody.

Jakob and Shuffles stood back to back, fighting off two gangsters who both had knives. Lashing out hard, Shuffles managed to cut one of the mugs, but he forgot about the fella on his left who drove a knife deep into his arm. Crying out, Shuffles fell to the ground and the kid stood over him, ready to put both knives into Anino.

With a scream of rage, Stanley launched himself at the gangster, grabbed his neck, and head butted him in the face. Blood flew out of the galoot's nose. Dropping down, Stanley landed four hard punches on his kidneys, and the kid went down in a groaning heap.

Stanley tried to ignore the throbbing pain in his head and fought off his churning stomach. He could barely move, but he stumbled toward the guy fighting with Jakob. By the time he got there, Jakob had wrapped the kid in a chokehold until he went limp.

Breathing hard, Stanley looked at the five gangsters lying on the floor, moaning and nursing their wounds. He grimaced and held his left arm close to him. The welt had begun to throb. A groan to his left made him turn and he saw Shuffles on his knees, knife protruding from his forearm. Stanley went over to him and asked, "You okay?"

"Oh yeah, aces. I got a new decoration to show off to the ladies."

"We gotta get that thing out." Taking the knife handle, he jerked it out hard and Shuffles groaned, eyes fluttering in his head as he fell forward. Stanley caught him and laid him on the ground. He found his jacket, and cut a makeshift bandage from it with his knife, binding Shuffles' arm wound. It didn't look too good.

Jakob came over; he only had a few cuts on his arm. "He okay?"

Stanley nodded. "I think so. We're gonna have to get him to the doc. Jakob, can you do that?"

Placing his hands atop Stanley's shoulders, he asked, "What about you?"

"Shuffles can't wait. Try to wake him up and take him. I'll be okay."

Jakob nodded, patting Stanley on the arm. "Go, pal." He turned and helped Shuffles to his feet and they made their way back the way they'd come.

Stanley got up and headed over to the stairs that he was pretty sure led to the basement.

"Hey, numbskull, where do you think you're going?" He turned to see Anino and Arthur running to catch up with him.

"To get Hazel, dummy. Anino and Artie, spread out to search

and watch for more goons. Not sure where the girls are."

Arthur gripped his arm hard. "If you run into the hooded guy you don't want to face him alone. I know him."

Stanley stopped and turned around. "What do you mean?"

"His family. They're the ones who wrecked my dad and mom. Stanny, it's Charles Chouteau," Arthur said, his face as white as a sheet. "And when I went to get my revenge on them, Charles caught me and beat me almost to death. Me, who ain't ever lost a fight. That cat has had some kinda training; that's facts."

Stanley swallowed hard. Anyone who made Arthur scared wasn't someone he was keen on meeting. "How do you know it's him?"

Arthur wiped his face. "Larry. I heard some of his swell friends call him that before. I been watchin' him awhile, see. But he's slippery. When you said that name today, I nearly lost my lunch. He's not a guy to pull punches."

Stanley knew the story of what happened to Arthur's family, but his friend had always refused to tell him names. He couldn't let him down in those tunnels with this Charles. No telling what Arthur would do.

"Then we really need to hurry and find those dames," Anino said.

Stanley raised his voice to Jericho and his four minions, "Hey jerks, the coppers are coming. They paying you enough to go down for kidnapping? It's old sparky if you do. Bet you'll light up like a Christmas tree."

The injured gangsters moaned and grumbled, pushing up to their elbows or knees.

"Say, didn't you hear what Stanny said? Cops are coming. Get your asses out of here," Arthur yelled at the remaining gangsters.

Jericho picked himself up, helped his friends, and together they limped out of the building. Arthur turned to Stanley, lit a cigarette, and said, "You're bleeding all over the place and that eye is gonna swell shut. You can't go in there alone, palsy. This guy could fit you for a Chicago overcoat, get me?"

Touching his eye, Stanley groaned. "Think I'm almost there anyway. But I'll manage. We need to split up so we can find them quicker."

Anino put his hand on his shoulder. "Take Artie with you, Stanley. You need him. I can guard the entrance and make sure those goons don't come back. I ain't injured and I got my two little friends." He held up his sticks with a dangerous expression on his face.

"So, yous gonna take me on this hunting trip, or what?" Arthur's face was hard and his eyes blazed with the eager fires of revenge.

Stanley looked at his friend as he puffed on a cigarette. He still worried Arthur might lose control at some point. However, he didn't want to admit it, but he was also scared to go down in the tunnels alone because of what he might find: Hazel beaten to a bloody pulp or dead. He bent his head and said a quick prayer of protection for her, his heart hammering in his chest.

Stanley took a deep breath and opened his eyes. "Okay, come on then, Artie. Anino you keep everyone else out. And watch your back."

"You got it, boss." Anino stood tall, holding his fighting sticks, ready for action.

Arthur took a drag on his cigarette, and threw it to the floor. "Let's go."

The boys made their way to the basement stairs of the former brewery. A strong smell of mold wafted from below and grew stronger with each step. Stanley asked, "Is Charles really that good?"

Arthur didn't say anything. "Let's put it this way, Stanny. As much as I want revenge against that snake, I'm shaking in my boots a little. Last time we met, I was afraid I was gonna die."

Stanley nodded as his stomach churned. When they reached the bottom, Arthur took out his metal lighter, flicked it, and light flared in the darkness.

"Can I see that?" Stanley reached over and took it. He held up the flame to find the cave opening. After a few minutes of searching around the large, empty room, they finally found the entrance, blocked with an iron gate and bound with an iron chain and lock.

"Damn it," he said, kicking the gate. Looking closer, he realized the lock was rusted and didn't look to be in very good shape. "Whoever is down there, this isn't the way they came in." Picking up a copper pipe he'd found, Stanley lifted it up to break the lock. Arthur caught his arm.

"Don't. It'll make too much noise," he whispered. He took off his bowler hat, pulled out a hairpin, and knelt in front of the lock.

"Light," he said, and Stanley held the lighter up. After a few minutes of working with the lock, they heard a click, and it came undone.

"See, I ain't all hit first and ask questions later." Arthur grinned.

Stanley nodded as they slowly opened the gate and went into the tunnel. They had to stoop to avoid hitting their heads on the limestone ceiling as they walked. He kept Arthur's lighter in his pocket as they stepped further into utter darkness.

The further they went, the more Stanley tried not to panic. According to just about everyone on the street, there were miles of tunnels. How would they know which was the right one?

He tugged on Arthur's shirt and whispered, "How're we going to find them?"

Arthur gave a low laugh. "I know these tunnels, boss. This is where I found him the first time. Just follow me."

After walking for what seemed like forever, they came to the end of the tunnel. Two paths branched off, one to the right and the other to the left. He could hear low voices echoing through the stone, but he couldn't make out what they were saying.

Arthur turned to Stanley and whispered in his ear. "Both of these tunnels lead to rooms but they all seem to connect. It's a bit of a maze. I'm gonna take the left and you take the right. My guess is that he's holed up like a rat in one of the rooms. You come in one way and I'll come in the other way. Let me distract him and you rescue the girls."

"How are you gonna do that?"

"I dunno. I'll think of something," Arthur said, taking off his bowler hat and wiping his brow.

Stanley gripped his arm. "You're not just doing this to help a couple of swells or to protect me, are you?"

Arthur snorted through his nose and whispered, "You know why I gotta do this, Stanny. I want to stare him in the face as he kicks the bucket. I want him to bleed and suffer for what they did to my family. I want to savor every twitch. And," he poked Stanley's shoulder, "I owe you, pal."

"Killing isn't the answer, Arthur. It will ruin you. Just stop him, that's all." Stanley handed the lighter back to Arthur with a handshake.

His friend leaned in. "I'm already ruined." Without another word, Arthur squeezed Stanley's hand, turned and went down the left tunnel.

Taking a deep breath, Stanley followed the stone tunnel on the right as it angled downwards and to the left. Taking care not to make any noise, he crept along the brick walls. He passed through one room full of old broken barrels, which smelled of damp wood, mildew, and stale beer. Hearing voices, he turned toward a long adjoining room. A dim light flickered at the end, and he heard Hazel cry out, "Please. Please, don't hurt her."

He clenched his fists at the sound of desperation in her voice. Everything in him wanted to burst out to protect her and beat the stuffing out of this freak. But he took a deep breath and steadied himself. *No point in getting her and Sandy killed by being rash*, he thought. He needed to wait for whatever Arthur was going to do. He squatted behind a barrel and searched the darkness. He thought he saw a shadow move across the light.

He closed his eyes and thought; *I'm coming, girl, hold on.*

A male voice, Charles, he guessed, responded, "You've really given me no choice, you know. I had to bring her out here, so you could see. Like the pretty cut on her face? She'll have the scar for life."

"That won't be anything like the one I'm about to give you, Larry." Arthur's voice echoed in the cave. Stanley peeked out and saw his friend emerging from a tunnel entrance about forty-feet to his left, his bowler hat on and cocked to the side. He lit up a cigarette as he stood at the entrance of the tunnel. The flicking light made Arthur's face look like a skull on fire.

Charles replied, "Well, well, if isn't little Artie. How are Mummy and Daddy lately?"

Stanley winced and prayed that Arthur would control his temper.

"Just dandy, Mister Shit Pile." Arthur kept his voice even.

The killer replied, "So, I hear you're a knight. Too bad your new friend Stanley doesn't know you like I do. Remember when I used to play trucks with you in our garden?"

"Yeah, well, our smooching days are over, Larry."

"Stop calling me that."

"Oh, sorry, Larry, don't like to hear the words of your dead girl coming back to you?" Arthur laughed and tossed his cigarette to the ground. "Why don't you make me come shut my gob?"

Arthur backed into the tunnel and disappeared from view. A figure ran over to the entrance and disappeared. Sounds of yelling and the crunching of rock came from the darkness. Stanley wanted to help Arthur, but he didn't have a choice. The girls had to come first.

Taking a deep breath, Stanley crept out into the cave. The Lemps had kept their beer in this room once, but all that was left now were the wooden keg shelves that lined the walls. A few beer barrels occupied some of the cradles. Candles lit one side of the room with a weak, wavering light, as what looked like a bundle of blankets on the far right moved a little. Just as he started forward, he heard Hazel crying from a wooden chair on the other side of the room. He hurried toward her, sidestepping the broken copper pipes, which littered the floor, to avoid making noise. He paused when he thought he heard footsteps.

Stanley took a deep breath. Hazel wept, and he wanted to reach out and soothe her in his arms. He didn't care that she was a swell, didn't care about all the girls who came before her. All he wanted was Hazel and to save her from this hell, so they could go on a real date like a boy and girl should.

Taking out his knife, he walked up quietly behind her watching for any movement in the tunnel, the sounds of Arthur and Charles fighting receding.

Hazel yanked against the ropes that tied her to the chair. "Get away from me!"

Stanley knelt and whispered, "Shh. What's a nice dame like you doing in a place like this?"

Hazel sobbed. "Stanley, thank God. I just knew you would come. I heard you in my head … " She continued to cry.

He wasn't sure what to think of that. "Did he hit you on the melon or something?" Stanley grimaced as he cut through the first two strands.

"I'm not crazy, Snoopy. I'm telling you, I heard you," she babbled in a loud whisper.

He furrowed his brow. What had this psychopath done to her anyway?

"Okay, okay, keep your hair on. I'm trying to cut these ropes," he said, trying to keep his voice calm.

She turned her head, urgent. "Sandy is alive. She's over there. We have to get to her."

Stanley glanced over at what he'd thought was a pile of blankets and made out the form of a girl on the floor, leaning against the wall. She wasn't moving. He swallowed. "We will, Haze. Don't worry. We won't leave without her."

Hazel let out another sob and nodded. "Okay. Okay. I'm so glad you came … and I'm sorry."

Stanley almost dropped his knife. "You're … sorry?"

"I was a beast. Forgive me? You can date whomever you want."

He snorted as he kept cutting through the ropes. "Look, dollface, I'm not sweet on Maggie. I kissed her a couple times, and she's threatening to tell her gramps. But that's over now. She doesn't matter." *No other girl matters.*

How in the world could she yak about all that now? He wanted to tell her how he felt, but he didn't think this was the time or place.

Hazel sniffed back her tears. "Arthur … that was a brave thing he did; will he be okay?"

Stanley furrowed his brow as he sawed through the next rope. The sounds of scuffling and fighting had stopped. Arthur must have led Charles further away. "I don't know, but we've got to make tracks. He did that on purpose, so I could get you."

Finally, he cut through, stood, and put out his hand. "Ready, Bananas?"

Her body shook a little as she took his hand to stand, forcing her to lean on him. "I think the ropes cut off my blood flow."

He squeezed her hand, warm relief flowing through him. "Let's get Sandy and get outta here. Arthur will get out, don't worry. I want to expose these VP nutters, and strip off the veil."

As Hazel stumbled toward her injured friend she said, "Stanley. There are other people here. Boys—I heard voices. Maybe they need—"

"Did you really think your bowler-hatted friend could stop me, Stanley? Do you think that you can really stop the Veiled Prophet and the power of Legion?" Charles's voice cut through the darkness.

Hazel gasped. They whirled to see Charles, a tall black silhouette in the tunnel opening. His dark form seemed to pulse and expand, merging with the shadows. Stanley's stomach dropped when he thought of what may have happened to Arthur. He held on to Hazel and whispered, "Think you can get to Sandy?"

She nodded and started to back away toward the motionless body of her friend.

"Well, considering he hides in the darkness, a little light might do him some good. Maybe he should show his fat, ugly face," Stanley said, rolling up his sleeves.

Charles chuckled as he walked across the floor toward him. "You don't get it, do you, street rat? The Veiled Prophet is faceless. You might expose the man wearing the veil but not the Prophet himself. Another will take his place. You can't defeat the Veiled Prophet because he never really dies. May be a different man, but he never changes. You're a Catholic; think about the Pope. It's never ending. And now the Veiled Prophet's plan is in motion and can't be stopped."

Swallowing hard, Stanley realized he couldn't see out of his left eye at all.

"Yeah, well, my Pope would think you're all wet. He shows his face in public while your Veiled Prophet is a twisted loony who hides behind secrets."

Walking to him with his arms hanging loosely at his sides, Charles didn't seem to have a care in the world.

"You're interesting to me, you know," Charles said, smiling. "It's a real shame that I've got to end you this way. If you weren't so low class, I'd see about taking you on as a student. You're smarter than the others. You're a leader. We've been observing you."

Stanley raised his fists and he bent his knees. "Maybe I can teach you a few things."

Charles crouched into a stance that Stanley had never seen. Before he could even get set, Charles jumped into the air and landed hard on Stanley's leg. Pain exploded in his thigh, forcing him down on one knee. Flipping backwards, Charles landed on his feet, and threw two straight punches at Stanley's face. Both connected, and Stanley staggered back, wiping the blood off. His vision blurred and pain shot through his head. Blinking a few times, he got his balance, launched himself at the killer, and grabbed hold of his arms. Wrestling around, Charles gripped onto Stanley's shirt and tried to bring him down for a head-butt. Spinning away, the shirt tore in half and Charles grinned as he held it up like a trophy.

"Nice moves, Larry," Stanley said through gritted teeth.

Charles let his guard down for just a second and Stanley kicked toward the killer's knee. Connecting, Charles groaned in pain but didn't go down.

"Nice moves, Sir Stanley," he said, mocking him.

He stomped on Stanley's thigh and dug in his heel. Stanley gasped but couldn't move. Blood flowed from his nose and down his chin. He wiped it away with the back of his arm.

"Now, where is that diary?"

"Up your sister's ass," he gasped between breaths full of pain, the taste of blood on his tongue.

A soft scraping sound caught Stanley's attention. He looked around Charles' legs and saw Hazel pick up a copper pipe. She twirled it in the air so fast it looked like a fan as she crept up behind Charles.

"So, this is what you like? Beating people? You should've just come out on the streets instead of kidnapping nice girls. I get into fights all the time," Stanley said, trying to keep Charles' attention away from Hazel.

Charles chuckled. "I don't expect a street rat like you to understand. My whole life, my will is wrapped in him. It is beyond your petty mind and morality."

Stanley smirked. "Well, rich boy, if that's the case, I'll keep my petty mind, thanks. Meanwhile, I wouldn't turn around if I were you."

Charles spun around, and with a lightning-fast twirl, Hazel hit him across the chin with one swipe. Blood flew out of his mouth. The killer stepped back, moaning, but unbowed.

"You little minx. I'm gonna kill you now," he growled.

Trying to stand up, Stanley felt the world spin a little. Every part of his body hurt, but Bananas needed him.

Or did she? As he stumbled toward the battling pair, every kick or punch Charles threw at her, Hazel parried with the copper pipe, spinning and ducking his punches.

Stanley stood still, mouth open. He'd never seen anything so beautiful.

She took a wide swing that threw her off balance; Charles took advantage of it and knocked her to the ground with a leg sweep. Stanley gasped and lurched toward her. Pain shot up his leg and his knees buckled. He fell hard to the dusty, stone floor.

Charles chuckled. "Well, well, the little debutante has some bite. Excellent. Now, I'm gonna use you to make your boyfriend tell me where the diary is, and you'll look much worse than dear, precious Sandy."

As Stanley struggled to get up, someone pushed him down on the ground, leaped over him, and clocked Charles on the head with a copper pipe. The cracking sound bounced off the cave walls. With a groan, the killer went to the ground, and the figure struck him again in the back.

"Now I'm going to bash your head in," Arthur roared.

Stanley got to his feet and stumbled forward. "No, Artie, no. This is not you. Stop."

The pipe wavered in the air, giving Stanley time to stand between his friend and Charles.

"He's not worth it, pal. It won't change anything."

Arthur's face contorted in rage as he yelled, "Ya know what he's done. What he is. He'll just do it again. Let me finish it."

Stanley held up his hands and limped over to his friend. "I won't let you do that, pal. No. You can't." He gripped Arthur's arm and then took away the pipe.

Breathing hard through his nose, Arthur stared at Stanley and then ran off to the opposite end of the room. He disappeared into the darkness.

Chapter Twenty-Two

Hazel stared in horror and relief at what Arthur had done to Charles. He lay unconscious and bleeding on the dusty floor. She dropped the copper pipe, and it clanged to the stone ground, the echo bouncing off the walls.

Stanley shook his head. "He did it. Didn't think he would stop … "

"Should we go after him?" Hazel asked without emotion.

"Nah. Let him be," Stanley said, his voice tired.

Hazel felt the urge to throw up. She swallowed a few times. "Charles can't hurt us anymore," she whispered, trying to calm herself.

Stanley gave a weary smile. "Thanks to you, Bananas. What was all of that anyhow?"

"Baton twirling." Hazel stared down at her hands, not recognizing them. It had just happened, as if her hands knew what to do and didn't need her at all.

Stanley gave a weak laugh, still watching her. "Wouldn't have believed it if I hadn't seen it."

"Ye of little faith," Hazel said, a faint smile on her face. She was dizzy, and everything seemed suddenly ridiculous. The mad impulse to laugh rose inside her, but she fought it. Her teeth chattered, and her whole body felt frozen.

Stanley crawled over to the body of the killer. "Haze—get me the rope."

Like a robot, Hazel picked up the rope that had tied her to the chair and tossed it at Stanley. As he bound Charles' hands and feet together, Hazel watched, her heart still pounding; nothing felt real.

She turned to see Sandy, slumped against one wall, her hands bound together and not moving where Charles had dragged her. Hazel stared, momentarily afraid to see if Sandy was dead or alive. She grabbed a candle off one of the barrels and went to her. "Sandy, it's me, Hazel."

Her friend didn't respond. In the flickering light, Hazel examined her. Dried blood caked around her nose and smeared across her cheeks. It looked as if her nose might be broken. A fresh cut oozed down one side of her face. Both eyes were blackened and swollen. Hazel cringed and blinked back tears. One arm seemed to bend at an odd angle and there were bruises on Sandy's throat. It was awful; he'd given her the works. Who knew what else had happened to her. Hazel was relieved to see her friend's chest rise and fall with shallow breaths. She was out cold.

"Son of a—" Stanley whispered, at Hazel's side now. "Gimme that pipe and I'll finish what Arthur started," he said, staring at Sandy.

It was bad, but what would have happened to them both if Stanley and Arthur had not shown up? Hazel's whole body trembled. She fumbled to untie Sandy's hands, fresh tears flowing down her cheeks. "It's going to be okay, Sandy," she hiccupped. "Stitches … she'll need … We have to get her to a doctor. Now."

Stanley didn't answer. Hazel turned to see him hunkering on the ground, his eyes squeezed shut in pain. He opened them and tried to smile at her. "We'll get her fixed up. Don't worry."

Hazel's heart squeezed. She grabbed the battered newsie and hugged him, pressing her face into his neck.

"Stanley," she choked out.

"You're okay now, Haze. I gotcha." He pulled back and winced. Blood tricked down his forehead and nose. His face was a beat up but beautiful sight.

"No. I got you," she breathed.

"You had me worried something awful." He touched her cheek. "Let's get outta this place."

"Yes, please." Hazel wiped her tears, a little embarrassed at her outburst. "B-but Sandy, we can't leave her down here with that, that monster."

Stanley looked back over his shoulder. "He can't touch her now. And I can't carry her out. We'll send someone back for her right away." He winced in pain as he moved.

Hazel nodded. "Okay." It felt wrong to leave her there in the dark with her torturer, but they didn't have a choice. Stanley would need her help to walk and she couldn't carry Sandy by herself. At least her friend wasn't awake and wouldn't know. Hazel looked over at Charles. Stanley had tied him up like a calf at a rodeo. He wasn't going anywhere.

"Follow me," Stanley ordered. "It's a maze."

A shudder ran over Hazel's body. How far into hell had she been dragged? Stanley hobbled a few steps and made a hissing sound through his teeth. He had to be in a lot of pain.

"You okay?" Hazel steadied him with one hand on his back when he wobbled.

"He knocked me on the head and my leg." His voice shook with the effort of walking.

Hazel grabbed one of his arms and put it over her shoulders, encouraging him to use her as a crutch. His arm was hot and damp with sweat on the back of her neck, but she didn't care.

"Thanks, Bananas." He leaned some of his weight on her, and as weak as she felt, Hazel propped him up. They stumbled their way through the cave and turned into a dark tunnel. Stanley's breathing became increasingly ragged as they went. But when Hazel tried to stop to let him rest, he grunted and continued forward.

Focusing on putting one foot in front of the other, Hazel tried to ignore thoughts of everything that had just happened. But the more they wound through the darkness, the more Hazel realized how close she'd been to death, isolated in this place so far from the light, in the clutches of a madman. It reminded her of stories she'd heard of how alligators killed their prey, dragging them down, down, away from the surface of the water and rolling them around, playing with them until they died. The image of that terrified her and a sob escaped her mouth. She hiccupped and cried as they walked, her shoulders shaking.

"It's okay, Haze. It's all over. We did it." Stanley's voice was gentle.

Had they done it? They had survived, and they had caught Evelyn's killer, but it was only the beginning. The chilling things Charles had said would always haunt her. She could never go back to life the way it was. Even if they had stopped Charles, there was still the Winnowing. Hazel shivered. With Stanley at her side, Hazel felt safer for now—but they couldn't lean on one another forever. This was far from over.

They wove through empty tunnels, the decaying wooden barrels, copper piping, and rusting machinery abandoned and useless now, like the Forgotten Man whom FDR talked about—men left to rot because nobody needed them for the work they used to do.

Shouts came from ahead, and Hazel saw the entrance of the cave. Her heart sped up with relief and anxiety. Who was out there? They passed through an old metal gate and struggled up some steps into the glare of bright lights.

"This isn't the way I came in," Stanley said.

Hazel looked at Stanley, just grateful to be out of the darkness. In the light, she saw his battle wounds and noticed Stanley's bare chest where his shirt had been torn away. There was a tattoo there—a heart on fire. Blue flames spread across the left side of his chest. She reached out to touch it, and their eyes met. Her own heart did a little flip, and Stanley gave her a small roguish smile.

"Step away from the girl, and hold your hands up!" somebody shouted.

Hazel startled, afraid of what new mess they had stumbled into. Stanley groaned and removed his arm from Hazel's shoulders. Losing contact with him, Hazel had a moment of panic, and she gripped his arm. "Don't let me go."

"Take is easy, Bananas. I'm not going anywhere," he whispered. He gently pried her hands from his arm.

"Miss, you okay? You Hazel Malloy?" one cop called out.

She turned to face the voices. "Yes, I'm fine." Hazel was blinded by the headlights of a few automobiles pointed at the entrance of the caves. It was night, and there were several men standing around.

"Back away from her and put your mitts where I can see them," another voice called out.

Two policemen approached, one pointing a gun at Stanley. He raised his hands over his head. "Okay, fellas. Okay."

Hazel glared at them, wanting to step in front of him. Instead, she grabbed onto his shirt with one hand as if that would somehow protect them both.

"Say, it's Stanny," said the fat policeman with the big mustache.

The tall, skinny cop with the oversized chin squinted at Stanley and lowered his gun. "Hey, Seamus," he yelled over his shoulder. "It's your scoundrel of a nephew!"

A small, wiry man with red hair shoved his way past the other two. "Step aside, Laurel and Hardy," he muttered. When he saw Stanley, he grimaced. He eyed Hazel and raised his brows. "Ya okay, then, boyo?"

Hazel let go of Stanley. She was so tired, and her body hurt, but she was embarrassed to seem helpless.

"Yeah." Stanley nodded, but he looked like he might cry. He swallowed and held up his chin in defiance. One eye was swollen shut, and his bottom lip was split open and bleeding.

The red-haired man let out a sob of relief and grabbed Stanley in both arms. "Foolish boy. I've got half a mind to give ya a lickin' myself. I thought you'd be killed—"

"Ouch … I'm aces, Uncle Seamus. I'm fine." He hugged the man and then pulled back. "But Sandy Schmidt needs help," he said with a shaky voice. "You're gonna need a stretcher to get her outta there; she can't walk. And the bastard who done it and killed Evelyn is in there too, tied up like a Christmas present."

Seamus looked at Hazel. "Good to see ya in one piece, Miss. We'll get ya patched up."

There was a flurry of activity as more policemen swarmed the entrance of the cave and sirens announced the arrival of an ambulance. Hazel blinked back tears, and she reached over to grab Stanley's shirt again. He glanced over at her, and they locked eyes for a long, silent moment. The chaos around them blurred. His eyes were the one stillness in that moment. Blue anchors that pinned her in place and kept her from coming apart.

Several policemen came and went asking questions, but Hazel hardly remembered what she said. It was like déjà vu, standing there with Stanley again, swarmed by the police. The lights from the squad car slanted across the tall boy beside her.

Stanley seemed to wilt as the minutes passed. He was worn out and had endured a beating. Hazel took his hand and held it tight. She felt pretty worn out herself. A paramedic looked at them both, shining a flashlight in her eyes. He asked some questions about their injuries and then taped some gauze to her forehead. The man in white spent more time with Stanley and then walked over to talk to Seamus.

"I ain't going in that meat wagon," Stanley said to his uncle as he approached.

"You need it, boyo. Ya look like you been thrown into a meat grinder."

"Time for that later; I wanna see Haze home first."

At that moment two men carrying a stretcher, flanked by several officers, emerged from the caves.

"I'm not going home. I want to make sure Sandy is okay." Hazel let go of Stanley's hand and rushed over to where they loaded her friend into the back of the ambulance. She had a brief glimpse of Sandy, battered and still unconscious before her view was blocked.

"Stand back," one man in white said as he closed the doors.

Hazel clapped a hand over her mouth. Tears stung her eyes.

Seamus was at her side. "Sorry, Miss. Don't ya worry now. Your friend is in good hands. Your parents will be eager to have ya back safe. Let's get ya home and then I'll take your official statements."

Hazel bit her lip. She wanted to follow Sandy to the hospital, but Seamus was right, she had to get home. All at once, she felt drained. Stanley appeared beside her and put his hand on her back.

"You can see her first thing tomorrow, Haze. It will be all right," his voice soothed.

"Okay. And will you go in and get looked at too?" She reached up and softly touched his swollen eye.

He let out a sigh and nodded. "Later. I promise."

Seamus examined them both and shook his head. He glanced at Stanley's bare chest and shrugged out of his jacket, handing it to him. "Put this on, will ya?"

Stanley grinned. "Wouldn't want to stir up Lindell," he said, putting the jacket on and giving Hazel a wink. She blushed.

Seamus ushered them toward one of the squad cars. Nobody spoke much as they drove to Lindell. Hazel stared out the window at the streets teemed with people going about their night as if nothing had happened. Her whole world had changed. Even when they pulled into the driveway of her home, it just seemed like a big empty house instead of a place of refuge. No place felt safe now. Charles had been in her house; any of *them* could get in whenever they wanted, disguised as decent, refined citizens and friends.

"Almost there, Miss. Your folks have been beside themselves with worry," Seamus said.

How strange that she'd hardly thought of them while going through that ordeal. She'd thought of Sandy, Peggy, and Stanley, but her parents had only been a passing thought—that they'd be sad if she died but upset by the scandal most of all. Hazel wondered if they would have been devastated at all. In her heart, she hoped so.

Stanley limped beside her on one side and Seamus on the other as they approached the large front doors of her house. Stanley leaned close to her ear and said under his breath, "Don't mention the diary."

Hazel nodded. After what Charles had said about the Veiled Prophet not having a face, she realized they couldn't trust anyone. And it was not as simple as finding out who the Veiled Prophet was; he was Legion.

Hazel started when a figure darted out of the shadows and stood near the porch. The small red glow of a cigarette lit up Arthur's face as he stood with his arms crossed.

"Say, who's that?" Seamus narrowed his eyes.

"A friend of mine," Stanley said.

Stanley flashed a hand sign; when Arthur flashed a couple back, Stanley nodded. Arthur removed his bowler hat and bowed slightly. Hazel shivered when Arthur turned his dark eyes on her just before he slipped back into the night. She couldn't erase the image of his fury as he'd attacked Charles. Arthur didn't like her, but it was clear he was loyal to Stanley, which might be the only reason Arthur hadn't wrung her neck by now.

Hazel linked arms with Stanley as he hobbled up to the front porch. Seamus opened the door for them, and they entered. The familiar smell of polished wood and flowers greeted Hazel. It felt as if she hadn't been here in months.

"Why, I'll be. Get a load of this palace." Stanley looked around him and removed his cap.

Hazel saw the marble statues, shining wood floor, high ceiling, and chandelier with new eyes. "Home sweet home," she whispered.

"My baby!" Mumsy dashed down the staircase, a pink satin cape flapping behind her. Hazel had never seen her mother like this. Her hair was a mess, and she had cried off all her makeup. There were black streaks down her cheeks, and lipstick was smeared across her face. She never looked this mussed even after a bender.

Crushed in her mother's arms, Hazel felt every ache and pain in her body from the day's ordeal. Mumsy's perfume was comforting. "Mumsy," she whispered, tears rolling down her cheeks.

Hazel's mom pulled back and searched her face with wide, wet eyes. "What did he do to you?" She traced a hand across Hazel's forehead and down one side of her face. "I was so afraid … "

Hazel had no idea what she must look like, but her mother's fingertips were smudged with blood from touching her.

"Ma'am, your daughter has been injured but she seems to be all right," Seamus said.

The deep voice of Nicholas Malloy echoed in the large foyer. "Thank God."

Hazel's father came toward her, the top buttons of his shirt undone, and his tie pulled out slack around his neck. His dark bangs hung loose over his forehead rather than slicked back. His face tense with emotion, he pulled her into his arms. He smelled of pipe tobacco and safety. Hazel couldn't remember the last time Pops had hugged her, and it made her heart ache.

After several minutes of hugging and grateful sobs between Hazel and her folks, they all went into the parlor and sat while Hazel and Stanley recounted how they'd made their escape from the Lemp caves.

"I want to thank you, young man. You saved my daughter," Nicholas Malloy said in a strained voice, leaning forward in his chair.

"She's my friend," Stanley said as if it were no big deal. "Besides, she saved me in return; you should've seen her twirling her baton of death."

"I couldn't be prouder," Hazel's father said, smiling at her a little sadly.

"That's my girl," Mumsy said, wiping away more tears. "Horrid things like this make you think, you know?"

Hazel had forgotten about this side of her parents. The soft side she recalled from her younger days.

Her father nodded. "Yes. It makes you examine the important things." He looked at his daughter as if he might cry.

Hazel's insides warmed. Of course she knew her parents loved her; they just weren't big on compliments and were too busy being adults. She wiped fresh tears away and nodded.

Seamus and her father had more questions. Hazel and Stanley left out the details about the diary, but when they mentioned that Charles said he worked for the Veiled Prophet, Seamus interrupted.

"He sounds like a nutter. The Veiled Prophet is just a symbol." Seamus shrugged in dismissal.

"Then why do you think he did it? You think he killed Evelyn for kicks? And then he grabbed Sandy and Hazel on a lark?" Stanley glowered. "Open your eyes, man. You cops are looking the other way and ignoring evidence. Don't you see there is something going on here?"

Seamus stared at Stanley, a grim look on his face. "Listen, boyo, we have no evidence to connect that crazy Chouteau boy to the VP, see? Maybe there is something to it, but we can't just make claims like that based on the ranting of a lunatic."

Nicholas Malloy cleared his throat. "The people this would implicate are very important and very powerful."

Hazel waited to hear the lecture about how one doesn't simply malign prominent people who are upstanding citizens. The cream of the crop will not tolerate slander.

But her father continued, "You'll need proof before going public with it." He stroked his mustache in thought. "It's like stomping through the brush when you hunt pheasant—you have to wait until your gun is loaded, cocked, and at the ready before scaring them from hiding and making them take flight or you'll miss your mark."

Seamus and Hazel's father exchanged a knowing look. Mumsy blew her nose into a handkerchief and said, "Then it's our little secret until the right moment." She leveled her gaze at Seamus. "And then we'll make them all pay for what they've done." Mumsy's voice was like ice, though the next moment it was champagne. "Besides, secrets are much more fun." She smiled at the others, and they nodded.

Hazel didn't know her mother in that moment; it was as if a mask had slipped and she was a flapper again. Both of her parents seemed different somehow.

Stanley looked at Hazel. "I think they're right: whatever this is, it's big. And if you really did hear boys' voices in that cave, maybe you aren't the only one taken by these people. We have to be smart about this."

"Don't trust anyone outside this room with what you just told us," Seamus said.

Hazel shivered. "They know who we are. How can Stanley and I ever go anywhere?"

Mumsy covered her mouth, eyes wide. Hazel's father played with his mustache, thinking. "No … they dare not bother you. Not now. Evelyn's murder and two kidnappings were perpetrated by a man who is now in custody. It would raise too many questions if the two kids who found the body and took down the man who did it were to suddenly come to harm. You're local celebrities now, or will be as soon as this hits the papers."

"They will watch and wait." Seamus nodded.

"So, we act like we know nothing?" Stanley asked.

Hazel hated the idea that maybe they would be watched or followed. But if they kept the diary hidden and she could successfully play the debutante, maybe the Veiled Prophet would not see her as a threat. After all, the Veiled Prophet had no evidence that Hazel and Stanley knew anything past the fact that Charles was a psychopathic nut.

"So, we just act like none of this happened?" Hazel stared at the swirling pattern of the Persian rug on the floor. She just wanted to go to bed and not think anymore.

"We'll figure this out. Together," Hazel's father said.

She sighed and leaned against her mother. "Okay," Hazel said. Mumsy put an arm around her and gave her a soft squeeze.

The weight of it all seemed so heavy, but an unspoken pact bound the room in silence; Hazel knew she wouldn't bear this alone. Still, everything had changed.

Stanley straightened his hat in the mirror and put on his new sport coat, a gift from Mr. Malloy. "I want you looking nice if you're going to escort my daughter to the ballgame," he'd said. At first, Stanley wanted to refuse, but Hazel had said, "Don't be a donkey. He's showing you how much he thinks of you. And anyway, there's not a thing wrong with looking good."

He smiled. Only she could talk him into looking like a swell. Still, he had to admit, the black jacket did look aces. Too bad his face didn't. The bruise on his forehead had begun to yellow and blacken along with the other war wounds on his body. A week since the caves, he still felt every ache and pain.

Still, he was going to game three of the World Series with Hazel, Sandy, and the Knights, another gift from Mr. Malloy. He'd gotten them tickets behind home plate. Stanley smiled at the thought of the swells staring at the kids they'd been reading about in the papers. No doubt, the Veiled Prophet's people would be watching. Chuckling to himself, he remembered what Arthur had said: "Anything to rub their nose in their own mess."

He limped downstairs and found Seamus in his dressing robe, sipping coffee and listening to the news on the radio.

"Well, look at you, boyo, regular Park Avenue swell."

Stanley frowned. "Not funny."

His uncle smiled and rubbed his wild uncombed hair. "Ah, just taking the mickey, ya look good. Wish your ma and da could see you."

Stanley furrowed his brow.

"I still have questions for you about my folks. Why all the secrets?"

Seamus paused. "To protect you."

"From what? Legion?"

"You've seen from what, so don't be stupid. Your ma and da were mixed up in this same stuff that you've gone and poked your Irish nose into. Peggy was a part of that. She fought with them. Ah well, the fat is in the fire now. Let's just hope we all don't get burned."

Stanley wrinkled his forehead. "So, my mom didn't just up and leave? And my dad didn't die fighting the English?"

Seamus looked at his pocket watch. "Your dad died, and it broke your ma's heart. Ya better get movin' if you're gonna pick up Hazel. I get the impression Mr. Malloy don't like late boys."

Stanley frowned. "This isn't over, Seamus."

His uncle took a long sip of his coffee and stared back at him. "No, boyo, not by a long shot. It's just beginning. And it'll be the grace of our Lord if we all survive it. But you saved an innocent man from ole sparky. That's something."

The ballplayer had come by two days ago and thanked Stanley. After a brief conversation, Paul had told them he planned to quit baseball, head out west, and go into his cousin's furniture business.

Shrugging, Stanley said, "I guess I did."

Seamus smiled. "No guessing, Stanley. Now, go, before you're late. Don't keep Nicholas Malloy waiting."

Stanley left and got lost in his thoughts as he walked to Hazel's. He couldn't ignore his uncle's words. Still, he, Hazel, and the Knights would be ready. They'd already done more than anyone thought they could. That had to mean something.

When he got to the gate, he found it open and walked right up to the door. Knocking lightly, Stanley waited until Roberts answered.

"Heya, Roberts, how's things?"

"Welcome, Master Stanley. Hazel is finishing getting ready; I'm to take you to the parlor."

"She isn't ready? What's the matter?"

Roberts gave him a thin smile. "You have a lot to learn about ladies, Master Stanley."

The butler led him into the parlor where he found Mrs. Malloy all done up in a green feathery dress sitting on a couch, sipping wine. Peggy was dusting the furniture and gave him a nod.

"Stanley! Don't you look dashing? The coat fits you, I see. Nicky can be so fussy about those things. Come, please sit. Hazel will be down in just a minute," Mrs. Malloy said with a big smile.

He took off his hat, bowed, and said, "With pleasure, my lady," and sat on the couch next to her.

Mrs. Malloy giggled. "Such a gentleman, don't you think, Peggy?"

Peggy gave her a broad smile. "To be sure. No wonder Miss Hazel fancies him so."

Stanley felt the heat rush to his cheeks.

Glancing around, Mrs. Malloy lowered her voice. "Better keep that to ourselves. Mr. Malloy is still getting used to them being friends." She grabbed Stanley's hand. "I'm so glad you are Hazel's beau."

Stanley stammered. "Er, um, we aren't—"

"Mumsy, leave Stanley alone. He's nervous as it is."

He looked up to see Hazel float into the room, wearing a white sundress and a ridiculous green hat with her blue eyes glowing. She looked triple aces, and he couldn't talk.

Stanley stood and stared, unable to say anything. She gave him a slow smile. "Cat got your tongue, Sir Snoopy?"

He cleared his throat and bowed. "Apologies, Lady Bananas, I think I'm still a bit foggy from the blow to my head."

Hazel beamed. "Or you're just being yourself."

Sandy stepped from behind Hazel, wearing a black dress and a simple black hat. "Hello, Stanley."

He looked her over and his smile faltered. Her wounds looked okay; the doctor did a good job sewing her up. But, there was something else there, a vacantness, he'd seen that look plenty of times in the slums. Broken.

A German shepherd puppy bounded into the room, followed by Mr. Malloy. The dog ran right to Stanley and leaped up on him. He laughed. "And who is this little fella?"

Hazel laughed. "That's Henri, the dog Daddy bought for me last night. He said that if I'm going to insist on going out by myself, I should have some sort of protection when you're not around."

Nicholas strolled over and shook Stanley's hand. "I have no idea where she got the name. French names are no names for dogs."

Stanley shot a glance at Hazel who gave him a slight smile.

Huh. She named the dog after her hat, the one that brought them together.

"All right, you three better get going. Are the other boys going to meet you there?" Mr. Malloy asked.

"Yeah, most of them still had to sell newspapers yet this morning. I took the day off."

They went outside where a fancy black car was waiting for them. An old man got out to open the door, but Stanley stopped him. "That's all right, I can get a door for myself."

Stanley had only agreed to the car ride to the game if they could take the trolley back. Mr. Malloy only agreed after Mrs. Malloy had told him not to be a pill.

He opened the door for Hazel and Sandy, who climbed in. Stanley followed, seating himself next to Hazel. Hazel's leg pressed against his, and she didn't move it. Breathing in her sweet perfume, he didn't know if he would be able to concentrate on the game.

As the car pulled out of the estate, Sandy said, "He's not going to suffer for what he did, is he? I want him to, you know. I want him to suffer."

Hazel glanced at Stanley and then back at Sandy and said, "Who do you mean?"

"Charles. Daddy read in the paper today how his lawyers are saying he's insane. They want to send him to a private loony bin. Said all his crazy ranting, they didn't say what about, proves that."

Stanley swallowed hard. "They won't go for that. The coppers have all the stuff they need."

Sandy turned to him, eyes blazing. "Haven't you been paying attention? Don't you get it? Hazel knows. Charles will never see the electric chair. At worst, he'll spend the rest of his life in some comfy mental ward in the country. No matter what he did to me and Evelyn, these people will never lose."

Stanley opened his mouth to say something sharp, but Hazel touched his arm. She took her friend's hand and said, "Let's not think about him now, okay? We don't know what's going to happen."

Sandy slumped into her seat and stared out of the window. Glancing at Stanley, Hazel pressed her leg tighter against his.

Yeah, he thought, *not like other dames*. Every little thing was magic.

Finally, they arrived at Sportsman's Park where the rest of the Knights waited at the main gate. Shuffles had his arm in a sling, but he was doing a dance for a gathered crowd. Jakob was reading a newspaper while Anino talked with Arthur, who stood a bit to the side smoking a cigarette.

Stanley got out and helped the ladies onto the sidewalk. As they walked up, all the Knights smiled at them except for Arthur, who took a long drag on his cigarette and stared at Sandy.

"Hazel, this is aces! I ain't never sat behind home plate before," Shuffles said, taking her hand and kissing it.

"Easy, there, boy," Stanley said without thinking.

All of them walked through the gate, gave their tickets to the usher, and made their way inside. Sandy offered to buy them all hot dogs and lemonade. As they all got their food, Vinnie came up to Stanley and Hazel.

"Oh, uh, hey, Hazel, this is Vinnie," Stanley said.

Vinnie nodded, and Hazel smiled. "Thank you for telling Stanley about the caves. I owe you my life."

Vinnie blushed a little and said, "Wasn't nothin'. Glad to do it." He shrugged. "I gots another message for you from the Raven. Don't want to tell you here."

Arthur came over and gave Vinnie a cold stare.

"Just you two, if you don't mind." Vinnie motioned to a spot behind the concession stand.

Stanley nodded to Arthur. "Take everyone to their seats. Try not to sneer at any swells until we get there, got it?"

Arthur nodded without saying anything as he gave Vinnie a final glare. He walked back over to the Knights and Sandy.

Vinnie shook his head. "I don't get it. Why do you keep that guy around?"

Stanley shrugged. "I have my reasons. Now, let's go over here, and you can spill it."

When they got to the corner of the concession stand, Vinnie lowered his voice. "The Raven wants to say he's going to have to do something about how you took out his boys."

Stanley set his jaw. "Well, if doing something means sending us more of his rats to beat up, I'm not worried."

Vinnie rolled his eyes. "He also wants you to know, our gang has been asked to keep an eye on both of you at all times."

"By whom?" Hazel asked, hand over her mouth.

"Can't tell you. I don't even know. The Raven won't say. But he did say that all of this is big. Very big. Scary big. He don't like where it's all going."

Stanley frowned. "Gee, that's big of him. But he's still gonna follow us around."

Vinnie shook his head. "I dunno, Stanley, but we ain't the only ones who'll be watching. He's gotta do it. They ain't givin' him much choice. Besides, there are others. New people are on the streets. Ain't never seen them around before."

"What do they look like?" Hazel asked, gripping Stanley's arm.

Frowning, Vinnie said, "Ain't what they look like. They blend in, and you'd never notice if you didn't know what to look for. They look like they're from Europe or somethin'."

Stanley waved his hand. "Immigrants. We get those all the time."

Vinnie shook his head. "Nah. Ain't like that. These people, men and women, goin' around asking a bunch of funny questions, educated types, no poor dumb beasts off the boat. Seems random, but put together, it all adds up."

"What are they asking?" Hazel asked, frowning.

"Weird stuff, like health, work status, and all that."

Stanley glanced at Hazel who nodded. "I bet it has something to do with the Winnowing. But what does that have to do with us?"

Vinnie frowned. "Dunno for sure. But the Raven says act, pretend, and don't let on you know you're being watched."

Hazel nodded. "I'll try. I suppose fear is a great motivator to get good at something. They'll be watching me the most, anyway."

"You'll get it." Stanley nodded.

They heard the announcer start to list the starting lineups. "We better go, or we'll miss it. Can't be late for my first game," Hazel said with a smile.

Stanley turned to walk with her to the seats when Vinnie said, "Stanny boy, one more thing, gotta just tell you."

Hazel frowned.

"It's okay, go sit with the fellas and Sandy. I'll be right there."

She walked a few steps, turned her head, and gave him a small smile. Stanley watched her go.

"Ain't no good, Stanny. Remember what I told you? She's like a piece of art. They ain't gonna let you take her out of the museum."

Frowning, Stanley said, "She's high class in her heart and in her head, but she isn't an object to be gawked at."

Vinnie rolled his eyes. "Listen, pal, I'm tellin' you, these rich folks, they ain't gonna like you takin' one of their own, get me?"

Stanley looked at his friend and smiled. "I get you. We're just friends." There was no way he was going to admit to Vinnie what he felt about Hazel.

Sighing, Vinnie said, "For a guy who's kissed a lot of dames, you're sure stupid." He looked up when the crowd started to roar. "I got to get to the scoreboard. Too bad your lazy butt won't be up there. It'll be the best view in the house."

Smiling, Stanley said, "I get to watch from behind home plate with a pretty girl. Think I win."

They slapped each other on the back, and Vinnie walked away. Stanley didn't want to think about Vinnie's warning or any of the rest of it. Not today. He'd rather think about being at the World Series with Hazel.

Hazel didn't want to think about gangs, murder, the Veiled Prophet, or any of the rest of that business today. She just wanted to spend some time with Stanley that wasn't about life and death. Just a boy and a girl at a ballgame with their friends. But it was hard to forget all that had happened. Stanley had filled her in on some of the things he had learned from the diary. The Winnowing was some kind of sorting out, but not the kind life did on its own, like what Pops had talked about. No. It reminded her more of things that Father Timothy had said about people playing God.

Hazel sat in her seat staring at the ball field, trying to shake the tickly feeling of being watched. She'd never seen a game before. Sometimes her dad listened on the radio, but this was new. Some of the players were out, throwing the ball around. They were a ratty looking bunch, but they were fun to watch. There was something satisfying about the thump of the ball landing squarely in a leather glove. The sun warmed Hazel's skin as a slight breeze played in her hair. She sipped her lemonade and closed her eyes, taking a deep breath. Although she hadn't slept well since her trip to hell, Hazel was lifted by the excitement of the crowd and the smell of popcorn and cut grass.

It was swell of her dad to get tickets for the gang. Lately, Hazel's folks had paid more attention to her than any other time she could remember. Even Mumsy stayed in at night to listen to radio programs and play cards rather than her usual round of wild clambakes. Hazel noticed that Pops spent less time in the office and more time staring at his wife. Grownups were weird. But it sure felt good. Even if things were uncertain, at least there were a few pluses to come out of the mess.

"Say, this is gonna be a scream. It's a lovely day," Hazel said, determined to be sunny despite the cloud that hung over them.

Sandy sat beside Hazel, lost in her own head. "Yeah," she mumbled, picking at her hot dog.

Her pretty face was mottled with purple and green bruises; a red scar stitched in black ran down the right side of her face, and one arm was in a sling. Most of the swelling around her eyes had gone down, but Sandy was barely recognizable as the girl she'd been. A bob with bangs replaced her long, wavy, honey hair. Her gaze never really focused on anybody anymore but seemed to look past everyone to some unknown place, a place that cast a shadow over her once bright, golden eyes. She didn't say much about their time in the caves when they were together. Hazel missed her smile.

Earlier that week had been Evelyn's funeral. The Schmidt family swam in a pool of misery. All the bouquets of flowers and fake friends did nothing to comfort them. It infuriated Hazel how many people didn't bother to show, afraid to come into contact with so much disgrace and scandal. But Stanley and his Knights had come, dressed in their best, hair combed, and faces washed. All except Arthur, who waited outside the church and at the edges of the cemetery.

Hazel looked over at the fellas. They were good boys. Anino, Shuffles, and Jakob were over the moon about their "fancy-pants seats." Somehow, they found a way to be jolly no matter how tough their lives were. They felt like big stuff being in the papers as the pack of kids who helped rescue the two kidnapped socialites.

From the corner of her eye, Hazel saw Arthur watching her and Sandy with narrowed eyes. She shivered. He leaned forward in his seat, cigarette hanging out of the side of his mouth and bowler hat cocked at an angle. Everything about him was off kilter. The dark Knight dug into his pocket and took something out. Hazel flinched when he shoved a scabby fist at Sandy.

Sandy turned and the two of them locked eyes. She lifted her open hand, and Arthur dropped something shiny into it.

Evelyn's ring.

Hazel jumped a little in her seat. *How'd he get his hands on that?* She was afraid to even ask. Arthur blew a plume of smoke to the side and sat back as if nothing had happened.

Sandy stared into her hand for several moments then closed her fist around the Veiled Prophet's gift to her dead sister.

Hazel touched her friend's knee. "Sandy?"

Sandy's hard eyes glossed over with tears, but she shook her head and tightened her lips. She was not going to talk about it.

"Hey, dollface, is this seat free or do you have a hat buying you popcorn?" Stanley plopped down beside her with a goofy smile on his face. He looked handsome in his new coat.

Hazel sighed. "Actually, it's reserved for somebody named No Good Bum. That you?"

"In the flesh." He shifted his cap and handed her a pretzel

wrapped in paper.

"Thanks," she chirped, her heart skipping. "These are the tops."

Stanley gave her a wink, biting into his own pretzel.

"Stanley Fields." The blond girl Hazel had seen him with before stood in the aisles, hands on her hips.

Bananas.

"How do you do?" His bright blue eyes widened, but he gave a casual nod.

"Don't 'how do you do' me!" Margaret glared daggers at Hazel. "What are ya doin' down here with the swells? Grampy won't like that you ain't at the scoreboard."

"Hm. You may be right. Vinnie not up there?" He made a show of looking confused.

The blond shrugged. "Guess you'd better get up there. Come with me." She let her scowl relax, and she licked her lips.

Hazel felt like her nails grew an inch. She fought not to make a face and took another bite of her pretzel. Hazel didn't like the idea of Stanley going off with that girl.

"See here, Maggie, it's my day off." Stanley rested his feet on the seat in front of him. "Relax."

"I see." She turned to Hazel. "Say, who are you anyway?"

She swallowed the bite she'd been chewing. "Hazel Malloy, and you are?"

"I'm Stanny's girl, Margaret Seable. You begin to see the picture?" She crossed her arms, an accusing tone in her voice. "Stanny and I had a date; he was supposed to take me dancing."

"Sorry about that." He cleared his throat and bounced his knee. He was in a fix. Stanley and his dames. What a silly boy.

"Sorry, huh?" the blond huffed.

Shuffles gave him a sock in the arm and said under his breath, "You never learn, do ya?"

Hazel raised her voice to the angry pin-up girl. "I suppose that's my fault. He was busy rescuing me from a murderer," she deadpanned.

The Knights snickered. Stanley pressed his lips together, fighting a smile.

Margaret was unfazed. "Every day?" She sneered. "Well, I guess my grampy won't like what I have to tell him about you, you bum."

After a moment Stanley stood. "Can I talk to you, alone?"

She grinned. "Sure."

Hazel fidgeted while the two headed up the bleachers to talk. After a while, Margaret flounced off with an angry expression on her face. Stanley returned to his seat his cheeks flushed.

Stanley sunk into his seat while his Knights taunted him.

"You're in for it now, boyo."

"Sucker born every minute in Dogtown."

"Way to go, Casanova."

"I had to come clean and lay it out for her. I should have from the beginning," he said.

Hazel smiled, her heart warming.

Sandy shook her head. "Fellas. Can't trust any of them," she said under her breath.

Hazel knew why Sandy felt that way. Charles had fooled them all. It made her a little nervous that maybe you never really knew anyone. Maybe everyone was a fake. But Stanley always seemed so familiar and so real.

"Whew. That was no picnic," he muttered.

She didn't know what to think about Stanley and his dames. But when they were together, she never got the feeling he was pining to be someplace else. "I suppose that's what you get for your wild ways." She wagged a finger at him.

He sat up straight and ran his hands over his new coat. "Do I still look too wild, Bananas?" Their blue eyes met, almost like a reflection of one another. He smiled at her. It was beautiful.

"I see the real you under all of that, boy," she said, scrunching up her nose at him.

Stanley chuckled. "I don't doubt it."

Hazel relaxed into her seat, filling with an unnamed hope. "She certainly is a looker. Why didn't you take her dancing, anyway?"

Stanley didn't say anything, just shifted his cap. Then he took Hazel's hand in his, as the Cardinals ran out on the field to start the game.

"You really gonk me. You know that, Bananas?"

Heat spread through Hazel's body, and she smiled. "Silly boy."

A crackle came over the speakers and the familiar nasal voice she'd heard on the radio said, "Before we sing our national anthem, let's all take a moment of silence in honor one of the Cardinal's own, Paul Duncan. It seems the tragic turn his life took was too much for him. He was found this morning, drowned in the Mississippi. God rest his soul."

Sandy gasped beside Hazel and the stadium hushed.

"Those dirty, rotten, rats … " Arthur breathed.

Paul hadn't gotten away. Or maybe he had, the only way he could. Hazel's heart raced. "Stanley, do you suppose … ?"

Stanley shook his head. "That was no suicide." His knee bounced up and down, nervous.

Hazel's body trembled. "We're next." She felt like crawling out of her skin. Suddenly everyone in the crowd seemed sinister.

Stanley turned to look her in the eyes. "Listen, he was up to his neck in all of this. Now remember what your dad said: they can't touch us right now. They don't know what we know, and it would just cause trouble for them." His blue gaze steadied her.

She swallowed and forced herself to breathe. "Are you sure?" she whispered.

"Yeah." He nodded and gave her a small smile.

Hazel searched his eyes. "Okay, Snoopy," she said. "Just stay close, huh?"

"You got it, Bananas. I'm not leaving you in the lurch. I'm in this with you."

Hazel nodded. The swelling of the national anthem seemed to a call to arms. She and this ragtag group of friends had won the first battle. But she knew there was more to come. Her history teacher, Mr. Wren, got it wrong. It wasn't a waste of effort that the people in the Great Strike didn't get their way and some lost their lives. When something isn't right or unfair there is no choice but to fight.

"The land of the free and the home of the brave."

Hazel squeezed Stanley's hand and he squeezed back.

"Play ball!"

Author's Note and Acknowledgements

I love classic film. Some of my favorite movies are from the silver screen era in Hollywood. The snappy dialog, drama, and comedy of movies from the 1930s, like *The Thin Man* series and *It Happened One Night*, were a major inspiration for this book.

When I first started writing this story, I envisioned it as a cozy little murder mystery, but as I dug into the history of St. Louis and our country, I found some things that would change that. Disturbing accounts of classism, bigotry, eugenics and the forced sterilization of over 60,000 Americans who were deemed "unfit" stain our country's history in ways that are seldom remembered or addressed.

I was disturbed to find out how close we came to a Nazi Germany situation here in the States, as the ideas behind eugenics are the seeds of Hitler's worldview. After I explored all of this, and discussed it with a good friend of the same mind, I knew that I would have to write a different story.

That said, it's a work of fiction and even the real organizations, places and people mentioned in the book are used for the purpose of telling the story. This is not a history book. Anyone who wants to know the history of American eugenics or the Veiled Prophet's place in St. Louis history can discover that for themselves.

In order to write this book, it took a team of people who loved and supported me through the process.

Special thanks to the Missouri Historical Society and their helpful librarians who provided a ton of great information, fascinating insights and little known facts about St. Louis history.

Thank you to all the friends and family who read and provided helpful criticisms of this book. In particular: Jennifer Jenkins, Ali Durham, and Gwen Holt. You all made the story so much better.

Big thanks to Amy Jameson and also the Teen Author Boot

Camp gang, Jen, Margie, Tahsha and Lois, who provided early encouragement and motivation to write this book.

To all the Month9Books crew: Shannon, Cameron, and Jennifer. You've been a dream to work with and I couldn't appreciate you more. And, most certainly, Georgia McBride, whose brassy courage and business savvy I admire beyond measure. Thanks for taking a risk on me.

Thanks to my big amazing family for always supporting me in my unconventional ways, and particularly to my parents who made me that way by raising me on classic film, old jazz, the love of books and a life of faith.

I am grateful for and honor the bravery of the victims of forced sterilization and eugenics who have shared their stories of the grave injustices done to them.

Lastly and especially, thank you to Jonathan who loves research, history, old movies and without whom this book could never have happened.

With love,

Jo

Jo Schaffer

Jo Schaffer was born and raised in the California Bay Area in a huge, creative family. She is a YA novelist, speaker and a Taekwondo black belt.

She's a founding member of the nonprofit organization that created Teen Author Boot Camp, one of the nation's biggest conferences for teens where bestselling authors present writing workshops to nearly a thousand attendees.

Jo loves being involved in anything that promotes literacy and family. She is passionate about community, travel, books, music, healthy eating, classic films and martial arts. But her favorite thing is being mom to three strapping sons and a neurotic cat named Hero.

They live together in the beautiful mountains of Utah.

www.joschaffer.com

OTHER MONTH9BOOKS TITLES YOU MIGHT LIKE

YELLOW LOCUST
THE SPONSORED
PRAEFATIO

Find more books like this at http://www.Month9Books.com

Connect with Month9Books online:
Facebook: www.Facebook.com/Month9Books
Twitter: https://twitter.com/Month9Books
You Tube: www.youtube.com/user/Month9Books
Tumblr: http://month9books.tumblr.com/

Neither quick fists nor nimble feet can save Selena Flood, a fighter of preternatural talent, from the forces of New Canaan, the most ruthless and powerful of the despotic kingdoms around.

YELLOW LOCUST

JUSTIN JOSCHKO

THE SPONSORED

DON'T BREAK THE RULES.
DON'T FOLLOW YOUR HEART.
DON'T GET CAUGHT.

CAROLINE T. PATTI

BOOK 1 IN THE PRAEFATIO SERIES

PRAEFATIO

A NOVEL

"This is teen fantasy at its most entertaining, most heartbreaking, most compelling. Highly recommended." –Jonathan Maberry, New York Times bestselling author of ROT & RUIN and FIRE & ASH

GEORGIA McBRIDE

CPSIA information can be obtained
at www.ICGtesting.com
Printed in the USA
FSHW01n0840140518

9 781946 700650